OBLIVIOUS

GHOSTMAKER BOOK 2

KRISTA WALSH

Raven's Quill Press

Ottawa, ON

Raven's Quill Press

www.kristawalshauthor.com

Publisher's Note: This is a work of fiction. Names, characters, places, and incidents are a product of the author's imagination. Locales and public names are sometimes used for atmospheric purposes. Any resemblance to actual people, living or dead, or to businesses, companies, events, institutions, or locales is completely coincidental.

Cover Design © John Wenzel/Chris Reddie
Model: Thomas James

Oblivious / WALSH -- 1st ed.
Print ISBN: 978-1-9994923-7-3

To the City of Ottawa

If it weren't for your sinkholes, your storms, your public transportation, your construction, your walking paths, your geese, and your increasing number of high-rises, I might never have been inspired to write this series.

Chapter 1

Jet

I EASED MY foot off the gas pedal before I blew too far over the speed limit. We needed to get to my apartment building, pack, and get out as quickly as possible, and being pulled over for speeding would not only slow us down but also attract attention from people we didn't want asking questions. If the blood on my hands didn't get us hauled in for questioning, the injured man in my passenger seat would, and there went our secrecy. We had to keep our heads down, avoid notice. Anything to buy us a bit of extra time to disappear.

But as soon as the engine slowed, I caught myself paying more attention to the rear-view mirror than the road ahead, every moment expecting a black SUV to pull up behind us.

They won't be that quick. They can't have tracked us down yet.

I figured we had about half an hour before the security offi-cers pulled my name from the records. Thirty minutes before it became known that Captain Bridget Dawson had used her registered security key to free an American spy from custody. Eighteen-hundred seconds until Supernatural, Magical and Occult Affairs Canada declared me a rogue agent.

Possibly a murderer.

Maybe even a traitor.

Thirty minutes was a small window, but I'd never been more motivated to perform a miracle.

My stomach twisted with uncontrolled nerves, and bile burned the back of my throat at the reek of blood trapped in my nose—not all of it from the man sitting beside me.

My gaze strayed to the passenger seat, to the half-naked Gideon Leigh bleeding on the upholstery of my Mustang. Bruises and dark stubble shadowed his pale face, his expression pinched with pain. Every few seconds, part of his body dissolved into mist, his cellular makeup pulling apart only to come back together in slightly better condition than before.

He'd been working on healing himself ever since I'd removed the metal collar blocking his supernatural ability. His dislocated shoulder now sat properly in its socket, and the thousand cuts he'd received, the dozens of lashes on his mangled back, looked a few days old instead of the ravaged, weeping mess they'd been twenty minutes ago.

I didn't know how he was still conscious.

"How are you holding up?" I asked. "You going to stay with us?"

"For a while yet," he said through clenched teeth. His back arched and he groaned as another surge of pain passed through him. His left arm dissolved from shoulder to elbow, and when it took shape again, the gash along the back of his bicep had thinned, though fresh blood soon welled to the surface.

I returned my attention to the road and ground my teeth as I sped through a yellow light. Only three more minutes and we'd reach my apartment, but those three minutes stretched ahead of me like a decade after a week that felt like it had already lasted seven years.

Two days ago, the minister had ordered that Gideon, a foreign agent working unauthorized on Canadian soil, be taken into custody. From what Gideon had managed to tell me between grunts of discomfort and wavering consciousness, he'd spent the first day undergoing a gentle interrogation at the hands of my lieutenant, Eric Sampson, and the second trapped in the dark, naked and collared, while a man recently recruited to my task force—to *my* team—tortured him to the brink of insanity. All under my nose in my own goddamned detainment centre.

For fourteen years, I had been a loyal SMOAC agent, a proud member of the department that took care of Canada's vast supernatural population. For fourteen years, I had dutifully followed orders, putting my faith in the people sworn to keep us safe, hidden, and supported. I loved my job, I loved my hand-picked team, and I loved the sense that I was serving my country in a hands-on, ass-kicking way.

Within the past week, all my pride and deepest-held beliefs had been blown apart. What should have been a routine raid to wipe out the country's biggest supernatural crime organization had resulted in the massacre of half my team. Instead of the drug deal we'd expected to interrupt, only the drugs had waited for us—strapped to a time bomb that had detonated, releasing a roomful of ghost, the latest trend in street drugs that gave mundanes a glimpse through the perception filter at the true face of the world and gave supernaturals a boost to their abilities. A fantastic party drug. Except that the tiniest amount over the safe limit—somewhere less than three milligrams—could send your brain into overdrive and kill you within minutes.

No rushing to the hospital to deal with the overdose, just death. A horrible, bloody, painful death.

For ten out of my twenty-member squad.

So many days later, I still hadn't wrapped my head fully around my loss.

And that had only been the start of my week. In the past twenty-four hours, I'd uncovered a possible connection between the Death's Head Syndicate and our department, learned that six of our best informants were dead or missing, found our minister murdered in his office, and saved my best friend, Madison Prince, from a mad chemist looking to send some kind of message over the unseen wall.

Now I was on the run because, in choosing to save Gideon from the new-recruit-slash-syndicate mole who'd taken great joy in tormenting him, I'd painted a target on my back. The only thing the members of the department *not* involved in the conspiracy would know was that I'd helped a detained private security officer escape on the same night Minister Bastien had been killed, while the actual guilty parties would no doubt guess I'd put togther at least part of the truth and have an easy time pinning the crime on me.

Everything was fine.

I could handle this.

I took the next turn too fast and nearly struck a pedestrian crossing the street against the light. She flipped me off, and I hit the gas as soon as her foot touched the sidewalk.

Two minutes away from home now. Once there, the real strain would begin as we waited for Madison, now my literal partner in crime, to call me and tell us where to meet her. She was arranging a safe house for us, somewhere we could recover and figure out how the hell to deal with this disaster, and the sooner we vanished, the better. Although we'd left the office building less than five minutes ago, I had my cellphone in my lap, checking the screen every other second to make sure I didn't miss her.

A little more than an hour ago, she'd been strapped to a ghostbomb, staring into the eyes of the Ghostmaker himself, Peter Dougall, and already she'd put it behind her to focus on keeping us safe. There weren't a dozen women in the world like her.

I just hoped she was quick about sorting out the details, because the last thing I wanted to do was feel trapped in my home watching the clock, knowing every tick of the second hand brought us closer to discovery.

Another grunt from Gideon pulled my thoughts away from the mayhem I'd found myself in, and when I looked over, I saw he'd passed out, his head slumped to one side and his chest slowly materializing.

I slammed my palms against the steering wheel. "*Fuck!*"

Shouting didn't make me feel any better, but at least it vented some of the energy threatening to tear me apart.

My frustration wasn't only over the state of him. The sight of anyone in his condition—inflicted in *my* detainment centre—would get to me. But he couldn't be some stranger I'd rescued from SMOAC's creeping corruption, could he? It had to be more complicated than that. Because of course.

Two years ago, I'd booted him out of my life. A week ago, he'd wheedled his way back in. When we'd first met, he and I had been all thriller novel—sex and spies—and although I'd sworn that part of our relationship was over, I'd had more than enough reason to doubt myself over the past couple days. The arrogant son of a bitch was a charming, intelligent private security officer. He was also a lying, manipulative skeezebag.

I hated him, I wanted him, I hated that I wanted him, and now I was stuck saving his life so I could figure out whether I hated or wanted him more.

Bastard.

I hung a final left and pulled around the back of my apartment building, a squeezed-in alley that hid my car from view and provided three exit points, one of which only the people who lived here knew about. It was a tight fit, but I was willing to risk a few scratches on my baby if it meant reaching a main road quickly and without anyone seeing.

Once the engine was off, I rested my hand on a healed patch of Gideon's arm and gently shook him awake, careful not to jar him too much. I was afraid one more shock to his system would undo all his work.

His eyelids fluttered open, his chest heaved, and he bolted upright, eyes wide and nostrils flared with panic. When he turned and saw me, his shoulders relaxed, and I pretended I hadn't noticed his terror, knowing he'd hate for me to see his weakness.

Which was bullshit, of course. Twenty-four hours stuck in the dark, cold and bleeding—I would have been concerned if he *weren't* haunted by nightmares.

"We need to get moving," I said, keeping him focused on the here and now. "We don't have a lot of time."

He jerked his head in a nod and groaned as he attempted to pull his stained white T-shirt over his head. His movements were slow and stiff, and I held back a wince with every stretch and tug on the wounds he hadn't yet stitched back together. I wanted to help—not only to speed things along but also to save him some of the agony of brushing crusted cotton over his open gashes—but didn't want to insult his pride.

A voice in the back of my head scoffed. *Pride.* That was why he'd wound up in SMOAC's hands to begin with, because he'd taken too many stupid risks, confident he wouldn't get caught.

Part of me, I was ashamed to admit, was still pissed off he'd lied to me about why he'd come to Ottawa. Not a risk assessment as he'd said but an attempt to work his own case, using my resources, without my knowledge. How long would it have been before he'd taken everything back to his firm, interrupted my operation of shutting down the ghost trade, and stolen credit for the work we'd done together? If Minister Bastien hadn't outed him, I would probably still be in the dark, helping him propel his career forward while he ran my reputation through the mud.

If you hadn't called him to meet you at Dougall's place, he wouldn't have been imprisoned and tortured, my infuriating brain reminded me, and I worked to smother my resentment. The man had suffered enough for his lies.

Gideon sagged against the seat, the effort of getting dressed apparently having exhausted him. He glanced at his wrist, and his fingers travelled over an inch-wide space of untanned skin. He tensed and reached for his jeans pockets, patting them down.

"I have it," I said, and leaned into the backseat for his black vest and the leather bracelet he rarely took off.

"Thanks." As soon as the bracelet was in place, he appeared

more at ease, as though it weren't so much a sentimental accessory as a talisman against further harm.

"Are you okay to walk?" I asked.

It had taken both Madison and me to get him into my car, but he looked far more alive now than he had when we'd found him on the cell floor.

"I'll be fine." His words were terse, and he didn't spare me a glance as he opened his door.

I left the car unlocked to save time later and came around to the passenger side to help him if he needed it. His gaze darted from one end of the alley to the other, and he jumped when an obnoxious laugh echoed from the building behind us. It wasn't quite four o'clock in the morning, and shadows filled with threats seemed to surround us.

I couldn't drag my feet to coddle him. Trusting he would keep up, I strode to the back door and let us in. The elevator ride to the fourth floor was slow and awkward, but eventually we made it, and I let us into my apartment with a few extra glances over my shoulder.

"What's the plan?" he asked as he headed to the kitchen. He turned on the water and ducked his head to drink straight from the faucet, a low moan escaping his throat as he chugged.

"A vanishing act," I said. "Clean place to stay, clean car, and from there we decide how to move forward. We have no idea how high in the department this goes. We found Bastien dead, but was he the one working with the syndicate and they double-crossed him, or is someone else in the department behind this and they needed to get him out of the way? One of the first priorities is to get you out of sight. I doubt you'd make it over the border in your current state, but we can keep you safe until we find a way to return you to SilverGuard."

As if it would be as easy as snapping our fingers. An entire department on our asses, a conspiracy to defraud the supernatural community, murder, torture, bombings, an injured American.

Easy as pie.

Gideon turned off the water and wiped his mouth with the back of his hand. "You work for a secret government agency, and you're telling me you don't have access to super jets or teleportation devices?"

A snarky reply tickled the tip of my tongue, ready to match his, but when I turned around, I saw his attempt to lighten the mood was offset by a hardness around his eyes and a tight, mirthless smirk.

"And just how would we explain that to the taxpayers?" I asked, preferring to respond to the joke instead of the anger I sensed radiating off him.

He ran his hand through his hair, the styled locks dark and thick with yet more blood. From the look in his eyes, he had something else to say, and I held my breath. I was exhausted, drained from my own mental and physical exertions over the past week, and didn't know if I was up for whatever rage he wanted to throw my way. Not that he didn't have every right to be furious at his situation, but other than getting him to safety and overturning every last rock to beat the shit out of the guy who'd hurt him, there wasn't much I could do.

After a moment, he turned away, splashed some water on his face, and returned to what had to be the excruciating process of stitching himself back together, fading into mist and rematerializing without pause.

I watched in fascinated silence. Gideon's ability had blown me away the first time I'd witnessed it back in New York. The way his limbs dissolved, clothes and all, and came back with everything in its proper place. I had full control over the air molecules around me, giving me what looked like a blend of super strength and telekinesis, but Gideon was able to break himself down to an atomic level, changing out of his solid state into little more than a cloud. He could drift through the air unseen or as an opaque fog, as he chose.

I'd asked him once how he carried his clothes and weapons with him, and he'd told me he could affect anything he understood well enough to change. The more he brought with him, the more effort it took, but he'd been practicing his skills since he was a kid.

I'd asked if he'd ever taken another person with him.

He'd said he never got close enough to anyone to know them as well as he'd need to.

At the time, I'd thought he was being coy. Then I'd learned it was the most honest he'd ever been with me. Gideon Leigh did not do partners, he did not do relationships, and he most certainly did not do intimacy.

That I'd saved his life, shifting the uneasy balance between us, had to rankle his ever-sensitive ego.

Good.

Now that I was sure he wasn't going to die, my fury over his lies and manipulation swept over me in a wave, heating me from the roots of my hair down into the pit of my stomach.

He'd played me. He'd come to me asking for help and kept the most important information to himself. When Bastien had ordered him to be taken away, I had said nothing, happy he would face the consequences of betraying my trust again. I never imagined he would wind up getting tortured, but knowing he wouldn't get away with screwing me over had been sweet vindication.

After all that, I was stuck with him again. I couldn't direct my attention solely to finding the mole in my department, I had to watch my back and second-guess every move this double-crosser made. He'd believed SMOAC wasn't good enough to bring down the syndicate and that he had to do the work for us.

Now that he was free, would he carry on with his task? Use me for whatever information I provided and act behind my back? I didn't want to give him the chance. My goal was to make sure he stayed alive long enough to get home.

The only thing he had going for him was that, as far as I knew, he'd never tried to kill me.

Sadly, it was the most I could ask of my allies right now.

Even as my anger grew, I sensed his frustration rising from the other side of the island. No doubt Madison and her empathic ability would have been able to pinpoint the exact cause of his fury, but all I picked up was the way the air vibrated between us, like an electrical current that prickled my skin.

Was his fiery glare directed at me, or was I projecting? After all, what the hell did he have to be pissed at *me* for? I'd just saved his ass.

"I'm going to go clean up," he said, his tone short. He didn't wait for me to give permission. As though he owned the place, he headed for the bathroom, pulling off his T-shirt as he went. I glared at his passing figure, not saying a word, but before the door shut behind him, my anger evaporated into remorse at the barely healed gore of his back.

I'd said nothing when Eric had taken him away and look what they'd done to him. If Madison hadn't noticed they'd buried all official trace of him, pushing us to track him down, who knows what state he would have been in when we'd found him. *If* we'd found him.

I steeled myself against regret. It served no purpose. We'd gotten him out, and he would be fine. Like hell if I would let him see I was worried.

"Don't get blood in my bathroom," I called to him through the door. "And be quick about it."

Chapter 2

Gideon

A S SOON AS I closed the door to the bathroom, my legs gave out, and I sank onto the edge of the claw-foot tub. My hands trembled, and the shake spread up my arms and down my spine in a wave of uncontrollable shivers. I wrapped my arms around my middle to hold myself together.

Pain crept in from everywhere—not a single type of pain, either, but everything from sharp to throbbing to burning. The fucker who'd held me in that cell had messed with my head, playing with my nervous system with every little nick and cut. What had felt like gouges and slashes were nothing more than small slices now that I saw them clearly—something that had been denied to me in the small, dark room.

For twenty-four hours, I had either hung from the ceiling, chained and collared, or lain on the freezing stone floor. Only twenty-four hours, but it had felt like forever. Every time

Carstairs had left and returned, another piece of me died, and I wasn't sure how much of my soul was left. Even being here in the relative safety of a clean, warm bathroom did little to fend off the monsters chasing me.

I couldn't close my eyes without seeing his leering grin. The son of a bitch had gotten off on my pain. He had taunted me every moment as he screwed with my perceptions, mixing pleasure and pain, controlling each tiny reaction of my nervous system. His enjoyment made it that much worse. It told me I hadn't been able to hide my terror. My years of training and experience had counted for nothing. I had lost all control, all sense of self, and nothing seemed real anymore. Jet, this apartment, the ceramic underneath me, might be nothing more than illusions designed to trip me up.

What could I rely on—what could I *trust*—if I barely believed the floor underneath me would stay stable enough to bear my weight? My whole world had crumbled, and somehow I was expected to find the strength to pull myself to my feet. To get home, make my report, pretend as though everything was normal.

Worse, Jet knew. She'd tried to hide it, but I'd seen the pity in her eyes when I'd freaked out in the car. All because I'd heard something my frazzled brain had interpreted as heavy boots clomping down the hallway, the creak of a cell door opening.

She talked about getting me across the border and home to SilverGuard, the private security firm that —for now—

employed me. For what? Would I feel any better looking my fellow agents in the eye and explaining to them how my mind hadn't held steady under Carstairs's twisted ability? I didn't want to see them. I wanted to crawl to the far reaches of the earth and stay there until the shadows creeping around the edges of my thoughts went away and I was alone in my head.

The idea that I might never be alone up there again, that Carstairs might have made himself comfortable in the dark corners of my skull, made my stomach heave, and it was only with luck I made it to the toilet in time to bring up all the water I'd downed at the kitchen sink.

I tried to stay quiet, not wanting Jet to come check on me, but she left me alone, and eventually the nausea and trembling subsided, leaving me a sweating, bleeding mess on her grey bathmat.

I must have fallen asleep, because when Jet knocked on the bathroom door, I was still lying there.

"Gideon? You all right?" she asked.

"Fine," I said automatically as I struggled to sit up. A hint of dawn had spilled into the bathroom while I'd been out. The fog in my head, a throbbing, cloudy ache, dulled my thoughts, but underneath lurked a streak of irritation that Jet was treating me with kid gloves. We should have been out of here ages ago, even without Madison's call. "I'll be out in a minute."

I waited for her to give me shit or tell me to hurry up, but only silence came through the door.

Using the edge of the vanity to ease myself to my feet, I worked to steady my legs and threw my bloodstained T-shirt on the counter beside the sink. The mirror gave me a full view of the damage. Blood all over my face and chest, mostly dry now except for a few deeper wounds that had reopened in my weak attempt to stand up.

My nap hadn't done much to help me regain my strength, but we didn't have the luxury of time for me to hold off on stitching myself back together. Bracing for the strain, I misted one limb at a time, conserving more energy than if I tried to dissolve all at once. The slashes and gouges shrank, but I had a long way to go until I returned to full fighting form, and I'd have a new array of battle scars to add to my already impressive collection. Some wounds ran too deep to heal.

Carstairs's face rose behind my eyelids as I closed my eyes against another wave of pain. The SMOAC tactical gear he had no right to wear, the smirk on his lips, the amusement in his eyes. He was a ghost following me around, never far out of sight.

I spat into the sink, bringing up the blood that had seeped into my lungs and mouth with all my dissolving.

He would never have another chance to play inside my head. The next time I saw him, he would be the one to suffer. To scream. To curse my name as the life drained out of his eyes.

I looked down to find I'd curled my fingers into the edges of the vanity, my knuckles white and the cuts on the backs of my hands bleeding again. I ran the water and shoved them under the cold stream. From my hands, I moved on to my arms, and then my chest, my face, and a pathetic attempt at my hair. Jet's grey towels were red by the time I finished, but to hell with her.

She could have gotten me out of that mess, told her lover boy lieutenant to go easy on me, and she'd said nothing. She'd allowed Sampson, the action figure with the blond hair and blue eyes, to stuff me in a car and hand me over to the monster who'd done this to me.

By the time Carstairs had finished our last round, I'd given up hope she would come for me. She had in the end, but what had she rescued? Not the man she'd known in New York. Not the man who'd knocked on her door a few days ago looking for information. That man was gone, and in his place was this broken fragment of what he'd been.

She'd saved me, but she'd waited too long. And sure, she'd launched herself into the syndicate's crosshairs by freeing me, but as far as I was concerned, it was the least she could have done. I'd kept my mouth shut about what we'd learned from her informants, kept my SilverGuard handler in the dark about the situation up here to give her time to find answers, and covered her ass with all she'd been up to behind her colonel's back. Questioning the informants, trying to worm her way into the syndicate information stream, an unauthorized mission from SMOAC's greatest rule-follower.

I'd risked my job—the only thing that mattered to me—by

keeping quiet, so as far as I was concerned, we were even.

I thought about what she'd told me on our way out of the SMOAC building about the dead informants. Mark O'Malley, head of the syndicate, getting rid of anyone who'd spoken out of turn. She'd told me about Lafontaine and Rourke, the bloodstained house of one and the brutal assault on the other. Horrible, regrettable, but I almost envied them. At least they'd been able to go down fighting. At least their deaths had been quick.

Another shiver ran through me, but this time I relaxed into it, refusing to let the terror and nausea overwhelm me again. We didn't have time for that. We'd already wasted enough.

Because I couldn't stop here. As shattered as I felt, I couldn't curl into a ball and give up. I couldn't give in. Not when the fuckers who'd done this to me were out there thinking they'd won.

Somehow I had to keep going. Even if I had to lie my ass off to make people believe I was strong enough to stand on my own and face my terror. I wouldn't let them see me as broken, and I wouldn't—couldn't—let Carstairs own me.

I pictured Peter Dougall in his mess of a living room, surrounded by boxes and ratty furniture. He'd looked like a university kid who spent too much time smoking pot and earning a living hacking computers. Turned out he was the mastermind behind the country's greatest pharmaceutical threat, a rook in the Death's Head Syndicate's pocket.

Dougall, the Ghostmaker. The moniker was enough to raise the hairs on people's arms. This was the guy who'd created the drug that seduced and killed thousands in both the supernatural and mundane worlds. To have him be some puny twerp who didn't look like he could handle his own in a fight was offensive.

Enough so that I wanted to drive my fist into the guy's face. His, and Carstairs's, and anyone who threatened to lay a finger on Jet.

Because, goddamn it, as pissed off as I was at her for leaving me behind, I couldn't swallow the fear bubbling inside me that she was in way over her head. Danger was closing in on all sides, and if she didn't tread carefully, she would be pinned in the centre.

She talked about keeping me out of the way until I made it home, but I knew first-hand what O'Malley's people were capable of. I knew how far they were willing to go to reach their goals and how few fucks they gave about the lives they destroyed along the way. If our suspicions were right that this mess reached all the way up the SMOAC chain, she would need whatever help she could get. People she could trust to have her back and to make sure monsters like Carstairs didn't get within a million miles of her.

I stared myself down in the mirror, not for the first time asking my reflection why I would consider sticking around when my escape route lay right in front of me. But I couldn't leave. I was staying for myself, to battle my demons, but equally strong was my need to watch out for this woman who didn't want me around.

You're an idiot.

She was right. I should get the hell out of here. Head home, report to SilverGuard that Canada was in the hands of the syndicate, and help defend our border. Take O'Malley down with all the resources Jet lacked.

It would be the sane thing to do. The professional thing to do. And the job always came first.

Except when it didn't.

Shit.

Chapter 3

Madison

I COULDN'T STOP fidgeting. My finger tapped an uneven rhythm on the dining table and my leg matched the tempo. I'd tried to calm down. Meril help me, I'd tried. My grandmother's emotion-resetting herbal tea, some deep breathing, a few pep talks, but the bugs continued to crawl under my skin, refusing to let me fall still.

The moment I'd reached my condo apartment, I'd moved my laptop to the table by the window so I could monitor the street. Time was short. I had to get out of here. But my pace was set by my outdated computer. Getting to safety was only step one. Without guidance to help us zig the syndicate's zags, we would be stuck until not even hiding would protect us.

Fear threatened to strip me of all rational thought, but I had to muster my courage if I wanted to give me and Jet a way to move forward with our investigation once we slipped under the department's radar. Some advantage, even if it was a small one.

The cursor on the screen flickered accusingly at me as SMOAC's secured server denied my password for the second time. Had the security office already found me out and blocked my access? My heart raced and my palms grew clammy, but when I tried again, the cloud files opened. My hands were shaking so badly, I must have fumbled the sequence.

Relief wormed its way beneath the vise-like grip of my stress, stretching out the jaws that had clamped around my chest. We'd made it this far, but I couldn't assume our luck would hold much longer.

Soon enough, the security team would finish reviewing the camera footage, and the powers that be might see me and Jet hurrying away from Jean-Luc's dead body and disappearing down the stairs in time to escape whoever had come onto the floor from the elevator bay. Jet had wiped some of the footage clean, but had she gotten all of it? She was no tech whiz, so even if she'd removed us from the system's memory, I doubted it would take much effort for someone who knew what they were doing to bring us back.

Even without that, even if all trace of *me* being there was gone, there had been no way for Jet to erase the record of using her security pass to get us into the detainment centre or, more damning, using her registered key to remove Gideon's collar so we could get him out of that torture chamber.

Once security put those pieces together, how much longer

would it take for them to come up with a story that put the syndicate and their government allies on our trail?

We were so screwed.

Persephone, my tabby cat, leapt into my lap, butted her head against my chin, and fell into a steady purr as I navigated my files. With my free hand, I stroked her soft fur, knowing today could be the last time I saw her for a while.

I wouldn't let myself consider it might be the last time ever.

Panic thrashed against my ribs, but I did my best to ignore it by doubling down on the information in front of me. If I wanted to come home to my cat, my condo, my dinner date with the man of my dreams, I needed the evidence that would help make that possible. If only I weren't dealing with a system that moved at the speed of a sloth demon.

My hand trembled as I guided the mouse through the files that had opened my eyes to the corruption in the department. The files that proved what Jet, Gideon, and I already knew, and whatever information might help us learn the rest. As soon as I was cut off, we would lose access to the department's system and to any resources, contacts, or research involving the Death's Head Syndicate and the ghost epidemic that had swept through the country.

I printed all of it. It didn't help my troubled conscience to think how many trees I was killing in the process, but some-where in this paperwork, this shrine of bureaucracy, could be everything we needed to clear our names and point the finger at the real traitors.

In the files I'd spread across my office floor last night, I'd discovered a pattern of questionable activity. Money shifting hands and disappearing, approved projects that would have offered stability and safety to Canada's supernatural population getting shuttered with flimsy excuses. And on all of them, Minister Bastien's signature.

What I'd found had formed the outline of a picture—a nightmarish picture that twisted the image I held of the department I loved so much—but I needed more. Proof of where the money had gone. Proof that the projects had been cancelled deliberately to stir up dissatisfaction in the community and create tensions between the two sides of the unseen wall. Proof that the minister—my friend—had betrayed his people.

Somehow, by a path I didn't fully understand yet, I'd found myself in the middle of a government conspiracy, and to hell if I would sit back and let that big fat spider come and bite my head off. I was going to fight. Right now, based on the information we had, no one would believe me if I came forward—if I knew who to come forward *to*.

Ten years of hard work—ten years of trade negotiations, project management, helping Jean-Luc maintain the foundations of our shaky supernatural world—and everything I'd toiled over was on the brink of collapse. The department was unravelling, and Meril, queen of the realm and my great-great grandmother, was one ghostbomb away from dragging my behind back to court and putting an end to all the efforts I'd made to help supernaturals build their lives on this side of the wall.

I was a SMOAC employee. It was how I had defined my life. My great-grandmother had helped found the department as a way to support the supernaturals who wanted to distance themselves from Meril's court, and there was no way I would let her legacy crumble to pieces because some greedy sons of bitches would rather ally themselves with the syndicate than serve their country as they'd sworn to do.

Bit by bit, my anger overcame my fear, and my heart rate slowed enough to clear away the spots dancing in my vision. Persephone meowed and jumped off my lap, her tail twitching with indignation. I shifted in my chair to better see my laptop screen in the glare of the morning sun and picked up the pace of my printing.

I wasn't out of the game yet. I hadn't lost all control. I had to pull myself together, ground myself in the familiar paperwork, and I would find my way out of this maze.

While the documents spewed out of my printer, I rose from my seat and went into the kitchen to reheat the kettle. Mug from the cupboard, grandmother's herbs in the infuser, boiling water into the mug, breathe in the gentle aroma while the tea steeped.

The steps of my go-to calming ritual helped settle my nerves and see things more clearly.

None of my scattered, frantic thoughts were wrong, but I had to change my way of thinking. The department was at risk from an unseen power, but they didn't know who they were up against. Yes, I had made my career based on my ability to draw up a mean trade agreement and read the emotions in the room, but I was also the great-granddaughter of the woman who had stared Sir John A. Macdonald in the eye and told him in no uncertain terms that the world was the way it was and he could either accept it and cede some of his power to a new department or he could face the wrath of a queen who knew how to bend a man's will to her own.

I wasn't about to let some crime syndicate steal the strength of my family line away from me.

O'Malley's allies had found a way to go unnoticed in their path of corruption, and I would use the same method to stop them. Although I felt like I was trapped in a pit of vipers with no way out, I was prepared to disappear. My grandmother had put it into my head days ago that I should be ready to run, and my contacts had set me up with a tidy escape. A safe house and replacement car waited for me.

We weren't alone.

The apartment my contact had rented was a temporary retreat while we gathered our resources, but it would also give us an out if we needed to fall further back.

"You work for a secret government department," Nan had always told me. "Never put yourself in a situation you can't escape. No one will believe you if you get into trouble, so you have to watch your own back."

Not the nicest lesson to hear growing up, but now, with the end of my career—and likely worse—staring me in the face, I couldn't help but be grateful for her pragmatism.

I sipped my tea and stared at my laptop, allowing my thoughts to run through everything else I might need.

I wished I could call my family, give them a heads-up of the danger and ask for their advice, but to make any contact risked bringing the wrong attention to their door. If the syndicate had access to everyone's personnel files, as it seemed likely they did based on what we'd discovered, then they knew about my family in Manitoba. They knew who my connections were. Either they would try to use them to get to me, or they would try to cut me off.

There was always the option of throwing up my hands and going directly to Meril, as I was sure she hoped I would, but doing so would give her permission to take control of the department, not to mention strip me of my freedom, and if she did that, the country as we knew it would change forever, and I would be trapped on the other side of the wall, unable to help direct it. Even if I succeeded in finding the source of the corruption, sniffing out the rats, and bringing them to justice, the debt would be hers, and SMOAC would be the price we had to pay. It was the threat that had hung over my head with every failed trade deal and every new public relations nightmare over the past few months. A threat brought home more than once in the last week every time she'd told me I had to fix the problem quickly or an official summons would be sent to my door.

One last chance.

For over a hundred and fifty years, she'd tolerated the governmental oversight of our people on this side of the wall, but I had no doubt she would leap at the chance to regain control if the opportunity presented itself.

No matter how bad things looked right now, I wasn't willing to sacrifice the autonomy of our kind. Not when a smidge of hope remained that we might see this through ourselves. She hadn't reached out to me since Dougall had manhandled me into a chair last night and attempted to kill me, talking some nonsense about using my death to start a war with the realm, so I assumed she didn't know what had happened. Dougall's plan had failed, and I still had time. All I could do was make the most of it.

Much too long later, the last sheets came out of the printer, and I shut down my laptop. No point giving the security team any extra breadcrumbs to follow. Jet and Gideon had already been told: no computer, no phones. The only call Jet was to accept was from me. My contact would deliver new phones with new numbers along with the keys to the safe house, so as soon as I left my apartment, I was air.

My work phone pinged, and the sound dropped another stone into my stomach. Reluctantly, I walked over to the kitchen counter and looked at the warning notice on my screen. The message confirmed my suspicion: my account had been locked. I was shut out, with no resources except what I was clever enough to dig up.

At least I'd had time to print what I needed. Hopefully enough to put together more of the pattern I'd uncovered. With shaking hands, I picked up the thick stack of documents and stuffed them into my canvas satchel. There would be more than enough time to read everything after I reached our new refuge.

All that was left now was to drop Persephone off at my neighbour's apartment and leave. Jet and Gideon were waiting for my call, and the sooner we got away, the safer we would be.

I went into the bedroom and grabbed my bag filled with clothes, a safety box with extra money, and a few family heirlooms to keep me tied to something normal, however small.

Persephone brushed against my leg, and I scooped her into my arms, imprinting her warmth and familiar weight into my memory.

"Jenn will take care of you, little one," I said. "You'll be fat and spoiled by the time I come home."

My throat closed and tears burned in my eyes as I stood in the middle of my living room, surveying the life I had built for myself. I loved my condo and everything in it—items I had carefully selected to add pleasure and beauty to an otherwise work-focused and quiet existence. But they were just things.

Nothing I couldn't replace when everything settled.

And maybe next time, I'd find a place with a view that didn't wind up ruined by the construction of another high-rise. Miracles could happen.

Squaring my shoulders, I pulled my bag over my head, hugged Persephone tightly against my chest, and walked out.

Chapter 4

Jet

I FINISHED SHOVING a few T-shirts and underthings into a duffle bag, then threw it onto the bed and pulled a large wooden trunk out from under the metal frame.

I'd bought the trunk at the Great Glebe Garage Sale ages ago. One of those antique beauties you always saw in movies and wanted but could never find in real life. This one reeked of mothballs and old cigar smoke and contained the few treasures I carried with me every time I moved.

The photograph of me and my grandmother, her with her hands on my shoulders, both of us making silly faces at my dad behind the camera. I must have been ten years old, and he'd insisted on a memento of our day at the Calgary Stampede. It was the best memory I had of the two most important people in my life. The tiger's eye pendant my grandmother had given me when I'd left Alberta to make a life for myself in Ottawa.

My dad's hunting knife with the polished wood handle.

I slid them into the side of my bag, wanting them close. If the rest of my apartment burned, I wouldn't grieve much for its loss.

I checked my phone again, but there was still no word from Madison.

Where the hell was she? When we'd split up outside the SMOAC building, she'd said she would call within half an hour. It had been over sixty minutes since we'd reached my place, and we were getting dangerously close to what I considered our final cut-off point. Staying much longer risked us getting penned in on all the main roads.

Gideon's silence in the bathroom did nothing to calm me down. Had he passed out in there? Was he taking a goddamned bath?

I'd knocked once and he'd answered, which at least assured me he hadn't died. As injured as he was, I doubted he wanted me barging in to check on him while he patched himself up, so I gave him his privacy. Until Madison checked in, he could take his time. Probably for the best if he did. I would reassess if I heard any loud noises that suggested he'd collapsed on my tiled floor.

But if Madison didn't call soon…

I paced my bedroom, double-checked I had everything we needed, and started running through backup options to get us out of here. My car was outside, but the vehicle was on record, so we wouldn't get far with it. The plan had been to drive some-where the security team wouldn't think to look right away and have Madison pick us up in the clean car to drive us to the safe house. With time getting away from us, that plan was becoming less and less practical. We'd have someone on our ass the moment I turned out of the alley.

It meant I'd have to leave my baby where she was and hope whoever towed her took good care of her. One of the few losses to my material life that made my heart ache.

Without her, though, our options of where to hide were limited. Public transportation carried too many witnesses, same with a cab, and with Gideon in his current state, we would attract too much attention on foot.

No, the best option was Madison, but she had to direct us *now*.

I grabbed my phone off the bed and punched in her number, but stopped before I hit dial. She'd expressly ordered no outgoing calls and to accept no incoming other than hers.

"You never know who's watching or what might give us away," she'd said.

I didn't often let someone else call the shots, but this was Madison's plan. She'd always been cautious, great about thinking ahead, and the events of the past few days had made those instincts invaluable.

No matter how much I wanted to check my team's group chat to see if anyone had reached out, no matter how much I wanted to message them to beg them not to believe anything they heard about me, I had to trust her lead. My instincts screamed at me to run, to leave everyone and everything behind, pull a Gideon and vanish without a trace. Madison had managed to keep her head in this crisis, and if she'd prepared for the worst-case scenario, I was confident no one would track us down. My team would be safer if I made no contact.

I shoved my phone into my back pocket and trusted her to call me when she was ready.

Finally, I heard movement in the apartment and assumed Gideon had rejoined the land of the living. I grabbed a clean T-shirt—a plain grey one Eric had left behind at some point—and returned to the living room to find Gideon standing next to the window, hidden from outside view by the thick curtains.

I bit my tongue to stop myself from asking again if he was all right. In some ways, he looked worse now than he had when he'd gone into the bathroom. His face was nearly as white as the clean patches of his T-shirt, and his hand trembled where it clung to the curtain. His lips were pressed together, his eyes tight, and I understood that for all his healing, the pain hadn't let up.

He started when I came up behind him and half-turned to look at me.

"I miss anything?" he asked. No explanation for what had taken him so long, which told me his extended disappearance hadn't been intentional. If he'd chosen to make me wait, I would have found defiance in his eyes, but instead there was exhaustion and a glimmer of anxiety, as though he dreaded my asking.

I did him the courtesy of pretending I hadn't noticed the passing time and shook my head. "I've been watching. No sign of them yet."

"Think you gave them the slip?"

My throat tightened as I thought of the key in Gideon's possession. My digital footprint shouting to the world that I'd gone against my superiors and helped a foreign agent escape custody. "No way in hell."

"Then Madison or not, we'd better get moving."

In the dim light of the arriving dawn, I looked him over. Dark circles lined his eyes, and he stood with a distinctive stoop to his shoulders, as though he'd curled in on himself, protecting his vitals. But he was standing, and his voice sounded stronger than it had in the car, so I took that as a good sign.

"Do you have anything you need to grab?" I asked. "Anywhere we need to stop?"

He looked down at his shirt, still damp from what I guessed was a failed attempt to wash it out. "I wouldn't say no to a clean shirt, but it's not worth getting caught for it. I'll grab something on the road if we have a chance. I've lived with worse."

I thought of the state of his Brooklyn apartment.

"No doubt," I said before I could stop myself, and turned away before he reacted.

That's great, Jet. Antagonize the man who knows your crimes. Smart way to play this.

I didn't think Gideon would turn on me, but why chance it? In this twisted game of cat and mouse, there were no rules and anyone was free to play.

The sooner we got him home, the better.

In an effort to keep things civil, I handed him Eric's T-shirt and said, "Here, this'll tide you over for now. We can figure the rest out later. Madison no doubt thought ahead and stocked the closets at the safe house."

Gideon stripped off his ruined shirt, giving me a glimpse of the sleek lines of his stomach as they cut towards the defined vee over his black jeans. Even under these circumstances, I would have appreciated the view, but at the moment the dozens of cuts that criss-crossed his chest and belly and circled around his sides distracted me. He turned to chuck the dead shirt into the kitchen garbage behind him, and I took in the half-healed welts on his back, still red and raised but no longer weeping. Clearly he'd made some progress in the bathroom. I hoped it would be enough.

As he turned around, I tore my gaze away and focused on the faded pattern of my couch. He pulled the clean shirt over his head with a grunt, slipped his vest on, and returned his attention to the view beyond the curtains. His posture stiffened. "I hope whatever plans your friend is making, she's ready for us. They were nice enough to wait until I cleaned up, but it looks like we've got company."

Holding my bag close at my side, I peered around where he'd inched open the curtain. Sure enough, three black SUVs had pulled up in front of my building. SUVs I recognized. SMOAC task force vehicles.

I shouldn't have been surprised. It was what we'd said would happen. Even so, having my own people come to bring me in told me a lot about our situation. It meant Madison had been right: the security team had jumped straight to suspecting the worst, and someone higher up the chain had determined I was too high-risk to send a few security officers to find me.

I'd earned a red mark on my file. Armed and dangerous.

I closed my physical eyes and opened my supernatural one to the rest of the building, searching for anyone rushing towards the apartment with the same urgency that was driving me to flee. Madison would have sensed their emotions, their intentions, whether they were friend or foe. Without her insight, I had to assume the threat and use my skills to outrun them.

I flattened my palm on the wall and blocked out the initial burst of history that invaded my mind at the contact. With a concerted effort, I sent my attention through the building. The vision through my third eye grew murky, the whole world fading into shadow. In the haze, I made out Gideon's form beside me, clearer for being familiar and close. Beyond him was the blurred view of my apartment, the hallway outside, the neighbours across the hall going about their completely normal day.

I slid my gaze forward, taking in the stairs, the elevator. The farther I pressed, the foggier my vision became, until all I detected was movement. *Eight people coming into the building. Splitting into pairs. Three hitting the different stairwells. The last staying in the lobby.* Probably waiting for the clunky elevator. Just as I'd trained them to do. There would be another four soldiers circling the perimeter. Close in, block the exits, don't give the wanted party room to escape.

"We need to get out of here." My lips felt numb, my tongue unwieldy.

Gideon's brow furrowed. "They sent three full teams? Seems like overkill, doesn't it?"

"I guess they figured if I wasn't willing to sit around at the office and wait for them to find me, I wouldn't be too quick to turn myself over now. They were right." I raised an eyebrow. "I don't suppose you've learned how to mist the two of us away since the last time we saw each other?"

"Not if you don't want to risk losing body parts."

I wasn't surprised, but it would have made our disappearance a lot easier.

As it was, our best bet was to get to my car. If we could time our exit properly, we'd have a bit of a head start before they realized we were gone. I just didn't know how to get to the alley. Despite my forward thinking in parking behind the building, they'd covered all the ways down.

I'd planned on a smaller contingent. One, maybe two guys

swinging by to check out my place. Instead, the department had sent a full force, and in another minute, every route would be blocked.

"Then I guess I'll have to find my own way out." I started towards the door.

Gideon stayed close behind me. "You? What about me?"

I jerked to a halt and turned around, taking a step backwards when I found him closer than I'd expected. "What about you? You can mist away and meet me at the car."

He frowned, his brown eyes full of emotions I couldn't unravel. "You just broke me out of prison. I'm not going to leave you here without backup."

So many responses flew through my mind—*you idiot, get out of here* being among the top—but my tongue stuck to the roof of my mouth. Was he playing a game, one I didn't see yet, or was he seriously putting himself in danger out of some twisted sense of gratitude? Or was it possible he—no, I refused to go down that line. What we'd had in New York had been great, but it hadn't ended well, and it hadn't meant enough for him to tell me the real reason he'd come to Ottawa. No, I'd had to learn the truth in front of my colonel and my lieutenant from a man who'd now been murdered.

Gideon had his reasons for leaving it to me to get us out of here, and I couldn't take the time to guess what they were. I had to focus, stay open to every opportunity of escape. If he wanted to slow himself down and come with me, that was his problem.

"Let's hit the stairs."

With my third eye watching, I led the way out of the apartment. For a breath, I hesitated, wondering if I should take the extra seconds to lock the door in the hope it might make them think we'd left a while ago, but decided against it. We couldn't afford any delay, and if they thought I deserved three teams, I doubted they would bother trying the door handle. As soon as I didn't answer, they would kick it in, and Gideon's shirt in the trash, the blood not yet dry, would give away pretty quickly that we hadn't been gone long.

As we passed the main stairway, I detected two shadows making their way up. The loud clanging of the iffy elevator told me the fourth pair was also on the move.

Shit, shit, shit.

The walls were closing in. Another minute and we'd be trapped.

My heart raced, and I stood frozen in the hallway, a cornered animal ready to fight. But fighting wasn't an option. I hadn't done anything wrong, and making a show of force was the worst way to prove it. What I needed was time.

Focus, Dawson.

Gideon stood right on my heels, so on edge his tension rolled off him in waves that rippled through the air between us. But he didn't rush me, and in the silence, my training cut through my panic.

The exits were blocked, so we would improvise.

In the back of my mind, I made note of the irony. I'd always taught my team that improvisation would get them killed. But all our planning hadn't prepared us for the ghostbomb in the de Lauer subbasement, and my only way out of here was to trust my instincts.

If life ever returned to normal and I was lucky enough to resume my post, I'd have to make some changes to the lesson plan.

Closing my eyes, I mentally laid out the blueprint of the fourth floor. The only place to hide was the utility room, which was too obvious. They would clear it as soon as they checked my apartment.

We also couldn't stand still while I came up with an idea.

I tapped Gideon's hand to let him know we were moving and led him around the corner, as far from the incoming troops as we could get to give ourselves some flexibility to manoeuvre. At the end of the hallway was a window, and I peered outside to get my bearings as we passed. The west side of the building overlooked a small parking lot and followed the fire escape. If these guys were smart—and they were—they would have more troops waiting at the bottom of the metal stairs, either in the parking lot or ready to grab me once I hit the street.

My pulse raced so quickly I tasted blood in the back of my throat, and my breath came shaky and shallow.

Not the proper response of a conditioned soldier, Dawson. Shape up,

Michael's voice echoed in my head.

Across the parking lot stood another apartment building, a fourteen-storey high-rise. I'd been known to achieve some pretty impressive feats with heights and jumps, but that was out even for me.

My pulse leapt again as my third eye picked up four shadows reaching our floor. I jerked Gideon around the corner just before the stairwell door opened and the elevator pinged. Four sets of boots hit the curled, peeling linoleum, all moving towards my apartment. My heart was trying to tear its way out of my rib cage, and I worried the sound of it would give us away.

Breathe. Panic wouldn't help us. As soon as the opportunity opened, we had to move. I had to be ready.

As my calm took hold, I realized that in my rush to get out of sight, I'd locked myself between Gideon and the wall. He looked down at me, pupils dilated, every molecule of him ready to run and every hard muscle of his body pressed against mine. His hands rested on my hips, the tips of his fingers brushing my waist, sending electrical currents under my skin. My heart fluttered, the heat rushing through my veins waking me up to every sensation, every danger, real and imagined.

We had to get out of here. If the stairwells were blocked and the elevator was out, where did that leave us? Running in circles around the fourth floor, trying to stay one step ahead of them? That would work great until they had the genius idea of splitting up and leaving guards posted. The window in the hallway was locked, so there was no scaling down the wall that way.

Think, Dawson. There's always a route. Always a way out.

Thinking would be so much easier if I didn't feel so closed in. If Gideon weren't staring at me with such expectation and… No, I didn't want to think about that. I had to concentrate on getting us free.

I swallowed hard, blocked Gideon out of my mind, and shifted my attention to the four people creeping closer to my apartment door and the shadows of four more coming up the other two stairwells.

We couldn't get caught. Especially not now. It would have been bad enough if they'd found me at home, but I'd fled again, sneaking around with the man I'd freed from custody. How would they not see me dodging my team as an act of guilt? Every step I took away from them made it that much harder for me to explain myself.

And if I never found the evidence to clear my name?

I squeezed my eyes shut.

Being caught now could lose me my stripes, my uniform, maybe my freedom if not my life. It would also crush any chance I had to uncover the source of the rot spreading through the department.

I sensed them moving further onto the floor, close enough now to hear snippets of conversation.

"… you sure?"

"It's what the boss told us," said a voice I didn't recognize.

"They're looking at her for the minister's murder."

"The captain?" someone else asked. This voice I knew. Xander. "I don't believe that for a second."

"Believe it or not, it's what they're saying. So we find her, we bring her in for questioning. But from what I hear, she won't be your captain much longer. Now shut up, I think I heard something."

If he had, it wasn't either of us. Gideon stood frozen against me, and I felt incapable of making a sound. It was one thing to expect someone to accuse me of murder, but something else to hear someone say it. And for them to send my own team… Had Michael given the order? Was he one of the people who believed I was involved?

Couldn't be. He wouldn't.

No matter how hard I tried to convince myself, the fear lingered that it was true. I'd made the best decisions I could in the moment, but I'd been the one to watch Dougall strap Madison to that ghostbomb. I'd been the one Madison had shown her evidence to, and we'd been the ones to find the minister dead. The ones to find Gideon lost in the dark corners of our detainment centre, undocumented and at death's door. No one else had been there. No one else could know the choice I'd been left with or the truth that had hit me over the head that someone we trusted was behind it all.

Someone was setting me up, just as my team had been set up in the de Lauer attack, and I wouldn't let it stand. I would find a way to clear my name, to protect Madison and Gideon, and to point the finger at the real killer.

First, I had to get us out of here unseen, and every second that passed closed the window for our safe escape.

I crossed my fingers and prayed to every god I'd heard of that the pair moving towards us wouldn't come around the corner.

Chapter 5

Gideon

Jet's heartbeat raced against mine, and my pulse shifted to match hers until I couldn't tell whose was whose.

It was fear, I told myself. Fear of being found by the people coming after us.

It had nothing to do with how close she was or the thrill of the chase, even if for a change we were the hunted instead of the hunters.

Her body tensed, ready to spring, and I clung to her tighter to make sure she remembered to take me with her. Only when my fingers curled around the belt loop of her jeans did I realize I'd grabbed hold of her hips when she'd hauled me around the corner, and now that I'd noticed it, despite everything, my body responded.

Hockey, I told myself. *Think about hockey. That last trade deal was bullshit. What were the Rangers thinking? Fuck, her body's rock hard, but still so goddamned soft.* Memories poured through my mind of the long nights spent in my apartment. Rain falling, the smell of rotting leaves in the air, cool nights bundled under blankets, sweat dripping between her breasts as she—

For God's sake, Gideon, focus. Your life is on the line here.

Before I had time to switch to detailing every meal I'd eaten this week, Jet frowned and jerked her head towards the corner. We were clear to move.

I released my breath and followed her into the stairwell, expecting to head down, skirt around the guys in the lobby, and reach the street. Instead, we started up. Trusting her to have thought out a plan, I kept my mouth shut and let her lead.

The pace she kept was tough to match with my strained muscles and torn flesh, but I pushed myself to stay close. The lashes on my back, still not fully healed, burned as they chafed against my shirt, and my jeans were hell against the gashes on my legs, but all of that would be nothing if we were caught.

Carstairs's leering smile crept into my thoughts, and I almost tripped over the back of Jet's heel. For a quick second, darkness fell over me, and I was back in that cell, every tiny wound bursting into a thousand more.

At the idea of being his plaything again, all the fire rushing through my blood at the press of Jet's body turned to ash in my mouth.

I meant what I'd told Jet—I wouldn't abandon her when we were only in this situation because she'd saved me, but if our plans went to shit and I had to decide between misting away or becoming Carstairs's pet, she would have to forgive me, because I wouldn't stick around.

Can't think like that. Not caught yet.

I pushed myself harder and chased after Jet as she exited onto the fifth floor and led us around to the east side of the building.

She stopped short, paused, then grabbed my arm and jerked me around the corner to hurry us down the hallway. Her expression was pinched with concentration, watching something I couldn't see, and all I could do was cross my fingers she saw enough to get us out of here.

My heart raced, my tongue dry and prickling. Every instinct I had told me to pull out of her grip and save myself, and even when we stopped, I felt as though I were fighting against a riptide.

A door opened down the hallway, footsteps approached, and soon we were moving again. Back into the stairwell and down to the fourth floor, around to the north side of the building. What the hell were we doing? Did she have any actual plan to find an exit, or was our best chance to stay out of their way until they gave up the search?

I didn't know how much longer I could keep up with her.

We rounded another corner, stopped again. I wanted to scream at her to keep running, keep moving, but I clenched my teeth and stayed quiet.

"*Shit*," I heard her whisper, and at the intensity in her dark eyes, I shared her frustration. We still weren't safe.

Somehow they'd stayed on our trail, not close enough to see us, but always dogging our steps. As far as I could tell, we'd been dodging at random, zigging their zag. Was it a coincidence they were sticking so close behind us, or did they have someone on their team whose ability countered Jet's? If that were the case, we were fucked.

Her brow furrowed as she looked behind us, and her eyes widened. "Gideon."

She pointed at the floor the way we'd come, at the tiny dark spots leading right to us.

I followed the trail to the big red bloodstain that had soaked the hem of my T-shirt. To the blood that had pooled on the edge of my belt and dripped a steady pattern onto the floor.

"Fuck me," I said, and raised my shirt to see what had happened.

The gash down my middle had reopened, the angry mouth spitting red breadcrumbs at every turn. No wonder we hadn't been able to get ahead—I'd left a helpful path for them to follow.

My head swam with exhaustion, but I forced myself to summon my remaining strength. If we wanted to disappear, I had to stay with it.

I closed my eyes and sent my mind to the blood swimming in my veins, sank into it, connected with it. Normally the effort of doing something so simple would have been as easy as picking up a slice of bread, but pain burrowed deep into my side, my brain aware of the wound now that my eyes had seen it. Adrenaline surged beneath the sharp burn, clearing my head but also driving home the need to run.

Need to hurry. Can't slow down.

I sucked in a breath and focused harder, starting with one cell and then another, until the process came back to me and I dissolved the blood into mist. I stretched my mind beyond myself, grabbed every familiar bit of me within reach, and when I opened my eyes, the blood trail had vanished within three feet of where we stood. As long as I paid attention, all evidence of our route ended here.

Jet nodded, satisfied if wary, but before we could celebrate, another doorway opened. We were out of time.

She rushed us around the next corner to the western stairwell. Although we hadn't made much progress thanks to my unintentional handiwork, she'd kept us ahead of her people. It had been a long time since I'd seen her in action like this, and I remembered why I'd been so quick to follow her lead in New York. Despite the danger, despite the devil at our backs, she didn't appear flustered or fazed. Her sole focus was on the next step, adjusting her plan as she went. Living up to her rank.

Again, I expected her to take us down, but we went back up, bypassing the fifth floor and the sixth. I had no idea what to think when she pushed open the access door to the roof.

What were we going to do? Jump?

But I had to have faith she knew what she was doing. That she hadn't decided the only way out was a long fall.

I did my best not to get too close to the edge. I didn't like to dwell on it, but me and heights didn't get along so well. Misting only worked as long as I had the time and clear-headedness to do it, neither of which I would find during a sharp drop.

"Can we access the fire escape up here?" I asked, shifting my gaze to take in the beer cans and cigarette butts scattered across the tar surface. Clearly the roof was a popular hangout spot for the residents. Although, considering the beer cans and cigarette butts that littered the front entrance, the lobby, and the stairwell, I doubted there was an unpopular spot in this building to get one's buzz on.

"We're not taking the fire escape," Jet said, and when I looked her way, I found her scanning the buildings that neighboured hers. Her gaze jumped from one to another, and her fingers tapped against her thigh in a steady pattern I remembered well. She was debating something, trying to make up her mind.

I didn't like the way she eyed those other buildings.

"You have a plan, then?"

"Shut up," she said, but her order was detached, unemotional.

She closed her eyes, and I held my breath and looked over the ledge to the ground six storeys below.

Shit.

"Shit," she said, echoing me to such a perfect pitch I wondered if I'd spoken aloud. Her eyes were open, and she watched the door as she hurried to the eastern side of the building. Over here was another apartment building, this one about eight storeys tall. Far enough away and with enough of a height difference that there was no way she could consider jumping, but a lot more manageable than the shady high-rise to the north.

Jet jumped onto the ledge that circled the roof, and my first reaction was to lurch towards her, ready to catch her.

"Hoping to learn how to fly?" I asked, impressed by how casual I sounded when my insides had turned to water.

"I thought I might run."

I peered over the side to where her car waited below. "It's a far way to fall."

"All part of the adventure. Now shut up."

She screwed her eyes tight and raised her arms in front of her. The air around me tingled, making the hairs on my arms and the back of my neck dance. Jet's face turned red, sweat beaded on her brow, and her hands trembled.

"What—"

I didn't want to ask, I wanted to shut up and trust her, but whatever she was doing was taking too much out of her. Pushing herself was not a solution, not after the other close calls she'd faced this week. Three ghostbombs and a bar fight with a bull-man and a mountain were enough for a year, let alone a few days. What hope did we have if she burned out?

I glanced over my shoulder at the door. Still closed. No sign that anyone knew we were up here. We had time to come up with another plan. We could work together to get down the fire escape.

I opened my mouth to suggest it, but as I turned to face her, the words dried on my tongue.

In front of Jet, the air wavered, drawing together into a shimmering force that looked impossibly tangible.

"Either mist or move," she said through clenched teeth, not opening her eyes to see what I'd do.

I started to dissolve. There was no way I was crossing what I could only descibe as an air bridge created by her sheer force of will.

But halfway through misting, my strength ran out. The blood loss, the pain, the exhaustion—I was worn down to a point where my body refused to do what I told it to. Even if I succeeded in disappearing, there was no way I'd be able to hold it—or, worst case, no way I'd be able to bring myself back.

My heart thrummed. I'd left the ability-blocking collar back in the cell, but I may as well have been wearing it. My greatest advantage was useless, and any delay would put me back in Carstairs's grasp.

Come on, Gideon. What's worse—a possible fall to your death or him?

My choice was obvious: I had to run.

I closed my eyes as I stepped onto the ledge, but I couldn't keep them closed if I wanted to make it across without stepping off the side of nothing.

"All right," I said under my breath. "I can do this. I can do this. Why can't I walk on air? It's absolutely able to hold my weight."

If I said it often enough, maybe eventually I'd believe it.

"Come on," Jet hissed. Her entire body trembled, her face a dangerous shade of red.

She was holding on for me and still had to get across herself. *Stop fucking around, Leigh.*

I licked my lips and stepped onto the bridge, exhaling sharply when the air held firm under my boot. But the longer I stood still, the more the unseen surface gave way beneath me, so I stopped thinking and ran.

It was impossible to see the bridge if I looked at it directly, but if I kept my gaze glued to the roof across, I caught a glimpse of it in my periphery, a shimmering reflection in the sunlight of something that wasn't supposed to be there.

Thirty feet. Twenty-five. Twenty. I counted off the steps, not once pausing to think of what awaited me at the bottom if I fell. Falling wasn't an option.

My thighs burned with the uphill run, which would have been an easy dash on a good day. Sweat dripped down the collar of my shirt, and my lungs strained as I worked to keep my breath steady. I was pretty sure I was about to throw up.

And then, suddenly, there I was, standing on the roof of the next building. Alive. Free. Definitely about to throw up.

I collapsed onto my hands and knees and pulled myself to the ledge, peering over the side to watch Jet.

She opened her eyes, her brow still wrinkled with the effort of using her ability as she stepped onto the bridge.

Come on, Jet. Hurry.

Sweat shone on her face, and her legs wobbled as she sped into a jog. The strain of keeping the bridge intact was taking its toll. She'd only made it a quarter of the way across and patches behind her were fading.

Her foot slipped, and my heart jumped into my throat.

She caught herself, but her balance was too shaky, her pace too ragged.

She wasn't going to reach the other side.

Cement dug into the pads of my fingers as I tightened my grip on the sharp corner of the ledge. I had to be ready to grab her if the bridge collapsed. I didn't know if dissolving right now would kill me—or if I could catch her even if it didn't—but damned if I was going to watch her fall without doing whatever I could to prevent her from hitting the ground at full impact.

Keeping low to stay out of view, I braced my feet against the roof, ready to throw myself at her if she needed me. She'd reached the halfway mark now and was picking up speed, her gait smoothing as she shifted into a run. Watching her sprint in what appeared to be mid-air between buildings made my stomach do flip-flops. How was this possible? How was she holding on?

Come on.

I didn't care as long as she was able to keep it up for a few more seconds.

She hit the three-quarter mark. I moved over, positioning myself to grab her hand when she reached the ledge.

Just as I reached for her, the stairwell door on the roof across the way flew open.

Chapter 6

Jet

ALMOST THERE. YOU'RE *almost there.*

The air bridge stretched out in front of me, a fragile walkway held together by stubbornness and the dregs of my determination. My need to hurry seemed to slow time, as though I were running through molasses, stuck at an infuriating crawl while the world zipped by me.

I should have started across right after Gideon, but I'd had to make sure my strength held until he reached the other side. He'd put his trust in me, and I needed to see him safe.

But now fatigue tugged on my muscles, the strain of keeping the bridge dense enough to carry my weight more than I had the energy for after too little food, even less sleep, and no chance to recover after the last time I'd exerted my ability.

So close now.

My foot slipped through the bridge where the air had

grown thin. I caught myself mid-stride and kept running. It was a miracle I'd kept my hold this long, but in a few more seconds it wouldn't matter that I'd gotten myself wrapped up in a fight against the syndicate and a corrupt government department. I'd be nothing more than a splatter on the roof of my car seven storeys below.

We were almost out, away from my team and free to find somewhere safe to hole up until I was ready to approach them on my terms. Hopefully with enough evidence of my innocence to get them on my side.

When I was within two steps from safety, a slam rang out behind me as the door to the roof of my building flew open and struck against the brick wall. My focus veered towards the sound, my third eye instinctively opening to gauge the threat, and as soon as my attention shifted, my hold on the air let go and the bridge vanished.

My stomach leapt into my throat as my feet flailed on open sky, and the blood rushing in my ears drowned out all other sound. For a split second, panic wiped my thoughts, my training. My breath stopped, my heart stopped—every sense caught in the anticipation of what waited for me on the ground.

Instinct returned first, and in a wild scramble, I grabbed for the ledge. Just before I slipped out of reach, Gideon grabbed my wrist. My body slammed into the side of the building, and at the impact, my years of training pushed through the fear that had fogged my mind. Gritting my teeth, I latched on to Gideon's forearm and used my shoulder to shove away from the wall and give myself space to find my footing against the brick. Sweat dripped down my face, mirrored on his, but I measured my breaths, tightened my core, and concentrated on reaching the top, tearing up the side of the building at a pace that threatened to make me vomit up my lungs.

As soon as the ledge reached chest-height, Gideon gave me a final tug, and we both rolled onto the rooftop, hidden from view of anyone stepping onto the roof across the way.

I lay on my back and stared at the black spots swimming against the bright blue sky. My chest ached with sharp breaths I couldn't seem to slow, and the muscles in my back squeezed and released, an uneven, agonizing rhythm of spasms that sent sympathetic pangs down my arms and legs. The pain was a relief, keeping me from considering the emotional significance of the last few seconds.

Gideon lay still beside me, his expression open with shock and lingering horror.

I guessed we were even now. A life for a life. There went my advantage.

And now I'd have to thank him. *Shit.*

He recovered before I did and pulled himself to the ledge, peering over it to scope out the other rooftop.

"Did they see us?" I asked, keeping my voice low.

"Doesn't look like it. The door blocked most of their view. They're doing a tour of the roof, but not—oops." He ducked down. I glared at him, but he shook his head. "They're doing a scan, clearing the building."

I heard the clang and clatter of boots going down the fire escape and joined Gideon at the ledge, my hand pressed against my ribs to try to keep them in place. I worried they were about to collapse on me, taking my heart and lungs with them.

We watched two of the soldiers head down the steps towards the parking lot and meet up with two more once they reached the bottom. My heart sank into my shoes as I recognized them. Adam. Eric. Katie. They'd sent my longest-serving troops to bring me in.

What would they have done if they'd found me? Considering all we'd been through together, I wanted to think they would have stopped long enough to let me explain. Eric and I didn't see eye to eye about the dark truth behind the de Lauer attack, but maybe Adam, Katie, or Xander would have believed me and helped me convince Eric to take a chance and follow my lead. I wanted to think their loyalty would have stretched far enough to know I had nothing to do with the minister's death and that my freeing Gideon hadn't been an act of rebellion but an attempt to undo the injustice the syndicate had committed under our roof.

Would our years of training, our missions, our history have been enough for them to let me go, or would they have followed orders, turned on me, and dragged me in as a rogue agent?

Would they still see me as their captain, their packleader?

The thought that I'd broken their faith in me stole whatever calm I'd managed to regain. My palms turned clammy, and I collapsed with light-headedness, thankful I hadn't needed to find out whether I had lost the trust of some of the most important people in my life.

"They're gone," Gideon said. He sagged to the ground beside me, his back against the ledge, and dragged his knees to his chest.

More blood had soaked through his shirt, and he grimaced, pulling up the ruined cotton to expose the gash across his stomach. It stretched from his rib cage to his navel and must have sliced deeper than his other wounds if he'd failed to seal it.

I'd seen the way he'd tried to turn to mist before he'd run across the bridge, and now that we were safe, I had time to understand what it meant that he hadn't been able to. He might have stayed with me to have my back, but he'd been in no place to get himself away. He'd relied on me to keep him out of my team's hands—out of Carstairs's hands—and I'd almost failed him. All that running up and down stairs, him pushing through pain and exhaustion to keep pace with me, and we almost hadn't made it. He might be angry with me for letting Carstairs get his hands on him the first time, but I'd had no idea what waited for him when Eric took him away. This time, however… If Carstairs got him again, Gideon's blood would be on my hands.

Maybe it was the sight of him beside me, pale and sweating,

but suddenly I found it easy to say, "Thanks for catching me."

He grimaced as he pressed his hands into his side and shifted into a more comfortable position. "If you fell, my ticket home would be nothing more than a blood spatter on the concrete."

His words were casual, joking, but his tone gave away enough of his fading fear, enough of his relief, to take the sting out of his seeming indifference.

For a change—a very brief window—I didn't feel a desire to hit him.

While the two of us waited for our heartbeats to slow, I considered our next move. We needed to get the hell out of here before my team moved into phase two of their search for us. I knew them too well to think they'd let me disappear this easily. From here, they'd step up surveillance. Someone across the street, and someone on one of the neighbouring rooftops. Possibly this one.

A fleeting thought passed through my mind that maybe I wouldn't be in this mess if I'd trusted my JetPack to help me from the start. If I'd brought them in on my conversations with the informants, they might have been at my side right now instead of hunting me down.

I shoved the wish away as soon as I noticed it. If they'd joined me, I would have had to hold that bridge for a dozen people instead of two. They'd be in the same situation I was— if not suspected of murder, then at least as accessories. Hard as it was to stand on opposing sides, they were safer this way. I had to remember that.

My phone buzzed in my pocket, and with a sigh of relief and no small amount of irritation, I pulled it free, groaning with the effort of moving my arms. I didn't recognize the number on the screen but took the chance it was the call we'd been waiting for.

"About fucking time," I wheezed.

"Sorry," Madison said. "I had to—"

"Don't care. You're somewhere safe?"

"I just left, but what—"

"They know."

Silenced stretched out on the line. At last, she said, "Meet me at our place," and the phone went dead.

Chapter 7

Madison

THE MOMENT I hung up on Jet, I officially left my old life behind. Temporarily or permanently I couldn't say, but until we stopped the syndicate, the Madison Prince of Laurier Avenue with her comfortable condo, uncomfortable shoes, and latest-model Acura was gone, and in her place was the Madison Prince of durable footwear, large sunglasses, and whatever beater Gary had picked up for me.

I was least upset about the shoes.

I didn't bother to drive to Mooney's Pub. It was a ten-minute walk away, and though I risked being recognized by any co-workers who happened to be out hunting down breakfast before work, I was less conspicuous on foot than my car would have been parked on the street. Besides, I appreciated the extra time to get my thoughts in order.

In the early morning, the bar was quiet. Mooney's regularly

stayed open just shy of twenty-four hours, closed long enough to clean up and change the guard. Not because it was the most popular bar on a street full of bars, but because it was the only one in the area that catered specifically to downtown's supernatural population. The more nocturnal folk needed somewhere to go after standard last call, even if the mundanes believed it locked its doors at legal hours.

At this time of day, the few early birds had staked out their tables, but I'd either missed or beaten the breakfast rush. I was torn about whether the emptiness worked in our favour. There were fewer people to overhear our conversation, but it would be harder to go unnoticed.

Alyssa Mooney—owner, founder, witch—stood behind the bar filling orders for a couple of university students at the far end of the cherrywood bartop, the two young men unshaved, unrested, unmotivated.

Late-year postgrads were my guess, and I couldn't have asked for better company. They would be too desperate to escape their research papers to pay attention to whoever else might pull up a stool.

Alyssa delivered their coffees with an extra bowl of beernuts out of sympathy, then made her way over to me wearing a bright smile.

"Bit early for you, isn't it?" she asked. A glint of jade shone in her eyes, the unnaturally green irises one of the few signs of her magic-infused genes. "I don't think I've ever seen you here at the start of the day in all my years behind the bar." Her smile collapsed under a wave of concern. "Everything all right?"

This was where mundanes often overestimated their idea of supernaturals. Fans of fantasy media might guess Alyssa had reached her conclusions so quickly out of some latent psychic ability, but I knew it was simply her bartender attention to detail.

Or maybe I was wrong and bartending called to people with a particular ability—either known or unknown—to poke around in people's minds.

Either way, her skills were too good to bother lying to her.

"I'm in a bit of a jam, actually," I said, though I kept my tone light and conversational. "Me and some friends of mine. I don't suppose they're here yet?"

It worked to my advantage I only ever came here with Jet. Alyssa would know who I meant without my having to spell it out, and right now vagueness would be safer for both of us.

She shook her head and shifted to put her back to the students and the two occupied tables near the front window. One of the bleary-eyed postgrads had already finished his coffee, and the complimentary beer nuts were almost gone.

"What's going on?" She kept her voice low and pasted on an even brighter smile, giving her words a pleased, gossiping note for the benefit of any eavesdroppers.

Clever duck.

"Ran into a bit of a work sitch," I said, and threw in an inane laugh for good measure. "You know, the usual top-secret, confidential nonsense." The strain of maintaining my bubbly facade wore on me. "The sort of crap where, if I told you, I'd have to kill you and all that mess."

Would she catch my too-subtle warning? I didn't want to be any more overt.

As confusion crossed her face, I worried I'd have to take a step closer to honesty, but awareness dawned in the next breath, and she laughed through the stickiness of worry I sensed wafting off her. "I'll save myself the bother and skip the personal questions."

"I probably should have stayed home and gone back to bed, but to hell with it. It's noon somewhere, right? I needed a drink and couldn't think of anywhere else I'd rather be."

Last resort. I hoped she understood. The last thing I wanted was to put Alyssa in danger. She'd been a friend of mine and Jet's for a good many years, and I didn't want to lead the department to her door. But it had been the first and best place I could think of for me and Jet to meet up. I hadn't felt comfortable giving her the address of the safe house over the phone, not if the department had already come after her.

Hopefully Alyssa would forgive me for bringing trouble to her doorstep.

She grabbed a rag from under the bar and started wiping the surface, taking particular note of anything I might have touched.

"As far as I'm concerned," she said without looking up

from the bartop or losing her smile, though she did drop her voice to a lower volume, "the only people here right now are those two guys, who will soon be too overcaffeinated on free coffee to notice anything, and the two tables by the window. There's definitely no one in the loft at this time of morning. It's too quiet and out of the way." She pulled a bottle opener from the same place she'd grabbed the rag and slid it across to me. "And there definitely aren't a few bottles of craft upstairs in case anyone needs something to settle their nerves."

I wrapped my fingers around the cold metal and swallowed the ball that formed in my throat. Alyssa caught my gaze and gave me a quick wink before returning her attention to the students at the bar. She refilled their mugs and went to check her tables. My way was clear.

I took the opportunity and snuck up the stairs in the back corner to the overflow seating on the second floor.

The loft wasn't my favourite part of the bar. During the crowded evenings it was too hot and closed in, and during the day there weren't enough windows to brighten the wood panelling. But it was quiet and empty. Alyssa was right—just what we needed.

I chose a table in the corner out of direct view of the stairs. If anyone came up other than Jet and Gideon, I might have time to sneak out the window onto the roof to avoid being seen.

My newfound paranoia clearly thought I was an action hero.

The bottle opener pressed into my palm, and though I wasn't typically one for beer, especially first thing in the morning, at the moment I needed something to keep myself busy and save me from the cottony dryness that had taken over my mouth. I crossed over to the mini-bar fridge and pulled out a bottle, popping the cap and leaving both it and some money on the bar for Alyssa. Just because I was making use of her hospitality didn't mean I intended to take advantage of it.

Beer in hand, I sat at the table and checked my new smartphone. It, along with five other identical phones, had been waiting in my mailbox when I'd left my condo. Gary, my gnomic friend, had pulled through. New numbers, no history, no tracking. The best way to keep in touch with the increasingly few people I trusted and cut myself off from everyone else.

I set the phone on the table in front of me and stared at the screen, waiting for it to ring even though I knew it wouldn't. Once in a while, I looked towards the stairs, but they remained empty.

I sipped my beer, my nerves growing more frazzled with every passing minute. Where were they? Jet didn't live that far away, and by the sound of it, she'd been in a rush. How did she know they knew? Had they come for her? Called her? How much did they know? The questions piled inside my skull, growing more frantic the longer they remained unanswered.

Before I broke my own rule of radio silence and call her again, the stairs creaked, and her familiar face peeked around the corner. Her harried, tense face, with her dusty black T-shirt and uneven ponytail. What the hell had happened?

Her gaze darted around the room—paranoia had obviously hit her as well—and only when she was sure no threat awaited them did she step aside and allow Gideon to come in. The sight of him floored me. When we'd found him in his darkened cell, he'd been barely able to stand, covered in so much blood I'd had trouble recognizing the man underneath. Now, only a few hours later, he could have come out the victor of a nasty fight, bruised and stiff but otherwise unscathed. No wonder he looked so tired. That sort of quick healing would suck the energy out of anyone.

He wasn't completely in the clear, though. Although he wore a different shirt, it was already soaked through, blood and sweat staining everything not hidden by his black vest.

I raised my hand to catch their attention, and they joined me without saying a word. At the sight of my beer, Jet quirked an eyebrow. I gestured to the bottle opener on the counter, then to the fridge. She looked to Gideon. He nodded.

She went to the bar, grabbed two bottles, and left the caps and a few bills next to mine. It might not make up for the hell that would rain down on Alyssa if she were caught harbouring fugitives, but at least no one could accuse us of stealing. Beer, anyway. I stroked my satchel full of papers that, legally, I didn't have the authorization to read anymore.

Jet returned to the table, passed Gideon his beer, and took

a sip of her own.

Finally, feeling more confident we weren't about to be interrupted by some stray patron, I asked, "What's the news?"

She glanced at Gideon, who shrugged, and said, "Four cars, twelve soldiers." Her throat worked with a swallow. "My team, mostly."

I shivered against the chill of sadness that dripped off her, as crisp and bitter as a late fall morning, and did my best to block my awareness of her emotions. Normally she was better at guarding herself from me. I wanted to respect her privacy, but she was too distraught to keep her barrier up.

Gideon either didn't care enough to hide himself, didn't know how, or didn't know what I was capable of, because his emotions were an open book. The rage I'd sensed in him from the moment we'd first crossed paths was still there, a deep simmering heat he likely didn't notice anymore. It was too ingrained in who he was.

But there was so much more than that. Enough so that, if I allowed myself to pry, I'd be concerned about losing myself in the chaos. His superficial appearance, all casual arrogance, almost indifference, was nothing more than a thinly laid veil for everything swirling under the surface of his mind. There was fear—a complicated bouquet that ebbed and flowed with his shifting thoughts, and something… something warmer, something that sparked and smouldered whenever he looked at Jet. Something that went a long way to soften my opinion of him.

Though I would never tell Jet. It wasn't my place.

Overpowering all of that, though, was a sense of defeat that most certainly hadn't been there when I'd met him outside Dougall's house. Before Carstairs had gotten his hands on him. I didn't know how much he'd told Jet about what he'd gone through, but although he'd been pretty tight-lipped with me, I suspected he'd suffered more than physical torture during his twenty-four hours.

The back of my throat burned with horror and disgust over the possibilities, but more than that was my worry about what it meant for his psyche. That sort of soul-crushing hopelessness was enough to break the strongest person.

Unfortunately, I couldn't say anything to either reassure or sympathize without admitting I'd poked around in his head, so I turned my attention to Jet and hoped that, whatever existed between these two, she would be able to help guide him out of the darkness.

"What are you thinking?" I asked her. "That they came to arrest you?"

Jet dropped her forehead into the cradle of her palms. "From what I overheard, they were supposed to bring me in for questioning. And if the department convinced my team to turn on me…" She shuddered, and I understood her apprehension. Her team was her life. As she'd risen in the ranks to captain, she'd brought them together, trained them, supported them. They were her family. If they turned on her, her entire career would be washed away. If it hadn't been anyway, considering our situation. "I don't know if they believed I was involved before, but now that I've run away again, who knows what they think. If ever we'd considered reaching out to them, I think that resource is dead."

Her face took on a faint greenish tinge, and Gideon pushed her beer towards her. She chugged it back, but it didn't appear to soothe her fractured state.

She was falling apart, and the only way I could see to pull her together was to put her to work.

"Our options are limited," I said, "but we do have a few. My contact has an off-the-books apartment and a new car waiting for us, so at least we'll have a base of operations. Jet, do you have anyone you can bring in?"

She hesitated, staring deeply into her beer, and then nodded, and as she considered the possibilities, her expression cleared. Comfort spread through my tense muscles. We hadn't lost her to desperation yet.

"The syndicate made a mistake when they wiped out our informants," she said. "I know a few people through Rourke, and they won't be happy to learn he was ambushed outside the club."

"I have a few names I can bring to the table, too," Gideon said, as though each word were an effort. Beneath his fuzzy exhaustion, however, was an iron vein of determination. Regardless of what he'd endured, he wasn't backing down.

"You think your contacts are different from mine?" Jet

asked, her words laced with skepticism.

The corner of his mouth curled. "I know they are."

"Here. In my city."

A mischievous gleam came into his eyes above a tight, cynical smile. "You jealous?"

She sputtered. "What? Are you—no. That's not the point, Gideon. You were here, in *my* city, reaching out to *my* people, and you didn't have the decency to bring me in on it."

And we were right back where we'd been outside Dougall's house, Gideon on his high horse acting like he intended to take control of the operation, and Jet getting defensive that he was making independent moves in her territory. Emotions bounced around the room, strong enough to trigger the headache I'd been trying so hard to keep at bay. Gideon's anger swirled with a wild streak of enjoyment. Jet's fury steamed alongside her hurt and disappointment.

Navigating our way through a government conspiracy would be impossible if these two didn't work out their issues.

"All right," I said, interrupting, "it sounds like we're in a good spot. We have a place to stay, and we have a possible grapevine to tap into. What more do we need? Except to decide whether we're actually going forward with figuring this out on our own."

Jet fell silent, and her gaze dropped to her beer bottle, a crease forming between her brows.

Gideon frowned. "Why wouldn't we?"

"Because we'd be moving against our department," she said, speaking my biggest reservation aloud. The one that had stayed with me despite everything I'd learned, seen, done. "If we don't find the proof we need to uncover the mole, we could be charged with who knows what. There's already a murder investigation hanging over my head, but will they settle for that or try for whatever else the syndicate can pin on us? Anything to discredit us before we have a chance to out them."

"Time will be a factor here," I agreed. "They won't sit around waiting to see what we'll do."

"They don't know how much we have on them, right?" said Gideon. "They might suspect, but if they've got a plan, they won't let a few suspicions hold them back. They'll need to keep moving forward. The community is up in arms. How long before the riots get so bad their hands are tied? They'll need to shut people up if they don't want to risk being noticed by the muns."

I appreciated his perspective but didn't feel as optimistic. "Unless the riots are part of the plan. It's a lot easier to work in the shadows when everyone is focused on what's happening in the open. Not to mention the discord it's sowing. Pitting groups against each other."

Jet pinched the bridge of her nose. "If that's the case, we don't know how far ahead they are. We might already be too late to stop them."

"Or we might have a golden opportunity," Gideon pushed.

"If they're stirring up these protests to act as a screen, their window is limited. They won't want to waste their time or resources searching for us. We play this smart and we'll be able to come up on their blind side."

I exchanged a look with Jet. He had a point.

"We could still come forward," I said, proposing the alternative that needed to be shared. "We haven't technically done anything wrong. Even freeing Gideon was a human rights issue. The people behind this won't want to gain the bad press if word gets out the Death's Head Syndicate has infiltrated the department and is using the SMOAC uniform to torture a foreign agent. News like that would bring the Americans down on us. We didn't kill the minister, we didn't have anything to do with the ghostbombs. For all intents and purposes, we're innocent victims in this. Surely Michael and Lucien would believe us. At the very least they'd hear us out."

"Sure," Jet said. "Absolutely. I have no doubt they would have our backs. But who would they ask to investigate? How could we be sure we wouldn't be putting *them* in danger, too? Until we know who's involved, we don't know who we can talk to. Not on an official level, anyway. Michael might know more if I went to him quietly, but he would feel obligated to bring me in. I don't want to put him in that position unless I have to."

I understood her reasoning. Jet's commanding officer was a good man who cared for her as a father would, but while family counted for a lot in this department, rules and regulations had to come first. It was how we kept the country running.

It was how I would have felt about bringing what I'd found to Jean-Luc's door. If he weren't dead. If all signs didn't point to him being at the heart of the corruption.

Jet passed her hands over her face. "I hate this. I hate that we're having this conversation. I have spent my entire career taking orders from this department. To go against it…" She shook her head. "But what choice do we have? Someone is tearing our home apart. I can't let that stand. Whatever it takes, I'm ready to fight."

Everything she said hit me on a visceral level. The idea that someone I worked with—possibly chatted to or laughed with in the kitchen—was poisoning the roots of my family's legacy made me sick. For them to have done so in such a blatant manner—manipulating documents, guiding decisions—meant that if Jean-Luc hadn't been involved, or at least hadn't been the only executive involved, they had no reason to stop. Unless they were stopped. And how that happened could mean the difference between a few deaths or the overturning of two centuries of self-governance.

"There's more at stake than the department if the queen steps in," I said. "She'll bulldoze SMOAC, the syndicate, and any other threat to the ground, along with everything in their paths, before she lets anyone usurp her power at the expense of her people. As one of her representatives on this side of the wall, I need to act before that happens."

Jet met my eye, and beneath her queasy desperation was the steel that made her such a good soldier. Her surface might be fractured, but she wasn't close to breaking. Whatever walls stood in her way had better watch out.

"I'm in, too," Gideon said. Considering everything I sensed from him, his words shocked me into speechlessness. The murky fog of his hopelessness had convinced me he wasn't ready for this fight, but maybe I had underestimated the strength and depth of his anger and that warmer, unacknowledged emotion.

Jet stared at him in profound shock.

"You're what?" she asked. "Gideon, no. We talked about this. You're in no fit state to fight, and this is not your battle."

"It *is*," he said, curling his fist on the table. "You might have your nose bent out of shape about why I'm here, but my mission isn't finished yet. My orders are to stop the syndicate from stretching their roots across the border, and like hell if I'm going to leave before I've done it. So either I push forward on my own or I stay and help you, but I'm not going home until I have something to show for it."

I shook my head in disbelief. This man had been arrested and tortured, but when presented with an opportunity to, understandably and justifiably, run and get to safety, he didn't hesitate to risk another round. While I was sure he had many reasons, most of them a mystery, one big motivation lay open to me, radiating off him in sunstruck waves that made my stomach flutter. And she had no idea. Maybe he didn't, either.

They were both idiots.

Jet rolled her eyes, her lip curled with disdain, as though she would never consider taking such a step for her job, which we all knew was a lie. But underneath, I picked up a gentle hum of relief. She had to know as well as I did we needed all the help we could get. We were going up against a government department. Three no-names against some of the most power-ful people in our community. Very little support, no proof, and a crap-ton of prayers.

Meril help us, we would need to call in a lot of favours.

Chapter 8

Gideon

JET AND I left the bar as the early lunch crowd was coming in, both of us proud new owners of the smartphones Madison had picked up, all three programmed to reach each other and no one else.

What the hell had I done?

They'd given me an out. I could have been on a bus to the border within the hour. Misted past border patrol, reached my contacts on the other side, and waved a fond farewell to this sinking ship. Despite what I'd said, SilverGuard would have been happy with the information I'd gathered. They'd know about Dougall being the Ghostmaker, which would be their prime concern. The syndicate was a problem, but largely viewed as a Canadian problem. Without Dougall, there would be no ghost moving across the border—hell, no ghost being produced— which meant no American involvement.

Problem solved.

But no, instead of leaving this forest fire to Smokey and his friends, I'd thrown myself in with the underdogs, risking every-thing in the hope that these two knew what they were doing and that they had enough luck on their side to still be breathing after they'd won.

I was a world-class fool.

Yet despite the voice in the back of my mind yelling at me to run away from this suicide mission, I didn't feel I'd had much choice. Three wasn't much of an army to stand against a national crime syndicate and a government mole protected by money and resources, but it was a hell of a lot better than two.

Worst case, I could always leave if the situation got too hot. Jet had said it herself: this wasn't my fight. They couldn't fault me for choosing not to sacrifice myself for another country's oversights.

That was if SilverGuard didn't make a move anyway. My handler was probably suffering some kind of breakdown by now waiting for me to report in. Jet and Madison had found my clothes in the detainment centre, but my phone had disappeared, no doubt thrown in the trash after Sampson's people had tried to get whatever they could off it. Which wouldn't have been much. I wasn't so stupid as to leave anything valuable on it.

Without a phone, however, I had no way of contacting Dark Wire on a secure line, which meant they would be a real treat when I finally got in touch. Jet might be lucky if my people didn't ship a whole truckload of agents to Ottawa to wipe out Dougall, the syndicate, and anyone associated with them in one violent, messy sweep. Madison talked about the threat their queen posed to this side of the wall, but she'd never seen how efficient my people could be. They'd be in and done before Meril took her first step.

"Where to?" I asked Jet as we walked down the street. We'd left her car at her apartment, so unless she decided public transportation was the way to go, our destinations were limited.

"I have a few contacts within walking distance," she said. "Hopefully by the time we touch base with them, Madison will have arranged for our new wheels. Two sets if we're lucky."

It struck me as relying an awful lot on hopes and ifs, which wasn't usually how I worked my missions, but I said nothing. She was running this show—I was here to provide the pretty face and to watch her back. When you had to look in all directions at once, a second set of eyes came in handy.

We headed up Bank Street past a collection of pubs in the heart of Centretown. My stomach grumbled at the thought of a burger and fries, spurred on by the beer I'd half-finished at Mooney's, but Jet walked past them and stepped into a bookstore.

From the outside, the shop wasn't anything special, the windows full of poetry classics and art textbooks, local notices and sale announcements.

Inside, it looked like someone had flipped a library upside

down. There was hardly room to walk. Stacks on stacks of books on the floor; on desks; over, under, and around the bookshelves. It smelled musty, the kind of reek book lovers got high on but made me sneeze. I enjoyed a good le Carré as much as the next person, but preferred something short I could read on my phone and never spent more time than I had to surrounded by so many words. Jet had never come off as much of a reader, either, but she walked with ease to the counter and leaned over it to greet the man who was on his hands and knees organizing yet another stack of books on the floor.

"Hey, Shawn," she said.

He started and looked up, his round eyes large behind a pair of thick-lensed glasses. It took a moment, but a smile spread across his face. There was a tightness to it, a wariness, but I chalked it up to the tensions I'd sensed from most of our kind around here this week. "Bridget Dawson, how are you, my dear?"

"Oh, you know, can't complain," she said, rehearsing her entry for the Understatement of the Year Award. "I wanted to ask you a few questions. Do you have a minute?"

By the change in Shawn's expression, she may as well have asked if she could shoot his prize-winning poodle. His attempt at a smile vanished, replaced by a cold, hard stare that raised goosebumps on my arms. His eyes flashed red and his lip curled, and the change from friendly bookstore owner to feral demon was so sudden I had to stop myself from taking a step backwards.

"Excuse me?" he said, his words now lisped, as though working his tongue around sharpened fangs.

Jet frowned. "I just have—"

"You dare come in here with questions? You dare try to drag me into whatever problems you stirred up in this city?" He snorted at her obvious surprise. "Oh yes, don't think I'm ignorant of your involvement in all this, *Captain*. Mitchel called me after you went to see him. Told me you were poking around. Look what happened to him."

She paled and her lips parted, as though he'd punched her in the gut, and by the flash of horror in her eyes, she'd been sucked right back into the basement where she'd found Lafontaine's mangled corpse.

What exactly was this son of a bitch suggesting? That she was responsible for his death? Was he stupid enough to let his rage focus on the person who was trying to help instead of the people who had done the actual slaughtering?

Anger swam in my veins, prickling my skin, but I pressed my lips together. Jet had come here for a reason, and me throwing a fist into this creature's face wouldn't get us what she wanted.

A moment passed as she pulled herself together. "I'm sorry, Shawn," she said, her voice quiet, her sympathy a mask for her personal pain. I curled my hand on the counter, still debating the pros and cons of stopping this guy from making her feel worse than she already did. "I didn't mean for any harm to come to him."

His eyes widened. "You didn't mean—" he sputtered. "It doesn't matter what you *meant*, it's that you didn't *think*. And poor Mac would still be grieving in the basement if I hadn't come forward as Mitchel's next of kin to claim him and bring him home."

Confusion clouded my thoughts until I remembered Lafontaine's Rottweiler.

"Forty years I knew that man," Shawn continued, tears spilling over his cheeks. "What am I—how am I—"

He turned away, and Jet bowed her head, her eyes squeezed shut. Her jaw flexed as she battled whatever emotions his reaction had triggered, and when she raised her chin, her gaze was hard. "I'm sorry. I really am. But it was necessary to speak with him. The information he gave me could save lives."

Shawn spat. "It didn't save his. Or are other people's lives more important than one adlet? What about the lives that have been torn apart by this—this war that's suddenly being waged on our city?"

I clenched my teeth, holding myself back from grabbing this man by the throat. Not because he was angry and grieving, but because he had no idea how much Jet had lost in the same brewing war. More than he could imagine.

Jet said nothing. She was a wall, standing strong against his fury.

"Whatever questions you have, you can save them for

someone else," he said. "Too many people are getting hurt for no good reason, and I see no point in being one of them."

This last comment broke through Jet's patience as red crept into her cheeks. She rested her hands on the counter. "You're right. The city is in trouble. It's bullshit, but it's not going to change if people don't help. Will you really hole yourself up in here when you could make a difference?"

"Why should I risk my life for people who don't want to help me?"

"Mitchel did," she said, and I sucked in a silent breath as Shawn's red eyes narrowed. "He knew the risks, and he still did what he had to do, and thanks to him, we stand a chance of ending this conflict before it really starts."

"He might have believed blabbing was worth it, but I don't." She opened her mouth to say more, but he cut her off. "I want to be left alone to live my life. What's left of it. Isn't that what you guys at SMOAC promise us? That we have as many rights and resources as the rest of the country? Prove it. Do your job, fix the problem, and leave me the hell out of it. Now get out of my store."

Jet shoved away from the counter, her face flushed. I braced myself, ready to step in if she needed backup, but she turned on her heel and stalked towards the door. I kept up with her when what I really wanted to do was give the man a solid shake, but I limited myself to shooting him a dark look over my shoulder.

"I can't believe him," she said after she'd stormed a few blocks away. "If he and Mitchel were that close, how can he not want to prove who killed him? I've seen that man fight, heard stories about the role he played in the Magic Riots. He's no coward."

"Do you think someone threatened him?"

"Yeah." Her shoulders slumped. "He's threatened the same way we all are. Word is spreading that if you poke your head too far in the syndicate's direction, you'll lose it." She shrugged, raised her chin, and straightened her spine as she hit a second wind. "Come on. He might have been my best choice, but he's not the only one."

But we didn't have any more success with her next contact. We tracked down one of Rourke's old mates at the Legion, and he refused to acknowledge us. The syndicate had achieved their goal in silencing the people who had come forward. The message was clear—you talk, you die—and people were taking it to heart.

"These bastards are digging their own graves believing the shelter's going to keep them safe," she said when we hit the street, glaring at the Legion doors. "Staying quiet won't protect them, and if they don't want to take a stand, then maybe I don't want to put my life on the line for them if it comes to it."

My first thought was that she was venting, but when I caught the look in her eyes, I saw, in this moment at least, she was absolutely serious.

"Wow," I said. "You hate the whole world, don't you?"

She whipped around to face me, her teeth bared, and snapped, "I do not." Then, as though she realized how defensive she sounded, she relaxed her shoulders and added, "I take everyone on a case-by-case basis."

I couldn't help but snort as unexpected irritation swirled deep in my blood, a tide ready to come in. "Bullshit. I've saved your ass a million and one times since I came to town, and you can't see past what happened between us two years ago to appreciate it. One lie, Jet. One tiny lie that didn't even mean anything."

She froze but made no reply, her gaze boring into mine until it reached the faint glimmer of shame I had tried so hard to rationalize away. A flood of anger mixed with my guilt, and I had trouble holding her stare. Was she ever going to forgive me for what had happened in New York? After all we'd been through over the last couple of days, the lie I'd told her about being a federal agent felt like decades ago. A blip in the eternity we had known each other.

It took more than a slight effort to remember that, in reality, we'd spent a total of four weeks in each other's company. Enough to form a connection, but hardly enough for all sins to be forgotten. Frustration pushed both guilt and anger out of the way, and I did my best to shrug it off. We weren't going to resolve anything here and now, and our priorities were so much bigger than our messed-up history.

"Fine," I said. "Let's keep moving and try to remember we're not each other's enemy, all right?"

She didn't bother to say anything as she set off down the street, and I followed in answering silence. Eventually the conflict between us would come to a head, but until then, I had to take my own advice.

Our failed attempts to broaden our resources this morning had put one truth in glaring perspective: the fear spreading through the community up here meant Jet and Madison stood alone on the front lines, and if they failed... Drugs, murder, civil unrest—that kind of corruption spread like cancer. Maybe Dark Wire wouldn't agree with me, but ghost crossing the border was now the least of our concerns, and I refused to add myself to the list of people willing to let someone else handle it.

And maybe—just maybe—Jet and I would find some neutral ground along the way.

Chapter 9

Madison

I CALLED GARY before I left Mooney's and stayed out of sight by walking the quiet residential streets until he was free to meet me that afternoon. When I finally reached the safe house in the heart of Centretown, he was waiting by the front door—located at the back of the building—to meet me.

He wasn't much to look at. Half-gnome, he stood on the shorter side, with a brown wrinkled face, a large sharp nose, and beady black eyes. On a good day, he was the sweetest creature you could ever hope to meet, but gods help you if you crossed him. You know the garden gnomes you find around Halloween? The ones with the zombie faces covered in blood and gore? The inspiration for their design didn't come from nothing.

In a way, he was a perfect match for the building behind him, a walking lesson not to believe everything you saw.

It was a part of the perception filter I found so fascinating, the occasional feeling of living in a dream world where what you saw differed from what most people perceived. Sometimes I got glimmers of the mundane view. If someone's emotions ran exceptionally high, my vision skewed, and out of the corner of my eye, I spotted the illusion, the lie their non-supernatural brains told them to safeguard their sanity and our secret.

Part of the government's promise to its supernatural population was to guarantee safe housing. While some of us had no trouble renting in mundane-suited buildings, there were others who didn't trust that their identities would remain unknown, or who had a harder time keeping their true natures hidden. Those folks needed a place that was all theirs. A place where they could relax once they got home and drop the charade they played in public.

That was why the building that now housed my hopefully temporary residence existed.

On the outside, to a mundane, the three-storey complex looked like a dilapidated heritage building. Paper covering the windows on the vacant commercial ground floor, the walls above crumbled or torn down. Scaffolding leaned against the northwest wall to prevent anyone walking down the street from being crushed by the crumbling stone. It was a trash heap. A building the mayor kept saying would be restored, though they'd put it off for the last fifteen years. When asked why it remained a low priority, they claimed a shift in municipal priorities, a side effect of a little supernatural persuasion.

To someone of our blood, though, it was a beautiful urban apartment building, complete with two- and three-bedroom units, great views of Bank and Somerset streets, and no flyers in the mailbox. The brickwork was classic, full of character and artistic design. The lobby boasted marble tiles and stone archways, with detailed moulding around the doorways. A single elevator sat on the ground floor waiting to take anyone in need of a lift, but I wondered how many people bothered when the thrill of the wide staircase, like one you'd find in an old hotel, lent a touch of Hollywood to an otherwise banal climb.

"What do you think?" Gary asked as he led me inside. His deep voice rumbled through the empty foyer, his chest puffing with pride.

"This is perfect," I said.

"I've had my finger on the lease these ten years waiting for you to need it. Ever since your parents asked me to watch out for you."

My head jerked back as his words registered. A decade? I'd known my family had been nervous about me coming out here on my own, but I'd had no clue they'd taken their concerns so far as to include Gary. I wasn't sure whether to be touched by their love for me or offended that they thought I couldn't handle my own problems.

Never mind that they'd been right. I didn't want to think about how long it might have taken Gary to find something appropriate if he hadn't been so well prepared.

"I made sure you got one of the three-bedrooms," he continued, now in full tour-guide mode. "Figured if you had to move, it shouldn't be a complete downgrade."

I thought of Jet and Gideon and how well that had worked out. "It's like you read my mind."

From the way he beamed at me, I knew I'd said the right thing. Gary loved nothing more than being indispensable.

"Here are the keys to the apartment," he said, handing over a key ring with two keys. "I made a spare, but I don't recommend separating them if you don't have to. The fewer copies lying around, the more controlled the access."

He may as well have been channelling my Nan for all his words of caution.

"And these," he said, dangling a second set of keys in front of me, "are for your new ride. I know I said I'd lend you my Buick, but the wife made a point about noticeability, and she's so old she stands out. The car, not the missus. So I kept it low-key, but it's no beater. Older car, low mileage, won't get you anywhere in a hurry, but it's reliable, quiet, and has four brand-new tires. Just look for the beige Grand Prix in the parking lot."

He pulled a thick envelope out of his back pocket and handed that over next. "Finally, I have these. New driver's licence and credit cards, with a bit of cash to get you started." I accepted the envelope with gratitude. I'd arranged this setup before I'd known Jet and Gideon would need similar cover, but we would make do. We'd have to.

"Anything attached to your name should be tossed away before you go upstairs," Gary continued. "You got the phones working all right?"

I patted the unfamiliar weight in my back pocket and nodded.

"Good. So you should be all set up here as far as I'm able to help you."

My throat burned with gratitude, not only for all he'd done, but for the concern etched into his wrinkled face. "Thank you, Gary. I owe you more than you realize."

He shrugged. "I get the feeling there's more going on here than the media is sharing. Maybe more than they know. It true the minister's dead?"

I hadn't heard anything on the news about Jean-Luc being found yet, so I limited my response to a nod. The last thing I needed was to give away the fact I'd been the one to find him murdered on his office floor.

"Shit," Gary said. "Isn't that just a blow up a kelpie's nose. They know what happened?"

I looked over my shoulder to make sure we were still alone, then leaned in close. "I think it has something to do with the Death's Head Syndicate and their link to the Ghostmaker. I'm telling you this as a warning. Do yourself a favour and keep your head down, okay? Better yet, maybe get out of town for a few weeks. It's probably for the best if you and your family aren't associated with me, the department, or the realm right now."

Never in my life had I imagined every corner of our world would be under threat, so I braced for Gary to stare at me as though I were the worst kind of melodramatic, but he looked up at me with his sharp black eyes, his brow possibly furrowed though it was difficult to differentiate the wrinkles in his already impressive collection.

"That bad?" he asked.

I nodded, unsure how much more it would be smart to tell him or how much he'd already picked up from his myriad other sources. Did he know about the note we'd found outside the de Lauer Estates threatening more ghostbombs and attacks on anyone associated with the queen? Did he know the threat wasn't only on this side of the wall? That Meril had warned me more than once she was ready to take a stand if SMOAC should falter?

None of those details would influence his decision more than my recommendation, so I kept them to myself. The fewer people who knew about Meril, the less chance word would get back to her that I was stirring up panic.

"Think about how bad it might get," I said, "then multiply it by at least ten."

A black cloud of worry tinged with outright fear swept off him and mixed with my own.

"You sure you want to stay here, then?" he asked, glancing towards the front doors. "I have a cousin in Hamilton who could set you up off the grid until the scene cools down. No point sitting right in the middle of it if you don't have to."

Warmth stirred in my chest and a lump formed in my throat. I did my best to clear it and said, "Unfortunately, I made a promise to help fix things, so there's no other place for me to be than right here. But thanks to you, I already feel safer."

The gnome bowed his head, but a trickle of sorrow mixed with his worry, and it took all my self-control not to give him a giant, grateful hug. Considering how isolated I felt amid all this chaos, that sort of connection meant the world to me, no matter how fleeting.

"Well, stay safe, then," he said, and shoved his hands into the pockets of his slacks. "Be sure to let me know when you're done with the place, and I'll come by and clean it up. I might take your advice and go visit my cousin. It's been a few years since we've hit the Hammer."

A twinge of grief pinched my heart that he was so ready to leave, but it was an automatic reaction to losing something else familiar and reassuring. Ottawa was no place for him until this storm passed. He was an information-gatherer, and as essential a resource as he was, he would also be walking around with a target on his back if the wrong people found out he'd helped me. I couldn't repay his loyalty to my family by handing him a death sentence.

"As soon as I'm there, I'll set up a clean phone and shoot you my contact info," he said. "For emergencies. In case you change your mind and decide you want out."

I wished I could take him up on his offer and escape while I still had time, but he was doomed to disappointment.

"Keep yourself and your family safe," I said. "I'll take care of things here."

"Take care of your*self*," he said, then offered a brusque nod and waddled off, leaving me alone in the lobby. Gnomes weren't known for their emotional openness, but I'd picked up all the best wishes he hadn't spoken aloud.

Not wanting to run into anyone on the main stairs or by the elevator, I found a back stairwell and made my way to the third floor. I didn't meet anyone in the hallway when I stepped out, though I sensed various emotions coming through the doors as I walked towards the apartment at the far end. Frustration, anger. It seemed to be a common reaction to everything in the news these days. Mitigated, of course, by warmth towards family and friends, but always this underlying dissatisfaction. It rolled over my skin like oil, clogging my pores and making it difficult to take a deep breath.

The worst part was they were right to be angry. For months, I'd sensed the community's growing restlessness and thought everyone was being ungrateful, not appreciating how hard we were working to keep them hidden and provide access to essential resources. Now I stood here as angry as any of them—as betrayed and let down—and it hurt that my beloved department was the cause of our pain.

It was a relief to seal myself into my new home, gaining distance from everyone. Although it didn't make any difference as far as emotions were concerned, I drew the curtains, blocking even the thought of the rest of the world from my mind. Just for now, I needed a quiet place to think. So much was happening, so much was changing, and I needed a chance to piece it together.

I thought I'd gone over everything in my condo while I'd gotten ready to leave, but my talk with Jet and Gideon at the bar had brought our situation home in a new, more brutal light. At Mooney's, I'd needed to stay strong for Jet's sake, to help her see her way clear, but now that I was alone, a weight dropped around my neck, hunching my shoulders. A collar of fear and guilt and uncertainty. I was moving against SMOAC. Taking steps towards plugging a leak before the pipe burst. Was I up to the challenge? How long would it take before my habit of following the rules broke through this act of rebellion?

What rules?

What rules existed for putting a stop to someone using the department's authority to cause civil unrest? What rules had been put in place to stop a government official from using the syndicate to further their goals?

Unable to sit down and relax, I gave myself a tour of the apartment, poking my nose into every nook and cranny. Gary, bless him, had gone so far as to leave the fridge and cupboards fully stocked and the liquor cabinet wonderfully full.

I pulled out the bottle of scotch and poured myself a hefty

glass. The clock on the wall with its woodland-themed face informed me the day was closing in on five o'clock, and that was as much permission as I needed to down the whole thing.

The alcohol burned the back of my throat, but by the time it reached my stomach, it had settled into a warm blanket of courage.

We would figure this out. The three of us had proved how stubborn we were, how ready and willing we were to take risks, to endure and survive. If we were going to win against the syndicate and anyone working with them, that kind of foolhardy bravery was exactly what we needed. That and a plan. A really good plan.

With the clock ticking behind me, I picked up my new phone and scrolled through the empty pages of nothing. No apps, no photos, and no contacts other than the phones I'd given Jet and Gideon, and so far neither of them had sent any updates.

Although I knew it was a bad idea, the scotch muted my rational brain's objections as I went to the app store and downloaded a secondary messenger service. As soon as it finished downloading, I logged in with the email address I used exclusively for the app. The address had no affiliation to me, the department, or anything else I'd ever kept on my phone. Its sole purpose was to connect me with my family, and as their names popped up and their messages synced, the tightness in my chest eased.

For their safety, I wouldn't reach out to them, even set

my status to offline to prevent them from messaging me, but knowing I *could*, that the access was readily available, soothed the jagged pieces of my heart.

Only seven contacts existed on my list. My mother, my father, my sisters, my brother, my grandmother… and Malcolm Bishop. Not a family member at all, more of a what-if, and the only other person who knew this email address existed.

Seeing his name triggered a wave of regret about how I'd left things with him—not that I'd led him on, but that I didn't know if the hope I'd left him with was an illusion—and the squeeze on my heart grew a little tighter at the notification waiting for me.

JUST CHECKED INTO THE MLC. DON'T SEE YOU YET. YOU HERE?

Crap. In the madness of the past twenty-four hours, I'd forgotten all about the Managers' and Administrators' Conference. The Mid-listers' Conference, as Colm and I so affectionately referred to it. It was where we had met four years ago. Two wallflowers at a mandatory public service conference, and only one carrot muffin remaining on the catering table to share between them.

SAVED YOU A SEAT, he wrote. AND GRABBED AN EXTRA MUFFIN FOR YOU. SHH.

I tapped my fingers against the counter and stared at the unanswered messages, debating whether I should reply to him. I hated that stupid conference, but right now all I wanted was to be there with him, laughing at the emcee's droning voice and corny jokes and placing bets on how long it would take to fill some important vacant roles. Given the uncertainty of my life right now, it was the closest thing to a date I'd been able to promise him.

Bad enough I'd had to reschedule dinner, but now I was standing him up. True, since promising to meet him there, I had found my minister dead, almost been murdered, and gone on the run from our security team, but I still felt bad for not giving him the heads-up I would be a no-show today.

Colm knew nothing about my nature or my job. As a full-fledged mundane, he wasn't allowed to know most of it, and I'd never risked revealing the rest. The last thing I needed was his fear on my conscience—either of me or for me. It was better to let him think the busyness that delayed our date was also the reason I couldn't attend the conference, but I couldn't give up the wish that someday, maybe someday soon, we could bury ourselves in carrot muffins without worrying the sky was going to cave in on us.

Last-minute business trip, I replied. Be away for a week or two. Don't go eating all those muffins on your own.

My throat felt tight as I typed out my lies, wondering how hard they were going to bite me in the ass.

Split one when you get back? he asked.

The message flashed on my screen like an accusation, though I knew I was projecting.

You bet! I answered, because I had to. There was no guarantee I would be alive in a week or two, let alone free to put up my feet and relax with some sugary caffeinated beverage and delicious guilt-free carbohydrates—because to hell with calories if I survived this—but I couldn't say no. At the moment, the idea of seeing him was my faint ray of hope that everything would turn out all right. That Jet, Gideon, and I would get to the bottom of this conspiracy, solve Jean-Luc's murder, and drag Mark O'Malley and the government moles to justice.

As the situation spread out before me, my legs grew weak, and I slid into the dining chair to keep myself from collapsing to the floor.

Nothing about our situation was new. I'd known all of it from the time I'd decided to leave Persephone with my neighbour. But only now, faced with this unfamiliar apartment, in the position of making plans for my future, did the unknown slap me in the face with an icy hand.

I couldn't go home. I couldn't go to work. I couldn't contact my team or my boss or my friends or my family. If I did any of those things, I could be killed or arrested for murder depending on who found me first.

How the hell had we fallen into a such a deep, dark hole?

And how the hell were we going to dig ourselves out?

Chapter 10

Jet

MY LEGS SCREAMED at me, and my hips and spine ached from the effort of holding an air bridge together for a chunk of the morning, but as we still had no car and the city buses would land me in the hands of my team within the hour, the only option we had to track down my remaining contact was to walk.

We'd crossed from Centretown to Old Ottawa South within the last forty-five minutes, decent time given Gideon's condition, and were making our way up a shoddy street in what was considered to be a somewhat rougher neighbourhood. Though at the moment, at this time of year, with the sun shining and temperature rising, it seemed like any other part of town. The smell of burgers on the barbecue, kids out riding their bikes. Totally normal. Totally happy. No one with any obvious stresses or conspiracies on their minds.

Not for the first time today, a spike of envy drove into my heart, and I did my best to shove it away. Gideon calling me out on my bullshit had opened my eyes to my growing bitterness. It had pissed me off that so many people were prepared to sit back and do nothing, to either pretend nothing was wrong or hide from what they saw happening and leave me to fix the problem, and all I'd wanted to do was flip a table and tell them to work it out for themselves.

Gideon had stopped me short, the bastard. Without saying so, he'd reminded me this was my job. I couldn't expect some random supernatural on the street to put themselves in danger. They hadn't sworn their lives to protect their country. I had. So I could either let their self-preservation bother me, or I could focus my attention on people who had more to lose if they didn't help me.

"You sure about this guy?" Gideon asked as we walked down the street to a bungalow at the end. He wore a bright smile, as though we were enjoying a friendly conversation, and his posture was loose and easy—a pointed hint that I needed to drop my own regimented stiffness if we wanted to blend in. Over his grin, however, his gaze darted from one side of the street to the other, resting on yard gates, cars, parents supervising their children. I held back from pointing out he was the one using a vest to hide the blood on his shirt and was probably, next to me, the most dangerous person here.

"He's not as clean-cut as the informants we lost," I admitted, "but far from the worst. Petty crimes, mostly. Enough to give me some leverage if I can't rely on the goodness of his heart."

We'd come to the last name on my mental list, a car thief I'd taken down back in my early days. Thanks to the rumour mill, I knew he'd resumed his shady dealings, and I hoped I might get more than intel out of the guy.

We climbed the steps to the front door, and Gideon stayed at the top of the stairs, giving me space to start things off on my own. I knocked with the side of my fist. No playing around here. I wanted Travis to know I meant business right from the get-go. We didn't have time for honey.

But when the door opened, I found myself looking into the upturned face of a girl about six years old. She was missing a tooth at the front of her wide smile, and her golden eyes gave her away as her father's daughter.

At the sight of me, her smile vanished into a curious stare.

"Who are you?" she asked with the insolence only youth could muster.

"A friend of your dad's," I said. "Is he home?"

The girl dropped her gaze and twisted her toe against the tile. "I don't know." She dragged out the words. Six years old and the little one was already a pro at playing cagey.

"Maybe out back working on his Camaro?" I prodded, taking a stab in the dark that even after twelve years, Travis hadn't finished puttering with his pride and joy.

At the mention of the car, the girl cast me a suspicious look through her long blonde eyelashes. "You know the car?"

"Red, right? Metal bits on the front? I remember when all it had was a frame and a few working parts."

Travis's ability allowed him to manipulate metal. The last time I'd seen him, he'd hurled chunks of twisted scrap at my head to try to fend me off, tearing giant holes into the front end of his most prized possession. He hadn't succeeded in scaring me away, and when we'd dragged him to the detainment centre, he was more upset about the damage to the Camaro than about being caught.

"Becca?" a familiar voice called from inside. Travis's hulking shape came up from behind his daughter, and he wiped his hands on a stained white cloth, his fingers black with grease. "Who's here, baby girl?"

She shrugged and backed away, giving him room. At the sight of me, the lines around his eyes hardened, though he kept his smile easy. He rested his hand on Becca's shoulder and gently guided her behind him. "Go see Mama, all right? She's upstairs with Rory. Go on now."

"She told me to come downstairs so Rory could sleep," Becca argued.

"I'm sure he's asleep by now. Just be quiet. Please, Becca. If you ask nicely, she might bake you some cookies."

At that, Becca ran off. Children were so easy to bribe. If only cookies would be enough to convince Travis to come to the rogue side and work for me.

"Heya, Travis," I said.

Any trace of his smile disappeared. He manoeuvred into the doorway so his wide shoulders blocked any view of inside—and anyone inside from seeing us on the porch.

"What do you want?" he growled. "You come here, talk to my little girl? I haven't done anything."

"We both know that's not true," I said, and raised my hands. "Fact is, I don't care what you're doing in your garage these days. Killed anyone lately?"

His eyes widened and his skin paled, right down to his lips. "What? No! What the fu—what are you trying to lay on me?"

"Nothing. I just figure as long as you haven't crossed that line yet, we have no issues, you and me. No one's in trouble."

Well, you're not, I thought, but he didn't need that kind of hold over me.

His face turned from white to red, and he took a step closer, gripping the cloth so tightly at his side I suspected he'd punched holes through it with his fingernails. With his lip curled into a snarl, he said, "Get off my porch."

I closed the distance between us. If he wanted to play the intimidation game, he had to learn he wouldn't win. "I know you're still running cars, Travis. I know you've got yourself a sweet little workshop on Gladstone that does all kinds of shady things when the lights go out. That's great. One day someone's going to bust you for it and put you away so you don't get to watch your kids grow up, but it's not going to be me. Theft isn't my area anymore. Even if it were, I've got my eye on bigger fish."

He frowned, wary but with a hint of curiosity. "Like who?"

I shoved my hands in my jacket pockets, as casual as though I were nothing more than an old friend touching base. The floorboards of the porch creaked, and in the corner of my eye, I saw Gideon turn to lean on the railing so he could stare out over the street. Travis's gaze jumped from me to him, a silent question in his eyes, but I needed to keep him focused.

"The Death's Head." I got straight to the point, and he returned his attention to me, his whole body tensing.

"No way in hell. You're not getting me within a hundred metres of that syndicate shit."

"No one's asking you to get close. All I want to know is if you hear anything. Any word of them leaving town, any strange goings-on. New cars, new faces, new rumours. I know the kind of information that passes through your shop, and I need it. I'm out of the loop, Travis. Things are happening—things that'd keep your wife awake at night and terrified for your kids if she knew. The only way I can stop it is if people like you bring me back into the circle."

"No."

He stepped back inside the house and gripped the edge of the door to close it, but I grabbed hold of the air between us and shoved it forward so the door swung into him.

"That's not very nice, Travis."

He rubbed his cheek where the edge had clocked him, his golden eyes full of molten fire. "I got too much going on to get near anything those assholes are doing."

"Even if it means getting your record tossed?"

He froze. "You're not serious."

In a wave of exhaustion, I gave up trying to play hardball with him. I was tired of the push and pull of negotiation, trying to convince people that doing some good for their community would have far-reaching benefits, like justice and survival. That was Madison's job, not mine. My method was to kick in the door and put on the pressure until he caved, and right now, those skills wouldn't serve me. Just once, I wanted someone to step up and tell me they would help. Not because I offered anything, but because they would sleep better at night knowing they were doing something to keep themselves, their families, and their community safe. I pushed away from the doorjamb and met his gaze squarely.

"I've never been more serious. What I'm working on affects the country in ways I've never seen before and you wouldn't want to begin to imagine. So yes, I think a few stolen cars can be overlooked if you stop being so goddamn obvious about what you're doing and shoot me a message if you hear any news about O'Malley's movements, all right?"

I pulled a scrap of paper out of my back pocket and held it out to him. On it, I'd written my new phone number. Just the number—no name, no information to trace it back to me if he decided to screw me over.

"All right," he said, accepting the paper with a slow exhale. "But only on my terms. I'm not taking risks. I won't do that to my family."

I nodded. How could I argue with that? I knew what O'Malley was capable of doing to anyone who moved against the syndicate, and if Travis was as connected as I suspected he was, he did, too. I couldn't ask him to sacrifice everything the way Mitchel Lafontaine had for the sake of a few tips.

"Thanks, Travis." I debated quitting while I was ahead, but there was still the matter of my second goal for this visit. Deciding I had nothing to lose by trying, I said, "This is going to sound crazy, but I don't suppose you have an… off-the-books vehicle you could lend me?"

Travis blinked. "You're joking."

"Serious situation," I reminded him.

His surprise turned into a glower as he reached into his back pocket and pulled out a business card. "If you're setting me up—"

"I swear."

He huffed out a breath, his nostrils flaring. "Call the garage. Geordie will find something for you."

I took the card and slid it into my pocket. Getting caught with a stolen car would do nothing to support my story that I was one of the good guys, but there was no way in hell I would find the answers I needed if I had to walk across the city every day. I couldn't rely solely on Madison, either. We had to be flexible and ready to move at a moment's notice, splitting up if necessary. As far as I could see, it was the only way I could be sure of at least one of us getting out of this alive.

"Thanks again," I said. "So, how's the Camaro?"

"Red," Travis said, and he closed the door in my face. I couldn't bring myself to be too offended. A few minutes' work, and we had a new addition to our surveillance team.

"Well played," Gideon said as we walked up the street. A few people shot us dark looks on our way back—no doubt worried we'd spend ten minutes chatting on their porch, too—but I ignored them. The less we interacted with them, the less likely they'd be to remember us if anyone came poking around asking questions.

"We'll see if it was worth it. At this point, I'm braced to have to sell my soul to learn what O'Malley's next step is."

"Hey," he nudged me with his elbow, "at least it means you still have one to sell."

Chapter 11

Gideon

As Jet and I retraced our steps through the neighbourhood towards the small shopping centre, I spotted something I hadn't seen in a decade. Something that solved at least one of my problems.

"You still have pay phones up here?" I asked, gesturing to the glass booth on the corner. I knew Canada was a bit behind the times, but this seemed a little extreme. Convenient, but extreme.

"Out of nostalgia, I think. Or maybe as an art installation."

"Does it work?" I started towards it, and she didn't say anything to stop me.

I stepped inside and gripped the receiver with my bloodied T-shirt, happy to hear the steady ring of a dial tone.

The door stuck as I slid it closed, and I had to give it a solid kick to shut it the rest of the way, but when I checked my pockets, I found them empty and had to wrestle the door back open. "I don't suppose you have change?"

Jet rolled her eyes as she pulled her wallet out of her back pocket, unzipped the tiny coin purse, and dropped a few quarters into my palm.

"Quarters?"

"Inflation's a bitch."

I closed the door again, dropped the coins into the slot, and used the back of my knuckle to dial a number so familiar to me I could have called it in my sleep.

The phone rang four times before the call connected with a click, but no one spoke on the other end.

I readied myself for shit to fly. "Dark Wire, it's Nightwatch."

"You're calling from an unsecured line. Late." Although their altered voice sounded calm, my ear tickled with their restrained fury. I suspected my handler had been forced to come up with a bunch of excuses to explain to our superiors why I hadn't checked in. Did they suspect I'd gone rogue? Part of me had expected them to be worried for my well-being, but based on my reception, I might have overestimated their regard for me.

Fair, considering I was coming off probation from my last mission fuck-up.

A fuck-up that involved blowing my cover to a certain Canadian task force captain.

I was only just regaining my reputation, and here I was

about to ask for a few massive favours. No surprise, really, if Dark Wire hated working with me.

"I ran into some obstacles. Communication will be a bit of a challenge going forward."

"Negative. You're ordered to report home immediately. We have a dryad situation that needs your attention."

"Not possible."

My gaze fell on Jet through the glass doors. She'd leaned back against the side of the booth, arms crossed with her jacket draped over them, one foot over the other. A casual pose, but I knew she was surveying our exit routes. The muscles in her toned arms stretched out from under the sleeves of her T-shirt, and her black jeans hugged her hips in ways that made it hard for me to tear my attention away from them. But it wasn't only her physical qualities that tied me to her.

As angry as I was that she had thrown me into Carstairs's waiting arms, it was an anger that stirred my blood. She wound me up, kept me energized. The frustration of dealing with her made the moments where she relented all the more satisfying. We fought a constant battle of wills, but always with a hint that she enjoyed it as much as I did—that as hard as we pushed against each other, we were both waiting for an opening to give up, to fall in. And while that chance existed, I couldn't leave. Not again. Not without seeing what happened.

"The situation here has changed," I explained. "The players are moving, and I have a handle on where the cards will fall.

If we don't take the opportunity, we won't be able to contain the problem at the border."

Never had I been more grateful for the lack of a secure phone line. They wouldn't be able to ask many questions or call me on my bullshit.

When the silence stretched out, I pictured a dark shape hunched over a phone, a vague face growing redder as the mind behind it tried to work out whether I was playing them, and, if not, whether I was worth the extra money and paperwork. If they pushed the issue, I would have a hard time justifying my sticking around on foreign soil, but I hoped that whatever remained of my old reputation would push them to give me the benefit of the doubt. At least they had no way of knowing how deeply Jet was involved; otherwise, I would be on a plane to New York by end of day.

"You have five days," Dark Wire finally said. "After that, you better report back here or contact me with a damned good reason why you're still there. While on mission, you are under strict orders not to do anything that threatens the reputation or integrity of the firm, you are *not* to interfere with foreign politics, and—let me make this very clear—you are to maintain a professional relationship with any contacts you've formed, do you understand?"

"I do," I said. I understood very well, but understanding was not obeying.

"I mean it, Nightwatch. Ignore or circumvent any of

these rules, and the firm won't open its doors to you when you come home."

I froze, my aching fingers stiff around the receiver. Toe the line or lose my job. Leave Jet alone or get thrown out on my ass. The message was unmistakable, but what did it mean that at least one of the rules had already been broken beyond repair? The problem *was* foreign politics. No way to back out of that one.

In the end, it didn't matter. If this was going to be my last mission, at least it would be for a good cause. "Understood."

A pause, followed by a heavy breath on the line. "What do you need from us?"

I did my best to keep the relief out of my voice. I couldn't feel smug that I'd gotten my way—not when I might have just submitted my death warrant. "Permission for radio silence. My phone has been compromised and is no longer in operation. By chance, I stepped back in time and found a pay phone, but I don't think I'll be lucky enough to stumble across one on every street corner. I also need authority to grease some wheels."

"Authority denied," they said, barely hiding their disbelief. "We can't give free rein on information over an unsecured line, nor can we let you go around offering deals to people without thorough background checks and approvals." I must have given Dark Wire a real shock for them to let their neutral tone slip.

"Whatever you're able to give me, then. I might not need anything, but I have to leave the door open."

Another drawn-out hesitation. "Fine. But this better be worth it, Nightwatch, or you'll answer to head office."

The line clicked off, and I bowed my head. It was done. Permission to stay and work without oversight. Freedom to play with some bargaining chips Jet didn't have the power to offer right now. Small victories, but at least it was something.

Something that hopefully helped us wrap this up within the next five days, or else I would be forced to make a decision: keep my promise to help Jet or sacrifice the only identity in this world I felt comfortable wearing.

Fuck me.

I drew in a deep breath, let it out slowly, and stepped back into the twenty-first century.

"Good chat?" Jet asked. She pushed away from the phone booth and fell in beside me as I started across the parking lot.

"Good chat. Now there's one more person we need to see."

By the time we got back to Mooney's, my feet were killing me, and the injuries I hadn't been able to heal yet throbbed. How the hell did people go through life putting one foot in front of the other all the time? More than once today, I'd been ready to leave Jet behind and mist my way across town, but since I wouldn't get far without her, I'd resigned myself to the walk.

The idea of a cold drink made my dry mouth tingle and motivated me to keep moving.

At least she'd had the forethought to run into the shopping centre and grab me a clean shirt. The new cotton scratched against my open wounds, and I'd already bled through it in patches, but I no longer looked like I was about to keel over from blood loss.

"I don't think it's a good idea to be here," Jet said, her gaze darting around the now busy bar.

I wanted to warn her she would gain attention by acting so on edge, but since I liked the shape of my nose, I draped my arm around her shoulders and steered her towards the bar. She tensed under my touch, and I squeezed her shoulder. *This is business*, I tried to tell her. *Cover. Nothing more.* She seemed to understand, because her muscles relaxed, and although her gaze remained sharp, taking in every face and movement in the room, the obvious traces of worry around her eyes and mouth vanished.

To be kind to both of us, I removed my arm as soon as we escaped the worst of the crowd and found a place near the back of the bar.

"Is he here?" she asked.

I scanned the faces around me, and it took more than one pass to spot the man in the red plaid button-down. On anyone else, the shirt would have made him a shining beacon in a room of black suits and white dress shirts, but that was a side effect of being a sloth demon. You only saw them if you were looking for them; otherwise, they were negative space. Something you skirted without realizing it, something you forgot the moment you turned away.

"That's him."

Jet looked to where I'd nodded, frowned, blinked, looked again, and her nose wrinkled. "Daily Davis? I've heard of him. He's a worse drunk than Rourke." At the reference to her former informant and old colleague, her expression blanched. She wavered on her feet but quickly pulled herself together.

"He is," I agreed, overlooking her reaction for the sake of her pride, "but if you thought Rourke was good at going unseen, he had nothing on Davis. The man's practically invisible. He picks up more information in a single night than most teams gather in a week because he doesn't have to try."

We made our way towards him, me taking a place on Davis's right, Jet on his left. Davis looked up at me first and let out a groan. He tried to slide out of his stool the other way, but Jet closed in to stop him.

"Shit," he said, and settled back in his seat with a resigned sigh.

"Two visits from me in one week," I said with a smile. "Aren't you lucky."

"You say luck, I wonder what god's dog I ran over. What the fuck do you want, Leigh?"

"Answers."

"I gave you everything I had the other day. I told you—O'Malley's up and moved to Kingston."

"Bullshit," Jet said, leaning in. "He's right here, and I think you know that."

Davis's eyes flashed red, and he hunched closer to his pint glass. "Fuck you. Everyone knows it's true. The new bar's a place called Hell on Earth, Hell for short. I guess they figured The Afterlife was too neutral. It opened three months ago, and business is booming. Doing better than here. Ghost, coke, dope. Whatever you want."

"How could you possibly know that?" Jet asked, eying him over. "Everyone else I've asked about Kingston doesn't know their ass from their elbow."

"I dealt for O'Malley, didn't I?" Davis said, and her eyes widened. She looked at me, and I shrugged. It wasn't my fault she hadn't known.

But by the way her lips pressed into a thin line and her cheeks flushed a rich pink, I guessed she thought I should have done her the courtesy of passing that particular bit of information along beforehand.

Well, she couldn't have it both ways. She couldn't be upset I didn't do her job for her *and* be pissed I'd come up here to do her job. No wonder this woman drove me crazy.

Not that I blamed her for being unimpressed by Davis's career pursuits. The guy paid his beer tab by dealing death. He offered no benefit to society, did more harm than good, and probably didn't pay his taxes. If he weren't such a perfect information pipeline for the trash we were looking to take down, I would have bagged him up with the rest of the syndicate.

One thing he'd said, however, stuck out.

"Dealt, past tense?" I asked. That was new.

He slid me a nasty stare. "Didn't know it was any of your business, but yeah. Got the can a week ago. Bastards told me I wasn't needed. They'd 'streamlined.'" He sneered as he used his air quotes. "I'm tellin' you. They're gone."

Seeing that Jet was too angry with me to form any questions, I closed the distance between us a little more. "You know that's not the whole truth, Davis. You can lie to us—hell, you can lie to yourself—but deep in your gut, you know something's not right here. You've been one of O'Malley's lapdogs for years. If he dropped you to ship business to another city, that might explain why you've been nursing that beer since we got here instead of chugging back two or ten. Kingston might be true, Hell might be the next hot spot, but O'Malley is still in Ottawa, and I think you've done enough digging to find out what he's up to."

I spoke with more confidence than I felt, gambling on what I knew about people like Davis, and my act paid off by the way the demon closed in on himself, hiding behind a swig of beer.

Jet rested her elbow on the bar and trailed her gaze over Davis's face before landing on the eyes he was so deliberately averting.

"Where is O'Malley, Davis?" she asked, all hint of anger and disgust gone. "You seen him around lately?"

"Nope," he answered, but there was enough waver in his voice to give him away.

I crossed my arms, the two of us inching closer to him, caging him. Despite his determined attempt to appear nonchalant, I spotted the bead of sweat forming along his hairline.

"You sure you're telling us everything?" I asked. "He hasn't been around The Afterlife at all? Hasn't given you a call and let you know he has product to move?"

"That's not how this works, man, you know that," Davis said a low growl.

"No?" Jet asked. "Then who does his dirty work? Big Joe? Sammy G? Who supplies you with the ghost?"

He licked his lips. "I can't flap my mouth about this to you people. You might be all right with ending your life in a dumpster, but mine's worth more to me than that."

Jet winced at the reference to Rourke's fate, so I kept his attention on me, scanning him from his balding head to his beer-thick belly. "Really?"

Davis grunted.

I surveyed the room, caught the bartender's eye, and waved him down for two of whatever Davis was drinking. We said nothing while we waited, and even after my pint glass was in front of me, I took a moment to wet my lips, leaving room for the silence to stretch out and Davis to get more uncomfortable.

"What if I told you," I said after enough time had passed, "that I could get you across the border and far away from the syndicate? No one would know where you were, and you'd be free to find a new bar to fund, wherever you wanted. Would you talk to us then?"

Jet's eyes flickered with interest, but she buried her curiosity in a sip of beer.

"You're bullshitting me," Davis said.

"I'm not." I set my drink aside and turned to face him. "I have a one-time limited offer, and you have a very small window to accept it."

"Think about it, Davis," Jet said, her voice smooth, inviting confidence. "You know what O'Malley will do if he learns you talked to us, and you can't hide from them if they want to track you down. Work with us, and you're in the clear. No looking over your shoulder as the situation gets hotter. No getting caught in the flames yourself. I promise you, O'Malley's going down, along with anyone involved with him. If you don't want to be a fish caught in that net, I suggest you take Mr. Leigh up on his offer."

The demon's tongue darted over his lips, and for a moment he disappeared from view, his ability to blend in growing erratic with his increasing agitation.

"How do I know they wouldn't find me anyway?"

I smirked. "Who do you think I work for, Davis? If they're able to track you down, my firm may as well close up shop and send all our agents to work at fast-food joints, because they aren't cut out for any other job. No one finds the people we squirrel away. Ever."

He pinched his brow, and I caught Jet's gaze, which was filled with silent questions. I hadn't told her what I'd negotiated with Dark Wire, and she hadn't asked, so I understood her surprise that I had the power to make a deal like this. Not that I was thrilled about it. The last thing I wanted was someone like Davis setting up business for himself in my city. We had enough people like him already. But if he knew anything about where to find O'Malley, anything that would help us shut down the syndicate and weed out the mole within SMOAC, it would be worth it. Jet believed O'Malley was in Ottawa, and I trusted her judgement.

Even if I would never tell her so.

"All right," Davis said, and Jet and I exchanged a satisfied glance over his head. "O'Malley's still kicking around The Afterlife, sure. He's made some new connections, so he's been dropping his old ones like we've gone rotten. No severance package or fond farewell. Just silence. I can't pay my rent like that. Hell, I can't pay for this beer like that. So I stick around, keep my mouth shut, and wait for things to go back to normal. If you're right, then that's not gonna happen, so what have I got to lose? What do you want to know?"

"What have you heard about these new connections?" Jet asked.

"Not as much as you'd like," he said. "I don't have names.

They're suits. They're men. They got short hair and polished shoes. Not the sort I typically run around with, and not the sort O'Malley would usually deal with, either. Saw them having a meet once. They were in front of some office building downtown, fucking each other with deals and promises. O'Malley and some other guy. I think I recognized him from TV. Older, sharp dresser. Some government prick."

The muscles in my stomach clenched. The news didn't come as a surprise, but to have it confirmed, to have someone lay eyes on the mole…

"Was it the minister?" Jet asked. "Could you point him out if you saw him again?"

"Sure, maybe, but I don't plan to stick around long enough to find out, if you understand me."

"What about eye colour?" she pushed. "Could you tell me that much? Were they blue? Brown? Gold?"

There was so much desperation in her voice I doubted we'd get more out of Davis without more promises. People like him took what they could get, changing by the minute if they thought they held the advantage.

"Listen, lady, if I could tell you that much, I would, all right?" he said, surprising me. I hadn't expected honesty. He must have noticed my shock, because he scowled. "What? The sooner you take these assholes in, the safer I am. But I honestly didn't notice. It was dark when they met, and they were doing whatever they could not to be seen."

"Where exactly was this office building?" Jet asked.

He shrugged. "Laurier somewhere. O'Malley's car was parked on the street, and they were having a gab."

"When?" I asked.

"Last week or so. After I got canned."

"And you just *happened* to see his car?" Jet asked.

"All right, fine. Maybe you were right, and I wanted to do a little digging. Find out why I'd been screwed over. They came out of the building, heads together like they were planning the end of the world, all buddy-buddy, and I knew I was fucked. I have my ways, but I can't compete with a government type. They've got money, connections. Exactly what you want in ghost clientele. My customers don't have the money or the interest in that shit. They prefer to stick to the basics. So anyway, I see these guys talking, they shake hands, then O'Malley gets into his car and drives off. The other one watches him for a while, and another guy comes out, this one dressed all in black. That's as much as I can tell ya. They talked it out, then the suit claps the other guy on the shoulder and goes back in. Man in black follows a few minutes later. That's all she wrote."

Davis's story had Jet buzzing so much I could almost sense the vibration from where I sat. I didn't blame her. This was the closest we'd come to identifying the SMOAC traitors who were trying to ruin her. Who had wiped out her team and nearly killed her. The fact she wasn't shaking the information out of Davis was an impressive demonstration of restraint.

Especially now that he'd confirmed we were dealing with at least two moles. Two times the treason.

"The man in black," Jet said, "was he in a suit, too? Fatigues?"

Davis shook his head and sipped his beer. "Maybe? I didn't get a close enough look at him. Could have been either. But that's all I got. Everything I know. Now, what about my ticket out of here?"

To be so close to the truth only to come up short was a hammer blow, and if it was bad for me, I could only imagine Jet's disappointment. She hid it well, though, turning away from Davis to lean against the bar and stare into the wall.

"I'll make the call and get back to you. Least I can do," I said, and threw a few bills onto the counter. "Grab yourself another on me."

He hadn't given enough away to deserve his Get Out of Jail Free card, but Rourke, Lafontaine, and the other informants were evidence that the syndicate was plugging its leaks. It was only a matter of time before they tracked back to Davis. Helping him out would be a pain in the ass, but at least it would mean one less life on Jet's conscience.

By the time we left the bar, I was pumped over our progress. Much more hopeful than when we'd walked out of the Legion. Not only did we have confirmation that SMOAC was in business with the syndicate—real eyewitness evidence—but we knew there were at least two people involved, one who wore a suit and one who wore black.

All right, it wasn't much to go on, but even if the one in black was Carstairs, it was more than we'd had an hour ago.

"You and me, we make a good team," I said as we walked down the street towards Travis's garage. Jet didn't look too pleased about owing the man a favour—or was she upset Davis hadn't been able to give us more? It was hard to read the many moods of Bridget Dawson.

"Sure," she said absently, as though she hadn't heard me.

I didn't know if it was the rush of our escape this morning, the relief of finally having a lead, or the high that came from getting information out of someone who didn't want to give it, but in that moment, I didn't want our momentum to slow. I wanted to take a chance and see what happened.

"Hey," I said, and rested my hand on Jet's arm to pull her to a stop. Her skin was warm under my fingertips, humming with a current of energy that spread through my veins and made the hairs on the back of my neck stand on end. Or was that the adrenaline talking?

She turned on her heel and tilted her head to look up at me, her dark gaze mildly distracted.

"Why don't we call a truce," I said. "You, me—we're always going to do things to piss each other off. We're always going to put the job ahead of everything else. Why don't we accept that and find some way to be okay with each other?"

In response, her eyes cleared, and I felt like she saw me for the first time since I'd strolled back into her life. At that look, a glimmer of hope glowed like embers in my stomach. The desire to kiss her and pull her against me set my body shaking. This woman, who in so many ways was everything I needed, was right here for the first time in two years, and all I wanted was to get back to where we'd been in New York. Before I'd gone and fucked everything up by waiting too long to be honest with her. Which I would do again if the job called for it.

Maybe she realized it, too. Maybe that was why the clarity in her eyes dimmed, replaced by a shimmering anger as she turned away from me.

"It would make our lives a lot easier, Gideon," she said, "but I don't know you well enough to trust you that far."

With that, she walked away from me again.

Chapter 12

Madison

IROLLED MY neck to work out the kinks that had formed while I sat hunched over the papers spread across the dining room table.

After my text exchange with Colm, I'd thrown myself into my work, needing a distraction from the disappointment that I wasn't at the conference with him and the overwhelming fear that Jet, Gideon, and I would never find our way out of this net. Even now, those doubts lingered in the back of my mind, and the only way to shut them up was to double down on the work in front of me and press forward.

Somewhere in these documents was a clue to the truth. Some logic behind which community projects were approved and shut down, some idea of who might have had access to the disappearing funds.

Some explanation for why Jean-Luc might have gotten

involved in anything like this.

My heart twinged at the thought of my friend—the man I'd looked up to since I was a child, who'd always seemed bigger than life, a stalwart hero standing alongside my father as they fought for the rights and protections of the Canadian supernatural population—turning his back on everything he'd believed in. What would have pushed him to do it? Greed? Desperation? A knife through his heart had guaranteed I'd never get to ask him in person, so I had to trust that somewhere in these piles of paper, I'd find the answer.

I'd printed as many decision and funding notes from the past six months as I'd been able to, as well as contracts and negotiations with stakeholders, corporations, foundations, and organizations from the past two years. As far as I could tell on my first pass through the documentation, the corruption didn't go that far back. Not to this scale, anyway. And widespread ghost distribution had only become a problem within the past ten months. My hope was that in comparing the old funding and policy decisions to the recent ones, I could pinpoint when the change had happened, and who'd had a hand in it.

So far, I'd found nothing but the bottom of my scotch glass and the fact that Jean-Luc's name was on everything.

My eyes ached, a throbbing had taken up space behind my left ear, and my stomach sloshed with alcohol, fatigue, and very little food.

I leaned back in my chair and stretched my arms over my

head, relishing the cracks and pops that loosened my shoulders and straightened my spine. My gaze roved over the cupboards, and I wondered if I should throw together some kind of snack. A break wouldn't be the worst thing. A few minutes to step away from the bleak joke my life had become.

With a sigh, I slid my chair back and went to the fridge. My situation definitely called for comfort food. Ten minutes later, after raiding the cabinet for anything unhealthy, I returned to the table with a bowl of bright orange macaroni and cheese and a refilled glass of scotch. Let no one say I wasn't classy.

As I sat down, the edge of my glass hit the table, and liquor spilled over the spread-out papers.

"Shit."

I hurried to get a cloth and dabbed up the liquid, trying not to destroy anything potentially critical. As I wiped the scotch off the date on a briefing note, my hand slowed. A note signed by Jean-Luc on the fifth of December last year.

That didn't make sense.

I dropped into my chair and set the glass and my bowl aside.

Holding the date in my head, I pawed through the other papers on my desk until I came to a negotiation debrief Jean-Luc and I had attended last winter. The first week of December in Vancouver. Had he brought this briefing note with him and signed it there?

I pulled out the note again and checked the date stamps on the cover sheet that had to be signed off by the full chain of command before it reached the minister's office. Deputy Minister Gagnon had signed it on the third of December before passing it on to Jean-Luc's office. The minister hadn't been there to sign it. He wouldn't have seen it until he'd returned on the seventh.

As the connection slowly formed in my mind, I thought back to the complaint files Phyllis had gathered the night of her death. The ones she'd given me to collate and report on to save the minister time. So many of those files had struck me as odd additions, not fitting with the pattern of recent complaints Phyllis had claimed they were.

Riffling through my papers, I tracked down half of them, and sure enough, every one of the minister's signatures—with the exception of those in the assessment report that had left me so confused—fell on dates he hadn't been in the office.

What had Phyllis and Jean-Luc really been searching for?

A conversation with Jean-Luc came back to me, one that felt like it had taken place decades ago but had been less than a week. Him in my office telling me he would have Phyllis look into our recent failed negotiations, so sure there was some cause other than bad luck or our department's lapse in judgement.

Had she discovered the same irregularities I had?

Exhilaration buzzed through my blood, joined by what I refused to acknowledge as hope. What would it mean if Jean-Luc hadn't actually seen these papers? I took a bite of mac and cheese, then moved the bowl to the counter so I could reorganize the stacks on the table. Now I had a goal, an aim for what I was looking for.

I set the December fifth notes into a pile and began my search in earnest, cross-checking dates with the calendars I'd printed off, lining everything up in chronological order and marking the notes it would have been impossible for Jean-Luc to sign. Page after page moved through my hands, and I felt like I was seeing the entire government process in a time lapse, including all the places where the corruption had leaked in. For a second, I swore I sensed a shadowy figure hovering over my shoulder, a figment of the person who had orchestrated every bureaucratic sleight of hand.

"What is this?" Jet asked, and in my surprise, I threw the papers I was holding into the air as I whirled around.

At the sight of her and Gideon standing by the dining table, I pressed my hand to my heart.

"Meril's grace, you scared the crap out of me," I said, and frowned at the door. "How did you get in?"

"We knocked," she said. "When you didn't answer, Gideon picked the lock."

Her lips twitched with a smirk, though beneath her amusement, I sensed her stress and a streak of anger. From Gideon, I detected similar tension, twisted with deep, frustrated longing. I glanced between the two of them, wondered what I'd missed, then decided it was none of my business. That I hadn't noticed them coming into the apartment was enough of a reminder that we had more serious issues at hand than their emotional immaturity.

"Sorry for scaring you," Jet said. She nodded at the table. "Did you find something?"

I released a heavy breath to slow my heart, then turned around and reclaimed the papers I'd thrown. "I think so. Not quite what I was looking for, but in some ways better. And maybe what we need to set us on the path to the source. To the mole. There are a bunch of briefing notes here signed by Jean-Luc that he couldn't have signed. So I went through everything again, and see?"

By their identical bewildered expressions, they did not see.

"Up here," I pointed to one row of papers, "are the monthly calendars going back to last year. They show all the days the minister wasn't in the city. Now, for some of these trips, he could have brought notes with him to sign, or the matters might have been urgent enough that they were sent to him en route, but for the most part, that wouldn't have happened. Not with requests from foundations and organizations that could have waited until he got home."

My words sped up as my excitement grew. The idea that my discovery might clear my friend intoxicated me, and I hoped Gideon and Jet were keeping up.

"These here," I pointed, "the marked ones, these are notes it would have been impossible for him to sign when the date stamp says he did."

"Couldn't someone have accidentally stamped them with the wrong date?" Jet asked, moving closer to the rows laid out on the table to check for herself.

"Sure, once or twice, but I counted twelve instances in the past few months alone. Even more telling is the evidence in this pile right here from eleven, twelve months ago. In these cases, the date stamp is the day *after* the minister would have been back in the office. If Phyllis had noticed the incorrect date, she never would have let it slide. It means she never saw them."

"Phyllis?" Gideon asked.

"The minister's admin," Jet said.

Gideon nodded his understanding and returned his attention to me. "How do you know the dates are wrong? Couldn't he have signed them the day they're stamped?"

"No, because the manual stamp doesn't match the digital one." I pointed to the date at the bottom of the page, now included in the file name. "The system automatically marks the file when you upload it. See? These files were uploaded into the system *before* Jean-Luc supposedly signed them. Six months ago, the discrepancy stops and the manual stamp matches the digital one, even though the minister would have been away at the time. If I had to guess what happened, whoever arranged these forged signatures started by pretending the papers were signed once the minister got home, but must have noticed their mistake with the digital stamp, so gave up fudging the manual one. It looks more suspicious to have a signature happen after an upload than to have them match during a time when Jean-Luc wouldn't have been available. And their plan worked. No one caught on." My mouth went dry. "Although now I'm wondering if that's why they were killed. Phyllis had some of these files on her desk that day. It's possible she noticed and pointed it out to Jean-Luc."

I was glad I was already sitting down, because my head swam and black dots danced in my eyes. Now that I'd said it out loud, I realized how likely my theory was.

"What does this prove?" Gideon asked, and I wanted to kick him for his confusion. Wasn't it obvious?

"That Jean-Luc couldn't have been involved," I said, the words coming out calmly even though I wanted to shout them from the rooftops. "He was set up, just like we were."

The truth tasted sweet on my tongue, though the aftertaste was bitter.

"Why wouldn't whoever did this wait to upload the notes into the digital system until the minister was back to make sure the dates matched?" Jet asked after a moment had passed.

I cleared my throat and dragged my thoughts back to the papers. "And risk being caught forging Jean-Luc's signature? Again, why change the game if the rules worked for them?"

"What kind of briefing notes are we talking about?" Gideon asked, and something about the way the two of them bounced their questions back and forth caught my interest. I knew they'd been busy trying to reboot our investigation, but by the smoothness of their interrogation, the way they fed off each other's inquiries, splitting my attention, I guessed they'd fallen into whatever groove they'd formed in New York.

Jet was right—they did work well together. The energy between them buzzed like electricity and made my skin tingle.

"Take this one, for example." I drew out a collection of papers in the most recent date range. "It's a standard funding request for a community centre in an at-risk area. I read the note. Everything appears to be in order. They requested millions of dollars to build it and get some programming off the ground. Last month, it was raided as a suspected ghost lab. The story is similar across a bunch of these notes. 'Coincidental' ties to ghost or other criminal activity, the money going missing, and the projects never being completed. Someone was forging Jean-Luc's signature on projects that, on the surface, looked legitimate, but were actually a cover for illegal activity."

"And you're sure it wasn't Jean-Luc himself?" Jet asked.

I brushed my hair behind my ear, then crossed my arms over my chest, then rested them on the table. "Maybe I'm deluding myself, but why would he mess around with the dates if he'd signed these documents? That so much of this happened while he was out of town screams someone going behind his back." The greasiness of doubt slithered through my stomach. "Sure, it could be he was trying to deflect suspicion if anyone caught on to the pattern, but if that's the case—if he was the one signing off on all these millions of dollars—then whoever stabbed him killed their gift horse and they're finished. We have nothing more to worry about. Their plan is over, and we can focus on clearing our names instead. If it wasn't Jean-Luc, then the trouble will continue until we weed out the forger. Do you want to take that risk?"

Gideon and Jet exchanged a glance, and she puffed out a breath. "How high do we think this goes?"

I saw the way her thoughts were running and shook my head. "None of these requests required prime minister approval. They're all low-profile projects. Billions in total, but not enough money at once to require anything more than the minister's signature."

I empathized with the wave of relief rolling off her. If the corruption had gone all the way to the top—if the mundanes were involved, if the prime minister couldn't be trusted—then there was nothing we could do on this side of the wall. I shuddered as I considered the alternative, but it needed to be said. "If we don't uncover how deep this corruption runs and put a stop to it, we won't be able to contain what's happening as a departmental issue. Word will get out, the queen will be forced to step in, and we're going to have an even bigger problem on our hands."

The weight of my reminder of what was at stake—as if a

drug-dealing, embezzling government mole wasn't enough—effectively shut down the conversation. What else was there to say? The others couldn't argue with me, but I didn't want them to agree, either. It was too big. Like an avalanche tumbling towards us, gaining speed and mass, and there we were, the three of us, at the bottom of the mountain trying to prevent the snow from crushing everything behind us… without getting buried ourselves.

It was impossible.

Yet somehow we were going to try. Eventually. First, we opened another bottle of scotch, Gideon doing the honours of pouring while I scraped my forgotten mac and cheese into the compost bin. Once we'd indulged in some liquid courage, Gideon headed up to the roof, a pack of cigarettes in his hand.

"I think this calls for one," he said to Jet on his way out, and he'd already turned around by the time her brow folded into a frown.

She turned her back on the door and tapped her glass against her thigh.

"So," she said, approaching the dining room table as though she'd put Gideon out of her mind the moment he'd left. "What do you think? With Meril on the verge of rising from the depths, how do we move forward? Has she reached out to you again?"

A stone formed in the pit of my stomach, and I rubbed at my chest to loosen the tension around my lungs. "No. Nothing since her last warning. I don't know if that means she's giving me more time or if our next encounter will be as she storms across the wall."

Jet's throat bobbed with a hard swallow, and her lips twisted into a grimace. "Terrifying. All right, well, I guess we hope for the first one and work our asses off to make the most of it. Is there a way to find out who uploaded these documents into the system?"

I didn't need empathic abilities to know her mind wasn't on paperwork. The surface of the scotch in her glass rippled from the tremors in her hand, and her shoulders had climbed towards her earlobes.

"Unfortunately not. Not without full access to the system, and even then, if they were smart, they've hidden it under someone else's account. Mine for all I know. Another finger to aim in my direction." At some point, Jet's attention had slipped into the middle distance, and I doubted she'd heard half of what I'd said. "Jet, talk to me."

She needed to get out of her head. We'd known each other for ten years. We'd bitched about guys before. I'd been there when she'd come home from New York, there to witness the mess she'd been despite the successful mission. Gideon was her weak spot. Had been from the moment she'd met him. And now something new had happened.

She shook her head. "There's nothing to talk about."

"No? Not even that you found your ex-lover bloody and

broken on the floor of a prison cell in your detainment centre, tortured by someone who was recently recruited to your team without your say-so?" I leaned my hip against the table, careful not to dislodge any papers. "Not even that you spent a day with him, and the two of you came back here riffing banter like it was scripted from a Barney Miller episode?"

Jet's head jerked up, eyes wide and lips parted, and her shoulders tensed again. "No."

I sighed and took my drink over to the deep grey sectional in the middle of the room. "You didn't ask for it, but I'm giving you my two cents anyway. After everything we've been through, I think I'm entitled, even if you chuck it out the window. You should forgive him and admit you have feelings for him. At least to yourself."

I expected frustration and dismissal, not a sharp laugh as Jet sat on the couch beside me. "The only feeling I have for him is the desire to kick his ass back to Brooklyn."

Despite her attempt to sound annoyed, I picked up everything running underneath. The confusion, the inner debate running through her head, warring between guilt and longing, anger and regret. Only partially thanks to my ability, the rest because of how bad she was sometimes at schooling her expression.

Her response made sense. There was a lot to take into consideration, and my advice didn't stem from the fact that Gideon was the greatest guy in the world or a person I particularly wanted my friend to be with. For one thing, he was a liar, a spy, and was Gideon even his real name? He was the sort of person who put his job first, and though I couldn't fault him for that, did Jet really want to be with someone who couldn't make her a priority? Always coming second? Then again, whoever she chose would have to be comfortable with the same, which was one reason I was all right letting that point slide.

In spite of all his flaws, I saw the way he shifted around her, giving her space even while he stayed aware of every move she made. Knowing she could take care of herself, but ready to step in if anything tried to take her by surprise. And she did the same with him. There was a symmetry to them, as though their broken pieces fit together.

And if that wasn't enough, the waves of emotion I got from him, the same I detected in Jet, buried under everything else, would have been a real shame to waste.

It made me think of the string of text messages on my phone from a man who seemed to be made up of everything I wanted, even if at the moment I had no idea how to have it. Or if I should. Or could.

"What do you think about Colm?" I asked before I could stop myself.

"Colm?" Jet asked, her eyes glinting with a knowing stare. "Mr. Carrot Muffin?"

I laughed. "Yeah, him."

The corner of Jet's mouth curled upwards. "I think you

would make beautiful babies."

My drink sloshed over the side of my glass, and I used the back of my hand to wipe my chin. "What—oh for goodness' sake, Jet. I'm not talking about having my way with him up against the photocopier."

Her smile grew wider as she gave a slight shrug, suggesting she didn't think it was a horrible idea. I pushed away the images her suggestion brought to mind, remembering the many hours I'd spent playing similar reels through my head.

Any sort of romantic tryst was too far from the realm of reality, or even possibility, right now for me to enjoy the fantasy. The truth sucked the amusement out of my bones, and I said, "I mean about whether I could trust him."

With what? I didn't know. With the truth, with my heart, with my secret? Trust him to help us? Trust him not to run away?

I didn't care. I just wanted her to say yes. All I needed was a push to call him, invite him over, and tell him everything. For the past few hours, he'd remained at the back of my mind, his questions going unanswered for so long, his patience and care in not pushing me for any sort of confidence. And all for what? For me to lie to him? The only honesty between us was that I loved carrot muffins and that the sight of him in the lobby made me smile. And, I guess, that I was an employee of the Canadian public service. Everything else was either an evasion or a straight-out tall one, and I hated it.

My reasons were sound—I wanted to keep him safe—but if Jet wasn't concerned, maybe there was room for me to drop my guard as well.

But when I read her expression, my hopes crumbled. Her brow was furrowed, and her sharp gaze locked on mine. "You know my answer to that," she said. "He's one of them. Mundane. Trusting them is never worth the risk."

Chapter 13

Jet

I DON'T REMEMBER what time I fell asleep. One second I was on the couch watching some mindless crime drama to escape the dumpster fire my life had become, and the next, I was waking up in a bed that wasn't my own, the curtains open when I usually kept mine closed, and the sun up.

To top off the shitshow of disorientation, my entire body ached. From head to toe, my joints creaked, an inch away from popping in their sockets but never quite getting there. Hips, ankles, shoulders, wrists, not a single bendy part of me felt bendy. My knuckles were stiff and swollen, the tendons around my elbows and knees on fire. Every muscle felt stretched, torn, mangled, and I hadn't even moved yet.

Lingering drowsiness and pain of a dozen varieties prevented me from remembering what had caused my battered state, but slowly the events of yesterday came back. The effort of keeping my third eye open during our flight from my building, the air bridge I'd held together, our slog across town.

No wonder I felt like death warmed to a slow simmer.

Unfortunately, I didn't have time to lounge in bed and wait for my body to be ready. We had traitors to smoke out and a queen to avoid. I'd have to grit my teeth and bear it.

To start slow, I wriggled my toes, wincing as they cracked, then rolled my ankles to wake up my feet and calves. From there, I bent my knees and veered them from one side to the other to get the kinks out of my back. When all of that seemed to be okay, I stretched my arms in front of me, then over my head, startling myself when my fingers brushed against a headboard, something I'd never had.

I still hurt, but at least some of the stiffness had eased.

One part of my disorientation dealt with, I turned my attention to the room. A simple bedroom, decorated in throw pillows and furniture I wouldn't have picked out for myself. Sort of inn-like. Impersonal, but homey. Pale green curtains fluttered over a green-and-white bedspread. The traffic sounded so familiar, I may as well have been at my apartment. Probably because we were a whole ten-minute walk away.

So different for all it remained the same.

That left the question of how I'd made it to bed when I'd passed out in the living room. In a panic, I checked under the covers. Underwear on, but no pants. There was no way Madison would have been able to move me alone, so Gideon must have helped her. If he'd done the pants removing, he would be lucky to have his hands when I got through with him.

But when I spotted my jeans neatly folded on top of the dresser, my concerns vanished. From what I remembered of Gideon's Brooklyn apartment, he wouldn't know how to fold laundry.

I braced my hands against the mattress to push myself into a sit, and a groan escaped my throat as the room spun around me. Not from the alcohol—I hadn't drunk enough last night for a headache this bad—which was almost disappointing. It wasn't fair I should be in this much pain without the fun that usually caused it.

On shaking legs, I stood up and crossed the room. My mouth tasted like butt and felt about as clean, and my eyes were crusty. I needed a shower. I needed to feel like a living person again, not like a corpse freshly risen from the grave. I needed it to happen before anyone saw me.

This was why I didn't have roommates.

I grabbed my jeans, a clean shirt and underthings, and the bathroom gear I'd brought with me, and inched the door open. From here, I could make out the kitchen around the corner and a sliver of the living room. No sounds filled the apartment, so hopefully that meant no one else was up and about.

Where the hell is the bathroom?

I had a vague recollection of where it had been last night, but the layout was hazy in the fog of my uncooperative brain and body.

To hell with it. As long as I didn't stumble into Gideon's room, I was fine.

I stepped into the hallway and scanned the open doors, spotting the bathroom across the hall and one door down. Easy.

Not wanting to wake anyone up, I carried my weight on my toes to keep my steps light. Despite my efforts, the floor creaked beneath me, and I paused, straining to hear anyone else moving around, about to encounter me in all my morning glory. When the apartment remained quiet, I kept going, making it to the first door.

So far so good.

But before I could relax, the floor creaked again as someone got up in the room beside me. I was too far from my room to dart back in and not close enough to the bathroom, leaving me trapped in the hallway as the door opened to reveal a sleepy, shirtless Gideon. In the second that passed before I fully registered my horror at being caught pantless and cottonmouthed, my brain took in his brown hair sticking up in bed-mussed spikes, the rough stubble along his jawline, the lines of muscle over his chest and stomach, the hardness of his arms and the leather bracelet around his left wrist, the grooves of his hips where they disappeared beneath the band of his jockeys… my gaze shot back up at the evidence of his morning situation.

His eyes grew wide at the sight of me, and I realized I wasn't the only one getting a good look.

"Morning," he said, his voice a grumbly bass that rattled its way down my stomach and between my legs. He passed a hand over his face and scratched his stubble. "How'd you sleep?"

"Can't remember, so must have been well. You?"

"Good, yeah."

God, we sounded as awkward as two teenagers who'd spent the night together and had no idea how to behave the next morning. And we hadn't even had sex.

Nor will you, I reminded the deepest places in my body that had suddenly stirred to life.

In spite of myself, my thoughts flew to New York. How often had I seen him in a similar condition in our little hideaway of his crummy apartment? At the time, it had been nothing, a side effect of the way we'd spent our evening. Warm, sleepless nights filled with passion and laughter, the uncomplicated connection between two people who held the same values when it came to work and casual relationships.

It had been easy then. Now, I felt so confused about what I wanted and thought and felt that seeing him in his present state left me even more muddled. I had to get away from him. Clear my head and focus on the whole country-potentially-collapsing problem.

I half-turned towards the bathroom. "I was just…"

"Oh, yeah, of course."

"Unless you wanted to…" I made a vague gesture towards his nether regions, and when his gaze travelled down, his cheeks turned pink and he cleared his throat.

"Uh, no. You go ahead. I can wait a minute. Thanks."

He stepped back into his room and closed the door. The sound of the latch catching was followed closely by a *thunk* that might have been his head hitting the door, and I bit down on a smile as I closed myself in the bathroom.

My amusement withered as last night's conversation with Madison came back to me. Sure, most of my evening was a blur, but *that* part stood out in word-for-word detail.

I wasn't the type of woman who got sloshed and talked about boys. Never had been. Madison had caught me at a low point, and the discussion had been a waste of time. I scoffed as I peeled off my shirt and turned on the water in the shower stall. Forgive him. She couldn't be serious. The man was a thorn in my side, and all I wanted was to resolve our problem quickly so he could go home and lie to some other poor girl.

But as I turned on the spray and stepped into the shower, moaning with pleasure as the hot water soaked deep into my muscles, I wondered if I should give Madison more credit. Had I been lying to myself? Yes, he had hurt me. Yes, it had been a shitty thing to do. But working with him again made me remember why I'd been drawn to him in the first place. He was good at his job, he was quick, he was brutal, and he *got it*. He got why the work was so important, and why being able to trust your team was the only thing that mattered when you poked your nose into the unknown.

That counted for a lot in my books. There was also a balance of evils happening right now. He had lied about his identity to shut down a supernatural smuggling racket. A shit move for a decent motive. Someone in my department was lying about *their* identity to earn some money while they watched their country fall to pieces. For now, I would choose the lying sack of shit who followed some kind of moral compass, however shaky.

So, fine, I would agree with Madison that far. But goddamn if I would acknowledge anything more than that. Not when the chances were so high he would screw me over again if he had to. Or that I would have to do the same to him. What kind of future was there for two people whose priorities were so often at cross-purposes?

I rested my head against the cold tile of the bathroom wall as the warm spray pelted my back.

Why did everything in my life have to be so complicated?

When this was over, I was taking a vacation away from everyone. No people, no problems—just a bottle of Jack and a New York-style cheesecake all to myself.

But first I had to survive the darkness to come.

Though my joint pain had eased by the time I got out of the shower, my head was no clearer, and my confusion only increased when my phone rang halfway through a heaping breakfast of bacon and eggs.

I didn't recognize the number, but when I answered, Travis's agitated voice said, "They're calling for a protest."

My brain rushed through the five W's before I landed on, "Who?"

He'd jumped straight to the punchline with no setup. What had I missed in the last twenty-four hours?

Madison set her fork down and crossed her arms on the table, her gaze glued to my face. Gideon barely spared me a glance—had hardly looked at me since our run-in this morning—but by the subtle tilt of his head, I knew he was listening.

"Whoever's leading the bitchfest," said Travis. "Word came through the shop half an hour ago. They're trying to draw more people in to fluff up the crowd or some bullshit. I guess some of the local busybodies held a meet last night and voted to march on Parliament Hill. People from all the surrounding areas. Calling for the protection of supe rights, slamming the queen for being useless. Fucking asshats."

I took a second to take in what he was saying. Protests had popped up across the country since the de Lauer attack. They were a big publicity draw, but we had the same right to gather as any other group. The perception filters that covered anything magic-touched would prevent the mundanes from seeing details they shouldn't, and the prime minister would get an earful. Interesting, especially about the anger towards Meril, but hardly enough for Travis to set aside his loathing and give me a call. "What else?"

He paused and his voice dropped, growing muffled as he spoke closer into his phone. "Could be something is set to happen while all those people are there."

The suggestion between his words, the warning in his tone, was enough to make me sit up. Madison's brow furrowed and Gideon pushed his plate away, his shoulders tense, ready to get up and run if I gave the order.

"What exactly have you heard?"

"Nothing specific," he said. "Honestly, I don't know. But SMOAC must have heard something, too, because they beefed up security around the Hill. I know because Dawn—my wife— she works downtown. She's in a shop on Sparks, and she's been watching these agents prowling around." I heard the first hints of concern in his voice. Whatever rumours had reached him, he wasn't bullshitting me. "She's worried, and fuck if I'm not scared for her. Protests can be good for business, but if some- one's planning to cause trouble…"

A grinding screech echoed down the line, and images filled my head of car parts and heavy machinery warping out of shape with Travis's rising anger.

"I'll get down there and see what I can find out," I said. "Thanks for the heads-up."

He hung up without saying anything else, and I clicked my tongue against the roof of my mouth as I set down the phone.

The other two stared at me, waiting for me to share, but

I was already busy trying to piece together a plan of action. I would have to get downtown without being recognized, avoid security, and put a stop to whatever might happen, all without creating a panic in the crowd. How the hell was I supposed to do that on my own?

Madison broke first. "What is it?"

I pulled my thoughts back to the table, no closer to an answer. "Rumours. Nothing concrete, just words circulating and making everything worse."

Following rumours was how I'd wound up here—half my squad dead, on the run from my superiors, and under suspicion of murder—left with two friends to watch my back and no idea who else to trust. Travis sounded sincere, but how much did that count for? How could I be sure his source was any good? Would innocent people die if I acted on his information, or would the greater evil be to ignore him?

"I don't understand," I said, pinching the bridge of my nose. "He's talking about someone making trouble at a protest. Does that sound like something a drug-dealing syndicate would do? We talked about the unrest being part of O'Malley's plan, a distraction for the news to cover up whatever his actual goals are, but this kind of public show? Why? Security will be there. My team is supposed to be there. They'll step in to prevent any disturbance and haul away anyone who tries to cause it. Where is the benefit to O'Malley except to lose some lackeys?"

"Maybe he thinks your team won't be fast enough to catch

them?" Gideon suggested.

"Possibly, but for what? To hurt civilians? Draw more mundane eyes our way? How does that tie in to ghost dealing and money laundering?"

We were missing something. A large, blurred patch in the middle of the picture.

"Unless…" Madison started, then she shook her head and sipped her coffee.

"What?" Gideon asked, beating me to it.

"It's just a theory," she said.

"That's all we have to work with right now," I said. "Maybe one more will clear the haze."

She shifted in her seat, her gaze moving from Gideon's to mine before dropping back to her mug. "What if their purpose in stirring up discontent is darker than using it as a distraction?"

I tried to guess where her thoughts had gone, but the path forward was too murky. When I looked at Gideon, he shrugged and shook his head.

"We assumed this was all about the ghost, or the money the ghost earns," Madison said. "The labs, the bombs, the Kingston rumour. Everything we've followed has been the drug trail. What if the ghost has nothing to do with it? What if it's the convenient hot topic that draws the right kind of headlines and sets off the right type of groups? The type that makes noise, that forms mobs. What if the riots aren't intended to cover the movement of the ghost, but the ghost is being used to set off the riots?" She looked from me to Gideon, seeing if we were following.

At first, her logic escaped me, but as I formed the question, the horrifying possibility pooled at the base of my spine.

"They're trying to cause chaos," Gideon said, voicing my fears. "Destabilize the balance of the country."

"That's why they're targeting Meril," I said. From the start, I'd been curious about the sudden open hostility towards the queen considering no one had heard from her in decades. "Causing trouble between both sides of the wall. To cut us off from each other? Channel power somewhere?"

Madison nodded. "What if whoever's signing these briefing notes and shutting down projects isn't working *for* the syndicate but working *with* them?"

I swallowed around the rock in my throat. "If so, we have to assume Travis's information is good. Something is going to happen at the protest today. Up until now, they've been using Dougall to attract attention…"

Madison blanched. "They wouldn't. A ghostbomb near all those people?"

Gideon scowled. "Right now, I think we need to plan for the nightmare scenario."

As much as it turned my stomach, he was right. "Let's hope we get lucky. If they're planning something that huge, whoever's behind it will want to be close enough to watch the fallout."

Maybe we would end this before anyone else got hurt.

Chapter 14

Jet

THE WEIGHT OF Madison's theory crushed all speech for a good minute, but as soon as the shock wore off, a heated argument began that left my blood buzzing with no way to vent the excess energy except to take it out on the table lamp in the corner.

"Of course I'm going," I said, astounded it was even a question. The lamp rattled against the wall. "And I'm going alone. You can't be seen in public, and I know this city. I can get around more easily if I'm not worried about watching out for you."

"Not a chance in hell," Gideon said, bracing both hands on the counter. "You shouldn't be within a fifty-block radius of that crowd. They're searching for you, Jet. Have you forgotten the little thing about a *murder investigation*? Where would you even start? You have no idea what sort of trouble they're organizing. If there's another ghostbomb in the middle of the crowd, what would you do? If whatever happens turns a peaceful protest into a fucking riot, you'd wind up trapped in the middle of it. Stay home. Call it in."

My thoughts flew to Eric Sampson, my lieutenant. At any other time, he would have been my go-to in a situation like this. Someone I trusted with my life. Zeke, Ellison, Sara—a week ago, I would have counted on any of them. Now Zeke was in hospital, Ellie was dead, and Eric and Sara probably agreed with the majority that their dear packleader had lost her mind.

Gideon was right that I should call to warn them, but would they listen? I suspected they'd give it as much weight as an anonymous tip. Until we shut down O'Malley and anyone working with him, I had lost their trust, which meant I couldn't be sure they would take me seriously. What if they did a half-assed sweep to appease their grief-stricken captain? What if they ignored my report altogether, assuming it was more of my paranoid ravings, and missed the signs of a planned attack?

I would call to make the report, but there was no way I'd take the risk of a potential threat being overlooked.

"This isn't my first protest," I said, "and if it goes that way, it won't be my first riot."

Gideon opened his mouth, no doubt to spout something sharp and witty, but as the lamp on the table grew rowdier in response to my rising anger, Madison stepped between us.

"What *is* your plan? I know you're not thinking of walking in and seeing what happens."

She wasn't siding with Gideon, but by the satisfaction on his face, he certainly thought she was. And, frankly, it was hard not to feel attacked.

I set my hands on my hips and focused on Madison, willing the lamp to sit still so it didn't give away my uncontrolled frustration. I didn't want to admit I hadn't sorted out the details yet. Though now that I'd been put on the spot, ideas fluttered through my head, organizing themselves into the most practical options. Fourteen years of experience had given me that advantage at least. I might not have a team behind me, but I could come up with a dozen battle tactics in a three-minute span.

Another spasm of pain around my heart stole my breath. If I had played things differently, I would probably be corralling what was left of my team right now, patrolling Parliament Hill, preparing for the protest. I would be on the inside, with the full strength of SMOAC resources behind me.

But if I'd gone that route, Gideon would be locked in a cell at Carstairs's mercy. Madison would be at risk of Dougall using her to make a fake political point to follow through on a fake threatening note. I would have to walk around with a smile on my face as though I didn't suspect every person I crossed to be in league with the syndicate. And I wouldn't have had the forewarning that something might go down at the protest.

I'd made the only decision I could, and though it hurt like a son of a bitch to be out here on my own, I had to work with what was available.

My emotions tried to get the better of me, so I cleared my throat and focused on logistics. "My primary mission will be to observe. If Michael is organizing security, he'll do a thorough job of it, especially if they receive word of a potential attack. Likely I won't have to step in at all. Our security team is good, and my task force is the best. I know how they're trained. They know what they're looking for and how to be discreet. I'll set up on a rooftop, somewhere out of sight."

"To what end?" Madison rested her hand on my arm. "I know you want to help, but it won't do us any good if you're found. We have a better chance of protecting ourselves by figuring out the connections and significance behind these briefing notes."

My gaze shifted to the papers piled in the middle of the dining table. Madison had stacked them by month. A chronological view of all the ways someone had messed with our community. Hundreds of documents, and those were just the notes Madison had been able to pull before IT blocked her access. We only had a snapshot of how far this corruption went back and how widespread the problem had become, and of that brief glimpse, we'd only begun to dig into it.

She was right. Paperwork was tangible evidence, and therefore had to be the priority… but the idea of being cooped up inside reading page after page of bureaucratic bullshit created knots in my stomach that squeezed my lungs and guts.

"I can't do it," I said. "I have to see with my own eyes that security downtown is ready for any possible outcome. My troops are good, but they don't know about Dougall. Would *you* have believed Dougall was the Ghostmaker?" I posed the question to both of them but didn't wait for an answer. "Besides, I can't—fuck." I bowed my head, hating what I was about to say. "I can't trust that the right people are calling the shots."

My stomach turned at the idea that someone I worked for might be dirty, but we couldn't afford to be naive. "We know someone in the upper echelon is involved. If it benefits them to have this protest fall to pieces, we can't be sure they'll order the troops to move in time. Someone has to be there who knows what's going on. I know I need to stay out of sight—I *know* I can't be caught—but if you're right, Madison, and someone in our department is vying for power, then this could be one step towards stopping them. If I can save lives, I need to try."

Madison cast her gaze down, and I guessed her thoughts weren't so far from my own. For a moment, she said nothing, white lines forming around her mouth as she pressed her lips together in thought—or possibly in an effort not to throw up—and then she met my gaze and said, "You're right. You need to be there."

I was halfway through a sigh of gratitude that I had her support when she added, "Gideon's also right. He has to go with you."

My jaw dropped, and I sputtered out a few failed arguments. Had I not been clear? How the hell was I supposed to keep an eye out for unusual activity if I was busy making sure Gideon wasn't recognized by anyone in the crowd? Or that his half-healed wounds didn't reopen and bleed him dry before we got him to safety?

In fact, why was I being questioned at all? Madison knew how to negotiate, but I was the captain here. I gave the orders and worked out the strategy.

I also knew when and how to pick my battles, and by the look in Madison's eye, this wasn't a fight I would win.

Gideon looked downright smug about it, and the desire to clock him, a desire that had faded over the course of the last twenty-four hours, resurfaced within me.

"Fine," I said once I'd found my voice, "but the rule stands. My country, my lead."

He nodded, his smirk fading into seriousness. "Nothing's changed, Jet. You lead, I'll follow."

There was nothing in the words themselves that caught my attention, but the intensity with which he said them and the look in his eyes expressed more than enough. He might not agree with my decision, but he would be there for me. Something that, so far, despite all our problems, had always been true.

By the time Gideon and I got downtown, a large crowd had already formed. The lawn on Parliament Hill was a press of bodies waving signs that read *Respect our Rights* and *Marching for Magic*. Through my peripheral vision, I glimpsed what the mundanes saw, the text on the posters re-forming to read things like *Dental Care is Health Care*. A safe, standard point of contention where the greatest risk would be drawing interested mundanes into the crowd.

The numbers concerned me. Either the authorities hadn't heard anything about Travis's rumour, or they had, and they'd decided to let things play out. I'd called in the tip before leaving the safe house, using a false name and number, but didn't feel confident anyone would put much stock in it.

I wondered what Michael thought of the situation. Trouble or no, he had to see the danger in letting people gather like this. We were already at three ghostbombs. A protest this large was asking for Dougall to step in and shake things up. Unless Michael didn't believe O'Malley would shake things up that publicly.

Gideon and I kept to the far side of Wellington, getting a feel for the crowd before we decided whether or not to step into it. As we walked, I checked the faces of the uniforms we passed, and though I glimpsed a few people I recognized, I didn't spot any of my team or anyone in SMOAC kit.

We paused on the corner, and I stood on tiptoe to get a better look at the screens draped over the podium. The prime minister stood on the steps in front of the Peace Tower addressing the questions being shouted by a handful of reporters and journalists, most of them representing supernatural news streams, with a few mundanes having come out because of the crowds. Mostly small-time papers and outlets. We supernaturals tended not to use anything too sensational to cover our real purpose.

A few weeks ago, the Minister of Supernatural, Magical and Occult Affairs would have stood at the prime minister's side, interpreting questions and offering answers and spins, but since he was dead, Deputy Minister Lucien Gagnon had taken over the role.

Although the questions were vague and the answers generic to hide from the mundane media, it was easy for someone in the know to follow the source of the crowd's outrage. Our people demanded answers about how the government intended to protect them. With the recent attacks, the minister's death, and the rise in ghost-related incidents, they wanted reassurance that they were safe, that the people responsible would be caught, that their lives could continue as normal. The department had let them down by not making their security, either physically or as supernaturals, a priority. I agreed with them but hated that they might be falling into the syndicate's trap by making such a public outcry.

The prime minister tried to field their questions without revealing the true nature of the discussion, and Gagnon did his best to keep the answers coming at a steady pace, but the situation in the department had changed too quickly, and deputy minister hadn't had much time to get up to speed as acting leader. The supernatural community, like SMOAC, was a microcosm of the rest of the world, and the minister had been the last word on everything. His death was a destabilizing force. With his removal, a power vacuum had opened, and we had to hope Gagnon was strong and clever enough to fill the void.

Gideon glanced at me, and I nodded my chin up the street. Standing around served no purpose. We didn't have a good view of the crowd, and I was in no mood to listen to the prime minister give assurances to a problem the department didn't understand—or refused to acknowledge.

While we walked, I played with the brim of my black baseball cap, making a show of adjusting it to better display my apparent love of the Ottawa Senators, but in reality working to keep my face hidden from the sharp gazes of my team. I hated hockey, but my opinion had struck Madison as an even better reason to use the cap with my disguise, adding to the bright pink *Ottawa* T-shirt she'd made me wear. I'd also changed my walk from my usual determined stride to more of a hip-swinging swagger, as though I were some tourist checking out the city with my honeybun of a boyfriend.

Any member of my pack would be as quick to recognize me as I would them, so while we were this close to the crowd, I had to become someone I wasn't—someone they wouldn't look at twice.

One high point of Madison's costuming choice was that Gideon looked as miserable in his red *Canada* T-shirt as I felt, even though he'd refused the loose plaid shorts she'd wanted him to wear. His cap matched mine, except that it sported the logo for the Montreal Canadiens. Habs versus Sens. A reason not even our fictional relationship would work… unless we joined together in our hatred of the Toronto Maple Leafs.

"It's impossible to see anything from down here," he grumbled as a flock of camera-toting tourists pushed past him.

He was right. No matter where we stood on the street, we'd only be able to see a few metres in any direction.

"We need to get higher," I said, though the suggestion came with its own set of problems. We could find our way into one of the office buildings to reach the roof, but our response to any trouble would be slowed by the need to get back to ground level. There would also be the risk of more eyes on us than I was comfortable with.

I looked up. Government buildings took up most of the block, but not all of them were the oppressive high-rises that had consumed much of downtown. Right across from the Peace Tower was one such four-storey building. Easy enough to get to the roof and avoid the curious stares and awkward questions of the commissionaires. Once up top, we would be able to see all of Parliament Hill and not need to wait for any elevators to get back down.

"Come on," I said, and Gideon followed me around the corner and up a side street towards an alley.

"A government building? Really?" he asked. "I thought we were trying to avoid the feds."

"I don't plan on getting close enough to let anyone see me," I assured him. "Besides, everyone knows I would never be caught dead in a pink tourist T-shirt."

I couldn't deny Madison's idea had been a good one—lucky for us our safe house was right next to a dollar store for cheap, easy access to the throwaway gear—and I was extra relieved none of my team would know me. Disguise or not, I'd never live it down.

We reached the alley tucked between two buildings—a common smoking spot based on the number of cigarette butts lying around—and I shoulder-checked to make sure we were alone before setting my fingers against the stone wall.

"Meet you on the roof?"

Gideon raised his finger to the brim of his cap, and in a breath he dissolved, becoming nothing more than lingering trails of mist that drifted to the rooftop.

At least he had his strength back. Mine was still in question.

Gritting my teeth, I closed my eyes and connected to the air molecules around me, drawing them closer, folding them into a security strap across my back to hold me close to the wall. Once I felt confident that if I slipped I wouldn't immediately fall and shatter a bone or two, I found spots for my hands and feet to grip and started to climb.

The first few steps were fine, my muscles strong enough to get me moving, but by the time I reached the second storey, the effort of keeping the air net intact had drained me. My arms trembled and sweat dripped into my eyes. I ignored the pain and pulled myself from one handhold to another, my toes finding grooves in the stone to push me up.

If I'd had the energy, I would have created steps in the air and run to the roof, but after containing two ghostbombs and holding an air bridge in place, my stamina was running on empty. I needed to make sure I could wrestle someone to the ground if we spotted any of O'Malley's people, and if I pushed myself too hard now, the odds weren't good. The wall-climbing was physically exhausting, but at least my muscles were primed for that sort of activity.

I passed the third floor and did a quick scan of the alley below to make sure I was still alone. As I shifted my grip, my foot slipped, sending shards of rock skittering down the side of the building. I hugged myself closer to the wall, the press of air holding me in place, and guided my foot to a stronger lip.

A door opened below me, and my heart stopped, my breath catching in my lungs.

Don't look up. Don't look up. I prayed to all the gods I could name that whoever had stepped outside would carry on without taking in the view. Their reaction if they found Little Miss Tourist climbing the side of a government building would not make our task any easier. I wanted to rush out of view, but until they left, I was stuck. I couldn't risk sending more stones down the wall.

Multiple voices floated towards me, and I peered down again to watch three people in suits leaving through a side door and heading towards the street. It had to be lunch time.

As they reached the end of the alley, one of them shielded their eyes and looked up and down the street. I squeezed my eyes shut, my heart racing as I prepared to make a quick getaway over the rooftop before the RCMP arrived, but a moment later, another laugh echoed between the buildings, growing fainter as the source of it moved away.

I opened my eyes to find them gone and released my breath. As my terror subsided, my hands loosened their hold on the wall. I lurched backwards, but the strap of air caught me, and I threw myself forward. My poor heart galloped against my ribs, the taste of blood filling my mouth from my throbbing pulse—or had I bitten my tongue?—and I bowed my head.

Focus, Dawson.

I channelled my training, tightened my grip, and continued my climb.

When I reached the roof, my legs were shaking and my shoulders screamed with every small movement. This wasn't me. I should have been able to make this climb without issue.

Get it together, Dawson, I thought, Michael's voice in my head. *Better keep training if I don't want to be caught with my pants down.*

Gideon was already in place on the other side of the building, peering over the ledge into the crowd below. Gravel crunched beneath my shoes, and he looked over his shoulder.

"You finally made it."

"Asshole," I grumbled, not in the mood to think of anything more creative. I sank to my knees beside him. "See anything?"

He shook his head. "Nothing but a bunch of pissed-off supernaturals. I can only imagine the inferno it'll set off if Travis's intel is right and no one steps in."

"Let's make sure that doesn't happen."

For a while, neither of us spoke, our attention directed outwards. I finally spotted the SMOAC task force organizing a perimeter around the Hill, lining Wellington, which was reduced to a single lane this close to Centre Block, and ducking down the side streets. The slowed traffic created a creeping sensation in my stomach.

Stop it. You're reading nightmares in shadows.

Slower traffic meant less chance of protesters getting hit by cars if the crowd swelled off the Hill. It didn't foretell anything else. It didn't matter that the streets were clogged, which gave less room to manoeuvre an evacuation if we needed one. If the security team didn't expect anything to happen, their decision made perfect sense.

But I couldn't shake my uneasiness at seeing all these people penned in, their exits blocked.

If something went wrong in this packed, dense crowd, it

would be a massacre.

I scanned the scene more than once before I spotted Eric. In his tactical gear, his features obscured under his black cap and sunglasses, he was difficult to recognize, but I knew the line of his shoulders under his vest and the gestures he used to arrange his troops how he wanted them. Blond hair peeked out from under his cap. The man was due for a haircut.

My heart twinged at the sight of him. The last time we'd seen each other, we hadn't left on good terms. He'd refused to see the red flags pointing to corruption in the department, and I'd refused to trust the people I'd worked with for fourteen years. Maybe that did make me a stubborn ass with a dead career ahead of me, but considering why I was here and all I'd learned since then, I stood my ground that I was the one with my eyes wide open.

I wished I could have convinced him. Eric was as loyal to the department as I was and would have gone to whatever lengths to help me save it. There had been a moment—an oh-so-brief glimmer—where I thought he saw things my way, but he'd retreated into the security of the life he'd built for himself, too afraid to consider the possibility that the people he served no longer deserved his devotion.

"Jet?" Gideon nudged me with his elbow. "You okay?"

I forced a smile. "Peachy. You watch over that way, by the hotel. I'll keep my eye on the stage."

He shot me a look of concern, his dark eyes full of questions I didn't want him to ask, then he nodded and did as I said.

I spared one last glance at Eric before he melted into the crowd. Despite where things stood between us, I was relieved he was working this shift. No matter how I felt about the rest of the department, I had faith that whatever corruption was oozing its way into SMOAC hadn't touched him. Any plans he made to protect the people here today would be to keep them safe.

Which meant I was free to scout for whoever might want to hurt them.

From up here, we had a clear view of the street, the Hill, all the way past the Château Laurier and the Rideau Shopping Centre. It was a beautiful day, the sun warm but not too hot. The crisp breeze, touched with the smell of river water and the various flavours of the market, cooled the back of my neck. It was the best time of year to be in Ottawa, and people knew it. At this time of day, the sidewalks were packed with public servants, tourists, and people out shopping. Thousands of people, even outside of the protest.

Chaos.

Gideon and I sat and watched as the reporters asked their questions and the prime minister fumbled through some answers, the same sort of vague platitudes and assurances Gagnon had heaped on me in person at our last meeting.

The crowds were obviously as satisfied by those answers as I had been, because as the day grew warmer, the masses grew more restless, pressing forward, signs waving, closing whatever gaps existed between them until all breathing room vanished.

I felt claustrophobic watching them, unable to imagine how bad it would be standing in the middle of it.

That's when I spotted Peter Dougall crossing the street towards us.

He was there and gone so quickly, I doubted my eyes, but the memory of the loose red-and-black plaid button-down shirt over a white T-shirt and saggy blue jeans remained with me.

In a crouch, I hurried to the far end of the building, desperate to find him again, but he'd lost himself in the crowd.

"Shit," I hissed. "Not good, not good."

"What is it?" Gideon asked.

"Dougall."

He sat up straighter, leaned over the ledge to look for himself. "Where?"

"He was right there on the corner," I said, fear twisting my nerves. "But I don't—no, wait. There."

I hurried to Gideon's side and pointed Dougall out as he moved away from Parliament Hill. His dirty blond hair was pulled into a low ponytail, and he moved erratically, as though afraid of touching anyone or anything. Nervous, just as he'd been the first time we'd spoken to him.

But now I knew it was all a show. The man was high energy but as cool as a snake when he needed to be. And if the Ghost-maker was here…

"Fuck," Gideon said, as though reading my thoughts. "You

were right. You think there's a bomb? You really think he'd go that far? There's got to be a few thousand people here."

Bile crept up the back of my throat at the thought of what would happen if he were to play supervillain. All these people—all these supernaturals—crammed so tightly together. If a ghostbomb went off, their abilities would be heightened. Paranoia and aggression would set in. I knew the effects all too well. The screams of my team as they destroyed each other, as their bodies broke down, haunted me in my sleep so many days later. These people would tear each other to pieces, and the media would be there to catch everything. How the hell would the prime minister explain such a catastrophe? Tentacles and toxic spit, magic spells and sheer brute strength. Shifters, demons, witches, all reacting on pure defensive instinct.

First at the de Lauer Estates and then at Dougall's house, I'd been able to contain the powder, prevent it from reaching any civilians, but there was no way in hell I'd manage anything like that out in the open.

"We need to move," I said.

"Jet, you can't. If you go in there, security will see you. They won't give you a chance to explain."

"And if we stay here and Dougall's planted a bomb? Do you really want front-row seats for that carnage?"

"Call Eric. Call *anyone*. Let them deal with it."

I hesitated, then ground my teeth and pulled my phone out of my pocket. He was right, and I hated it, but I'd promised

Madison I would stay out of the way.

I kept my eye on Dougall as I jabbed the first digits of Eric's number, but before I finished dialling, the son of a bitch broke into a run. "We don't have time for this. If he's running, there's something he's running *from*. You get into the crowd and search for the bomb. Don't be seen. If you find it, get it to the team before it goes off."

Gideon grabbed my arm as I made to move away, his palm warm, the lines around his eyes hard. I told myself he was only thinking about what had to be done and tried to ignore the obvious emotions swirling in his gaze. "Where the hell are *you* going?"

I held his stare, refusing to show any of the fear snaking around inside me. "I'm going after the Ghostmaker."

Chapter 15

Gideon

J ET RAN BEFORE I could stop her, which left nothing for me to do but run in the opposite direction. If Dougall was on his way to deliver a bomb, Jet would catch him. If he'd already delivered it, he would be rushing as fast as he could away from it. And thanks to this crowd, I had no idea where he'd started from. Every time I pushed forward, someone pushed me back. I'd earned more than a few nasty looks for my trampling of people's toes and liberal use of elbows, but nothing I did created an easy path for myself. The crowd was crammed in too close and getting more impatient the longer their leader blathered on about how aware the party was of their concerns.

This was ridiculous.

I flung my hat to the ground to better see the space around me.

There could be a ghostbomb ready to go off, and I was

caught in the middle of a potential stampede. I had to mist through them. My senses would be limited, but speed was more important. I could hold myself together, keep as much of my spatial awareness as possible, and bring myself back if I noticed anything suspicious. I might miss whatever Dougall had left behind, but I wouldn't find it the way I was going, either.

Fuck it.

With a breath, I dissolved the atoms of my clothes, my knives, my body, until I was able to pass between protesters as though they stood miles apart. Without the distraction of finding my way around obstacles, I was hit with an overwhelming terror of what would happen if our suspicions were right about the bomb and we weren't fast enough to get rid of it. Thousands of people dead in front of the country's leader. Caught on the news. Our secret revealed to the world.

Why?

If we followed Madison's theory, distraction made sense. Civil unrest made sense.

Risking the divide between supernatural and mundane? If that was their goal, we were screwed. Unless they believed the perception filter was strong enough to hide the truth. A protest-turned-mob, a terrorist act, a tragedy, nothing more.

Every molecule of my being vibrated with nervous energy. Whatever their reason, we would do what we could to prevent it, which meant I had to concentrate on finding that bomb. Panic wouldn't help me.

Think, Gideon.

I had to work on the assumption that Dougall would have been strategic. Hit the centre of the crowd for maximum damage. So that was where I started. Hoping I was wrong, hoping we'd overreacted, I made my way to the Centennial Flame. A first sweep revealed nothing, but I materialized to get a closer look. No sign of any ticking clock or unwanted mechanism.

Where else would he go? Think, think, think.

I scanned the area again, and my gaze fell on the rigging in front of the Peace Tower. A stage. It took me a second to realize we weren't far from Canada Day and I was standing at ground zero of their big celebration.

Wouldn't that be a huge kick in the ass.

Gritting my teeth, I dissolved again until I reached the stage. The protesters crowded right up to the edge, but on the far right side was enough of a gap for me to spot the red LED panel shining out from underneath. Jet had been right. O'Malley was insane, and we had three minutes before the world suffered the consequences of his insanity.

Fuck.

I pulled my phone out of my pocket, but who was there to call? Jet had gone after Dougall and could be anywhere. She'd said to get the bomb to her team, so that's what I would do. Pass it off and disappear before they got their hands on me.

I whirled around and strained to see over the crowd for any

SMOAC troops. Anyone who could take over and leave me free to get my ass out of here.

When I finally spotted Jet's toy soldier lieutenant, he and a few others were organizing, moving at a swift pace away from the crowd. Towards the main road.

In the direction Jet had gone.

What now?

I looked at the timer. Two minutes thirty.

I wanted to call Jet, find out what the fuck had happened, but I had no time. If no one was around to help me, I had to deal with it myself.

A quick glance to make sure I hadn't attracted any attention, then I ducked under the stage to get a closer look at the bomb. Not that there was much point in me poking at it. I didn't know the first thing about bomb disposal. I was a spy. I gathered information, sometimes kicked some ass, and knew who to call to make problems disappear. None of those skills would help me here.

I wiped my sweaty palms on my thighs.

"All right. What am I looking at?"

Digital clock. Many kilos of ghost.

Enough to affect if not kill everyone in the crowd and within a five-block radius if it got airborne.

I puffed out a breath. All I had to do was stay calm.

A mess of wires connected the clock to the detonator, though the attached charge looked small. Of course it was. The blast only had to be big enough to tear the plastic and send the powder flying. No big explosion, just an anticlimactic *poof* and a reign of terror no one would be able to contain.

A minute thirty.

I couldn't dick around figuring out what wires to cut. By the look of it, some weren't even attached to anything, just there to confuse the issue. Easier to throw the whole thing into the river.

If I'd given myself enough time.

I pulled my knife out of my boot, flipped it open, and sliced through the duct tape strapping the bomb to the underside of the stage. It dropped, but I caught it in my arms before it hit the grass.

Forty-five seconds.

There was no way I could dissolve it with me. The risk of releasing the powder was too high.

Without thinking about how I would do this, only knowing I had to, I sprinted away from the protesters, over the barricades, towards the river.

As I ran, my heart pounded against my rib cage and my thoughts raced with every possible disaster. What if this wasn't the only bomb? Dougall could have planted a dozen throughout the crowd, and if they were all set to three-minute timers, there was no way in hell I'd get to them fast enough.

My breath grew laboured, my muscles screaming at me to slow down, stop, rest. I pushed harder. The healing wound down my chest tore open, pain slashed across my middle, and I pushed through that, too. A bloody shirt would mean nothing if this bomb went off in my hands.

Keep moving. Faster.

Voices called after me and footsteps pounded behind me as a pair of uniforms gave chase, but I held on to the rhythm of my boots hitting the grass, the tickle of sweat dripping down the small of my back. All I had to do was outrun them, reach the water. And accept that if Dougall had planted more bombs, even at staggered times, I would never find them in time with these mundanes on my ass. My best option was to hope there was only the one, keep running, and find Jet. I had to make sure she was all right.

My thoughts of her pulled me out of my rhythm. I tripped, stumbled, re-secured my grip on the bomb, and found my stride. She was fine. She could take care of herself. As soon as I destroyed the curse in my arms, I would track her down and we'd get the hell out of here.

Ten seconds.

The water came into view up ahead. The cops behind me loomed closer. A spasm shot through my shoulder, strong enough to make me grind my teeth.

Five seconds.

I jumped the railing around the walking path and landed with a grunt on the rocks along the river.

Three seconds.

I hurled the bomb and watched it sink into the current but

couldn't stick around to see if my plan worked. If the pouches opened, would the ghost poison the water? Kill the mers?

Questions for later.

With the cops hot on my tail, I ducked out of sight along the walking path and misted away. They would wonder where I'd gone, wonder what I'd been up to, and hopefully never know how close they'd come to enjoying their last day on earth.

The vibrations running through me earlier were even worse now, adrenaline so thick in my blood that as my cells split into microscopic particles, the effects were still there. I had to find Jet, tell her what had happened. What I'd done.

Had to make sure she was okay.

I travelled over the protest in the direction the SMOAC troops had gone, and my thoughts—free of the bomb threat—homed in on Jet. Had she caught up with Dougall? Had the bastard hurt her? Had her team spotted her running through the crowd and gone after her? If so, was it to help or hinder?

I'm coming.

She had to be all right. We needed her.

I refused to allow myself to think what it would mean for me personally if she were in trouble.

All I could do was move.

As soon as I passed over the crowd, I materialized and continued on foot, sacrificing speed for the ability to see. The pain I'd felt during my earlier sprint returned, worsened, but I didn't give myself room to think about it. Pumping my legs harder, I spotted the SMOAC troops running towards the shopping centre. I started to follow them but pulled back when a flash of pink caught my eye. Pink shirt, black cap. Jet. Running down the stairs beside a solid piece of Beaux-Arts architecture. The old train station.

I opened my mouth to call after her, then snapped it shut. Shouting would gain attention, and she was flying so quickly I doubted she would have heard me anyway. Tearing after a plaid-shirted, baggy-jeaned blond. Dougall. She'd found him, and neither appeared injured. I'd made it in time.

I ran faster and watched Dougall disappear through a side door into the building. Jet followed him. By the time I reached the door, it was closed. When I tried it, it was locked.

Anger sparked in my blood and my vision flashed red, but I centred myself to clear my head and see my way forward. Again I melted into mist, forcing the change as my exhausted body resisted, slipped through the crack under the door, and reformed once inside.

I found myself in a brightly lit stairwell, the cleanest stairwell I'd ever seen in a public building. Footsteps echoed in the distance, and I closed my eyes to track the sound. To my right. Going down. I started after them, my footsteps mingling with theirs. One steady pace, one shuffling sprint. I knew whose was whose, and when the shuffling sprint stumbled, I also knew it wouldn't be long before Jet had him. The bastard was a weasel, and I didn't trust what he would do if cornered.

I picked up speed and raced into the bowels of the building.

A door slammed ahead, and I followed the sound into an underground parking garage.

The place reeked of old oil and gasoline, and although white fluorescents flickered along the ceiling every few feet, the shadows were deep and menacing. No cars filled the space, nothing to block my view but a few concrete pillars.

Up ahead was the Ghostmaker. He'd drawn to a halt, and Jet had stopped a few feet away. She stood with her arms extended by her sides and her feet braced, ready to follow if he ran again, but by the way she'd tilted her head, she had widened her awareness to check for any other threat. I understood her caution. Why had he stopped running? Why was he wearing that wide, shit-eating grin?

I checked over my shoulder, then cursed myself for letting myself be distracted. The jerk-off had gotten into my head.

"Give it up, Peter," Jet said, and her shoulders rose and fell with panting breaths, her voice straining to regain control. "There's nowhere for you to go. I can keep running as long as you can, but the only ending here is you in a SMOAC cell crying for your mother."

Dougall's grin grew wider.

"Dawson!"

The call came from my left, and Jet turned to look. Dougall fled. Jet saw it, started after him, but drew to a sharp halt when another shout rang out. "Stop right there, Jet!"

I recognized the voice and, when he came closer, the face that went with it. Sampson, Jet's lover boy lieutenant. The man who had roughed me up trying to get information I didn't have. The man who'd handed me over to Carstairs. Had he known what would happen when the cell door closed? Was he in on it? Jet had faith in him, but the sight of him turned my blood to ice.

Especially as I accepted the likelihood that I would soon be in his hands again. We'd been caught. I could mist out of here, but Jet had no escape.

"Dougall, he's here—he went that way," she said, but if she expected her lieutenant to leave her to chase him, she was mistaken.

Sampson nodded, and one of his team jogged in the direction Jet pointed, but the rest remained where they were, disapproving and stern.

Jet's eyes glimmered with desperation, and I wanted to reassure her everything would be all right. I'd found the ghostbomb. The evidence that Dougall had been at the protest was bobbing somewhere in the Ottawa River. How could they believe she was trying to bring down the department now that we'd saved the supernatural community from being outed on the evening news?

But all hope I had that we could turn this around evaporated and the ground fell out from under me when the rest of the team arrived. Headed by Carstairs. Still in that SMOAC uniform with that stupid, ugly-ass facial hair. Looking relaxed.

Confident. Like he was meant to be here.

Vomit burned the back of my throat, but I fought through my rising panic. I had to get away. Get myself to safety.

I prepared to dissolve, but when I looked at Jet, all I could think was she didn't know about the bomb, so she wouldn't be able to use it to prove her case. I couldn't leave her in their hands without them knowing. It was her ticket to freedom. I wanted to tell her, give her that weapon to defend herself, but my mouth was so dry, the words caught in my throat. I was too terrified of doing anything that might direct Carstairs's eye my way.

Jet stood with her chest heaving, her hands eerily still at her sides, and, by her expression, waited until she had control over her anger before turning around to face her right-hand man.

As she did, Eric raised his weapon and trained it on her. Her eyes widened, and every cell in my body froze. He made a quick gesture to the soldier at his side, and she closed the space between them to pat Jet down, taking her cell phone, her keys, and the knife in her boot. As though her captain were nothing more than a criminal.

He'd turned on her. That was the only explanation. That was why they'd let Dougall escape and why they hadn't searched harder to root out the truth of the protest rumour. It didn't matter that I'd found the bomb or that I'd gotten rid of it.

In that moment, I knew I had to get out of here. Staying wouldn't benefit Jet—would actually make it worse for her—and I couldn't go back to that cell. I couldn't let Carstairs step deeper into my brain, turning my nervous system into his personal playground, taking control of my pleasure and pain.

My insides twisted into a thousand tangles. I tried to catch Jet's gaze, but she'd fixed her attention on Sampson. No chance to let her know, then. No chance to say goodbye. I would get to Madison, and we'd come up with a plan. I wouldn't abandon Jet, but I had to get out.

I started to mist away, but with my concentration so scattered, I wavered, and in the microsecond my body solidified, a cool metal weight slipped around my neck.

No. NO!

The collar snapped shut with a click, and the rest of me rematerialized, the electric current shooting through my body preventing me from dissolving, stripping me of my ability, my freedom. If they left it in place much longer, my sanity.

"Kind of you to patch yourself up while you were away," Carstairs's voice rumbled in my ear. "Means we can start from scratch."

My legs gave out. My knees struck the concrete with an impact that rattled my teeth as dread sank into the pit of my stomach, and only my paralyzing terror kept me from screaming.

He had me. Again. And by the rough glee in his tone, the inside of that cell would be the last thing I ever saw.

Chapter 16

Madison

How did I always get left behind with the paperwork?

I'd spent most of the day sorting and re-sorting briefing notes, playing it like a puzzle that needed the correct order to reveal its secrets, and with every new shuffle, I asked myself if I should have gone downtown with the others. I could have been an extra set of eyes. I might have helped soothe the crowd if emotions ran high.

I would have known what was going on.

I'd had the TV set to the news since this morning, but it had only touched on the protest long enough to say it was happening and people should expect traffic delays. I spotted Lucien standing next to the prime minister, saw a few SMOAC agents monitoring the event, but no sign of trouble.

I hoped Jet and Gideon were bored out of their skulls somewhere in the horde. That they would come home in another hour or two complaining about the heat. Maybe even having worked out one or two of their problems. One day of reprieve to charge us up for the next day of chaos.

My ringing phone jarred me out of my reading. I stretched my back, moaned in sweet relief as pops and cracks rippled down my spine, and reached over to answer it. The screen read *Unknown Caller*, but that didn't mean much. We'd turned off caller ID on all three burner phones, a downside for us even if it kept us safer.

"Hey, any news?" I greeted.

"Madi?" Not a voice I expected to hear on the other end of the line. Not Jet's brusque tone or Gideon's gruff forwardness, but Uncle Sercario's smooth tenor, though today he sounded strained. Tense.

My heart stopped. He shouldn't have been calling. Not only had I not given him this number, but we'd agreed I would be the one calling with the updates. Whatever measures possible to maintain distance between Meril and myself. Not that it mattered when the woman could barge her way into my dreams, but every bit helped.

"Don't be upset," my uncle said. "Gary told me how to contact you. When your line got disconnected, I knew you'd been smart and disappeared."

Gary. Of course. The gnome was loyal to my entire family, not just to me. If he thought ratting me out to Serc was in my best interest, he wouldn't have hesitated.

"How is he?" I asked. "Did he get out of town?"

"He's safe," Serc said, and I couldn't help but notice the subtle emphasis on the pronoun. My mouth went dry. He paused, and in his silence, I heard everything he was about to say, and my coffee curdled in my gut. "The queen wants to see you."

I squeezed my eyes shut. I'd known this was coming. Since her last visit, I'd accepted that every hour of freedom was a gift. Even so, hearing him say those words hurt. I'd fought so hard to avoid this moment, working around the clock, pushing myself to the brink to prove I was doing everything possible to resolve our problems without her involvement. But despite my efforts, the call I'd been dreading for the last few days had come.

"The protests?"

"Among other things. She's made it clear she isn't ready to make a stand in any grand way yet, but she wants you to return to court. As an adviser, she says."

I swallowed around a tongue that felt three sizes too big. Responding to her summons would mean saying goodbye to this side of the wall. If not forever, then for a very long time. As long as my life extended in the realm. Long enough that the life I'd built for myself would be gone, along with any hopes I had for a future once the syndicate was crushed and the department stabilized.

The horror of the alternative stretched out before me, numbing me to my core. Years of doing the queen's bidding, surrounded by political intrigue, backstabbers, spies, and always Meril's watchful Eyes. Life on the other side of the wall might have been bearable if I'd been a regular supernatural, but as the queen's descendant, I would stand among the ambitious alligators with Serc as my only ally.

"I know you've already done it once, but can you delay her?" I asked, knowing the answer but needing to ask anyway. If only to tell myself I had. "Say you couldn't reach me?"

"I can try," he said, "but you know her, Madison. That she asked me to call you is a show of respect. If you reject the gesture, she won't be as gracious next time. Nevertheless, I'll do what I can. It might gain you a few days, but any more than that, and it's my neck on the line."

I heard the meaning beneath his words. The queen had made it clear she wouldn't be happy if he failed in his mission. My freedom would mean his life.

I wouldn't be that selfish.

"A few days, then."

A few days when I'd planned on years. Decades. The clock on the wall morphed into a challenge, a screaming reminder that each minute was precious.

If days were all I had, I couldn't waste them poring over papers. Jet couldn't do this on her own, not even with Gideon's help. I had to do more to give her a fighting chance. She'd reached out to everyone she knew, but I had a few contacts up my sleeve. People I had put off because the risks were too great—for them and us—but that now stood as our only recourse. O'Malley had set the game board, putting his pawns into play, but I wouldn't leave here without making sure we had a few extra players of our own.

I wished Jet and Gideon were here to help me talk through my idea, but I couldn't wait for them to get home. And maybe it would be easier to present everything as a done deal. Less space for arguing.

"Can I see you?" I asked my uncle, who'd been waiting patiently on the other end of the line while my panicked brain scrambled for footing. "Whether I'm here or over there, I can't step back and let things unfold as they will, and we can't do this alone."

Serc sighed, and I pictured him passing a hand over his aging face. "You know there's not much I can do, Madi. Not without her approval. And if you want to extend your time there as long as possible, dragging me into it is probably not the best idea."

"You might not be able to do anything directly, but there has to be some way you can help. Please?"

I didn't want to admit I was afraid and wanted to see him, the only family I had within easy travel distance, but I suspected he understood anyway.

"Tell me when and where," he said gently. "I'll be there."

We made our plans, and I ended the call, but when I turned my attention back to the papers spread across the table, the black letters sprawled across the white pages were blurred under my inability to concentrate, their significance gone.

A few days.

Either the three of us saved the country with no resources and no reinforcements within the week, or I would be forced to abandon my friends and family to the syndicate's plot and Meril's wrath.

Gods help us all.

Chapter 17

Jet

A SCREAM OF desperation caught in my throat.

Not for my sake, but for Gideon's.

Why had he come after me? He shouldn't have come. He should have been at the safe house recovering from his wounds and far away from the man who'd delivered them. Instead, he was right back in Carstairs's hands. The man who had tortured him. The syndicate mole who had burrowed his way into my team because of our need for new recruits.

A need that only existed because his syndicate had created the void at the expense of ten people I loved.

But what could I say to convince Eric to let Gideon go? As far as he was concerned, Gideon was an American spy and I had helped him escape. He had no reason to believe me.

Which was made crystal clear by the gun aimed at my chest.

By my own lieutenant. My friend.

Even more than Gideon's hangdog look and the way he flinched whenever Carstairs got too close, Eric's reaction shattered me. Did he really see me as a threat? As someone who would hurt him?

His gaze jumped from Gideon to me, his blue eyes full of sadness, but he must have asked himself the same questions because he holstered his weapon and took a step towards me. I might have been more reassured if he hadn't walked with his hands raised, the same way he would approach an on-edge witness or a scared dog.

Well, he should be afraid I would bite. Now that my shock was wearing off, anger was setting in.

He stopped within a few inches of me and, in a low voice, said, "Jet, where the hell have you been? The colonel's been trying to call you. I've tried to call you. Your phone's been off." As though he hadn't drawn his weapon on me. As though he hadn't handed Gideon over to the man who'd nearly killed him. Did he know how Carstairs amused himself?

By all that's sacred, please don't let him know.

That I couldn't answer the question with confidence pained me, but until I knew for sure, I had to keep my secrets close. Though that didn't mean I couldn't test the waters.

"I already told you, I was chasing Peter Dougall. The Ghostmaker. I would have caught him if you hadn't stopped me." Some of my anger slipped through, and I reined it in. If I wanted Eric to listen—if I wanted to detect any hint of his role in the department's growing shadow—I had to keep a cool head.

"How did you know he'd be here?" Eric asked, brow furrowed in confusion.

I shuddered as I remembered my last view of Dougall. The smile on his face… What had he known? That we were being followed and he was safe? That I was already too late to stop whatever chaos he'd hoped to cause?

"I followed him here from the protest. He was running away—" We didn't have time for all these explanations. "You might want to sweep the Hill for another bomb."

My gaze flicked towards Gideon, and as our eyes met, an expression of bitter satisfaction curled his lip.

"The river," he said, his voice rough, almost choked. "I found it under the stage and threw it in the river."

Pride swelled in my chest that we'd succeeded, that Dougall would go home pouting tonight, and my fury returned in a wave.

I turned back to Eric. "You hear that? This man saved *thousands* of people today. Get that collar off him and track down the man who ran out of here thinking he was free to go."

Pain flickered across Eric's face, and he dropped his gaze to the floor. "I can't do that, Jet, I'm sorry."

Jet, I noticed. Not captain.

"I'm to bring you in for questioning, and Mr. Leigh is supposed to be in our custody."

"So he can be tortured again?" I snapped, my patience slipping.

Eric jerked as if I'd slapped him. "Tortured? Jet, come on. I may have roughed him up a bit, but other than a few bruises, he was fine. You get more hands-on than that." Awareness dawned in his eyes. "Is that what he told you? Is that why you busted him out of there?"

Only now did I have reason to regret that Gideon had been so thorough in patching himself up. There was hardly any evidence of what Carstairs had done to him, the bloody mess he'd left on the floor. It was his word against mine, and by the smug look he gave me over Eric's shoulder, he knew it.

Fucker.

Before this was over, I would enjoy watching the son of a bitch burn.

"He didn't tell me anything," I shot back, and Eric's face hardened again. "What I saw with my own eyes was telling enough, whether you believe me or not. Send a team to check the river. If the bomb is still there, we can't leave that much ghost out in the open, even if it's soaked."

No one moved, and my blood ran cold. I'd been giving orders for so long, I was used to having them followed without hesitation. To have them go ignored was an unexpected twist of the knife.

Eric looked over his shoulder, nodded, and a handful of my team stepped forward. Some faces I didn't recognize— more new recruits, I guessed, and I wondered how many had been sent to us courtesy of the syndicate—but also Xander and Katie. They stared at me with confusion and questions in their eyes before heading off with the others to confirm Gideon's story.

I hoped they found whatever was left of the bomb. It would not look good for us if it was gone.

"Sorry about that," Eric said quietly, for my ears alone. "Orders came down from the top. You're on suspension. I'm leading the team."

I swallowed hard. "They couldn't have made a better choice."

This was what I'd wanted, wasn't it? My team to be in good hands. It's why I hadn't asked Eric to join me when I'd made my decision to fight back.

It still felt like a punch to the gut.

He shifted closer, close enough for me to inhale a hint of sweat and body wash from his skin. My memories tumbled to the last night we'd spent together, back when the team we'd seen as unbreakable had just been broken. We'd found comfort in each other's pain and passed the early hours of the morning trying to piece ourselves together. Now I didn't know if I could trust him. It felt like a year ago and yesterday all at once, and I would have given anything to go back to what we were.

"Where've you been, Jet?" His breath tickled my ear. "You've got to know we were looking for you. You're not an idiot. You were there the night the minister was killed. We found the boardroom full of ghost. We need you to come in and make a statement. The colonel's *pissed* the deputy ordered such a big team to go after you when a phone call would have been enough. He knows you must be freaking out that you're going to be arrested for Bastien's murder." I narrowed my eyes, and his widened in horror. "Gods, do you think that's what this is? Of course not. No one believes you had anything to do with it. You're going through some shit, we all know that, but never in a million years would we think you'd go so far as to kill the minister."

I did my best to keep breathing at a steady pace. He might believe I hadn't committed the crime, but if he wasn't involved, he couldn't know someone higher up than him might spin the situation to prove exactly that if it served their purpose.

"Though," he said, "I gotta say, finding you with this guy is going to be harder to explain." He shifted on his feet to face Gideon, who raised his head and glared at Eric with a hatred I wondered if my lieutenant deserved. I hadn't pushed Gideon too hard about what had happened before Carstairs locked him in that cell. Eric said he'd left him with a few bruises, but was that really as far as it had gone?

Any strength of will Gideon showed shrivelled when Carstairs tweaked his ear, and rage snaked through my stomach. I wanted to fly at him, grab him by his Kevlar and pound his face into the concrete.

All I could do was stay where I was and bite my tongue. So far, in public, he hadn't done anything our team didn't usually do. Little tweaks and shifts to keep prisoners off balance. Nothing for Eric to call him out on or to justify the pain I wanted to inflict on him.

In disgust, I stepped away from my lieutenant. He didn't know the truth, but it was only because he was too stubborn to hear it. He was happy in his ignorance, and in the face of Gideon's terror, his passive acceptance sickened me. I'd always preached critical thinking and the dangers of taking anything for granted. Although Eric had supported me and helped me instil that way of thinking into our troops, he obviously didn't practice it himself. How had I never noticed?

Easy, Dawson. He always followed orders. If anyone's blind here, it's you.

I clenched my fists at my sides and looked at Gideon. He had to get out of here. Whatever happened to me, so be it, but he couldn't let himself be taken again. I stared at the collar, the same kind I'd taken off him when we'd rescued him. When I'd given Gideon the key.

He'd kept it. Clung to it like a talisman when we'd left the detainment centre. Did he still have it on him? I crossed my fingers he'd had the foresight to treasure it even more closely than his bracelet. All I had to do was remind him we still had hope and pray that what little luck we clung to didn't abandon us.

"He isn't what you think he is," I said to Eric, keeping Gideon in my periphery. "He's not the *key* to this whole thing."

Would that be enough? Would he understand?

I needed him to get it. Back and forth we'd gone in the crazy see-saw of our relationship, and although my anger towards him continued to burn bright, hot, and pure, it mixed so closely with my need to argue with him I didn't know where one feeling ended and the other began. The thought of Carstairs ending what we had… Nausea bubbled and seared my insides. It couldn't happen.

But just as I was starting to worry I'd been too subtle, there it was, a slight widening of his eyes as my message landed, and the tightness in my chest released. He dropped his gaze to the floor, bowing his head in a show of defeat, and I turned my full attention to Eric, whose lip had curled in a sneer.

"So he's not working for an American private security firm, up here on a contract without federal permission, poking his nose into our issues so he can return with information to his handler?" he asked.

Hard to argue with that.

"That's all true, but there's more going on than you know. He's trying to help."

A click echoed against the cement walls of the empty parking garage. Everyone's attention leapt to where Gideon had knelt, but he was gone, leaving an empty collar on the ground. Carstairs's face twisted with anger—probably the closest he'd come to showing his true colours in front of his new squad— but I held back a crow of victory. Gideon was safe. Whatever happened now, he could go back to Madison, and together they'd figure out what to do. I trusted them to move forward without me however they needed to.

In one smooth motion, three weapons were drawn and trained on me, but the betrayal in Eric's eyes was worse than the barrels staring me in the face.

"You're making this so much harder than it needs to be, Jet. I don't want to believe what they're saying about you. You don't know—you can't imagine—they're calling you a traitor. They're saying you're working with this spy against the interests of the department. I keep telling them they're wrong, but this?" He gestured to the empty collar. "Is it true?"

Traitor. The word landed like a punch to the sternum, robbing me of breath. I'd suspected it. I'd tried to brace myself for it, but nothing could have prepared me for hearing the accusation from Eric's lips.

"I told you, nothing is what it looks like," I said, raising my hands in an attempt to remind everyone to keep their heads. "This is so much bigger than a spy and a syndicate. Betrayal depends on your point of view. Talk to me, Eric. Give me a chance to explain."

"Explain more of your conspiracy theories?" he demanded, his face turning a deep shade of red and his eyes growing bright with unshed tears. "I don't want to hear them. You helped this son of a bitch escape and gave him the tools he needed to stay out of our reach. You can spout whatever stories you want, but the evidence is *right here.*" He jerked his finger towards the collar with a shaking hand and drew in a sharp breath through his nose.

"Or are you going to tell me you had no idea he had your key?"

I held his stare and said nothing. There was nothing for me to deny. I had helped Gideon, would do it again, and if Eric didn't want to hear my reasons, he wasn't the man I thought he was.

"You want to bind her, Lieutenant?" asked one of the new recruits, a woman I'd never seen before. She'd picked up the metal ring and let it dangle over her middle finger as though afraid to touch it.

My vision narrowed and my lungs squeezed tight. I couldn't look away from the collar that had stolen Gideon's freedom. That would block off my molecular control, my third eye.

Eric half-turned, looked at her, looked at the collar, and as her words sank in, his expression flared with horror. "No," he sputtered. "*No*, I don't want to bind her. Put that away, it's not needed."

She backed off, and he faced me. His shoulders sagged, and in a voice strained with resignation, he said, "I may not use the collar, but you need to come with me. Will you do it quietly, or will you force me to give an order I really don't want to give?"

He could barely meet my eye. How much had his mind changed in the past few minutes? Was he asking himself if I actually did have something to do with the minister's death? The ghostbombs?

My stomach turned.

If I had any chance of convincing him I was telling the

truth, I would take it. They wouldn't throw me into a cell with Carstairs right away, that much I was certain of, so I had time. They'd want to build their case against me before they tossed me into the shadows. Public humiliation, the scapegoating, then the torture.

But if I got Eric to hear me out, if I laid out everything we'd learned and made him see what we did, I would have another ally. I still had hope.

I stepped forward, prepared to give myself up. My sudden move took one of the recruits by surprise, and her trigger finger slipped. The shot echoed through the garage, the sound bouncing off the concrete, ricocheting in my ears to block out all other noise.

The air around me wavered, and a hand grabbed my arm and pulled me away just before the bullet reached where I'd been standing. If I'd been a half-second slower, it would have pierced my neck.

I stared at Gideon in horror. What was he doing here? Why hadn't he left? He should have misted away and gone to Madison the moment he was free.

The answer stared back at me from his deep brown eyes, a swirl of emotion I only partially understood. He'd stayed to watch out for me. To help me.

We could escape this. If we were quick, maybe we could—a second shot rang out. Gideon's eyes widened, and his gaze dropped to the red stain spreading across his chest.

"No."

The word slipped through my lips, and I looked from him to Eric, who stood with his weapon raised, his finger still on the trigger.

I turned back to Gideon, threw myself forward to catch him as he fell, but I wasn't fast enough.

He hit the concrete, and two pairs of hands grabbed me before I reached him. I struggled to get away, needing to know, to feel for myself that he was gone, even though the evidence was right there in the way he tried to dissolve, his body fading in and out without the strength to do it, in the way his gaze landed on me before the spark of life in his eyes flickered.

My legs gave out, and if someone hadn't been holding me, I would have fallen. There was no way he could survive that shot, no way he could pull himself together in time, and I couldn't even go to him. I could only hang there, numb, as the man who had barged his way into my life gave a final burst of effort and misted away like a dog dragging himself off to die, leaving nothing of him in the parking garage but a bullet fragment and a bloodstain.

Chapter 18

Jet

I DIDN'T KNOW what to feel.

It seemed like just the other day I was sitting on a concrete slab watching blue lights flash around a cordoned-off crime scene, everyone going about their business as though their business wasn't death.

Last time, though, I was one of the survivors. This time, I was the enemy.

Eric stood at my side, not talking to me and refusing to let anyone else come near me. If I were anyone other than his captain, I would have been in cuffs.

Gideon was dead.

The look on his face. The blood on his hands, spreading across his chest. The expression in his eyes before he'd disappeared. And now he was gone. Nothing of him left behind. Not even that damned leather bracelet. I would have sent it to his brother. Or maybe I would have kept it.

I tried to convince myself he might pull through. He'd misted away, right? That proved he retained some control. But even as I consoled myself with the idea, I remembered the stories he'd told me of when he was a child, of all the times his ability had taken over in stressful situations. He'd been conscious enough to dissolve, but after seeing the blood that had pooled beneath him, knowing who had fired the shot—my lieutenant with the supernaturally perfect aim—I held no hope I would ever see him again.

My chest grew tight, each breath an agony, and my cheeks were soaked with tears I'd given up trying to hold back. A shiver ran down my spine, and once the shaking started, I couldn't get it to stop. I wanted to call Madison. I wanted to warn her about what had happened and order her to get somewhere safe. She had to be careful. Gideon gone and me about to be taken in on suspicion of treason. She had to get out of the city. She had to be prepared for them to come after her next.

No matter how much she stood to lose, the safest place for her would be across the wall. At least there she'd be under Meril's protection.

But I had no way to warn her. I crossed my fingers she'd see the writing on the wall when Gideon and I didn't return to the safe house.

"Dawson." Michael Torrence's voice boomed through the parking garage, and I closed my eyes.

I wasn't ready for his anger or, worse, his accusation. It was bad enough coming from Eric, but I couldn't handle it from my commander. Not on top of everything else.

Despite my best attempts to pretend I was anywhere other than here, his large shape blocked the light in front of me and a boot crunched dirt as he rested his foot on the concrete beside me.

"Are we going to talk about this?"

I opened my eyes to take in his concerned and sympathetic face. The man who had taught me everything I knew and who now had to see where it had led me.

I tried to pull myself together. My decisions and judgement had brought me to this point. I couldn't demand understanding for what I had lost or been through. Nobody here would consider it justification.

Steeling myself for an interrogation, burying the knifepoint of my grief as deep as I could, I pulled my shoulders back and said, "I guess we should."

He nodded towards the black SUV parked well away from the milling soldiers and security officers who had arrived to clean up the scene. "Come on, let's sit somewhere private. We don't need everyone and his dog hearing this."

My insides curled and coiled. I reached for my identification in my pocket, prepared to hand it over when asked. If Michael suspected I was involved, he would have no choice but to take it.

As I walked to the vehicle, I couldn't bring myself to look

anyone in the eye. They had watched me crumble over the death of the foreign agent I had released from our custody. Dougall had evaded me for the third time, and now my freedom—at the very least my career—dangled on a thin wire. The last thing I wanted to see was curiosity, sympathy, or satisfaction over another corrupt officer being taken down. Especially when their triumph was misdirected.

Eric plodded behind us. I glanced over my shoulder and found him staring straight ahead with a blank expression. His detachment did nothing to settle my nerves.

Michael opened the backseat passenger door for me, and I climbed in. Then he slammed the door shut, and I wondered if this was it. Would he go around to the driver's seat and take me in? Throw me in an interrogation room and make me sit through the song and dance we performed for all our guests?

When he climbed into the backseat with me, the muscles in my chest relaxed, but I couldn't satisfy my need for a full breath, and my hand wouldn't fall still, tapping a steady beat against my thigh.

I glanced out my window, where Eric had taken a position outside the door. Had Michael ordered him to stand guard? What were they afraid I would do? Run? Or was he there to make sure we weren't interrupted?

"I think these are yours," Michael said, and he placed my keys, phone, and knife in my lap. I wrapped my fingers around them as though they would keep me afloat. "So, what have you got to say for yourself?"

Here we go. No more anticipating what was about to happen. No more running away.

My throat was tight as I swallowed. I peeled my sweaty hat off my head and stared at my fingers as I picked at a loose thread. He wanted to know what I was doing here, where I'd been, how I was involved. He didn't want to watch me breaking down over Gideon getting shot because he'd tried to save me. I had to push through. I had to find the iron spine I'd built over my years in this job and set my pain aside. If I stood any chance of getting Michael to understand, I had to stay strong.

Yet even after a few deep breaths, when the vise around my lungs and the burn in the back of my throat had eased, I still couldn't look him in the eye. Explaining things to Michael felt similar to confessing to my father when he'd caught me sneaking home after curfew. The consequences were so much greater, but the emotional stakes were just as high. He sounded tired. Sad to be having this conversation. So was I.

"I heard a rumour there was going to be trouble at the protest," I began, and my voice wobbled. *Dammit, Captain, tighten up.* I cleared my throat and steeled myself. "I called in the tip but came myself. I wanted to do my part. And then I saw Dougall, so I gave chase. I nearly had him, too." It came out sulkier than I'd intended, and I raised my chin. *Enough of this.* I was a task force captain acting for the benefit of her country. I had a right to be angry. Troops I had trained had overlooked the greater threat. A recruit had accidentally fired on her superior. A seasoned veteran had killed a foreign agent. Damn right I was pissed off. The iciness of grief melted into a blazing heat, and I tapped into it like fuel.

"Did they find the bomb?" I asked, wanting to make a point.

He nodded slowly, his lips pursed. "They did. Right where Leigh said it would be." He looked at me sidelong. "Why didn't you call us with the rumour directly? You're supposed to be on leave."

"Yes, sir." I left it at that for now. It seemed smarter to limit my answers to what was necessary. On top of that, I had no idea yet how to word what needed to be said.

"And you've been avoiding my calls while I've had to hear about you running around with the American we locked up and evading people the deputy minister sent to bring you in for a statement. Now—" he raised his hand to stop me when I tensed "—I agree they messed up sending three teams to your apartment. Gagnon overreacted, and I told him as much, but you know what they found on the twenty-fifth. You were there. You understand how serious this is."

"Yes, sir," I said, my words strained. I remembered all too well what had happened in that office building. Madison strapped to a chair with a ghostbomb on her lap, Dougall ever so calmly setting her up to die. Blood splashed across the minister's office, his assistant with her throat cut and him with a SMOAC-issue blade lodged in his chest.

Yes, I knew how serious this was.

I wished I could relax. I'd been braced for a fight for the past six days, in a constant state of apprehension. I was exhausted. Here, of all places, with this man who had taken care of my physical and mental well-being for fourteen years, I wanted to pretend, even for a moment, that everything was fine. And I couldn't.

Michael shifted in his seat and rubbed his fingers along his creased forehead. His white hair was matted against his scalp, and he pulled his cap back on, covering the ever-thinning hairline.

"I can't believe O'Malley took out the minister." There was a fatigued tremor in his voice I'd never heard before, but I barely registered it under my relief that he'd taken me at my word. "He must be off his fucking rocker if he thinks we won't nail him for this. And then the ghost in the boardroom… When we heard you'd been there, all I could think was you'd been hit by the blast."

"Dougall made it into the building somehow. He had—" I stopped myself from mentioning Madison's name. "But if you know I was there, you must have seen him on the security footage."

Michael shook his head. "Someone wiped the footage. All we have are the access records. We know you swiped your pass. We don't know how he got in."

Disappointment and satisfaction waged a war in my head. Knowing who had let Dougall into the building would have helped us pinpoint the mole, but no security footage meant Madison might be safe. I'd been brought in, but as long as they didn't know she was involved, she would be free to stay on the offensive—or at least have an escape route if the syndicate closed in. Dougall had tried to kill her to further their plans, and I didn't want him to get a second chance.

"Dougall had a ghostbomb," I continued. "He was setting it up when I found him in the boardroom. I tried to stop him, but I had to let him go to save myself."

I bowed my head as guilt crept through me, sapping my energy. I'd done what was necessary, but it ate at me that he'd gotten away. If I'd thought of a way to stop him and save Madison at the same time, we wouldn't be here right now. Gideon wouldn't be—

"You made the right call," Michael said, and he reached his hand out as though to pat the back of mine, then changed his mind and rested it in his lap. "I don't know what to do, Dawson. Everything's gotten out of hand. The syndicate's crossed a line, the department's falling apart, and my own troops are turning on each other. It's like I'm stuck in a nightmare and can't wake up."

He sounded as broken as I felt, haunted by the same ache that had spread across my heart and made it so difficult to navigate through the twisted logistics.

"Tell me about the other night," he said. "We can take your official statement later, but tell *me*, Dawson. What were you doing there?"

I snorted. "You don't think I murdered Bastien?"

"What? Shit, Dawson, not a chance in hell. What would make you think that?"

"You tried to bring me in for questioning. I overheard my team talking about it when they came to get me."

"Son of a—no wonder you fucking ran. Idiots. Of course I don't think you *murdered* the minister. We wanted you to come in so you could tell us what you'd seen or heard. Your side of how you found him dead."

If that was true, maybe I had made a mistake by running. Maybe I could have claimed my life was at risk and asked Michael to come to my apartment where we could have talked in private, off the record. Not that it mattered anymore. There was no going back. Now I had to try to untangle the path ahead. I smoothed my palms against my thighs. Where did I begin? How much did I share?

Whatever happens, protect Madison. Gideon was dead, so telling Michael about Carstairs, opening his eyes to the growing corruption, would be a start to make him realize the true horror of our situation.

I cleared my throat. "I went to the Peaview to see my guys. It had been… a rough night. Rourke was beaten to death and thrown in a dumpster for fuck's sake."

I scrubbed my hand across my mouth as bile burned the back of my throat, flashes from my third eye sweeping past me. Had Michael heard about the cleanup by now? Did he know about Lafontaine and all the other informants we'd lost? I pressed on, figuring if he had questions, he'd interrupt and ask.

"After I checked in on Zeke, I went up to the twenty-fifth to see if Madison was in her office. She wasn't." True enough. "That's when I found Dougall in the boardroom, and he admitted he was the Ghostmaker. I already told you what happened next." I frowned as memories of that night surfaced. "He wasn't the only one on the floor, though. When I got off the elevator, two men were on their way out."

"Did you see who they were?"

I shook my head. "I stepped into a cubicle so they wouldn't see me." I'd been a coward, too afraid of getting hurt if my abilities gave out on me. What would have happened if I'd stood my ground? Who would I have seen?

"What happened after you left the boardroom?"

"I—" How was I supposed to do this without mentioning Madison? The missing gaps of information were too wide. I hoped they were only obvious to me. "I performed a sweep of the floor to check for Dougall and to see if anyone else might be in danger and wound up in the minister's office. That's where I found Bastien and his EA."

All that blood.

"He was killed with a SMOAC armoury blade, sir," I spat. "Someone with access to our gear." Even with everything else, that detail made me see red.

"What next?" Michael asked, calmly, rationally. I did my

best to channel his detachment.

"I thought of Leigh."

Madison had told me he'd gone missing in the paperwork. She'd warned me what it would mean if we freed him. All eyes on us.

"Dougall was loose in the building, and I knew Leigh was somewhere in the detainment centre, so I went to find him."

"You didn't call security from the office."

"I knew how it would look. I was supposed to be on leave. I was already in deep shit because of what happened at Dougall's house, and I didn't want to risk anything worse." I huffed out a breath. "I'd also just missed death by my third ghostbomb and found the minister slaughtered. I wasn't in the clearest frame of mind."

I didn't know who I could trust, I almost said, but swallowed it down. *Stick to the basics. Only what's necessary.*

"So you headed downstairs."

I nodded. "It took me a while to find Leigh. He'd been stashed in one of the high-security cells. He'd been—" I sucked in air, slammed by the vision of Gideon on the floor, naked and bloodied. "Sir, Master Corporal Carstairs, one of the recruits taken on without my approval, is a syndicate mole." There. I'd said it. Outed at least one of the bastards.

Michael's eyes flew wide. "Excuse me?"

"I found Gideon Leigh on the floor of that cell carved like a Thanksgiving turkey. Once he regained consciousness, he told me what happened. Told me what Carstairs said. He admitted to Leigh the syndicate sent him."

Michael frowned. "And you believed him?"

"Yes, sir, I did."

"That's why you disobeyed orders and released him?"

"I couldn't leave him in the state he was in. Sir, if you'd seen him—no one loyal to our department could have done that."

"What about the key? Sampson said he had it on him today."

I swallowed hard, mind racing to keep my story straight. "My head was such a mess when I found him, I must have dropped it. He must have grabbed it when I wasn't paying attention. I don't know." I hoped my flustered delivery sold the haziness of my memory. I didn't need him digging too deeply into my motivations as far as Gideon was concerned.

He pinched the bridge of his nose. "This puts us in a shit situation, doesn't it? I act on this, and Carstairs knows something's up. I don't, and we have someone watching our every move." He struck his fist against his thigh, and the kinetic energy in the SUV stilled, making it impossible for me to move. "Goddammit, Dawson, I'm sorry you walked in on all that. I wish I'd known. Wish you'd told me."

I pressed my lips together, fought to regain my emotional footing, and when his ability faded and I could shift in my seat again, I carried on.

"I got Leigh out, called security to report Bastien's murder, and we've been hiding ever since. When I heard there might be trouble at the protest, we couldn't sit around and wait to see what happened."

"Just the two of you?" he asked.

"Yes, sir."

"You sure about that? Gagnon tells me your buddy there, Prince, hasn't been seen since the body was found."

I forced myself to ease my hand out of the fist it had formed. Of course they would assume we were working together after Bastien reamed us out for going behind his back. "I've tried calling her a few times, but her phone's been off. I can only imagine how devastated she is about Bastien—they were close."

Michael made a noise of acknowledgement, and I took the risk of pushing the issue a step further. "It's possible she crossed the wall. Meril is family. She might have felt safer over there."

Take Madison out of the picture. Redirect their attention.

He scowled. "I don't see how that could be true for anyone. The queen's court is a dragon's den and anyone who crosses the threshold is offering themselves for dinner. The sooner the folks on this side of the wall see that, the sooner we can find a way to split off from her altogether."

I blinked. This was the first time I'd heard Michael speak so openly against the queen. He'd never hidden his opinion that SMOAC was better at handling the struggles of our kind than Meril, but I hadn't realized he held such hostility towards the court. Obviously the recent protests had struck a chord with him.

"Well," he said, his face smoothing, "if you get in touch with her, tell her Gagnon wants to speak with her. Someone's got to fill Bastien's shoes until we get a new minister, and there's no one Gagnon trusts more to help him wade through the mess the man left behind."

"Yes, sir."

Silence filled the car. I'd told him everything, and now we were right where we'd started.

For a while, neither of us spoke, Michael processing what I'd said, me waiting for the axe to fall. I'd laid out my case, the trial had been held, the jury was pending. The only thing to come was the sentence.

"I'm not going to fire you," he said at last, surprising me out of my wallowing. "I won't lie and say I'm not disappointed by your show of piss-poor judgement or that there won't be a shit-ton of paperwork for you to complete when you get back to work, but I think I can get Gagnon to see reason."

"You're serious?" I didn't know what else to say. I'd gotten into the vehicle expecting a private lynching, but my commander had my back. Again.

"You're damn lucky your team found that bomb. It gives me some leverage. Shows you're still acting in the best interests of the department."

"Won't you get shitcanned for keeping me on?"

"Gagnon wouldn't dare. He needs competent people to help him run this ship until everything gets settled." He breathed out heavily through his nose and glanced my way for the first time since we'd gotten into the SUV. "I'm going to tell you something I shouldn't be saying, but you deserve to know. This whole thing, it's not just about the syndicate. I think it's more than that. There's corruption in the department."

My mouth fell open, and I sat forward, eager to learn whatever he was willing to share.

"I have a lead on the issue, and I'm moving forward to prove it," he said, "but this is twice you've stepped in the way of an official investigation. I can't keep having that happen when it distracts us from the larger problem. So that's why, as of now, I'm escalating your suspension."

My hope for details shrivelled under my shock. After what he'd said, I'd prepared myself for a reprieve, to be brought back into the fold. Instead, I was being pushed farther out.

He held out his hand, and I bowed my head as I pulled out my ID and handed it over. He didn't spare it a glance before he slipped it into his pocket, as though taking it hurt him as much as losing it hurt me.

"You'll have no access to the building or your accounts," he said, "and anyone who sees you anywhere close to Laurier Avenue will know to report you directly to me. I want daily check-ins from you and regular reports from the department psychologist about your progress before I *think* of letting you back on active duty."

A gurgle of protest escaped my throat, and despite my best

efforts to stay quiet, knowing I was getting off easy, I couldn't hold back my dismay. "If we both know something is wrong here, how can you order me off it?"

"Trust me, I'm not happy about this, but it's for your protection."

I snorted a laugh. Protection?

"Not from the syndicate," he clarified, interpreting my scorn. "You can handle your own against whatever O'Malley throws at you, but for your career. You keep running in like this, and the fate of your job won't be in my hands. Gagnon already wants to give you the boot. I convinced him that once you've had time to grieve—properly—you'll go back to being the best damned agent SMOAC has ever seen."

My head buzzed so loudly I couldn't make sense of my thoughts. I wasn't going to be arrested, I wasn't going to lose my job, Michael knew the problem was bigger than one group, and he was going to take action. It was the best outcome I could have asked for from the worst week of my life. But where did that leave me? Stuck at home, beating myself up over listening to my gut instead of my reason and letting Gideon talk me into letting him come today.

He found the ghostbomb. He escaped. It was his choice not to run when he had the opportunity.

And if he had, I would be dead. Shot by a nervous rookie.

"Sir…"

He held up a hand. "Think before you speak, Dawson. It's

not only for your sake. Your lieutenant shot a foreign agent. If I keep using resources to save your ass, how am I supposed to keep the target off Sampson's back when the Americans find out what happened?"

My blood cooled, froze, and I pressed my lips together.

"If you lie low, I can use what authority I have to protect him, you understand?"

"Yes, sir."

I sat back in my seat, struggling to hold myself together. I'd made so many mistakes, trusted my instincts when time and again they'd pushed me to make the wrong call. I'd been arrogant, thinking I could handle everything myself instead of picking up the phone and turning to my team.

Gideon was dead because of my decisions. Shot by my best friend who couldn't even look me in the eye because of every bad move I'd made in the past week. And now Eric stood to lose everything.

Tears slipped through my restraint.

I could fix this.

Despite everything, I had to believe I could fix this.

I wiped my face and shifted in my seat to face Michael. I wouldn't hide from what I'd done or from whatever consequences waited for me when this was over. I couldn't. He stared back at me, the weight of the world dulling his grey eyes. The de Lauer blast had added years to his face, and every new disaster had deepened the lines around his eyes and mouth. Even his shoulders had rolled out of their perfect posture, as though he couldn't bring himself to stand up straight.

Nothing scared me more than the idea that he felt defeated, too exhausted to fight. I needed him strong, needed him to help me fight the battles to come. And if I wanted him to trust me, I had to trust him with everything I knew. He would need as much information as possible to bring this to an end.

"Sir, I think…" Gideon's face flashed in my mind, and I hesitated.

Look what had happened to the people I'd confided in. Would I be putting Michael in danger if I shared what I'd learned? Lafontaine, Rourke, and the other informants, Gideon—so many people who knew the truth were dead. Michael was more than my commander. He was a man who supported and encouraged me, the way my father would have done if he weren't halfway across the country.

Forewarned is forearmed, I reminded myself. Michael would move forward with or without my information. If I told him what I knew, maybe he would be better able to keep himself safe.

"I know I messed up, and I know you think the only smart move is to keep me away from this, but I think you're wrong. I think I can still help you."

He started to interrupt me, but I pushed through. If I stopped to consider what I was saying, there was a good chance I'd never work up the courage to keep going.

"Hear me out. I don't know what kind of lead you're chasing, but maybe it's similar to the one Gideon and I uncovered. Someone in the department is involved. Carstairs is a symptom, but it goes higher than that. Someone is working with the syndicate to carry out these attacks. We think they're trying to stir up unrest, maybe to distract the media, maybe for some other reason. We think they've been doctoring paperwork, cancelling projects. Money has been disappearing for over a year. Billions of dollars in total."

I rested my hand on his arm and offered my final volley. "You're ordering me to sit this out, but why not use me? Spread the word you've suspended me. I'll stay out of view, shrug my shoulders and sigh through whatever official hoops you need me to jump through, and help you hunt down these fuckers when no one's looking."

I didn't think it was possible, but Michael collapsed in on himself even more than before. If I'd felt like a kicked dog following him across the parking lot, he looked like one now.

But he drew in a deep breath and revived a little, turning his steady gaze on me. "I can't do that. I can't let you get yourself killed." He said it with such assertion, as though the result was a certainty, not a possibility.

My heart dropped in my chest, each word a ten-kilo weight, and my brain needed a moment to kick-start itself. For everything I thought I knew, he'd obviously learned so much more. Of course he had. He had a good twenty years on me with the department and would be in a prime position to notice the corruption soaking in. How stupid I'd been to think I was the first person to stumble across it. "How high does this go, Michael?"

"I don't know," he said. "Has to be executive levels for the things they're getting away with. You say Carstairs is one of them—at least that gives me an angle. Maybe I can find out who put him forward as a recruit." He cupped the back of his neck. "You talk about cancelled projects, money going missing… I think you're missing the obvious, Dawson. Shit like that happens in government. Don't get distracted by patterns that don't mean anything. It's the drugs. Someone in SMOAC is helping O'Malley distribute ghost across the country, and likely making a heap of cash doing it. And they're ruthless. You know they are. Rourke and the other informants. Weldon. That's what I'm telling you, kid, stay out of it. You've already got a target on your back the way you're going after Dougall. Don't give them more of a reason to get rid of you. I can't bear the thought."

He took my hand and looped my fingers through his. His palm was cool and dry, which made mine feel extra clammy. The buzzing in my head turned to a pulsing. Almost like bird wings flapping against my ears. I worried I might be sick.

I squeezed his hand in return, desperate to hold on to something solid.

"And I can't bear the thought of you facing this by yourself," I said.

"I'm not alone, Dawson. I've got—" He cut himself off, but I caught the way his gaze strayed over my shoulder.

"You brought Eric in on this?" I asked, hurt pinching my chest. Eric, who hadn't given me the time of day. Eric, who'd been ready to believe I would turn on my department.

"I needed someone I trusted," Michael said, "and you—" He squeezed my hand tighter. "You have been through more this week than anyone should have to go through in a lifetime. People who should have been there to help you weren't, and those you should have been able to trust, like our new recruits, betrayed you. I wanted to do whatever I could to keep you safe."

"Yet here I am anyway," I said, "so put me to work. Please. Let me help you save the department."

His gaze captured mine, boring into me as though trying to read my soul from the inside out. I screamed at him, begged, pleaded with him to trust me, all while never saying a word and hoping our history would be enough to convince him.

"All right," he said at last, and I let out a breath, releasing the pressure in my lungs. "You won't be as involved as you want to be because you cannot be seen, is that understood?"

"Yes, sir."

"One whiff of you being within an inch of this, and I'll have no choice but to take your stripes to save your life."

A shiver ran down my spine. I understood the necessity of what he was saying, but the thought of losing my position… Still, fear wasn't about to stop me.

"Yes, sir."

"Finally, you will not have any communication about this with the rest of your team."

I started. "Sir?"

"Like I said, Eric is going to be under fire because of this SilverGuard fiasco, which means I'll probably have to drop him under the radar with you. The more people I need to manage, the harder it'll be to hide our snooping from the syndicate. We know there's a mole in executive, and we know there's one among the recruits. Who knows how many others there are."

Did he suspect someone from my hand-picked team? One of my pack? I opened my mouth to argue with him, but clapped it shut before I uttered a sound. There was no point. Much as I hated it, he was right.

"Yes, sir."

"Good." He gave my hand one last squeeze and let me go. "Then keep your phone close, Dawson. Trust me to take the lead on this, and I'll be in touch soon. In the meantime, keep your head down." Gently, he nudged my shoulder. "I'm glad we're on the same page again, kid. I've missed you. Together we stand a real chance to kick these fuckers out of our home."

Chapter 19

Jet

IT WAS LATE afternoon by the time Eric dropped me off at my apartment building. Michael had asked him to play chauffeur, and although I hated the idea of being trapped in a moving vehicle with the person who'd killed Gideon, my need to get away from the stench and sounds of the parking garage beat out my revulsion.

I also thought it smarter not to mention I'd driven downtown in a questionably legal ride that was still parked on a downtown side street. Later I would call Travis, have him pick it up, and avoid any connection between us coming to light. What a great way to prove my speedy dip down the ethical slide *and* destroy one of my few remaining resources if it got out.

I sat in Eric's car and stared up at my building through the passenger window. Only twenty-four hours since I'd been here, and already it didn't feel like home. This was the home of a woman who had her life together, who had friends, a routine, a career. Who at least pretended she knew what the future held.

I didn't feel like that woman anymore.

The fluttering in my head hadn't stopped since my chat with Michael, and I couldn't bring myself to open the door. My hand rested on the door handle, my fingers teasing it but unable to apply the pressure to release the latch. Yet the thought of sitting here and getting sucked into a conversation set my heart thumping against my ribs.

I felt trapped, frozen in place, unsure what was worse: staying here with the agonizing but familiar or going inside to the void my life was quickly becoming.

"I hope you know I'm here if you need to talk your way through this," Eric said, no doubt noticing I was taking a hundred years to leave.

Suddenly the awaiting darkness of my bedroom was more inviting than a fresh cup of coffee and a hot bath. Anything would be better than hearing him sympathize with me—or worse, try to offer comfort. He had shot Gideon. I loved this man for all he was and all we had done and been for each other, but he had stolen the only other person who understood me the way Eric did. Maybe even better. Stolen him right when I needed him most, before I'd had a chance to be anything but horrible to him.

The desire to spin around and elbow Eric in the face, throw my fist into his gut, scream until his ears bled nearly overcame me at the hint of his attempted kindness, but as I turned towards him, the pained expression written across the features I knew so well smothered my rage. In spite of my hurt and fury, it was the gentlest he'd been with me in days, and my throat closed so tightly all I could do was nod.

"It—" He started, stopped, cleared his throat. "I'm sorry everything happened the way it did. I should have tried harder to get you talking before today, to be there for you. I was so wrapped up in my own shit, so… *angry*, I didn't have room to help anyone else. And that's a garbage excuse, because you've been there for me—for all of us—up until now. The fact that I wasn't strong enough for both of us—"

I couldn't listen to any more. He wasn't talking about Gideon, he was talking about everything else. I'd thought for one fleeting moment he might have registered what his most recent actions had done to me, but I should have known better. Of course he would think of the team, the attack, the way things had fallen out between us from that moment.

But for me, the de Lauer basement and Eric's visit to my apartment after the disaster at Dougall's house felt like years ago instead of days, and I didn't have the energy to revisit any of it.

I rested my hand on his arm, the fabric of his shirt rough under my fingertips. As exhausted and emotionally wrecked as I was, my control over my third eye slipped, and everything his shirt sleeve had been through over the last few hours spun through my head in hurried flashes. Surfaces brushed, arm rising and dropping. The most boring day-in-the-life, but I couldn't shut it out.

"Stop." At first I didn't know whether I'd said it to his shirt or to him, but when Eric lifted his gaze to mine, I could only go forward. "You did what you had to do to take care of yourself. It's all you could have done. It's all you *should* have done."

"But maybe I could have—"

I shook my head. "You couldn't have stopped me, Eric. Unless you'd agreed to help me, nothing you said would have changed my mind. Not after I learned as much as I did. Since then, there's only ever been one road for me. And now…"

I shifted my gaze out the window, wondering what "now" might mean. Michael had said to lie low and wait for his call. How close was his lead to what Madison, Gideon, and I had already figured out? What was I supposed to do in the meantime?

"Jet," Eric said, drawing my attention back to him. "I can't imagine what you've been through since we talked. The board-room, finding the minister dead… You shouldn't have had to go through it alone."

I wasn't in the mood for his apologies. What I *was* in the mood for was a drink, a bath, and to lock the rest of the world out of my head for an hour or twenty.

But Eric hadn't finished. In fact, by the tone of his voice, he was just ramping up. "But if you hadn't run into the fire trying to be some kind of hero, maybe Michael would have brought you in on his investigation as well as me."

I quirked my eyebrow in silent question, and the subtle movement sent a shot of pain through my overworked third eye.

My head ached, my shoulders had locked up, and the longer I sat here listening to my remorseless friend, the harder it was for me to block out the events in the parking garage.

Blood spray. Eyes widening. Body falling…

"Michael filled me in on some of what you guys talked about," he said, shoving the thoughts out of my head. "He told me you figured out about the mole. If we'd been working together as a group, we might have figured it out before Bastien's murder."

Was that accusation I heard in his voice? Anger at me for trying to clear this up on my own? Well, fuck him. The heat of fury swept through me, wiping out my fatigue, and I curled my fingers into a fist.

"Sure, *I'm* the one who slowed things down. *I'm* the one who refused to listen to evidence when someone brought it forward days ago. *I'm* the one who had a syndicate plant right under my nose and missed the fact he was torturing a man to within an inch of his life."

A dark thought crept from the pit of my mind where I had tried so hard to bury it. Even in the warm afternoon sunshine, the shadow of it chilled my blood and raised goosebumps on my arms.

"Unless you didn't miss it."

I had to ask. I didn't know if I could trust his answer, but I had to get the question out before the weight of it crushed me.

"Miss what? That Carstairs is a syndicate thug?" Eric asked, genuine confusion written across his face. My ravings seemed to have taken him by surprise, and I hoped that gave me an advantage. If I caught him off guard, I was more likely to catch him in a lie.

Please don't be lying.

"A thug that worked on Gideon like he was a fucking chew toy."

"So you keep saying, Jet, and I'm not saying you're wrong, but I saw the guy. He didn't look that rough."

A ball grew in my throat, and I forced sound out around it. "Carstairs left him in Cell I with the lights off, the camera off, the collar around his neck for *twenty-four hours*. We—" I stumbled over Madison's having been there and hoped he didn't notice. "I found him covered in blood, riddled with knife wounds, the skin of his back almost flayed. Did you know what would happen once Carstairs brought him to the detainment centre?"

Describing the scene I'd walked in on, reliving those images, made the air grow thin. I reached for the control to roll down the window, then thought better of it. The thick humidity outside the air-conditioned car would do nothing to settle my stomach.

Or Eric's, by the look on his face. He'd gone pale, almost green around the mouth.

"Jet, how could you even—"

"Because I don't know what to believe anymore," I said. "You were there. You let Carstairs take him away. You never followed up or asked why the paperwork for Gideon's detainment hadn't been done."

He jerked his head back as though I'd hit him, and I caught the flash of shame in his eyes. Regardless of how hands-off he'd been in Gideon's fate, he should have done more to ensure his safety, and he knew it.

"You wonder why I went off on my own, why I stopped trusting the people around me," I said, refusing to let the pressure of tears choke me, "but this is why. There's so much going on that makes me question everything I thought I knew about our system. Despite your obvious opinion, I was doing my job."

Eric rubbed the pad of his thumb over the bridge of his nose. "I know. You're right. And I'm sorry. I had no idea about Carstairs. I knew he was overzealous, and he wasn't my favourite of the new recruits, but it never occurred to me he was a plant. But I honestly don't know what I did to make you not trust me. If you'd come to me after you found the American, we could have—"

I glowered at him, filling my stare with the full brunt of my anger. "I tried talking to you before I found him, didn't I? More than once. But you needed a bloody, broken victim to prove I'm not insane. My word isn't enough anymore."

Eric caught my eye and his cheeks flushed. His silent admission that I'd come close to hitting the nail pinched my heart, but nothing I said would make either of us feel better. We'd both fucked up and would have to live with the consequences.

"Like I said," he continued, his voice softer now, "I'm sorry about Leigh. I'm sorry we missed that Carstairs is one of O'Malley's thugs. That's on me. I accept that. As for everything else, I hope we can get past it and work together again to finish what we've started. We always work best when we're together."

I bit down on my tongue to avoid the fresh surge of pain thrusting at my ribs. He was right. Eric and I had always worked as a team. As captain and lieutenant. Me giving orders, and him carrying them out. It hadn't been until Gideon returned to my life that I realized how much I loved having a partner instead of a subordinate.

Though the hierarchy had shifted, hadn't it? I was on suspension, and Eric was giving the orders. Michael had chosen him, debriefed him on his private investigation. Where did that put us now?

The familiarity in the car was no longer as comforting. Like an old chair that had started to splinter. A comfy sweater with a new hole in the sleeve.

A shiver ran down my spine, and I hugged my arms around my middle to fend off the chill. Everything was changing so fast.

"Jet?"

I shook off my uneasiness and nodded. "You're right. We

do. So bring me up to speed. What does Michael know?"

If this was my new way forward, it made more sense to dive in and get started. Work would give me purpose. Better than the alternative of sitting alone with memories and regrets.

But my stomach dropped again when, instead of answering my question, Eric frowned and looked out the window.

"What?" I asked, suspicion snaking around the back of my mind. "Did Michael tell you not to fill me in? What about what you just said? About us working together again."

He raised his hand, fingers splayed, to silence me. "I know. This is weird for me, too, all right? I hate not knowing where I stand with you. But the colonel told me not to say too much, to let him be the one to catch you up. I guess he's worried you'll take what we know and go off on your own again. I wonder why?"

He shot me a dark look, and my cheeks flushed red. The taste of blood slid down my throat, and I shifted my tongue from between my teeth.

"I wouldn't have had to take the initiative if people had been honest with me in the first place," I pointed out. "If we're supposed to trust each other now, one of us has to take the first step. Michael told you what *I've* learned, now it's your turn."

Silence sat between us, thick with tension, our gazes locked as we assessed the situation. On opposing sides for the first time in our careers. This was our chance to tear down the wall that had formed between us, and I didn't know what it would do for our friendship if we couldn't.

"I will say this," he said at last, as though he realized the same thing. His voice was still hard, his words clipped, but he was talking. "A lot of what you found confirms what we know. Projects being financed then shuttered, money moving hands. But it's not the muddled mess you think it is. You're mixing pieces from two different puzzles. There's no big government conspiracy."

"Then how do you explain it?" I asked. Madison had laid everything out so clearly that I wasn't about to dismiss our evidence based on his claims. I needed facts. Hard proof. A reasonable alternative to the picture she had painted for us.

"I don't know if I can." He shifted in his seat, resting his wrist on top of the steering wheel. As though he were completely at ease. As though our conversation were a perfectly natural one to have in the middle of a summer afternoon after he'd killed someone.

What kind of alternate dimension had I stepped into?

"Half of what you found is absolutely the syndicate fucking with us. Michael told me about the empty community centres being used as ghost labs. It was after the second one was raided a month or two ago that he started to suspect someone had gained access to our project files."

A month or two ago?

"Don't look at me like that, Jet," Eric said, rolling his eyes. "What should he have done? Marched into The Afterlife and asked O'Malley to stop? He had suspicions, that's all. Nothing substantial enough to take to the minister, and nothing he wanted to involve us in. But as soon as he noticed, he started paying attention. According to everything he's found, that's as far as the syndicate has gotten."

"What about all the missing money?" I asked. "The reason the projects were cancelled in the first place, swallowing billions of dollars."

Eric pressed his lips together, his nostrils flaring with a deep, grounding sigh. "The cancelled funding is part of a guinea pig project. If you'd brought this to Michael instead of running around breaking down doors, maybe he would have briefed both of us after what happened at Dougall's house. There's an international federation that wants to share their resources and help our supernatural population reach the same standards as our kind in Europe and Asia."

The recommendations from the assessment Madison had dredged up what felt like forever ago.

"The Federation of Supernatural Affairs," I said.

Eric raised his eyebrows. "You've heard of them?"

"I've seen their name. Who are they?"

"I don't know much. Just that they organize all kinds of services, taking the burden off government hands."

Something about the idea didn't sit right with me, but I let it go to mull it over later. "A committee suggested Minister Bastien speak with them. Gagnon supported the suggestion,

Bastien didn't."

Eric nodded. "Exactly. The minister wasn't sold on the idea of handing over control, so Gagnon was running some long-term tests, seeing how the numbers would work, wanting to approach him with a full proposal. The money wasn't disappearing, just being shifted across other projects to see where the holes were. That's why it looked like everything was off the books, but I'm sure there's paperwork somewhere to back me up. He wanted to make sure the federation's offer was worth considering before they signed anything."

My mouth absently opened and closed, but my thoughts spun too quickly to voice them. That couldn't be true, could it? I'd heard about similar programs over the years. Far-reaching ideas that analysts and executives had privately run through before making them public. It was standard practice to avoid the higher-ups shooting things down too early.

Michael had told me, Eric had told me. Bigger than the syndicate, but no conspiracy. No monsters under the bed. Two people I trusted more than almost anyone else. The syndicate had twined its way into the department to bury its roots deeper into the country and widen its ghost distribution. Michael was working to ferret out the moles with Eric as his backup.

But if that were the case, if none of what Madison and I had discovered was connected to each other, then it meant I'd been blustering about spreading lies, and Lafontaine, Rourke, and all the others had died for nothing.

Gideon was dead because I'd jumped at shadows.

Guilt wrapped its slimy fingers around my heart, squeezing tighter than it had in the back of Michael's SUV. Had we acted too soon? Taken too many risks on not enough evidence? Talking with Michael, I'd realized how many mistakes I'd made, but if everything Eric said was true, I'd made so many more, and I would live to regret them for the rest of my life.

A sob caught in my throat, and I pressed my lips together to hold it back.

Eric reached out to rest his hand on the back of my neck, then rethought it and pulled away. "I'm sorry about today, Jet. Leigh moved so fast, I thought he was coming at me. McCormick's been suspended. The recruit with the happy trigger finger. We'll see if she gets her weapon back. But I shouldn't have reacted like that, and I'm sorry. I'm sorry I pushed you away when you wanted to confide in me. I hate that I made you feel you couldn't trust me."

I wished he wouldn't push the issue. Any of it. I wasn't ready to face the reality of what he'd done, knowing that as my pain came out so would my anger, and I wanted to be alone when that happened.

This time he curled his fingers around mine, but my hand stayed tense and unmoving. "It's behind us now, though, right? Michael brought you in, we can work together. I'm glad about that. Happy, even." He squeezed my hand, then set it back in my lap. "Because if you keep pushing the law like you have, I'll have no choice but to bring you in officially. I love you, Jet, you know I do, but you also know where my loyalties lie. I won't hesitate."

I met his eye, and the impact of his stare cut straight through me. He meant every word. No matter how much he might regret what he had to do, he wouldn't let our years together sway his belief that the department was in the right. It didn't matter what I said, or what evidence I put in front of him, he would do exactly what he'd accused me of doing: make up a story that best fit within the framework of how he understood the world.

What if he's right?

Again the question prodded me, refusing to be ignored. Michael knew about the Federation of Supernatural Affairs. How could I dismiss the possibility that this whole situation was nothing more than a combination of misunderstandings? The drugs were the syndicate, the screwy paperwork nothing more than a case study for this organization. Madison could learn more about them. She could go through the files again to see if Eric's explanation fit with what we'd found. Maybe there was paperwork we'd missed that showed the transfer of funds.

Madison. I have to tell her about Gideon.

I swallowed a groan, tightened my grip on the door handle, and steeled my spine. I would give Eric's explanation the benefit of the doubt for now and let Michael send me after the lead he was following, but in the end, evidence would guide my steps.

So in response to Eric silently begging me to toe the line, I nodded and said, "I understand," and hoped *he* understood. No hard feelings. We both had to do what we felt was right. Let our consciences light the way.

I didn't give him time to say anything else. Finally finding the use of my fingers to open the door, I stepped onto the sidewalk under the bright afternoon sun and closed the door behind me. The car idled a while longer, but as I walked past the few people sitting on the front stoop, Eric drove away, leaving me on my own.

With shaking hands, I let myself into the building and, on wooden legs, climbed the stairs to my apartment.

It felt strange to be back. Yesterday, I'd fled from my team, using everything in my arsenal to help Gideon and me disappear. We'd made it out. We'd survived.

Now here I was, dropped off by the very people I'd run from, Gideon gone, and me stripped of everything. Our escape had been a false victory. I should have known the house would win in the end.

My apartment was dark and quiet. It didn't feel any more like home than it had from the car.

I tossed my keys on the side table by the door and stood in the living room, staring around as though I'd never been here before. A clock on the wall ticked the seconds away. Shouts and laughter came through the open window from the museum across the street. The curtains billowed gently in the breeze.

So peaceful. So at odds with the static in my head.

I needed to get out of here. To get back to Madison and tell her what had happened. To get away from the memories that crushed whatever part of me still had the capacity to feel.

But I clung to the voice that told me I shouldn't leave yet. Eric might have driven away, but if I walked out of here minutes after being dropped off, I couldn't be sure word wouldn't get back to Michael, and he would think I was going against his orders. I needed Madison's help, but I couldn't risk her safety or the newfound trust I'd formed with my commander. Now more than ever, we needed to play it smart. Michael was right: together we stood a better chance of stopping Dougall and O'Malley than we ever would separately. I needed to stay in the loop, even if officially I was in disgrace.

I forced myself to move around my apartment as though I were glad to be back, but when I turned away from the window, my gaze fell on Gideon's bloody T-shirt draped over the edge of the garbage can. I froze, my heart forgetting how to beat. I brushed my fingers over the stiff material, remembering what an asshole I'd been the whole time he was stitching himself back together. Recovering from what my department had put him through. Grief threatened to kick in, but I pushed it down, wadded up the shirt, and chucked it into the bottom of the trash.

Determined to think of anything other than him, I headed to the bedroom. The closet doors were open from our hasty getaway, a few clothes strewn across the bed. I ignored the mess, grabbed a clean outfit, and went into the bathroom. Although the apartment was empty, I closed and locked the door, then turned on the shower as hot as it would go. Steam filled the room and floated out the window, and I watched the way it danced on the breeze as I sat on the edge of the tub, not yet able to get undressed and leave myself so vulnerable. I felt bare enough as it was, naked without my authority, my dignity. Without my friends.

As my gaze landed on the blood-stained towel hanging on the rack, a small, broken laugh echoed through the steam. I'd even lost my anger at Gideon, the constant flame that had motivated me to prove I was smarter than the silly woman who'd fallen for his charms. Much as I'd been furious with him, that fury had pushed me to become stronger. Finding out he'd come here to do my job had given me the courage to stick to my guns and keep digging.

Look where it had brought me.

Now, though, that anger had burned up, leaving me cold. Having him far away in the States would have been better than not having him at all.

I wrapped an arm around my middle to hold in the lurking pain and raised my other hand to weave the water droplets through my fingers. With the barest effort, I manipulated the draft in the room, causing the water to ebb and flow around my skin, creating shapes in the air. For a brief moment, they might have formed a face, but I released them before I made out whose.

After a few minutes of sitting, I turned off the water and sank to the floor to rest my head against the cool tiled wall. Eric's explanation sat like a lead weight in my gut, and I couldn't help but wonder how badly I had fucked things up. If I had turned to Michael at the start, backed down and followed orders, would anyone else have died? Gideon might already be home. He'd only stayed to watch out for me.

Tears streamed down my face and my nose ran, and I rushed to the toilet to bring up all my guilt and confusion about what was real and what was bullshit.

I spat the foul taste from my mouth and sat back on my heels. In the car, Eric's explanation had made sense, but now that his sad blue eyes were gone, I saw it didn't cover everything. The syndicate's reach within the department was wider than mooching our empty community centres. They wouldn't have dropped Carstairs into the task force if all they wanted was warehouse space. The three of us might have been off base, but our assumptions weren't as far off as Eric and Michael claimed. The monsters were real, and they were growing, and if we didn't stop them soon, they would consume us, just as they'd done to so many people already.

When my stomach finally settled, I returned to my spot with my head on the tile. I had to think of anything else. I would drive myself crazy if I imagined how bad things could get. But when I wrenched my thoughts away from Gideon and the others, they had no happy place to land.

I knew I couldn't give up. Even as I stared down the barrel of my shame, I knew I had to keep moving for the sake of those who had fallen, but for now, I could only sit here, paralyzed, needing to face the inevitable truth: my decisions had cost me allies every step of the way, and the harder I pushed, the more I would lose. Whoever was behind this, they were winning, and from where I stood, I didn't see any way of catching up with them.

I was boxed in. One foot out of line and not only would I lose my stripes, but Michael would have to choose between protecting me from myself or Eric from SilverGuard. I couldn't reach out to my team because one word to them about the conspiracy and they would be in the same line of fire as I was—my poor remaining pack that hadn't heard from me in days. I couldn't even check in on the group chat now that I'd ditched my phone.

When I'd visited the hospital, Zeke had given me his support to push as hard as I had to. Luvy, Mandy, Ray, Marc-André— they'd looked at me with faith and confidence. Would they look at me that way still, or would I find the same confusion I'd gotten from Xander and Katie? The same doubt.

But there was nothing I could do yet to confirm how far I'd lost my team.

I could only wait.

My stomach curled in on itself, and I pulled my knees to my

chest, wrapping my arms around my legs to hug them closer.

Wait for the syndicate to make another move.

Wait for Michael to get his lead lined up so he could give me some direction.

Wait for the world to stop spinning for one second so I could regain my balance and stop myself from spiralling out of control.

Chapter 20

Madison

Hours had passed since I'd hung up with Serc, and I was still waiting for an update from, well, anyone. Over an hour ago, a news reporter had announced the protest on the Hill was being broken up for security reasons, and after receiving no explanation from either the media or Jet or Gideon, I was doing my best not to worry. We had agreed radio silence was the way to go, and I cursed myself for recommending it. Until they were sure the coast was clear, they would neither get in touch nor return to the safe house.

Which left me trapped in a spiral of uncertainty, and the knots in my stomach wouldn't loosen.

To distract myself, I made more phone calls. I'd gotten things started with Serc, but he was right—he was limited in what he could do. Most groups would be. For some, their allegiances were tied too tightly to the queen's court; for others, the personal stakes were too high. That didn't stop me from trying. At the very least, I could warn people of what might be coming.

So far, of the five groups I'd contacted, I'd recruited a total of none. The goblins had already evacuated the city and debated leaving the country. Of course they were. They were usually the first to see the writing on the wall and the last to offer support or forewarning to the rest of the community. The brownies had hung up on me, either not wanting to face the truth or believing they wouldn't be affected. The witches had called me a traitor to the queen and told me I should step aside and let her take her proper place.

"Maybe a war is exactly what we need," their coven leader had said. "A chance to strike a new balance."

I doubted anyone on the Shadow Council would agree but hadn't bothered to argue.

The fae had thanked me, and although they didn't intend to leave the safety of their borders, they would pass along any information they heard. Only the shifters had caught on that they should take steps to ready their defences. Whether they would help us directly was another question, but at least they would be prepared to fight.

Not that it would matter much to me. Soon enough, I would be saying my goodbyes and doing Meril's bidding for the rest of my long, long life.

I checked my phone again, scrolling through my read messages hoping a new one from Jet would pop up, and meandering over to my private messaging app, crossing my fingers for a new message from Colm. I didn't expect one, but I hoped. I also feared, because when the time came to leave, I couldn't disappear without saying anything. Somehow I would have to say goodbye to him and to everything that might have been or could never have been. How the hell was I supposed to do that?

Doesn't really matter. Break his heart, make him think you're crazy. He'll never see you again, so who cares what his opinion of you is?

I closed my eyes as my chest tightened. I had to stop. Stressing over the inevitable was a waste of energy. I had to make peace with my situation, erase whatever desire I had of maybe, one day, letting him into my life and doing everything in my power to protect the world I was leaving behind.

Another scan of the news and more of the same nothing, just a brief commentary about security concerns cutting the protest short.

Had Jet reached out to Eric and convinced him to clear the place out, or had they found something?

I tapped my fingers on the dining table in an impatient rhythm. Only a few days left on this side of the wall, and I was sitting on my ass waiting for someone else to bring me news?

To hell with this.

I stood up and went into the bedroom to grab my shoes. If no one was going to update me, I would head downtown and find out for myself. Enough waiting around.

I was on my way to the door when my phone rang.

"Hello?" I answered, but the line remained silent. I paused by the dining table and repeated my greeting, wondering if my caller was stuck in a dead zone. Some of the folk I'd called straddled the unseen wall, and the interference often caused issues with mundane electronics. The silence stretched on. "If you're speaking, I can't hear you. You might want to change location and call me back."

I started to pull my phone away from my ear to hang up when I heard a quiet voice say, "Gideon's dead."

I froze. "Jet? What do you mean? What are you talking about?"

Please tell me you misspoke. That you meant Dougall. O'Malley. Carstairs. Please tell me you found the mole and stepped on him. Tell me this is over. That we're safe. That I don't need to leave.

"He was shot. He's gone," she said, her voice strained, working so hard to be steady.

I dropped into the closest chair at the table, but the way the room spun, I still felt like I was about to fall.

"How?" It was the only question I could get out, though a thousand more ran through my head. Where was she? Was she all right? What the hell had happened at that protest? "Start at the beginning. Tell me everything."

"Dougall was there. At the protest. We were right."

Her voice carried a strange echo that gave an eerie quality to her forced, even tone. I tried to imagine what might create the tinny sound and guessed she was in a bathroom, every syllable bouncing off the tiles. Was she at home?

"He planted a bomb."

My heart caught in my throat and my gaze jumped to the television, expecting to see a breaking news report about mass deaths on Parliament Hill, but before my panic settled in, she added, "Gideon found it. Destroyed it in time."

Gideon had saved them all. So what had happened? How had he gone from hero to dead?

"Did Dougall…" I started. As if we needed more of a reason to throw him into a deep, dark pit.

"No. He got away. It was Eric."

I swore my chair was tipping. Eric. Jet's Eric. One of her favourite people in the world. I couldn't find my balance. I closed my eyes to block out the weight of her grief, the loss of our ally—our friend—but the spinning in my head worsened, and I had to open them again to steady myself.

Eric had killed Gideon?

"My team. They were there when I went after Dougall." She sounded as though she were dragging the words out from the void. I wanted to tell her to stop, worried she would tear herself apart if she kept going, but she had to say it aloud. She had to get it out and make it real before it destroyed her. "They followed me away from the protest and went after me instead of him. They think I'm a traitor."

Her voice hitched, and my throat closed. Why hadn't she come back here? I didn't think I had it in me to soothe her emotions when my own were so fraught, but I could have put my arms around her while she talked.

"Then Gideon… He wasn't supposed to follow me. He did. Carstairs collared him, but Gideon had my key. The look on Eric's face…"

"We knew they'd figure out you helped him," I said. "It can't have come as that much of a surprise." It was the only solace I could provide, though it counted for little.

"I thought he'd left, gotten himself to safety, but one of the recruits freaked out, fired her weapon, and Gideon pulled me out of the way. Eric thought—I don't know what he thought. He shot him."

The silence returned, and I couldn't tell if Jet had broken down into tears or lost herself in the numbness of her pain.

Although I didn't want to imagine the scene, didn't want to put myself in Jet's shoes, I couldn't help myself. Her agony was so deep, so primal, it sucked me into the moment and dropped me into her mind. Caught between my two partners. My two lovers. One who'd known me almost half my life and had shared every challenge of my career; the other who had sacrificed so much, suffered so much, and was still standing by me. Both of them fighting to protect me in their own way. Both of them willing to do whatever it took.

And one of them had paid the price.

And Jet. My poor, dear Jet left to watch as one person she loved snuffed the life out of the other. Not an attack, not an act by a heartless crime boss or a megalomaniac chemist, but a rational decision based on training and experience. Now she had to live with the memory.

The pain around my heart squeezed my lungs and I forgot how to breathe, as though every bit of her grief were my own, but I clawed myself out of the quagmire. I couldn't afford to get stuck in someone else's loss. By understanding it, I might help Jet through it, but I couldn't possess it. To do so would be selfish and a waste of time. And I couldn't afford to waste time.

Not now.

We'd lost Gideon.

Not only would he and Jet never have a chance to work out whatever crap had prevented them from being happy, but we'd lost the third piece in our fight against thousands. Jet and I were all we had left, and any hope I held that some miracle would let us save the department within a week evaporated.

After that, Jet would be alone.

How the hell am I going to break it to her that I've been called back?

Unless she came with me. Offered her services to Meril and helped us win the war from the unseen realm if we couldn't win the battle here. I doubted she'd say yes, but I would feel better about leaving if I weren't going by myself.

"I'm coming to get you," I said. "Where are you?"

No matter what she decided, she needed someone beside her, and we needed to come up with a plan. I didn't normally encourage distraction as a coping mechanism, but right now we we didn't have many other options.

"Home," she said. "But don't come here. It's not safe for us to be seen together. I told Michael what happened that night in the office and managed to keep your name out of it. Tried to put it into his head that you've left town. Let's keep it that way. You have to be safe."

I bowed my head against the cage slowly closing in around us. Every time we made a move, the department or the syndicate responded, and our room to manoeuvre grew smaller. If whoever controlled the mole knew Jet was onto them, that she'd allied herself with a foreign spy against her department and that she had uncovered evidence pointing fingers at the upper echelon, then all eyes would be on her.

All the more reason to get her out of here.

"What are you going to do?" I asked.

"I—" she started, then stopped.

I focused my attention on the background noise, straining my ears to pick up any static or clicks, anything to suggest Jet and I weren't alone on the line, but I heard nothing. I tried to assure myself I was being paranoid. These phones were off the grid. For all intents and purposes, they didn't exist. Even so, I would swap them out for our other set as soon as Jet and I met up. Caution would only help us.

"The situation has changed a bit," she said, and I narrowed my eyes, unable to tell from her tone if the change was good or bad. "It turns out we're not the only ones looking into the department. Michael told me some things. Eric, too. It's possible we have more allies than we thought."

I leaned back in my chair. Was she serious? They knew about the mole? Had they been working a parallel investigation? How much did they know? I cursed the insecurity of wireless networks that she couldn't tell me more over the phone.

"I promised Michael I'd wait to do anything until I heard from him. He says he's working on a lead. But I can't—Gideon's blood is on everything here. The fucker ruined my towels and my bathmat."

There was a catch in her voice, her criticism lacking any of the heat or passion the mention of his name usually carried.

"Are you sure you should be by yourself right now?" I asked, knowing what she would say even as I formed the question. "We could find a place to meet. Go for a drive somewhere."

"Not until I'm sure we won't be followed. I can't take any more chances, Madi. I can't risk losing you, too."

I knew my friend and how tightly she clung to the weight of the world, as though the responsibility to bear it was her burden alone. Especially when it came to her job, the greatest chunk of her self-identity.

She'd lost her squad, Lafontaine and Rourke were dead, and now Gideon, all in the line of what she saw as her duty. Her conscience had to be a mess.

"His death wasn't your fault," I said, knowing it was pointless.

"I'll talk to you later."

The line went dead.

I rested the cool plastic of my phone against my forehead. It wouldn't have made any difference, but I wished I'd said more. Found the right words to ease her suffering.

But there were no magic words. Talking, hugs, alcohol, walking the city—they might take the edge off for a moment or two, but the only thing that would make her feel better was time. And getting to the bottom of whatever had toppled us into this hellscape. If Michael and Eric could help us do that, maybe it wasn't as much of a lost cause as we feared.

On shaking legs, I pushed myself to my feet and crossed the room to the window. I'd stared out at Bank Street a hundred times in the past few hours, but now it looked different somehow. More sinister. I half-expected to see uniformed troops on every corner moving towards the building, ready to take me in and shut down whatever operation the three of us had so naively started.

Had we really thought there wouldn't be casualties? Someone in SMOAC had believed the deaths of the department's best soldiers were an acceptable sacrifice for their mission— what difference would three more corpses make?

Well, unless they hurried, they'd miss their chance to sacrifice me—and if Jet was right that Michael had a solid lead, then maybe their hidden tyranny was almost at an end.

As much of a relief as it was to know others were tackling

the mole from another angle, I wasn't about to sit idly by while we waited for them to get their ducks in a row.

I tapped my phone against my lip, running more lists of names through my head, sorting out who else would be best to contact. Between the protesters, his own goons, and the traitors he'd recruited from within the department, O'Malley was building an army. It was time we drew a line in the sand and built one of our own. We had to create a wall of defence so Meril didn't have to do it herself.

Some of the names that popped into my head came with strings, and all of them came with risks, but at this point in the play, a bit of risk could be what it took to win the game.

Chapter 21

Jet

IF I'D EXPECTED my call with Madison to make me feel better, it hadn't worked. My veins crawled under my skin, stretching and contracting like burrowing worms. I couldn't sit still, couldn't focus.

It would have been better to wait until I was back at the safe house to break the news to her in person, but the idea of seeing the expression on her face when I told her strained the already weak guard around my emotions.

But now that I'd taken a shower and made my phone call, I'd struck off the two items I'd added to my to-do list.

Desperate for anything to pass the time, I shot Travis a text. SORRY TO DINE AND DASH. PARKED ON BANK NEAR SPARKS. SEND ME THE BILL.

At least he couldn't accuse me of stealing the damned car or running out on the inevitable parking ticket or towing fines.

So that was another thirty seconds of my day.

I circled my apartment, tidying areas I hadn't touched in over a week. I wiped down the counters, rearranged my mugs so all the handles faced the same way, swept the non-existent dirt out of the kitchen.

I was just about to go so far as to dust my shelves when my phone buzzed on the kitchen island.

Eyes narrowed, hoping it wasn't Madison calling me back to check in, not needing her hovering concern, I approached the phone and stared at the screen. Not Madison, Michael. I'd forgotten I'd given him my new number. I hadn't wanted to, not wanting to compromise my only means of communication, but I'd had no choice. He needed to reach me to tell me about his lead, and my old phone was off and stowed away under my bed at the safe house. Besides, this phone had been out of my possession for at least an hour in the parking garage, killing its usefulness. For all I knew, Carstairs had taken the opportunity to glean everything he could from it. Fortunately, we'd been careful enough that there wouldn't have been much for him to find.

My heart thrummed in my chest with the possibilities that awaited me on the other end of the line—a goal, a purpose, something that might bring us one step closer to an end—and my hand trembled as I answered.

"Colonel," I greeted. "You have something for me?"

"Yeah," he said, and his voice sounded gruff, exhausted. "For the record, I'm not happy with you for twisting my arm on this. If it were up to me, you'd be on a plane to Alberta to spend the next six months with your family."

"Understood," I said, my eagerness for his order no less intense for his reluctance to give it. I had to get out of my apartment. Although I knew it was in my head, I couldn't escape the stench of Gideon's blood.

"I think someone on the twenty-fifth is helping O'Malley expand his business into the States."

My stomach dropped. The rumour Gideon had been following. The reason he'd come here in the first place. I swallowed hard. "You think we might find evidence of it?"

"It won't be out in the open, but if there's government involvement in his distribution, there has to be paperwork somewhere to make it look legit. I've been keeping an ear to the ground, and more than one person's mentioned that someone in the department is turning the security office's head the other way, making room for the syndicate to move around as much as it wants without anyone noticing."

"What do you want me to do?"

"Look through the files in the minister's office."

I blinked. "You can't be serious."

"You asked me for a task, Dawson. This is where we'll find the proof. It has to be. If O'Malley is getting that much slack, direction has to be coming from the top. Either from Bastien or someone close to him."

I tapped my fingers against the island, my nerves jangling

with uncertainty. "How am I supposed to get into the minister's office to snoop around? I'm supposed to be on suspension, remember? Anyone sees me, I'm toast. That's what you told me. No one's going to open the door to his office to let me riffle through his papers."

"I gave Aline a heads-up that you'll be going in today to sign your suspension paperwork. She'll escort you upstairs. Gagnon is acting minister, but he's working out of his own office, so ask for a quiet place to review the documents before you sign them."

Panic squeezed my throat closed. Suspension paperwork. Official documentation of my disgrace.

"Don't give me that silence, kid. It has to be done if we want O'Malley's people to buy that you're off their heels."

"I know, sir. You're right. I'm sorry."

The words came out, but I didn't mean them. My signature would make the black mark all too real. And depending on how the situation wrapped up, there was a chance it would mean the end of my career. No going back.

It's already done. Your name on a piece of paper doesn't change anything.

I breathed through the tightness in my chest and curled my fingers into a fist.

"I'll head over there now."

"You'll find the codes for Bastien's filing cabinets under his keyboard. He was never good at remembering them. Call me when you've finished, let me know if you've found anything.

If the syndicate's using our resources to peddle their bullshit, I want to know it."

"Yes, sir."

I hung up and straightened my shoulders. I'd asked for a mission, and this was it. Just because I didn't like it didn't mean it wasn't a necessary step. A few hours of misery for potential victory. It would be worth it.

Hell, it'd be worth it to get out of this apartment.

I slipped my wallet into my back pocket, my knife into my boot, and headed out the back way to get to my car.

If my baby was still there.

I imagined the various ways I would tear people apart if anything had happened to my Mustang, venting some of my frustrations on the made-up vandals, and was almost disappointed to find her unscathed. Not even a scratch.

Nothing except the bloodstains on the front passenger seat.

"Fuck."

There was no way in hell I could drive to the office with that mess on display. Probably for the best. My head was still reeling from the madness of the morning. The last place I should be was behind the wheel.

But I couldn't leave her here another night.

"Come on, sweetheart, let's put you to bed," I said as I climbed into the driver's seat.

I wasn't normally a "talk to my car" kind of person, but the constant babble as I pulled out of the alley and circled around to pull into the parking garage distracted me from the memory of a broken Gideon dragging himself out of his seat. Panicking about his missing bracelet, which was as lost now as he was.

By the time I turned off the engine, my car safe in its assigned spot, I was shivering through my sweat. Acid burned a hole through my stomach, and I scrambled to open the door, ready to vomit all over the ground.

The cool draft coming through the vents, reeking of the same lung-clogging exhaust as the garage where Eric had pulled the trigger, both helped and hindered. My chest squeezed, and the world felt as though it were tipping on its axis, but at least I was no longer pukey.

On shaking legs, I got out of the car, locked it, and marched outside, needing to get as far away from the ghosts in my mind as possible.

As I made my way up Gladstone, I spotted a blue shirt stopped on the corner behind me. The shirt on its own meant nothing, but part of my brain was aware I'd seen it on the corner outside my apartment building as well. Whoever wore it blended in well enough with the crowd that I couldn't make out a face, but I homed in on them with my third eye, pinpointing the shadowy details so I could follow them without giving away that I was watching.

Could be coincidence. The walk from Centretown to downtown was common for the people who lived here, and I'd chosen one of the most direct routes. Blue Shirt could be a university student looking to hit the shops, or a public servant on their way back to work. I had to remember that, for most of the city, today was a normal day.

Eric might have been right that my paranoia was getting out of control.

Regardless, being cautious couldn't hurt. Laurier Avenue was a good hike up Bank Street, but there were a lot of places to stop along the way. Being on one of the best thoroughfares for neat boutiques and coffee shops meant I could weave in and out of stores for the better part of the afternoon. Let anyone following me have fun with that.

With the aim of bringing my potential tail on a milk run, I ducked into the nearest coffee shop. The moment I stepped inside, I realized my mistake. The place was crowded, the air thin, the exits blocked by people and display stands. But I couldn't turn around and walk out without buying something. It was exactly the sort of move that would attract unwanted attention. I was a captain on suspension, licking my wounds and making the most of my first day of forced vacation. I didn't want anyone watching me to be able to say anything different.

I ordered a small black coffee and settled by the window to stare out at the street. Anyone else would see it as a perfect day. Sun shining, parents pushing strollers, couples holding hands. Business suits, summer dresses, laughter, and that look of extreme calm you really only see when the weather is just on the right side of too warm.

I felt like I was about to jump out of my skin. I caught myself jogging my leg under the table and pressed my heel into the floor to hold myself still. How was I supposed to spot anyone paying special attention to me if I was drawing the eyes of the entire room? I wasn't a junkie jonesing for my next fix or a woman waiting for her blind date to arrive. I was nothing to look at. Calm, in control, relaxed.

I sipped my coffee, leaned back in my chair, and scanned the street with both my waking eyes and my psychic one to spot the person who belonged to the shadowed details I'd picked out.

Blue Shirt was still out there. I glimpsed the increasingly familiar hue on my third sweep across the block. Our safe house was just across the street, sitting on the corner going ignored by the mundane masses as the neighbourhood's oldest eyesore. No one appeared to be coming or going, but that didn't mean much from where I sat. The door was at the back of the building, tucked deep into what the mundanes would see as a construction site, though it appeared to the rest of us as a bright, arched doorway.

I wondered if Madison was upstairs looking out the window. Had she seen me walk by? I debated calling her to warn her about Blue Shirt, but left it for now. No point making her worry when I hadn't yet identified the problem.

On my next pass, I swore I caught a flash of brown hair in a ponytail above the blue shirt before the figure disappeared around the corner, following the same trail as the details I was tracking. The height of the figure, the darting way it moved…

Is that you, Dougall?

I watched the corner, waiting for another peek, but either my imagination had played tricks on me, or he'd found a better vantage point.

I hated feeling like a bug under a microscope. What did my stalker want? To catch me? Hurt me? Track my whereabouts to update someone else? Although my frazzled mind had picked out a hint of that grungy ponytail, it didn't make sense for Dougall to be my tail. Why would O'Malley use his chemist for surveillance?

Why would O'Malley have me followed at all? Unless he knew I was onto something. Dougall had messed up by being caught in his attempt to kill Madison. His identity had been outed, and the witnesses who were supposed to be dead had survived. O'Malley had to be worried about what that meant for his plans. It was only a matter of time before someone believed poor, scrawny, nervous Peter Dougall was the mastermind behind the city's most lethal street drug.

Was Dougall waiting to get close enough before setting off another bomb? Something more personal?

If so, the bastard wouldn't get a chance.

I thought about the knife in my boot and was glad I'd brought it. If he laid a hand on me, he'd walk away a few fingers short.

I noticed my leg jogging again and gave up. My tail wasn't

leaving, so it was time to move on. There was no way I was heading to the office with this guy on my ass. Michael had told me to be discreet, which meant no leading the syndicate straight to our evidence and potentially tipping off the government mole that I was snooping.

First step: lose my buddy.

I dumped my half-finished coffee and headed out to the street, and within another block, my stalker returned. I continued up Bank Street towards Wellington, surrounding myself with the tourist crowds coming to check out the Parliament buildings. The crowds were heavy enough I thought I stood a chance of disappearing, but not so thick I couldn't move with ease.

To have come here again, so soon after this morning, was a mistake. I knew it the second time I spotted Gideon's face on some random person.

The area around the Canada Day stage was blocked off from the earlier bomb threat, but otherwise, people acted as though nothing out of the ordinary had happened. The protests, the clear-out—all in the past for these people who relied so heavily on the routine of the day.

I skirted Parliament Hill and made my way towards Rideau Street without losing my blue-shirted companion. If the trip here hadn't been busy enough to drop him, I hoped a shopping centre on a beautiful summer day would do the trick. I considered the mall itself, but there were too many stores. Too many dead ends. Instead, I veered across the street and entered the department store. Four storeys of clothes, appliances, and furniture. Lots of places to vanish.

But my tail was dedicated. He remained with me as I ducked around clothing racks in womenswear and after I stepped into the bathroom. Every time I tried to see who he was, he disappeared, only that streak of blue and the trace of him through my third eye to prove I hadn't gone completely off the rails. Was it a supernatural ability that made him so easy to miss, or was he that well trained?

Either way, I'd had enough. I was tired. Tired of not being able to let my guard down, tired of being hunted. Tired of someone feeling smug at my expense because I was too exhausted and too scattered to outsmart them.

If I thought I could track him down and deal with him without causing a scene, I was annoyed enough to do it, but I wasn't in the mood not to throw a fist at his head. It was time to get rid of him and get on with my day. No more running, going from one end of the city to the other searching for somewhere to rest. I'd take a lesson from him and disappear. Blend so well into the crowd, he'd blink and I'd be gone.

I grabbed a black graphic tee from the nearest rack and snuck a light blue one underneath it. With the shirts draped over my arm, I wandered deeper into womenswear, picking up a deep red sweater, a few pairs of pants, and a flowy summer dress. Let my tail think I was treating my grief with some retail therapy.

Once my arms were full, I headed to the change room, and on my way there, slipped a black *Canada* baseball cap and a pair of sunglasses under the clothes. It had been a while since I'd played dress-up and my skills would be rusty, but my limited options meant I'd have to brush up quickly. As it was, dressed all in black on such a beautiful day, I stood out like a… well, like a trained task force soldier who didn't feel comfortable unless she dressed to match the shadows she worked in.

Thankfully, the change room was women only, giving me a sweet reprieve from the constant eyes on my back. The moment I entered the stall, I set down the clothes I'd grabbed and dropped onto the bench with a heavy exhale. I hadn't realized how much of a toll being followed had taken on me. To be here, hidden from him in this tiny room, felt as liberating as running free in an open field.

Maybe if I stay in here long enough…

There was no point considering it. The guy outside was obviously a patient son of a bitch. He would probably wait me out until the store closed and find his way in. It would be better to take my chances and face the consequences if I failed.

But as I went through the clothes I'd grabbed, I realized my misstep. Even if the colours I threw on were different from the ones he'd seen me grab, the styles were all the same, and I had to assume he'd paid attention.

I cracked open the door of the change room, waited until a woman down the aisle left with her purse, then slipped across the way into her room. Her discards hung on their hangers, and I flipped through the tank tops and short skirts to find something worth wearing.

Landing on a pale green halter top as the least bad option, I slipped my T-shirt over my head and left it folded on the bench. My lip curled with distaste as I ripped the tag off the halter and tugged the tight neckline over my hair and as far down as it would go, unimpressed to find the bottom of the shirt only reached my midriff. And that my sports bra in no way, shape, or form worked with the shirt.

Well, dammit.

I wrestled my bra off and fought against the unfamiliar sensation of being without, but I didn't have much choice except to suck it up. To go back out and enter another empty stall might grab the attention of the change room attendant. I'd have to make do.

At least it wasn't a bright pink tourist tee.

My jeans were plain faded black with no telltale marks on them, so at least I could hang on to those, but the rest of me… I eyed my reflection in the mirror, working hard to ignore the circles under my eyes and the haggardness that had deepened the lines of my brow and around my mouth. I couldn't do anything about those without a week on a hot sunny beach away from all my problems, so I focused on my hair. With a quick tug, I released the messy bun and let the brown waves tumble to their shoulder length.

After removing the tags from the sunglasses I'd stolen from the stand, I brushed my hair behind my ears and rested the glasses on top of my head. There. Done. A whole new me. As long as he didn't notice my clunky boots.

A quick look at my phone showed I'd only been in here about two minutes. Perfect.

I returned to the other stall, grabbed the dress I'd picked out, leaving the rest of my faux shopping trip behind, and approached a young woman eying herself in a sundress in front of the full-length mirror.

"Try this one," I said, offering her the flowy garment. "I think the colour would look great on you. It was a bit too small for me, but should fit you perfectly."

She eyed the dress, and her face lit up with a smile as she accepted it. "Thank you."

No, thank you.

I hoped her brown hair and similar physique would be enough to give my tail pause when she appeared wearing the outfit he'd seen me pick out. I also hoped I hadn't put her in any danger, but I couldn't afford to worry about her well-being. I had to concentrate and keep my eyes open for my ride out of here.

A quick look around showed no sign of Blue Shirt—though I was sure he was here somewhere—and another two women ready to leave the change room. I fell into step with them as they reached the door. My pulse raced, and I crossed my fingers this would work. If he—Dougall?—spotted me, I'd have no choice but to confront him, and considering possibility that I was dealing with a whackjob who'd planted a ghostbomb at a public protest, I had to be braced for another demonstration of his insanity. The mall was too crowded, the chance of mass casualties too high.

Please let this work.

"I couldn't believe it," one of the girls was saying. "Here's this guy who's acted like he's into me for months, and he just vanishes. Like a light switch. Next thing I hear, he's in Maui with a woman he met at a show."

"Men, am I right?" I butted in, leaning towards them as though we'd been friends all our lives. "You're absolutely better off without him. If he can't see what he might have had, he's not worth your anger."

"*Thank* you," the other woman said, her voice laced with gratitude even as the first woman looked surprised at my sudden and, frankly, inappropriate intrusion. "I've been trying to tell her that for weeks, but she won't listen."

She stretched out the syllables of the last word and knocked on her friend's head in gentle reproof.

"But he's so *cute*," the first woman said, and the three of us indulged in a laugh at the difficulties of relationships. As though I hadn't a care in the world and men were something I had loads of experience with. The kind of conversation I remembered having in high school but that had stopped when I'd joined SMOAC's task force. The women in our unit weren't the type to sit around and whine about the men in our lives. We went to the range and enjoyed some target practice when someone pissed us off.

By now we'd left the change room and made it halfway through womenswear. I needed to make it upstairs, across the overpass, and into the actual shopping centre. From there, I could make my way through the mall, leave by the bridge on the other side, and slip back to Laurier through the busiest tourist spots.

"I don't suppose you guys could give me your opinion on these glasses," I said, and slipped on the pair I'd taken from the stand. "Too… round?"

With that one question, I'd guaranteed a flurry of compliments and critique for the rest of the way to the mall until I found an opportunity to part ways with them. Only once I was there did I scan my surroundings, and the tension washed out of me when I found myself alone.

Not wanting to lose my advantage, I hurried up the escalator and made my way to the other large department store, which teemed with people heading for or coming off the line of buses. Sticking to the crowds, I grabbed a thin white cardigan from a sales rack and tore off the security tag as I walked, kicking the scrap of fabric with its intact tag under a display as I passed. Cardigan on, I swapped sunglasses with a pair on another rack. Later I would deal with my nagging conscience over shoplifting, but guilt wouldn't serve me at all if I didn't find my way out of here.

Wearing my second wardrobe change in ten minutes, I headed out the door and hopped on the back of the nearest accordion bus.

As I turned around, I spotted Blue Shirt stepping out of the shopping centre. Yes to the brown ponytail, but no spindly slouch. Not Dougall but Sammy G, one of O'Malley's top-tier lackeys.

What the hell?

His wide frame took up too much space as he looked first one way, then the other, and a shudder ran through me at the sight of him. Why was the syndicate following me?

What would he have done if he'd caught me?

He clenched his hands at his sides, tossed his head back and forth to search for me in the crowd, and I crossed my fingers he'd call it a day and report his failure to O'Malley.

But as the bus pulled away, his scowl gave way to a satisfied smirk that froze me all the way to the tips of my toes.

I'd escaped. He should have been pissed. I should have been free. So why did I feel as though I'd closed the door to my cage and locked myself in?

Chapter 22

Gideon

THE WORLD TILTED. Vanished.

Awareness wavered, and I clung to it, terrified of letting go. Already I'd slipped further than I ever had, my body, my cells, my existence spreading thin, almost out of reach.

The memory of that bullet shattering my sternum, the agony as it tore through flesh and sinew, lingered with me even as everything else faded away. The fibres of my heart being pierced, shredded. The life draining out of me.

How much was left?

I didn't know. Didn't want to find out. Afraid it wouldn't be enough. Afraid it would be just enough.

I gathered what I could, only part of me caring that I might have lost pieces of myself on the wind that buffeted me left and right. Only part of me wanting to come back.

Jet.

The look in her eyes when the shot had rung out in the parking garage. The terror, the grief.

The pain.

Nothing else could have made me try to pull myself back together.

Awareness slipped again, oblivion taunting me, tempting me.

I pushed harder, but the more strength I exerted, the more my grasp on myself loosened.

I floated.

The world tilted again, coming back into view. Outside. Sun. People.

Someone turned towards me, as though they'd seen the impossible riding the air. How much of me had pulled back together? I wasn't conscious enough to guess. Another moment later, they were gone, and the wind was carrying me again.

But the brightness of the day, the physical reminder that death hadn't found me yet, gave me another boost of energy, and I drew my drifting molecules closer. Still frazzled, still on the brink of breaking their ties and fracturing my being into a trillion detached particles, but present.

I stretched my awareness across them as though they were the door in the ocean and I was the selfish bitch taking up all the space on it.

Then I rested. Drifted. All together, but with no direction.

Where could I go? Where was safe?

Awareness flickered again, lurching.

Again Jet's face. The horror in her eyes.

She was my safe place. My grounding point.

With her, I would be able to find myself again.

With a destination in mind, a goal to keep me from sinking into the black depths of the void, I grabbed hold of the wind and drifted across it, no longer aimless.

Once, twice, three times I drew myself together enough to see where I was going, twice I had to change course, but before long, the haven of the safe house appeared before me. I misted, pressed myself against the stone-and-brick exterior of the building, counted cracks, searched for my way in.

Finally, third-storey window.

My energy flagged.

A breeze picked me up and guided me inside.

Silence wrapped around me.

I pulled myself together, piece by piece, but the pain was too much. Every pump of my heart shot spikes through my chest and stole my breath. I collapsed to the floor, and lights flashed in my vision as I lay on the ground, staring at the ceiling.

Warmth leaked out the corners of my eyes and tracked down my face, but no sound escaped me except a wheezing gasp.

Burning, tearing, screaming torment.

I misted again. The pain disappeared, dragging conscious-ness with it.

I had to find a balance. If I wanted to survive, to live long enough to make sure Jet was free, I had to find the knife-edge between too much and nothing at all.

Bracing myself, I eased back, starting with my fingers and toes, my hair, my eyes, my nose, my legs, my arms. Bit by bit, gritting my teeth against the agony that tore at me as I got closer to my midsection.

A scream burst from my lungs. I rolled onto my side, grabbed onto the armchair, and hauled myself into it. The deep cushion padded my aching joints but did nothing for the pumping, pulsing, prodding ache behind my ribs.

My breath came short and quick, sweat poured down my face, and I pressed my hand over the hole near my heart that spilled thick blood into the red cotton. Red on red.

I'd made it this far.

For what it was worth.

At least for now, I'd found somewhere safe.

Blackness took me, and I knew nothing.

Chapter 23

Jet

I GOT OFF the bus on the third stop and jaywalked across the street towards the office building.

At this time of day, closing in on the end of business hours, the lobby was crammed with people eager to get home. I was grateful, because it meant no one had eyes for me.

Almost surprising given my outfit.

I'd considered swinging home to change, but on the off-chance Sammy G decided to start at the beginning and wait for me there, I'd chosen to suck up the humiliation and go as I was.

Unfortunately, my seeming invisibility ended when I hit the security point and remembered I'd handed my pass over to Michael, leaving me with no way in.

Holding my head high to avoid a total walk of shame, I headed to the two commissionaires behind the security desk.

"Hi," I said, feeling as awkward as a rookie on their first day. "I forgot my pass. Can I make a call?"

There was no point asking the woman in uniform to do me a favour and let me through. Even if she believed this woman in the tight halter top and torn cardigan was indeed Captain Bridget Dawson, one look at my staff profile would reveal I wasn't supposed to be within ten metres of the building. Thank you, I'll see myself out.

But Michael had said Aline knew to expect me, so while I hated the thought of her seeing me like this—or at all considering the circumstances—I dialled her extension.

The entire process made me feel small. Having to fill out the visitor's book as though I hadn't worked here for fourteen years with barely a single holiday. The way Aline looked past me when she arrived in the lobby a few minutes later, all smiles for the commissionaires and avoidance for me. We'd always gotten along well, but now the trip up the elevator—her with her pass clutched in her hand and me with my visitor's badge clipped to my inappropriate V-neck—made me feel as though I were trapped in a tiny, airless container with an enemy.

As though I were the enemy.

I'd wanted to ask her if we could pop by the Peaview first to see if any of my team was still admitted, but I thought better of it. Michael had said no contact, and now that I was here, the sooner I got out, the better.

We reached the twenty-fifth, and when we stepped onto the

floor, I immediately became the centre of attention, my blissful anonymity in the lobby crashing and burning into a mountain of hostility and contempt as everyone eyed my stupid crop-top halter.

I hated to admit it, but I would have preferred the pity I'd dreaded so much on my last visit to the office.

Anything would have been better than this mix of curiosity and accusation. This distrust.

Really, no one on this floor should know who I was. I was a soldier, a resident of the first subbasement and a stranger to the paper-pushers up here with a view. I wondered which item on my increasingly long list of questionable decisions had made me so infamous.

I kept my gaze trained on the floor and followed Aline like a leashed puppy.

"Deputy Minister Gagnon's EA has the documents you need to sign," she said when we reached the reception area outside his door. "She's expecting you."

"Thank you," I said, but she'd turned her back on me and was already heading towards the elevator bay.

I let her go, not wanting to dawdle out in the open where everyone could see me, their disapproving stares making me feel about three inches tall. Squaring my shoulders, I approached the open cubicle where a young woman with blonde hair tied up in a messy bun sat typing appointments into a calendar.

"Hi, I'm Captain Bridget Dawson. Here to sign some

paperwork?"

She looked up from her screen and gave me a once-over. Her lip curled. "Right. They said you'd be coming." She reached for the yellow file folder sitting next to her elbow, my name written on the tab. "This is for you to fill out."

With a quick look around as though to make sure no one else was within earshot, I leaned in close. "Is there somewhere I could go to read it? Somewhere private?"

I doubted anyone would hand me an Oscar for my performance of shamed special forces captain—I wasn't even sure Gagnon's EA bought it—but she huffed and jerked the file folder towards me. "There are quiet rooms around the floor. Pick an empty one."

Crap. Not the offer I'd hoped for. If Gideon had been with me, he would have charmed this woman into letting him use whatever room he wanted. Clearly I'd learned nothing during our conversations with the informants.

My stomach clenched, and I forced my thoughts away from him. This wasn't the time to grieve. I had to find a way into the minister's office.

The door to the deputy's office opened, and Gagnon stepped out. I cringed at the sight of him, having sworn today's humiliation had already reached peak levels. It seemed the Fates' horrible sense of humour knew no bounds.

His sharp gaze took me in, morphing from irritation at seeing me to understanding when he caught sight of the yellow folder, and he jerked his head in a nod. "Captain Dawson, good of you to come in."

"She wants a place to read the papers, so I told her to go to a quiet room," his EA said.

He pressed his lips into a tight line and his nostrils flared as he shot a quick glance at his assistant. Then he forced a smile and nodded at me again. "Follow me, Captain. All sorts of noise filters into those quiet rooms, so I think we can do better for you. Michael called earlier to tell me you might come in, and he suggested the minister's office. I quite agree."

With an apology to the Fates for thinking they had it in for me, I fell into step behind him as we crossed the floor to the secure area on the other side. Down the hallway sat Madison's office, her door closed. Only a few nights ago, she and I had been there together going through the pattern she'd found in the minister's paperwork… before we'd come to this very office and found the minister's EA with her throat slashed, the entire space covered in blood.

Today, I never would have believed anything so tragic had happened here. The place was immaculate: files where they were supposed to be, a new desk, new chair, new carpeting, new artwork on the walls. The department's clean-up crew worked quickly.

"You can have the office to yourself for an hour or so. We have a meeting in here this evening, but I don't think it should take you that long to read through the documents. They're fairly straightforward."

"Thank you, Deputy Minister."

"If you have any questions, feel free to ask Erin."

I doubted I'd be in much of a rush to ask the woman the time of day but nodded my thanks all the same. He closed the door behind him, and I sank into the chair beside the minister's desk. Just like the room outside, this space was spotless, though the desk and shelves hadn't been replaced, only carefully restored.

I set the file folder on the desk in front of me but couldn't bring myself to open it. At some point while I was here, I would have to sit down and read through my suspension requirements. I would have to read the citation on my file and sign my name to the reason for it. A black mark on my otherwise clear record.

For now, I turned my thoughts to my real reason for being here. The reason the contents of the yellow folder were a heap of bullshit. A smokescreen so the mole would feel smug and think they'd gotten the upper hand on me.

I looked forward to the day I could shove the folder down their throat and make them choke.

Setting it aside, I lifted the minister's keyboard, grabbed the sticky note with the filing cabinet combinations, and approached the wall of drawers.

My phone buzzed in my pocket, and I pulled it free to check the screen. A text from Madison waited for me. Heading out for coffee to meet a friend. Hopefully home later

WITH NEWS.

A friend? I understood why she couldn't be more specific than that, but curiosity burned at me until I forced myself to set it aside. With only an hour to go through what looked like hundreds of files, I had to get started.

I had no clue what I was looking for specifically, so I opted for thoroughness and opened the cabinet on the left-hand side, ruled out the drawers stuffed with office supplies, and made my way down the line.

The first thing I learned was that Madison was one hundred per cent correct about the minister's EA. Phyllis had been robotically organized. I didn't find a single folder out of order, the papers tucked inside straight and even. Larger files, which in Michael's cabinets were stuffed full to bursting, were separated into smaller, labelled segments, and there appeared to be some kind of colour-coded cross-reference system as well.

Intense.

Shaking my head at the dedication of a reputedly miserable woman, I skimmed through the budget files, the personnel files—wincing as I did at the names of my fallen team whose résumés and records remained here for the archives—and finally slowed as I reached the section on international trade.

I checked the clock on the wall and ground my teeth. Soon enough, Erin would knock on the door asking me how things were going, so I had to speed up.

Grabbing the stack of files in one hand, I pulled them out

and brought them to the desk. It took me more than a few minutes to get the hang of Phyllis's organizational system, but as soon as I did, it was easy to jump to the collection of documents on Canada-U.S. trade.

From there, I flipped through the various trade agreements, the negotiations with Madison's name written all over them.

The clock ticked closer to the hour. Sweat dripped down the back of my neck.

Bad time management, Dawson.

I skimmed faster, flipping through health and security agreements, resources, products.

My eyes blurred, and I buried my face in my hands. Why couldn't Michael have given me more to go on? Someone in the department was directing attention away from the syndicate, making it easy for them to expand. The tip was vague, and the proof of corruption could be anywhere. I might have already passed it and not known what it was.

Just as I was about to give up, sign my slap on the wrist, and break the news to Michael that I'd failed, my gaze landed on the date stamp of a sheet of paper peeking out from under the stack in the bottom file.

Four days ago.

Curious, I nudged it free with the tip of my finger and leaned over the letterhead-stamped document.

Permission for a cross-border shipment.

I frowned. This document was out of place. Given Phyllis's strict system, it should have been filed under government orders in the first drawer.

I leaned back in my chair and scanned the printed text, taking in details about three cargo shipments due to pass into the States next week via the Thousand Islands Border Crossing. Signed by the minister two days before he'd died.

There was nothing to say the shipments had anything to do with the syndicate, but the lack of detail about the contents of the shipping containers was damning enough in an office where every last speck of dust was itemized on these requisitions.

Added to that, the city of origin, glaring in its bold italics, was Kingston, Ontario. Centre of the longest-running, most confused rumour about the Death's Head Syndicate's movements.

This had to be it. Three shipping containers of ghost to help O'Malley gain a foothold in New York. All the time Gideon had spent with me trying to prove the syndicate's goal of spreading its reach into the States and here was the evidence right in front of me. My throat tightened, and I screwed my eyes shut against the pain that he wasn't here to see it for himself.

I fought against my rising grief, wrestled it into the dark corners of my mind, and drew in a long, ragged breath.

Voices sounded from the reception area, and I glanced at the clock. Fifteen minutes to the hour. Obviously a few eager beavers had chosen to get here ahead of time. Probably hoping the meeting would start earlier so they could get home before dinner.

They had to be new to government.

I snapped a photo of the shipment authorization and stuffed everything haphazardly into the folders with a silent apology to Phyllis's memory. Doing my best to move with purpose and not rush to the point of dropping everything, I shoved the folders into the filing cabinet, threw myself into the chair on the outside of the minister's desk, and wrenched open the yellow file folder.

I was just scrawling my name at the bottom of the page, with no idea what I was signing, when the door opened and Erin led a group inside.

"All done?" she asked. Her tone was pleasant, but beneath the smile lurked a clear message that there was only one answer.

"Just. Should I leave it on your desk on my way out?" Simple, professional, only a hint of embarrassment about sharing space with these overtly loyal and non-scandalous public servants.

Any one of whom could be a syndicate dung beetle.

I eyed them closely as I left, took in the details of their hairstyles and features, but recognized no one. The twenty-fifth floor was a whole other world.

I dropped off the file folder and headed straight for the elevator bay, giving no opportunity for anyone to stop and stare. Only when I reached the empty lobby did I let go of the breath I'd been holding, and I didn't relax until I'd stepped outside into the stifling summer evening.

Under any other circumstances, I might have been grateful I was only wearing half a shirt.

When I reached the corner, I pulled out my phone and called Michael.

"Dawson? What took you so long?"

"Took me a while to get to the office," I said, and checked over my shoulder as I crossed the street. So far no sign of O'Malley's pet, which I hoped meant he'd given up after the shopping centre.

"Find anything?" he asked.

"I think so. I grabbed a photo so you can take a look, but it's an authorization form for a cross-border shipment out of Kingston."

"Kingston again. That damned rumour is going to chase me to my grave. Though maybe not so much of a rumour anymore."

"Looks like."

I waited for the light to change, using the window of the pub to check my six.

Michael snorted. "No wonder Bastien was so pissed off at finding the American with you. If he was helping O'Malley cart ghost across the border, the last thing he'd want is SilverGuard looking into it."

Again that squeeze around my heart that threatened to stop me in my tracks, but I forced myself to focus on the bigger issue. "You really think Bastien was involved?"

"He must have been. The authorization was filed in his office. I assume he's the one who signed it?"

"It looks like his signature, yeah. I guess it makes sense." I tried to sound sincere, though Madison's evidence of Bastien's innocence barred me from believing it so easily. Both Michael and Eric had accused me of reading too much into the paperwork angle, and right now my primary goal was to prove to Michael I was ready and willing to help however he needed me to. I would follow his lead.

"So what next?" I asked. "Do we take this to someone?"

"Not yet. Text me the photo, and I'll show it to a few people who might be able to help us. We need to prove there's ghost in those containers before we charge in, and the department is out of resources to get it done. How are we supposed to uphold our promise to the supernaturals of this country and stop the spread of a growing syndicate when our people are stretched thin to transparent? It's about time we let someone else handle the day-to-day so we can take care of what really matters."

I drew to a halt in the middle of a concrete courtyard outside a small plaza. The smell of hot dogs filled the air and a child's laughter echoed in my head.

"You mean the Federation of Supernatural Affairs?"

A moment of silence followed my question. "How do you know about them?"

"Eric told me about the guinea pig project."

And I had never been so happy he had, as it let me keep Madison's name out of it. No one needed to know about the files she'd pulled or the evidence she'd found until and unless I guaranteed her safety.

"Good," Michael said. "He saved me some time. That's exactly who we need. FoSA can offer services to our people the department could never hope to match. Give us a leg up on this side of the wall so we aren't trembling in fear of Meril's shadow. And while they do that, we'll be free to do our jobs. Like track down the syndicate and ensure the safety of our country."

"But isn't offering services the department's job? Do we really want to outsource?"

"SMOAC as it is was a noble dream, Dawson, but our population has tripled since we crossed the wall and founded the department. We can't afford to do and be everything anymore. It's not realistic. Not if we want to thrive."

My legs unfroze, and I continued my walk up Bank Street. His words made me uncomfortable, going against everything I'd grown up believing, but I saw his point.

No matter how I felt, though, I wasn't about to make up my mind over a phone call.

"Do we know what they're offering? What are the strings?"

"There will be time enough to discuss all that. I want to sit down and go over everything in person with you, but first, I'm going to follow up on this shipment. Go home and get some rest. I'll be in touch soon when I have something else, but this is great work, Dawson. You did good today."

Warmth blossomed around my heart. It was the highest praise I'd received all week. At least Michael was on my side again, which set my world a little more to rights.

But the thought of going back to my apartment made my stomach acid bubble.

"Sir, I don't think I should go home. On my way to the office, I had a friend. One of O'Malley's right hands. It took me a while to lose him, and I'm not in a hurry to pick him up again."

"Shit. This is the kind of thing you lead with, kid. You all right?"

"I'm fine. Confused about why O'Malley would want me followed, but fine."

"Use your brains. You've been hot on his heels since the de Lauer attack." He groaned, and I heard a sigh that sounded like it came from the depths of his being. "I hate this. Helping me is not worth your life. You lost his tail, so who knows what he'll try next. Seriously, Jet, you should back away from this. Keep yourself safe."

"I'll be safe once O'Malley is eating dust."

"Damn your stubbornness. Fine. You have a place to go?"

The safe house on Somerset appeared up ahead, and I walked towards it on autopilot, as though a cable were attached to my jeans, reeling me home.

"Yeah, I'm good."

"All right. I'll be in touch."

I hung up and slid my phone into my pocket, then paused on the corner across from the apartment building. The silence and security of our temporary haven lured me in, but the idea of going back without Gideon, of having to find yet another new normal, made me shy away.

Another few minutes wouldn't kill me. I needed snacks, comfort food, and the grocery store was just across the street. One quick stop, and then I could attempt to reshape my life for the third time this week.

Chapter 24

Madison

I SAT IN the far back corner of the coffee shop watching the door, searching each face for one in particular but on alert for anyone familiar who might walk in. I'd chosen a meeting spot far enough from the SMOAC office that it was unlikely any of my colleagues would stop by for an after-work pick-me-up, but I couldn't afford to relax my guard.

I'd already finished my peppermint tea, having measured each sip by the ticking clock, and my anxiety refused to be contained.

Doubts about my decision to be here ebbed and flowed. Of all the risks I could have taken, I'd opted for one that would certainly catch Meril's attention and possibly turn my few days into hours. Minutes.

What difference does it make anymore? You're going anyway.

So I kept telling myself, but there was a difference between

Meril summoning me out of concern for my well-being and her being upset I'd called in her satellite troops without permission.

But her hands were tied with what action she could take on this side of the wall, and until I joined her court, mine weren't. Something had to be done—reinforcements readied, eyes and ears prepared to move should our people need to be protected—and as long as I was in a position to save my country from the syndicate, the mole, and the repercussions if the wall fell, I would.

Finally, the woman I waited for walked in. She was as stunning as I remembered, tall and tan, with perfect curves, pouty lips, and eyes that made most people do a double take. Only after a second glance did they laugh and call themselves crazy for thinking she carried the universe in her gaze.

Which she did, of course.

Lilith Cochrane, as she called herself in this world, was a fairy. Not the cute garden fairy type that frolicked amongst the daisies—those guys were incredible gardeners and knew how to throw an amazing summer party—but the soldier type. A pointy-toothed, super-strengthed warrior. She'd been in the queen's army for most of her life until she'd crossed to this side of the wall a few years ago and opened her own security firm. Concerts, galas, swanky affairs where the hosts wanted people who could fit in with the crowd while watching out for their guests—that was Lilith's sphere. Which was why I'd called her.

I hoped that her having built a life for herself over here, with a business and reputation to maintain, would make her less eager to rat me out to the queen, but I had to brace myself for how Meril would react if she thought I was rallying her people out from under her. Just because we were family didn't mean my recall wouldn't involve a sentence in the marsh jail.

Lilith stood in line to order her coffee, giving me a few extra minutes to ready my approach. Finally, venti latte in hand, she sat down across from me.

"Madison," she said, her voice like dark chocolate, rich and a little sharp. "It's been a while."

"How've you been, Lil?"

She raised a perfectly rounded shoulder in a lazy shrug. "You know how it goes. Festivals and outdoor concerts. This is my busiest time of year."

"Thanks for taking the time to meet me."

Her indigo eyes, swirling with stars, met mine. "I had good reason. You're not the type to call me up for a gab, and I'm not oblivious to the changes happening around our city."

"You've been watching the news?"

"Hard not to. Even the muns know something's up, even if their guesses are a million miles away from the truth."

No wonder Meril was getting impatient for my return. If rumours and interest had piqued among the mundanes, it was only a matter of time before the more perceptive among them dug deeper, and once we reached that point, clean-up became significantly more challenging.

"What have you heard?" I asked.

Lilith cocked her head. "All kinds of things. Hard to narrow down what rumours might be relevant unless you tell me what you want to know."

Damn the woman. A real gossip would have been eager to share every last detail, but Lilith was shrewd. I tapped my fingers against the sides of my empty cup as I debated, but in the end, I accepted I had no choice but to offer a degree of transparency. After a quick scan of the coffee shop to make sure no one I knew had snuck in while I wasn't looking, I uncrossed my legs and leaned forward.

"Ghostbombs and the Death's Head Syndicate. Someone looking to create unrest across the country. Could mean a few less concerts with nothing but cokeheads and drunks to worry about and a few more all-out brain-melting riots if we don't step in and put a stop to it."

Concern flitted over Lilith's face before her features settled into their neutral form. "What's your interest?"

Fortunately, I'd planned for this question. To tell her Meril had recalled me would immediately put her back up, and I'd be lucky if she didn't leave a Lilith-shaped hole through the door in her hurry to escape. There was no way she'd cross the queen, no matter the risk to her investments.

"Personal. Helping a friend who got caught in the de Lauer blast."

At this, Lilith's mask slipped. Behind her soldier-cold eyes— in the queen's army, there was no room for mercy—lurked an empathetic soul. Hardly a surprise. As a soldier herself, she understood the horror of losing half her troops. I was more than a little relieved that not even she was unaffected by the reality of the danger we faced.

Although I would have felt better if she'd remained hard and aloof, as though she thought I was making a big deal out of nothing. A small part of me held on to an infinitesimal hope that we were overreacting. That the situation wasn't nearly as dire as it seemed.

That final, lingering hope smashed to the ground when Lilith scowled, revealing a hint of her pointed teeth. "These sons of bitches." She sipped her coffee, pressed her lips together, and when she spoke again, her voice was low and strained. "Someone should have taken on the syndicate years ago. I've never understood why soldiers on both sides of the wall have been content to look the other way while their evil spreads. Now look at where we are, and how are we supposed to stop them? Their arms are getting longer. Toronto is completely overrun, and they've consumed the capital. What's next?"

"Kingston?" I asked, testing the waters. At every point, this rumour had come up, the answer flip-flopping, with as many people claiming outright lie as gods-sworn truth. Was the confusion part of the plan or just wiliness on O'Malley's part? Misdirection made sense to keep the authorities off his back, but with what I knew of his government connections, it could as easily be a symptom of something bigger.

Lilith snorted. "I know the bastard is ambitious enough to cross the border, but he wouldn't be so obvious as to move his dealings to Kingston. The guy's devious. Kingston is nothing more than a distraction."

"You know this for a fact?" I asked.

"I do. As much as anything is fact. I have a cousin out Trenton-way. A month or so ago, someone approached him about taking a package of ghost to the army base. Guy gave him a card to The Afterlife and said if he was interested, he should drive to Ottawa to talk to someone and get things started. Why send him all the way here if they've moved to Kingston? Hell on Earth is a rising party palace, but from what my people there tell me, O'Malley's keeping it legit."

I bowed my head. Our suspicions were right, then: Kingston was O'Malley's way of making SMOAC chase its tail. Nothing to it.

It should have been a relief to learn the syndicate wasn't any closer to crossing the border than we thought it was, so why did I suspect there was more to the story? Why was the rumour on everyone's lips? If some people were so certain the rumour was a lie, why hadn't the department quashed it?

"Your cousin didn't report the request to anyone?" I asked.

Lilith scoffed. "And get his ass hauled in for dealing?"

I raised my hands, conceding her point. "Off the books."

Her gaze bored into mine. "Off the books, he did. He told me he passed the information along to a contact with ties to the security office, but if your people didn't get the message…"

Drawing in a deep breath, I straightened my spine and stretched my shoulders to ease some of the building tension. "That right there is part of the problem, Lil."

So the mole had been burying leads about the syndicate. Not a surprise, but now we had a better idea how deep the connection between the two ran. Every extra detail brought us closer to discovering the source of the corruption.

"Have you heard anything about a man named Peter Dougall?" I asked.

A small furrow appeared between Lilith's eyebrows, a barely-there wrinkle in her flawless skin. "The name doesn't ring a bell. He works for the syndicate?"

"He's the Ghostmaker."

Her lip curled, flashing a hint of pointed canine. "I haven't, but I'll keep an ear out for the bastard. If I get my hands on him, he won't be a problem for long."

I tightened my grip around my cup. "For now, it would be best if you stayed away from him. I worry that getting rid of him too quickly will speed up the syndicate's plan faster than we can outrun it. That's why I contacted you." I bit my lip to steel my nerves. Having brought Lilith this far, I had to show her the rest. The reason I needed her. "The queen wants to speak with me. I've put her off for now, but if I'm recalled…"

She gave me a knowing nod. "You need to be sure someone's ready to man the battlefield."

"Or at least to help the people trying to stop the battle from reaching that field."

"Oh?"

I tucked my hair behind my ear and smoothed a long lock over my shoulder. Did I want to give Jet away? Reveal her involvement? Lilith would want to know who she'd be working with; she wasn't the sort of woman to take things on faith. But to bring Jet's name into it before asking her permission, especially when she was fighting trust issues with some of her closest colleagues, didn't seem fair.

"I'm trying to get a handle on this before it blows up. A few of us are—" I faltered. That wasn't right. Not anymore. "Were." I struggled to meet the question in her eyes, but pushed myself to explain. "We lost one of our allies today."

She had to know what we were dealing with. I might not be able to tell her everything yet, but if I was asking for her help, I couldn't expect her to remain in the dark about the risk she'd be taking.

"I'm sorry," she said, and her compassion sounded genuine.

I cleared my throat to remove the painful lump and pushed forward. "I know there's wisdom in acting quickly on the information we have—believe me, I'd love to tear a few throats out myself—but…"

I trailed off as I tried to put my thoughts together and wished I hadn't sped through my tea. How was I supposed to fill her in without sounding like we were making mountains out of molehills or creating plans on an unmarked field riddled with land mines?

"I wish we had more to go on, but so far all the evidence we have is circumstantial," I admitted. "We know it leads to *something*, but what that something is remains unclear. We know some of the players, but not who's leading the game."

"I see," Lilith said, her eyes narrowing.

Afraid I was losing any support I might have gained, I scanned the room and leaned further across the table. "We're doing our best to put the pieces together, but I need you to have some faith in me. If we stumble too far in the dark on this, we risk giving ourselves away to the people involved or raising enough panic that Meril feels the need to call you in herself."

Her eyebrows shot up. "That big?"

I nodded, and the muscles around my lungs loosened. At least she was willing to give me the benefit of the doubt. It was all I could ask when so much of what we faced lay in shadow. "That big."

Lilith sipped her coffee, her starry gaze gliding over my shoulder. "The wall falling would lead to chaos. Mundane versus human, one species versus another, each fighting to come out on top. We wouldn't recognize the country by the time the fires died out."

I pictured it as she spoke. Meril could lay claim to whatever she wanted, but her power would be limited as each group vied for superiority in a newly formed hierarchy. She could exert her will in the unseen realm, drag everyone on this side of the wall back to the otherworld, but there would be those of our kind who fought to maintain their independence. Fire and bloodshed. Destruction. Oblivion. No worst-case conclusion would be too far-fetched.

"You see why we need to figure this out," I said. "Before the syndicate gains another foothold or launches another attack, and before Meril rallies her forces."

Lilith's eyes flicked to mine, and I sensed her uncertainty. Her deepest feelings were blocked from me, but even so, I detected a hit of adrenaline. Fear, maybe, over what the future might hold, but also exhilaration, the thrill of the fight. Battle was in her blood. I clung to hope she saw our cause—and our chances—as worthwhile.

"What can I do?" she asked.

I refrained from releasing a breath of relief, concentrating on what needed to be done instead of celebrating my minor victory. "Once we have more names, a better idea of who's in play, then we can talk strategy. When we're ready for that, do you have soldiers to spare? We don't know how many people O'Malley has at his disposal, but I'd feel better knowing we had a few on our side to help push him back. Meril won't like the idea of us taking this on ourselves, but with a bit of persuasion—" I thought of Serc and hoped he was up for the task "—she's bound to see it's the smartest move."

Lilith pursed her lips. "I can think of a dozen battle-ready troops off the top of my head, though they won't stand on the front lines without the queen's express command. Still, I'll see what I can do. If it means protecting the wall, protecting our people, and tearing a gaping hole in the syndicate's dealings, it would be an honour to help."

I gave her the number for my new unlisted phone and stood with her. "Thank you. And if…" I looked around. "If our conversation could stay on this side of the wall, I would appreciate it."

Lilith nodded her understanding. "The last thing I need is a recall of my own. The queen won't learn of your preparations through me."

I touched my fingers to my heart, a gesture Lilith mirrored before she took her coffee and left.

I threw out my empty cup, wiped down the table to give her a few minutes to walk away, and left the coffee shop. That was one extra game piece on our side, at least. Now to see if I could convince one more to put his faith in me.

Someone in my department was looking to start a war, and I would do whatever I could to make sure they found themselves staring down an even field.

Chapter 25

Jet

After twenty minutes circling the grocery store aisles, mindlessly taking in the organized shelves and brightly coloured labels and avoiding all thought of going home, I ran out of excuses to linger.

Resigned, I paid for my snacks and left, prepared to crash on the couch and eat every last one of my newly purchased pepperettes and Oreos. Better than alcohol and would save me from having to make dinner.

Madison would also be there, and I'd had enough time with my thoughts that I was ready to face her. We could open a bottle of wine, curse the Fates, and lay out a new plan. We weren't finished here, not by a long shot. We couldn't be. What I'd found in Bastien's office gave us a whole new perspective on the issue. When this was over, when we'd brought down the traitors, then I could grieve and work on repairing some of the relationships I'd damaged.

What I needed more than anything was for Madison to tell me we still had some fight left in us. After my morning and the chase across town, I was drained. The feeling of being hunted hadn't faded. I was the deer in the crosshairs, knowing someone lurked behind me but unable to run in all directions at once to avoid them.

I hated it.

After so many years of training, tracking, teaching, I'd grown used to feeling strong and in control. Only now that I'd been stripped of all security, all my resources and technology, did I realize that control was an illusion. My rank had been my shield against every threat, something I could wield with absolute assurance, and without it, I'd become a shaking recruit just starting basic training. Enemies waited around every corner, and all I had were my wits.

I needed my friend to tell me they would be enough.

The lobby of the Somerset building was empty, and I didn't pass anyone on my way up the stairs. When I reached our apartment, my third eye twitched, and I rested my hand against the wooden frame. I picked up a single shadow inside, which should have made sense, except the shadow's movements over the past hour were erratic, limited to a single area.

Had Madison come home and fallen asleep?

I opened my third eye wider, pressing through time to search for more shadows, for anyone walking by the apartment that might have set off the alarms in my head, but saw nothing.

Pressing my ear against the door, I tried to listen for whatever I was unable to see, but everything inside was quiet.

You're exhausted, Dawson. Can't even trust your own mind right now.

I pulled my phone out of my back pocket and found a second text from Madison, sent half an hour ago, probably while I'd been wandering around the grocery store.

Heading to ESD for late dinner with more friends, she'd written. When we can, we need to talk.

Of all the times to read that phrase. *We need to talk* were the most anxiety-inducing words at the best of times, but when they came from one of your few surviving friends, they turned into nightmare fodder. What friends was she talking about? Was she safe? Should I go to her?

The more immediate concern shoved every other question out of the way. If she wasn't home, who the hell was in our apartment?

A sharp pain shot through my jaw, and I opened my mouth to unclench my teeth, then stretched out my hands to draw in the air around me. Our trespasser had made a huge mistake.

Keeping one hand around the air molecules, gripping them so tightly they would lash out like a whip when I released them, I eased the door open with the other.

The curtains were drawn and the lights were off, dousing the room in a twilit darkness. A quick glance around the kitchen revealed no one, and I didn't hear anyone moving in any of the bedrooms.

Just as it had been from the outside, the apartment was still.

I took another step and closed the door behind me, holding on to the handle so the latch made only a faint click when it caught. My skin crawled with awareness that someone else was here, unseen in the darkness. My physical eyes picked up nothing but shadow, and though my third eye detected something, it couldn't lock on to it.

Who could have found out about this place? Had Madison spilled the beans to whoever she'd met with? Had her contact, the one who'd prepared this safe house, been compromised?

Madison, you'd better be okay.

I reminded myself she was far from defenceless—unless the bastard had some kind of mind protection like Dougall did, the son of a bitch—and her over-cautiousness went way beyond my growing paranoia. She wouldn't have given us up, and by the time she got home, safe and in one piece, I would have dealt with whoever or whatever had invaded our space.

Drawing a deep breath to centre myself, I focused my third eye on the history of the room. *Stillness. Shadow.* I moved further back. *Someone coming in through the window. Sitting in the armchair.* Too long ago to see who it was, but they were still here. Within ten metres of me. If it weren't so damn dark, I would have seen them the moment I'd opened the door.

I thought about turning on the light and putting an end to this stage show, but if our intruder was armed, I didn't want to make myself an easy target. Not until I was close enough to make a move of my own.

The possibility that Sammy G—or worse, Carstairs—had found me created a ball of terror in my throat. Thanks to Gideon, I knew exactly what I could expect if the syndicate got its hands on me. If Carstairs was here, lurking in the darkness, all he had to do was get inside my head and it wouldn't matter if I were armed to the teeth, he'd be able to drop me. I would have to be ready to act fast.

My heart thrummed against my ribs and sweat trickled down my back from under my stupid green halter top.

I will not be taken down dressed like this, I said to myself, and it was motivation enough to recover my courage.

I firmed my grip on the air and moved through the kitchen, skirted the dining table where Madison's papers remained in their neat piles across the surface. Exactly how we had left them this morning. Fifteen years ago, or so it felt like.

I passed through the living room, my eyes slow to adjust to the darkness. Through the rush of blood pulsing in my ears, I picked up the faint sound of someone breathing, the airflow shallow and ragged. Their presence flickered through my third eye again, and my mouth went dry. There was something familiar about the way they sat in my mind. The sense of them being both here and not here.

Holding my breath, refusing to let myself feel anything resembling hope, I crossed one foot lightly over the other towards the wall and flicked on the light switch.

A warm glow spilled from the table lamp over the armchair and across the floor, its fingers reaching towards me, battling the shadows of the arriving evening.

Revealing the figure collapsed in the chair.

Dark hair above a pale face, long eyelashes on gaunt cheeks, red shirt soaked with blood over ratty black jeans and heavy black boots. A leather bracelet around a limp wrist.

My heart stopped. I couldn't breathe. Couldn't think. Couldn't move.

Gideon.

Tears filled my eyes, and my heart galloped, strained against my ribs. It wasn't possible. Eric was a crack shot. It was in his blood—his aim was perfect. He'd fired at close range. Right in the chest. Gideon couldn't have survived it. But he was here. Breathing. His eyes were closed and he was covered in blood, but he was alive.

Alive.

As though the word were the rush of fire I needed to thaw out, I flew across the room and knelt beside him. For a minute, I could only stare, terrified that if I touched him, he would dissolve, prove to be nothing more than a figment of my over-burdened mind. Forget the evidence of my eyes, my third eye, and my ears. The impossibility held me captive until the pain of not knowing, the ache of unconfirmed hope, pushed me forward, and I took his hand.

His palm was clammy, his skin was cold, but he didn't disappear, and I swallowed the rock-hard sob building in my throat. At my touch, he twitched and groaned.

"Gideon?" Though it came out as a choked whisper, I didn't have the nerve to speak louder, too afraid to startle him. Too afraid I would break down. "Gideon, it's Jet. Can you hear me? Can you open your eyes?"

This close, under the glow of the lamplight, he looked like death warmed over. His skin was pasty under his dark stubble, and deep bruises of exhaustion circled his eyes. I didn't care. A few hours ago, I thought I'd never see him again. He could have grown a second nose, and I would have thought he was the most beautiful thing I'd ever laid eyes on.

His eyelids fluttered, and I tightened my fingers around his.

Where was Madison? Did she know?

No, she wouldn't have left me in the dark about this or left Gideon on his own in the state he was in.

Alive!

But would he stay that way? The blood on his T-shirt glistened in the light, not yet dry. Was he still bleeding? Still slipping away? My heart raced, but I couldn't let him see me panic. I had to assume he would make it. That he hadn't dragged himself back here just to make me watch him die a second time. I wouldn't let that happen.

His eyes opened, though it took a moment for awareness to fill his dark gaze.

"You scared the crap out of me, you son of a bitch." I tried my best to sound inconvenienced. The tremor gave me away.

He squeezed my fingers, his grip weak, though stronger than I'd expected. "Had to make you realize how much you'd miss me," he said, his voice hoarse and jagged.

"I think the blood loss might have caused some brain damage," I retorted, but the warmth that had filled me at the sight of him burned brighter, and I clung more fiercely to him. "How are you doing?"

"Better than I look," he said through sharp breaths. "I've been healing slowly. Just got so tired. You think I'd let a literal broken heart stop me?"

As he spoke, his torso evaporated. The tendons in his neck grew taut with the effort, and when he rematerialized, a fresh layer of sweat coated his brow. I kept my grip on his hand, wanting to yell at him to pace himself even as I wanted to scream at him to heal faster. I settled for saying nothing, trusting he would only push himself as far as he was able to.

His deep brown eyes met mine, and a shaky smile curled the corner of his mouth. My stomach flip-flopped, and I bowed my head against the armrest at the alarming sting of tears. Relief and joy mingled together and created a buzz that filled me from the roots of my hair down to my toes. All my aches and pains were gone, all the grief I'd suffered on his behalf mutated into the fear that I might lose him again.

Beneath it, sharp, heated fury swelled in my bones, directed at my lieutenant. In his effort to protect the people who had betrayed our department, Eric had nearly taken this man away from me. Gods knew Gideon and I had issues and my feelings for him were a twisted, confused mess, but I had nearly lost any chance of untangling them.

As the boiling rage hardened into molten rock in my veins, the lamp on the table rattled, and a flutter of paper sounded behind me—Madison's neat briefing notes scattering.

They would never get that close to him again. Not to him, and not to Madison. I had staked my position when I'd freed Gideon from that cell, but now I would defend it. Eric had made his stance clear, but I hoped he understood I wouldn't back down either. Not when the people I cared about were in danger.

"Hey," Gideon said, releasing my hand to brush his fingers under my chin. "What's going on?"

"If they come for you again, you run, do you hear me?" I raised my gaze to his, and his eyes widened at whatever he saw, but I didn't care. Let him be scared. He *should* be scared. If he cared anything about me, about what we were fighting for, he would do as I ordered. "No sticking around to protect me, no sacrificing yourself. You get the hell out of there and find somewhere safe to wait, is that clear?"

And just like that, my rage ran out. The lamp settled, Madison's papers drifted to the floor, and I sagged against the chair. The tears that had threatened now spilled down my cheeks, and I didn't have the strength to wipe them away. "I can't stand the thought that next time they won't bother with the collar. They'll shoot to kill, and you won't be able to mist the damage away."

Gideon gave my hand a gentle tug, guiding me into his lap, and I followed his lead, unable to disobey. Although I was careful where I rested my weight as I straddled his legs, I needed to be close to him, to prove to myself he was actually here, healing before my eyes.

He kept a firm grip on our entwined hands and brushed my hair behind my ear with the other, sliding his fingers to the back of my neck and resting his forehead against mine.

For a while, we stayed there unmoving, neither of us willing to let go. Right now, in this second, everything was fine. We were good, there were no monsters at the door. I was almost afraid to breathe, worried a single small change would bring the ceiling crashing down around us.

I knew I should call Madison, let her know the good news. Let her have the same rush of hope that now ran through me. But I couldn't share him. Not yet. For this fleeting moment, he was all mine, and I wasn't ready for anyone else to join us. I wanted to stay right where we were, my heart beating close to his, our breath in sync, the warmth of his hands replacing the chill of my grief.

The fire his presence—his touch—had set off in my blood spread through the rest of me, and soon the press of our foreheads and our joined hands weren't enough. I released him and slid my fingers under the hem of his T-shirt, gliding them over the ridges and valleys of his stomach. His skin was sticky with dried blood, but when I reached the place where he'd been shot, I skirted my fingers around the wound. He was sitting here, conscious, lucid, so he must have been able to patch himself up, but I was afraid to see the truth.

I told myself my exploration was only to make sure he hadn't lied to me about his condition—with Gideon, one never knew—but as I splayed my hand over his fevered chest, over his heart that should have been still but by some miracle continued to beat, my breath hitched.

He pulled back to catch my gaze, and the same paralysis came over me as when I'd found him sitting here. The fire burned with so much heat I didn't trust it. What was I doing? This man who had lied to me—*protected me*—betrayed me— *saved me*. This man who had made me cry, doubt myself, feel angrier than I ever had. *Who made me feel alive. Strong.* Did I really want to go down this road again? I had no idea. What I did know was that right now, I needed him. His heat, his closeness. After the hell of the last few days, with the sword still hanging over our heads, I needed to not feel alone.

The question was there in Gideon's eyes. He hadn't moved, one hand on my neck, the other on my waist. Waiting. Giving me control. If I didn't want this, I could get up. Pour us some drinks. He'd never say anything.

But as I'd realized recently about my authority within SMOAC, it was an illusion of control. Any actual control had disappeared as soon as his fingers curled into my skin, at the stirring of his desire against my thigh and the darkening of his eyes as longing overwhelmed his pain…

I leaned in, paused. He tensed beneath me, his entire body rigid, and I checked to make sure I hadn't hurt him. The hand at my neck grew warmer, his breath becoming more ragged. Not pain, but need. And something else? A faint flicker in his eyes I recognized as fear. Uncertainty. He'd left the decision up to me, but what did he want? This man who had been first tortured then shot because of me. So it was my turn to wait, close enough to feel his shaking breath on my cheek, my hand over his racing heart.

I shifted my hips and pressed myself against him, staying careful of his wound. My answer was *yes*, without hesitation. Now it was his turn.

He edged forward, to the last giving me room to run, but when his lips brushed against mine, all self-restraint between us vanished, and the fire in my veins blazed into an inferno.

I freed my hand from under his shirt and wrapped my fingers around his collar as he curled his into my hair. I rocked my hips to remove any last space, grinding myself deeper into his lap, and he tightened his arm around my waist to pull me against him.

He hissed. I froze.

Desire—his and mine—throbbed between my legs, but I was ready to stop if his body wasn't up for it. His torso shimmered as he dissolved, a strange sensation having him disappear against me, and when he pulled himself back together, his lips found mine once more, giving me no time to question.

The deeper he kissed me, the familiarity of his mouth taking me back to New York and every pleasure I had to look forward to, the more I needed. The clothes between us—the air between us—were obstacles I couldn't stand. We had to move. Go somewhere private. Somewhere we could hide—where our problems wouldn't find us.

He moved with me as I pulled him out of the chair, and I had enough rational thought left to summon the air to cradle his back as I helped him to his feet. He stumbled as he stood, but I caught him without trouble. Again his torso flickered beneath my hands, sending tiny currents over my fingers, and when he returned, more of his pain seemed to have faded. The electricity, however, hadn't. It redirected to every spot where our bodies touched, his one hand stroking my back, the other still wound in my hair. His lean body pressed against mine, all muscle and heat.

My heart fluttered against my ribs, and my breath came quick and shallow, as ragged as his. I tilted my head back and stared into eyes that were nearly black with the depth of a need so rich and pure it set another blaze under my skin.

How long had it been since he'd held me like this?

Who was I kidding? It had never been like this. In New York, we'd been bored with the stakeout or flying with the rush of success. We'd lost ourselves in the roles we'd played, exploring each other as thoroughly as we had the people we hunted.

In this moment, there were no more lies. No cover stories to hide behind. He had nearly died, and my belief in his death had killed something in me. That we were both standing here, breathing, feeling, was a high I had never experienced.

He pulled off my torn cardigan and slid his fingertips under the back of my halter top and along my spine, setting off a series of explosions down my arms and into the pit of my stomach.

He was the one who'd been shot, but under his gentle caress, I nearly lost the ability to stand.

Just when I thought I'd reached my limit, that any extra stimulation would leave me senseless, he bent his head and caught my lips with his. A moan escaped the back of my throat as I wrapped my arms around his neck, making it impossible for him to escape me.

He didn't try. His fingers curled into my stolen shirt so tightly the cheap material tore, and I grabbed hold of the tatters and tugged it over my head. As soon as one barrier between us was out of the way, his lips came back, this time on the crook of my neck where it met my jawline. My eyes rolled back in my head as pleasure trickled through me. My bare stomach brushed against the stiffness of his bloodied T-shirt, and I tucked my hands underneath to ease it off him.

A muffled grunt came through the fabric as Gideon raised

his arms over his head, and I took the opportunity to get a closer look at what remained of his brush with death. The skin was red and puckered, not nearly as healed as he'd let on, though the bleeding seemed to have stopped.

He hooked his finger under my chin and raised my gaze to his. The desire was still there, burning just as hot, but beneath it ran a wave of understanding.

I didn't want him to read me so easily. I didn't want him to know how much his near-death had broken me. I'd sworn never to let anyone get that close. He was fine, he was here, we needed each other. That was enough.

I slid my hand to the back of his neck and pulled him down for another kiss. He wrapped his arms around my waist and squeezed me closer. In his weakened state, he lost his balance and toppled backwards into the wall. The impact shook all the way through me, vibrating every cell in the air and raising my skin into goosebumps.

What the hell were we doing? Under any other circumstances, I'd be taking him to the hospital right now, not to bed. Cold reason swirled through my clouded passion. "Gideon—"

He trapped my mouth with his, shutting me up before I could finish, and reason slipped away again.

My fingers found their way to his belt, and even as I teased his tongue with mine, I unclasped it, leaving it hanging around the waistband of his jeans as I unhooked the button and unzipped him.

The skin of his chest was so warm. Blood and sweat mixed between us, and all I could think was how appropriate it was. We had fought together, survived, and lived to fuck about it afterward.

He nipped my bottom lip and returned his attentions to my neck as he led us backwards down the hallway. I turned us towards my bedroom, the closest room with a door we could lock, but he tugged me farther along, into the bathroom.

I flipped the switch as he closed the door, and then my back was against the wall and his head was bent, trailing hot kisses down my neck, my chest, the tips of his fingers tracing one nipple as his tongue worked the other.

My legs buckled, but he gripped me tight around the waist with his other arm, his chest against my stomach and his dark head buried against me as he teased and taunted, bringing me so close to the edge I was amazed I hadn't already burst.

Finding a nearly forgotten pool of willpower, I pushed him back and spun us around. He grimaced as his back hit the wall, but the corner of his mouth curled into a smile as I kissed him again, venturing on my own exploration.

He tasted so good, like earth and honey, his skin tickling my tongue as I travelled downwards, following the path of clean, bare skin. His fingers wound through my hair, sometimes pushing me away, sometimes pulling me closer, but never hard enough to take control away from me as I reached my knees and pulled down his jeans and the jockeys underneath.

Just a taste, a teaser, as I danced my tongue over the length of him. To my surprise, he tensed, softened, and took me by the elbow to guide me back up.

My joints screamed and the muscles in my legs spasmed as I gained my full height, but I pushed the pain to the back of my mind, too confused by what had just happened. I started to ask what was wrong, but the haunted look on his face, that same glimmer of fear I'd spotted earlier, stole my breath.

He pulled me close, brushed my hair behind my ear, and kissed me. Tentative at first, seeking, exploring, growing more desperate as he hardened against me again. Whatever ghosts chased after him, they must have retreated for now, because he shuffled us towards the shower, his lips leaving mine long enough for him to step out of his jeans and start the water. By the time the spray had warmed, filling the bathroom with steam, I'd removed the rest of my clothes, standing naked and open before this man who made me feel the same.

He drew me carefully into the stall and slid the door closed behind us, shutting out the world.

The water was hot enough that every droplet stung my already sensitive skin, and a fresh warmth rose within me, melting me against Gideon as he edged me back against the cold tile. He was a devil. A demon in the form of a man tempting me to the very edge of myself. I hated him. I needed him. I hated that I needed him, and I knew I would never be everything I wanted to be if he left my side.

My curses left my head and filled the room as he wrapped his hand around my wrist and spun me to face the wall. The brush of cold against my breasts contrasted with the heat of the water on my back, and then Gideon's body replaced the water, a steady warmth instead of the steaming patter of the shower. He kissed my shoulder, kissed the base of my neck, between my shoulder blades.

His touch turned hesitant, gentle, lacking the urgency of a moment ago, and the slowness nearly pushed me to take over. I was always on top. I preferred being the one to set the tempo, call the shots. Gideon knew it. In New York, he'd enjoyed it. But somehow I knew, on an instinctual level, that today the control couldn't be mine. Whatever he had suffered, whatever Carstairs had put him through, he needed to reclaim what had been stolen.

And I trusted him enough to hand over the reins.

The realization left me dizzy, light-headed, and when he set himself against me, thrust himself inside me, the combination of dizziness and pleasure made me see stars.

Not only did I trust Gideon, but I was happy to hand control over to him. To stop fighting. To submit to someone else.

I reached my arm around and hooked his neck, drawing him in to kiss me as he moved inside me, now fast, now slow, but always in a way that anticipated exactly what I needed. Even after all our time apart, he remembered everything I liked, everything that drove me to the brink. And this time, he didn't tease. He reached one hand around and slid his fingers between my legs, working me from all sides.

I felt him smile against my mouth as I lost myself too far even to kiss him, and as the first wave crested, he kept me pressed between him and the wall, his arm tight around me, preventing me from collapsing into a puddle of melted butter on the shower floor.

And just as I caught my breath, he started again, not giving me any time to regain my senses until long after the water had run cold.

Chapter 26

Madison

BY NINE O'CLOCK, the Elgin Street Diner was packed with students either satisfying their poutine cravings or trying to load up on calories before they kicked off their bar hop. I'd been here for a while already, having felt too wired after my meeting with Lilith to return to the safe house but too leery about being spotted by anyone I knew to stay out in the open. I'd kept the server busy with endless orders of diet pop and fries while I waited, so hadn't earned too much ill will by hiding out here.

Except maybe my growing ill will for French fries.

As the time passed, the hour getting later, I had nothing to do but think about that ever-ticking clock, each second counting down until I had to say goodbye to my life of service and cross the wall into a life of servitude.

I prayed Serc had some good news for me when he

arrived—the queen had changed her mind and wanted to use my position on this side of the wall to her advantage; she'd decided she didn't want my dour face moping around court for the next century—but I couldn't cling to hope. She'd made it clear in the past couple of days that my time as a SMOAC employee was coming to an end.

As I sat here, the world around me shimmered with memories of the meadow where Meril had dragged my unconscious mind. The vivid hues of the flowers, the sweetness of the breeze. A promise of the world that awaited me beyond the wall; the honey to sweeten the bitterness of what I was losing.

My fingers tightened around my cup, and I took a sip, hoping the fizziness of the pop would settle my nerves. It didn't.

To distract myself, I turned my gaze out the window. The sun hadn't set too long ago, daylight leaching out of the sky, but the heat had started to die down and a hint of dark cloud lurked in the distance, threatening rain. The sidewalks were full of people heading to the bars, grabbing late-night dinner, going home. All the daily inanities I never thought I'd miss.

I had spent my entire afternoon going from coffee shop to coffee shop, leaving messages with the mermaids in the Rideau Canal and the treekins along the Rideau River. While I sat here, my cold fries being swapped out with fresh ones, my drink replaced, the students leaving and the thirty-somethings coming in for a snack before calling it a night, my phone remained silent on the table, no one responding to my requests for a chat.

I also hadn't heard from Jet since her phone call. I'd texted her when I'd left the apartment and again when I'd reached the diner, and so far hadn't heard back. If she'd gotten my messages, she had to be curious. If not anxious. I'd been vague in case someone intercepted my messages—I couldn't put Lilith or Sercario in danger like that—but knew how it sounded and hoped Jet trusted me enough not to panic too much.

That would probably come later, when I explained why I was rounding up soldiers. When I told her that soon enough she'd have to move forward without me. I prayed she'd be all right, that being back on Michael's team, having him and Eric at her side, would make my absence less of a blow.

Even so, Meril's timing couldn't have been worse.

Before I crossed the wall, Jet and I would have to talk about Gideon, no matter how hard she tried to put me off. Although I barely knew him, my heart broke at the thought that he was gone. He'd carried a soul so deep I'd barely scratched the surface of it. He'd lied to my friend time and again, but he'd also shown himself to be brave, kind, patient. His moral compass might have been skewed, but at least he'd had one, and from what I'd seen, it had usually led him along a path of lighter grey.

No wonder Jet had been drawn to him, though she'd argue with me if I ever suggested it.

Even though I wanted to help her through her grief, I accepted I would do more good working to discover the mole, and right now, that meant gathering allies. Lilith and her team would be a huge asset, but more than a dozen groups in this city had a stake in ensuring the wall—and their secrets—held. Groups that had established themselves pre-SMOAC and who thrived on their independence. Groups that, for the most part, were difficult to track down.

If they wouldn't listen to me, I hoped I could convince Serc to talk to them on my behalf. They had to know I wouldn't reach out to them lightly. Although they lived on this side of the wall, they'd sworn off our world as completely as many of them had sworn off life in the realm. They thought nothing of the department and even less of the mundanes. All they wanted was to be left alone to survive in this ever-changing world. So far, many of them had succeeded, but would that continue to be the case if O'Malley and his associates triggered a civil war?

The threat might not be enough to get them to sit down and negotiate, but I had to try. It was what I knew best, the only help I had to offer in the time I had left.

I sank deep into my thoughts, spinning scenarios first in one direction, then another, working to see each possibility from every angle. I tried to decide how much I would weave into my story for the mermaids, and how it would differ from the situation I laid out for the trolls. I didn't expect the vampires at all. They had their own issues, their own hierarchies, and their own ways of dealing with things. Frankly, as long as they stayed out of our way, I'd be happy.

My imaginary arguments carried my mind so far out of

the diner that when the server came to check on me, I was surprised to find the moon had risen, the soft blue light spilling across the street. My fries were cold again, my drink flat, and the thirty-somethings had mostly cleared out, replaced by an older crowd—the ones who had finished their late-shifts and were looking for a wind-down snack before going home.

A glance at my phone showed it was almost midnight. Still no reply from Jet, which made me worry, but I didn't have time to run to the apartment to see if she was all right. My appointment was due any minute.

Right on time, the door opened, and my great-uncle walked in.

I ordered another plate of fries and two coffees, and the server left with a nod, shooting a curious glance in Sercario's direction. His interest wasn't surprising. To mundane eyes, my grandmother's brother looked normal enough with his short steel-grey hair that matched his sharp steel-grey eyes, but there was no denying the aura around him. Skeptics would say he had presence; believers would say his energy packed a punch. I would say he was a man who had earned a prominent position on the queen's Shadow Council and had the power to show for it. He was everything I could aspire to be if I wanted to. Everything I had avoided my entire life.

I rose to greet him, kissing his cheek and pressing my hand to my heart. His movements mirrored mine, and we settled at the table as the server brought our food.

Serc raised an eyebrow at me, and I shrugged. "If my access to delicious, greasy food is about to be cut off, I'm taking advantage of it."

"You don't have to be so melodramatic, Madi," he said, picking up a fry and biting off the end. "I could bring you fries." He set the other half on the corner of the plate and folded his hands on the table. "Have you spoken to your grandmother?"

I grimaced and shook my head. "I'm still hoping to find a way out of this. Spare Nan that pain."

"Madi, you—"

"I know." I lifted my gaze to his. "No luck on your end, then?"

The sympathy in his eyes was answer enough. "She didn't say anything, but she didn't need to. She's not pleased. Don't be surprised if she loses patience with me and sends her Eyes to find you."

I shuddered. Her watchers on this side of the wall could be anyone and anywhere. Unless I stayed at the safe house, caging myself inside, I'd never escape her.

"Thanks for buying me the time you did." I tried to sound grateful, but it came out defeated.

He finished his fry. "Did you have any luck today?"

"Lilith stands ready to help if we need a strong arm."

Serc blinked. "That's brave. Her Majesty won't appreciate her soldiers marching to someone else's command. She might see it as an act of treason. Which wouldn't turn out well for you *or* Lilith."

"Lil knows that." I did my best to stifle the tingle of irritation that buzzed through me. "She's stepped back from the front lines, but has offered her people as reinforcements. She knows what she stands to lose if SMOAC falls."

I didn't mean it to come out as an accusation that Serc wasn't taking me seriously, but when he froze, a subtle change for a man of subtleties, I knew my comment had landed. I tried to read his emotions, but a thick wall lay draped around him—the kind only an expert empath knew how to conjure. Had he raised it for my benefit, to stop me from prying, or had the guard become such a regular feature for him at court he no longer noticed it?

Those sorts of walls left me numb, cut off from the world. But then, out here I was surrounded by mundanes who didn't know how to read me, so the necessity of barriers that strong was low. Once I was trapped in Meril's circle, I would need to learn to protect myself from the political moves at play.

My stomach turned again, and I swallowed hard. Vomiting all over my uncle wouldn't solve my problems.

"What is going on here, Madi?" Serc asked, leaning forward. "You've been vague on the phone—as you should be—but what have you learned? Why are you so sure the department is in trouble?"

I sipped my coffee, grimaced, added sugar, then began at the beginning. I shared more than I'd revealed to Lilith, telling him about Jet, the attacks, Gideon. While Serc was the queen's man, he was also family. My grandmother would flay him alive if he passed anything along to the queen without my permission.

By the time I got to the part about the paper trail and Gideon's death, Serc had gone a little green about the gills. It was one thing to suspect what was coming, but another to have the truth laid out in front of you.

It was strangely validating to know more than he did for once in my life. My research would carry a lot of weight in whatever battle he helped wage against the syndicate—a battle I wouldn't be able to fight myself once I was gone. I wasn't asking him to do all the heavy lifting. Only to finish it.

"You see why we need to do something, uncle. With time, Jet and I might have brought this further along, but I can't ask her to do it alone." I tasted the bitterness of betrayal as I added, "I don't think she could if she tried. Not against the Ghost-maker *and* O'Malley *and* a government connection we haven't identified. She'll need help."

Serc hadn't uttered a single word as I'd brought him up to speed. He hadn't even moved, his hands clasped on the table in front of him as though he were a judge about to pass sentence. A role he'd served on the queen's council for decades.

"How soon do you need this help?"

Tears pricked the corners of my eyes. I'd been braced for an argument or to be told I was way off base. To have him be so quick to offer assistance was a balm to my fractured soul.

I tucked my hair behind my ear, gaining a moment to compose myself. "I don't know. If we move against O'Malley before we've pinpointed the mole, the people involved will scatter. The more information we have before we act, the better our chances of success. I think shooting Gideon was a mistake on their part. It's only a matter of time before his organization comes sniffing around and someone has to scramble to cover up what happened. He was an unexpected player, and his death might flush these guys out. That's a big might, though. And there's no guarantee it will happen before they enter the next stage of their plan."

Serc pressed his lips together, his brow furrowed.

I swallowed again, working up the courage to ask, "Will you help me reach out to the independents? If we form an alliance here, on this side of the wall, Jet stands a better chance of shutting their operation down before any extreme measures are required by the queen."

Before I'm forced to go.

The look Serc gave me told me he heard my unspoken addition.

"I might be able to convince them to listen," he said, answering one question. He paused, then answered the other. "Regardless, she'll want to know about this. All of it."

I'd been afraid he'd say that. While he wouldn't breathe a word to Meril without my say-so, he would stare at me with those steely eyes until I saw reason. And he wasn't wrong. If

Jet—and I had to assume I wouldn't be here to help—failed, the trouble would run over the wall, and Meril would raze this country to the ground before she let her corner of the realm be destroyed.

"I will," I said. "I won't turn my back on you, uncle. Not when you've gone to such lengths for me already." My shoulders slumped. "I just—"

"You have decisions to make," he said, nodding. "Ties to sever. Trust me, Madi, I understand. I think Meril is being stubborn, but one can't argue with the queen. Use the time you have left. Do what you need to do."

As though it were that simple. He said he understood, but he'd returned to court with his father when he was seven years old. What did he know about severing ties? It had been Nan's choice to stay behind with their mother on this side of the wall.

My heart clenched. Nan. If I didn't prevent this war, she might also be forced to return to the world she'd avoided. If I succeeded, I would be trapped in the queen's court, unable to return to my family without ever having a chance to see them again.

At least I knew Serc would act as messenger to make sure I didn't go without her special tea blend. Small consolation, but more than I'd find anywhere else.

With nothing more to say, I nodded and ate a French fry. They'd cooled again over the course of my story, but the greasiness was a comfort in light of the weight on my shoulders.

"No matter what happens, you know I'll do what I can to help," he said, and I raised my chin to give him a grateful, if exhausted, smile. "Tell me what you need."

"Lilith can provide the weapons, but we'll need more than a dozen soldiers to ensure justice is served. We need troops, if you have them. People to help us contain the situation so it doesn't spill into the mundane news. Clean-up crew once it's done. What we need is an edge, whatever it takes to get in their way at every turn. They've spent so long being one step ahead of us. I want to take them by surprise and annihilate them."

Anger burned deep in my soul—at O'Malley, the mole, Meril. I channelled it towards the shadows we were chasing, when really, given the chance, I longed to destroy anyone who tried to steal my freedom.

Yet again, Serc seemed to read my thoughts. "Maybe it would be better not to point this out, but it's possible you might use your situation to your advantage. Not against the syndicate, but with the queen."

My mouth went dry as I stared at him, but he held up a hand to fend off my bubbling questions. "I make no promises. Her Majesty needs good advisers, and she will likely see your instalment on the Shadow Council as her wisest move, but she needs the problem here cleaned up by competent people more than she needs more bodies around her table."

I snorted, a most uncourtly sound. "Why, when she could barrel over the department and the syndicate with a snap of her fingers?"

Serc tilted his head. His brow creased and then smoothed as awareness filled his eyes. "You give her more power than she has. She's limited by the wall you refuse to cross. If she moves, there are no half-measures, and the consequences of the fall would be so much greater than the effects on one city—one country. You think she'd revel in such a change, but the balance is as important to her as it is to the department."

This surprised me. "I thought she was biding her time, looking for a reason to regain control. That's how she made it sound when she spoke with me."

"Despite what you seem to think, she cares about her people, Madi. On both sides of the wall. She knows how many would die if she were pushed to respond with force." He reached for my hand, his fingers warm, his skin dry. A rock in the flood threatening to sweep me away. His gaze was gentle as it met mine, but full of the weight of his truth. "You two have the same goal, and you can still play a role in reaching it, but the longer you wait to go to her with what you know, and the larger this problem becomes, the more a quiet solution slips out of her hands. If it comes to war, if the barriers we've built around us crumble, the whole world burns, and the magic we seek to protect, and everyone and everything connected to it, will perish."

Chapter 27

Gideon

OR A MAN who'd recently survived a shot to the heart, I felt pretty fantastic.

Sure, my insides were on fire, and every time I raised my left arm I had to wait for the nausea to pass, but for now, the pain was secondary to the buttery looseness of my joints and the warmth of the naked body pressed against me.

I nuzzled my nose into Jet's hair, the spot behind her ear that trailed down to her neck. Her contented murmur at the contact made me smile, and I slid my arm tighter around her, closing the gaps between us.

From the moment I'd taken her in the shower, I hadn't been able to stop. The rush of being alive to experience the feel of her again made up for every twinge and spasm. Every time she'd hit her climax, my desire had increased. So we'd moved from sex to sleep and back again, pausing only to give me a few minutes to heal, both of us needing more and neither ready to turn our thoughts to reality.

She was exhausted, I was beyond tired, but even now I was inside her, moving slowly, barely moving at all. I slid my hand between her legs. Her sleepy mew spurred me on, and I kept teasing, as slow and gentle as my self-control allowed me to be.

My own pleasure built, a tightening deep within me that crept up my back and through my stomach. I held on as long as I could, but the second Jet's body shuddered with release, a shiver that ran from the base of her neck down to her calves, I let go, squeezing her so tightly that for a few rapid heartbeats we were no longer two people.

As soon as her shivers eased—taking far longer than mine—she relaxed into me, every angle, curve, and valley fitting so perfectly she may as well have been made for me.

I hadn't realized how much I'd missed her.

What we'd had in New York had been so much more than the bedroom romps, though those had been pretty amazing. Working with her again, I'd enjoyed the same rush, but here, with no one else in the room and no guns pointed at our heads, I remembered how strange it was to be able to… breathe. My guard was as low as I knew how to make it. If we could have stayed here forever, me inside her, both of us safe, I would have willingly given up everything else.

Considering how thoroughly I'd broken the second of Dark Wire's restrictions for my time here, I might have already done so. We could safely say I'd thrown any professional relationship with Jet out the window. Again.

But the briefness of our peace made itself known as the muscles in Jet's back tensed. Every ridge of her hardened against my chest, and the result was a similar reaction in my own. I winced as my gut flexed, the flesh around the bullet hole refusing to cooperate with my attempts to heal it.

Although I didn't want to lose even a moment of contact with her, I closed my eyes and misted from neck to navel, willing the tissue and muscle and bone to knit themselves together as I brought myself back. The effort left me queasy, and I drew in a few slow breaths until I was sure I wouldn't throw up.

Jet shifted in my arms, and I was prepared to let her go if she wanted to leave, but to my surprise, she didn't jump out of bed, eager to return to her planning. Instead, she rolled to face me and smoothed out the pillow between us. Her distracted gaze scanned my body, and her brow furrowed when her attention stopped at my wound.

I wished I'd gotten myself into a better state before she'd found me. She didn't need to worry about me when she should be concentrating on looking after herself.

Her fingertips trailed over my skin, her touch having the same effect on me now as it first had so many hours ago. I did my best not to think of where I wanted her exploration to end up and said nothing as she circled what was now a fresh, obviously bullet-shaped scar, her touch light enough that I felt it more as an electrical current than physical contact.

"Does it still hurt?" she asked.

It was the first non-sexually explicit thing she'd said to me all night, but the drowsy concern in her voice made me want to kiss her all the more. I compromised by pressing my lips into her hair as I stroked the smooth skin on her back.

"Like a son of a bitch," I admitted. "But it's getting better."

Her gaze rolled up to meet mine, and the guilt I found there pinched my heart. "Earlier," she said. "In the bathroom. When I—when you—"

My lungs closed on air, choking me, and my skin rippled until it felt like I was rising out of my body. I didn't want to talk about that. Didn't want to think about it.

But when I didn't answer, Jet didn't let it drop. "It's because of what happened, isn't it? What Carstairs—"

"Stop," I said, aiming for firm but gentle, though I suspected I'd missed the mark. The sound of his name sent bugs crawling through my veins. Even as Jet had landed in my lap, her fingers under my shirt, his face, his leer, his voice had haunted me. Taunted me. I'd had to work to keep him out of my head, only able to block him when I had Jet in sight.

She needed to know my reaction hadn't been because of her. I would have preferred to bury my fear and deal with it later, but I didn't want her thinking my response was because of anything she had done.

"You know some of what he did to me," I said, struggling

with every word, "but the knife wounds, the lashes… they were the least of it." I ground my teeth together, and pain spiked from my jaw into my skull. Jet shifted again to look at me, but I couldn't look back, terrified to find pity in her eyes. "He twisted my mind. Small nicks hurting like he'd impaled me, deep stabs filling me with ecstasy. Pain and pleasure, to the height of both. He wanted me to know nothing about my body was my own anymore. Anything he wanted me to feel, and all it would take was a flick of his ability." I shuddered and had to swallow hard to get the rest out. The important part. "Earlier, with you, I—"

"Hey." Her turn to interrupt. "You don't need to say anything else."

"No, I do." I eased onto my side and finally worked up the courage to look at her. The pity was there, and so was the guilt, but no judgement. No disgust. "Being with you gave me a chance to prove he doesn't control me. To remember you were there before he was. He may have had his fun, but he lost me, and he won't get another turn."

Jet closed her eyes, and when she opened them, she revealed a well of unshed tears. "I'm so sorry," she said. "I never should have let them take you away. I should have kept a closer eye on what they did with you. Followed up. None of this should have happened."

I brushed her hair behind her ear and kissed her forehead, the gesture not nearly enough. I wanted to bundle her against me and help put our pieces together, but worried the effort would crack whatever strength I was pretending to have. I caught her eye again. "You have nothing to apologize for, you hear me? This isn't on you. We all made decisions, and we're not done yet. You can't hold yourself responsible. For me. For Sampson. For anyone."

"You could be done. You could call it a day. Go home." I heard the sincerity in her voice, the hint of hope that I would take her up on the suggestion and protect myself. There was something to it. How much help would I be as I healed? All I had to do was call Dark Wire, and as soon as they learned what happened, they would order me back without hesitation. My remaining three-day grace period gone. Twice now I'd gone above and beyond what the mission required, for the second time in my career hanging everything on the line for this woman. Risking everything.

It would be so easy to set things right by SilverGuard.

I couldn't do it.

Beneath Jet's sincerity, I heard her desperation. She had me and she had Madison, not only to act as reinforcements but to help her hang on to her strength, her sanity, and there was no way I would leave her.

"I'm not going anywhere. Not until we drive that final nail into O'Malley's coffin."

Jet blinked her tears away and shifted so the front of her thigh pressed against mine. She didn't have to touch me. The bed was wide enough that she could have pulled away and lain comfortably. The fact that she seemed to need the contact as much as I did warmed every cold corner of my heart, and I guided my hand down her leg, pulling it over me so it rested on my hip.

"I hate this," she said. "I hate that I don't know who to turn to. That people who once turned to me no longer do. Michael says he knows how big this is, but does he? The way he talks about it, the way Eric tried to explain it, it still seems like they're only seeing half the picture. Part of me wants to have faith in them, the evidence Michael sent me to find reinforces his theory… but something feels off."

Michael had sent her after evidence? Clearly I'd missed a lot in the hours I'd been gone, but we had time now for her to catch me up. Time I never thought I'd get.

"What do you think it is?"

She dropped her gaze, and the furrow on her brow that had begun to disappear returned. The change lengthened the faint, scar-like traces of her third eye, transforming the pupil into a vertical slit, like a suspicious snake eye staring out at me.

"Eric says the inconsistencies Madi found in the paperwork are linked to some guinea pig secret project the deputy minister is running."

I flinched at her reference to her lieutenant, imagining them discussing the situation after the bastard had shot me, and swallowed the acid creeping up the back of my throat. He was her second-in-command. Of course she wouldn't cut him out of her life because of what he'd done.

But there was a tension in her voice at the mention of his name that told me they hadn't left things on the best of terms, and a small thrill of satisfaction fizzed through me.

"Michael said the same thing," she continued. "Testing to see if this third-party organization could take some weight off the department's resources. He says he knows there's a mole, but that the mole is connected only to O'Malley, and O'Malley is connected only to the drugs. He sent me to the minister's office, and I found a signed authorization form to ship what's likely ghost over the border into New York."

I stiffened, cringed, forced myself to relax, and Jet nodded. "I know. Exactly the proof you were looking for. And it might be true, something you can take back to SilverGuard to prevent the shipment from landing, but I don't know. There are too many unanswered questions. Did the minister actually sign the authorization? Was it his signature on all those couldn't-be-him documents, or is it Madi's wishful thinking that someone forged them? If he didn't sign them, then this has to be bigger than drugs, right?"

Her furrow deepened, and the snake eye narrowed, becoming more hostile. I waited for her to lead me down whatever rabbit hole she'd fallen into, but she'd zoned out, and by the darkening expression in her eyes, not to any happy place.

"What's going on in there?" I asked, gently tapping her forehead above her third eye. Now was not the time to be travelling alone when nightmares waited to pounce at every turn—even in her mind.

She drew her eyes up to meet mine, and though the furrow eased, her expression remained troubled.

"Is Michael right? He says the department's overreached itself. That its usefulness as it was is finished, which is why the syndicate was able to gain so much power over the last couple years."

"Is it so wild to think your mandate needs an update? Everything changes, Jet."

"Sure," she said, "but changes so much we need to bring in some out-of-country third party to look after our people so we can maintain law and order? SMOAC's purpose is so much greater than protecting our people from being outed—it should protect them in all ways. Services, resources. Otherwise, what's the point of there being a divide? We'd be better off across the wall."

I stroked her hair behind her ear. "You don't really believe that."

"No, I believe in SMOAC."

"Then what does it matter what Michael thinks? Prove him wrong. Uncover the mole, destroy the syndicate, free up the department to put its focus elsewhere. Exactly what you've been doing."

She huffed a laugh, and the corners of her eyes crinkled. "Not daunting at all, is it?"

I planted another kiss on her forehead. "We'll get there, Jet. We're closer now than we were."

Her faint smile faded, overpowered by fatigue. "Are we? From the start, O'Malley's kept his people ten steps ahead, and now…" Her frown returned.

"What is it?"

"Now it's like the department is ten steps ahead of me, too."

"What do you mean?"

"Just…" She raised her shoulder in an uncertain shrug. "Don't you find it all a little coincidental?"

I smirked. "You know I don't believe in coincidences, so you're going to have to be a little more specific."

"Twice we've gone after Dougall, and twice someone has been there to stop me from catching him—but only after he's planted his bombs."

I tried to follow the path her thoughts had taken, but it escaped me. "The first time, at his house, they got a call from him asking for help, obviously some kind of lure so he could launch another ghostbomb, right? In the parking garage, Sampson followed you."

"He didn't though," she said. "I followed Dougall through the side door. Eric accessed the garage from somewhere else. Almost like he knew where Dougall would be. And when they found us, they focused on *me*, not on Dougall. Every time I get close to him, someone gets in my way."

"Or you get in theirs."

Jet grunted in frustration and rolled away from me, but I looped my arm around her waist to stop her from getting too far.

"I'm not arguing with you," I said, my lips brushing her ear as I hugged her against me. Her hips fit so well against mine, but although my body responded, I ignored the rush of longing. "I'm trying to see what you do."

She resisted for a moment, then yielded, and her fingers played with the back of my hand, ran over the muscles of my forearm.

"I don't *know*," she said, "and that's what's so goddamn infuriating. Because you're right. At every point, we could be getting in each other's way. If that's the case, then if I stepped aside, the team could sort this out without any obstruction."

The team, I noted, not *her* team. It was the first time she'd disconnected herself from them, and it worried me. Up until now, fighting for them had been her greatest motivator. What did it mean if she no longer felt attached to her people?

"But if they have been hunting him," she went on, "why haven't they caught him yet? Why do they only get close to Dougall when I do? I'm tired of all these might-be coincidences, especially when people keep getting hurt. Task force orders come from somewhere, and whoever's giving them has to know more than they're letting on."

She huffed again and fell silent, and there was nothing more for me to say.

Two days ago, I was afraid to touch this woman, her fury

pushing me to keep my distance. Now it was nothing to slip my other arm around her and pull her closer, holding her against me, her dark thoughts the only barrier between us. She was aloof, not completely in the room, but the detachment didn't stop me. Was it my recent brush with death that made me realize I would happily brave her anger to be close to her again? When this was over, there would be a lot to talk about. Explanations and apologies, maybe goodbyes, but all of that seemed so far in the future. For now, we lived in this bubble of truce where our history didn't matter, and I wanted to stay here as long as possible.

She nestled into me, the warmth of her body contrasting against the cooler summer night. Sweat tickled the back of my neck, but a breeze came in through the open window and stole it away. The air smelled sweet, touched with food from the collection of restaurants on the corner across the street, and my stomach grumbled. The first thought I'd given to food in hours.

Jet must have heard it, because she rolled her head to face me. "Hungry?"

"Always," I said, and bent my head to kiss her, the taste of her stirring my desire for the umpteenth time that night.

She smiled against my kiss and pulled away. "At this rate, you won't have the strength to heal yourself before tomorrow."

I focused on my chest and misted away, but drawing myself back took more effort than it had since I'd returned to the safe house. "You do more for me than food."

Amusement danced in her eyes. "I never took you for such a romantic."

Neither had I. "Me? I'm a regular Romeo."

She raised her head to kiss me again, a quick, darting nip. "Well, I'm no Juliet. For starters, I'm of legal age. Come on, let's see what we can raid from the cupboards."

I didn't want to let her go. Right here, we were safe from anything the world might throw at us. It didn't matter if that safety was an illusion, that at any moment someone might track us down and have an easy time getting rid of us, as unprotected as we were. But she was already pulling away. She moved slowly enough that I wondered if she wanted me to stop her, so I did. I took hold of her wrist as she sat up, and when she looked over her shoulder, the light glinting in her dark eyes, I eased myself up and caught her lips with mine. She melted against my mouth but kept enough distance that I didn't pull her back down. I released my grip and shoved away the slight pang of loss as she broke contact. Her small smile washed over me like the warmest rays of the sun.

I collapsed against the pillows and enjoyed the show as she pulled on a pair of underwear and grabbed one of my white T-shirts from the chair in the corner. She slid it over her head so the hem dropped below her butt and tugged her thick hair free so it fell in raven waves just below her shoulders.

Gods, she's beautiful.

She quirked her eyebrow at me, and I winked at her. I was

fine. Just needed a minute to pull myself together before I made any attempt to stand. She chuckled, left the room, and closed the door behind her.

I groaned as I sagged into the mattress. Exhaustion tugged me towards oblivion even as my body left me in an uncomfortable state of want, but I fought against both. Right now, Jet needed me to be strong, and I was determined to be there for her. She was right that I had to heal, and food would be a good start. Then I could grab a few hours of solid sleep.

As for the rest, there would be loads of time for us to pick up where we left off once we wiped out the syndicate.

My chest strained as I rolled myself out of bed and bent over to grab my jockeys, the pain nowhere near as agonizing as it had been. Less like I was about to be split in two and more like someone had driven a knife between my ribs. An improvement, if still a problem. I glanced at the scarring tissue. No more blood or seepage. It had finally sealed. I would be fine. I would make sure of it.

Never had I been more motivated to make sure Jet survived this fight. It was the only way I could find out what came next.

Chapter 28

Jet

I KNEW I should get dressed. If we needed to make another quick getaway, I would waste precious minutes putting on pants or risk gaining all kinds of unwanted attention on the street.

Not to mention the questions Madison would ask if she strolled through the door and found me standing half-naked in the kitchen.

But however much practicality begged me to change, I didn't want to lose the way Gideon had stared at me on my way out the door. As though he'd unravelled. I'd been willing to let him take over for most of the night—guilt and horror screamed in the back of my mind over why he'd needed to reclaim his power—but it felt good to regain some balance. Even if it was a pretense. I'd honestly thought I was over him, but he'd left me undone.

My pulse raced at the memory of his brown eyes going dark, the same eyes that had stared at me as though I were a fresh-made chocolate cake for the past eight hours. Heat pulsed between my legs, and I opened the refrigerator to cool my flushed skin. Somehow I had to dredge up what remained of my self-control before I gave up on food and returned to bed to forget reality for another few hours.

Get a grip, Jet.

Here we were in the middle of a national crisis, and I was acting like a hormonally charged teenager. Madison would probably say it was normal, a way to vent my stress and ground myself in something positive.

A dangerous distraction.

I'd let my emotions get in the way when I'd told Gideon to go home. I'd meant what I'd said, but his pause had been telling. He'd read between the lines, heard my fear that he would leave. That was on me. I had to be firmer with him. Yes, we wanted him—*I want him*—to stay, but we would have to make do without him. He was in no shape to fight, so he would do more good by going back to New York, talking to his handler, and preparing for the worst if Madison and I failed.

And until he left, there couldn't be anything more between us. I had to keep my eye on the target, and that target couldn't be him.

I swore it to myself, but my resolution threatened to evaporate when the bedroom door opened and Gideon stepped out. A clean white T-shirt covered his healing wound, a pair of black Jockey shorts hugged his hips and left not much else to the imagination, and his leather bracelet squeezed his wrist. As though he hadn't been shot and risen from the dead. As though he'd just rolled out of bed, his dark hair mussed and the stubble on his jawline a touch longer than he usually left it.

I wanted him as much now as I had two years ago, and damn everything that made having him so fucking complicated.

"Sandwich?" I asked, gesturing to the contents of the fridge.

His eyes twinkled and the corner of his mouth curled upwards. "You offering? I would never dream of asking."

I tried to hide my smile as I flipped him off and set to work with mustard, mayo, and deli meat.

"What are these?" he asked, and I glanced over my shoulder to find two phones sitting on the counter that I hadn't noticed on my way by. "There's a note from Madison. *New phones.*"

"I told you the woman always thinks ahead. She must have gotten two sets in case one was compromised. Considering the recruit who almost shot me swiped mine and I had to give the number to Michael, I'd say she's right."

Gideon pulled his phone out of his pocket, threw it in the trash, and turned on one of the new ones. "She already programmed the numbers."

"Of course. The woman is nothing if not thorough."

I returned my attention to the knife in my hand, then brought two plates over to the island. My first bite was as sweet as ambrosia after so many emotional—and physical—ups and downs.

"Not bad," Gideon said around a mouthful. "Never would have pegged you as handy in the kitchen."

"You've now experienced my full range, and it doesn't happen often."

Silence fell between us, as comfortable as if we'd eaten midnight snacks together every night for years, and I forced myself to concentrate on my food. Sandwiches were simple. They didn't come with years of baggage or questions about tomorrow. They were all about the delicious, nutritious now.

Fortunately, Gideon must have had the same reluctance to talk about what the past few hours meant because he kept to himself, wiping mayo off the corner of his mouth with the side of his thumb.

When he wavered on his feet, nearly dropping his plate, he nodded towards the dining table. I followed his lead, careful not to upset any more of Madison's papers as I sat down.

"Any word from our resident bureaucrat?" he asked.

"No. Not since her text." I searched the room for my old phone and spotted it on the edge of the kitchen island. It had been a few hours since I'd checked it, but when I got up to grab it, there were no new messages from Madison. Only a text from Travis saying he'd picked up the car, another would be available if I needed it, and the bill was waiting for me at the garage.

At least he hadn't cut me out altogether.

"I hope she's all right," I said.

"Do you know what she's doing?"

"She said something about finding allies?" I shook my head. "I have no idea." To be fair, I hadn't given it much thought, having been distracted first by the suspected intruder in our apartment and then by the hours of I'm-happy-you're-not-dead sex. But even now, when the intruder had been identified and my lust temporarily sated, I couldn't figure out what she might have meant.

Gideon frowned. "She's only thinking about allies now? I thought she had no one else to call in."

I chewed the inside of my cheek. "That's what has me worried. She doesn't. Not unless she wants to risk the queen hearing what we're up to. She also said we need to talk."

"Is she breaking up with you?"

"Seems like pretty shit timing, doesn't it?"

The banter was so easy, so natural. As though finding each other in the bedroom had put us in sync everywhere else.

He still has to go.

I couldn't lose sight of what was important—safeguarding as many aspects of my life as possible.

"Can you call her?" he asked.

I checked the time on my phone, surprised to discover it was closing in on three-thirty in the morning. I didn't want to take the chance that a phone call might interrupt something important, but I replied to her text with a quick HOME NOW. READY TO TALK WHEN YOU ARE. No details, nothing to give anything away. Enough to let her know I was alive and wanting to make sure the same was true of her.

I had to have faith she was all right and that she knew what she was doing. But after what had almost happened when Dougall got his hands on her, I was concerned. Despite my attempt at a chill message and my determination to stay positive, my patience strained when thirty seconds passed without a reply.

"This is such a mess," I said as I dropped my head into my cupped hand. "I feel like we've been boxed into a corner. All I want to do is barge into The Afterlife and force O'Malley to talk. All this sneaking around, putting pieces together when we don't know the picture…" I snorted a bitter laugh. "Eric says I'm combining pieces from two different puzzles. That there's the syndicate and the drugs, and then there's this secret project with the FoSA group. Is he right? Have we ever been on the right trail, or did we veer off the path ten suspicions ago?"

Gideon didn't answer, but I hadn't expected him to. What was there to say?

I finished my sandwich, and as I set my plate aside, my elbow struck the papers closest to me, toppling the organized stack.

"Shit, shit, shit." I jumped to my feet and tried to put them back in order before more of them got mixed up in the pile. Madison had been so particular about how she'd laid everything out, and here I was, undoing so many hours of work. "Was it by date? But there was something about two dates. Did she have them by date stamp or digital mark?"

"Jet, relax," Gideon said, rising from his chair and grabbing my plate along with his. "If one stack is out of order, you can help Madison sort it out when she gets home. This is not a crisis."

He was right. I was losing my mind over blips. Somehow it seemed easier than losing my mind over the more serious issue, which was still too big for me to see.

I sank into my chair and flipped through the pages one at a time, hoping to find Madison's pattern and at the very least cleaning up my mess.

Water ran in the kitchen as Gideon scrubbed the dishes. "Anything interesting?" he asked over his shoulder.

"Not to me. Madi has a better grasp on this side of things. It's all political bullshit. Suits spinning their stories to get what they want. Some more than most, obviously."

"I never took you for a cynic."

"Careful, Leigh, your lies are slipping," I said, but the accusation carried no heat, none of the bitterness of old grudges. Had I actually forgiven the bastard? Hard to say if his near-death had wiped the slate clean or if the high of finding him alive just hadn't worn off yet.

He returned with two bottles of beer, already opened. I glanced at him, and he tapped his bottle against mine in a silent toast before returning to his seat.

"So if Madison has some surprise allies up her sleeve, what about you? Anyone you haven't thought of yet?"

I stretched my arms out in front of me to crack my back.

"I'm tapped out. We've contacted every person on my list, which covers most bases across the city. As you know, only one agreed to keep in touch. I like to think he would have called if he'd heard anything else, and if he hasn't, then the people we're looking for must be great at keeping their mouths shut."

"And have all the resources they need."

I nodded. "A full in-house play. If Madi doesn't have any luck, we can only cross our fingers Michael is able to do something with that shipping authorization. His reach is wider than mine."

I flipped through a few documents, more to give my hands something to do than out of actual interest, and sipped my drink. The beer was cold as it slid down my throat, but I nearly choked on it when I noticed a name among one of the annexes I was browsing.

"Michael?"

I set my beer down and brought the full document closer.

"What is it?" Gideon asked, but I was barely aware of him.

The funding document in my hand was for a project proposal my commander had worked on almost a year ago—a new task force surveillance unit. For the most part, our special forces took on more of an enforcement role. Once in a while, we were called on to provide a security detail for high-risk situations, but typically our local security office handled the day-to-day. As soon as the Kingston rumour had reached us, however, Michael took the stand that we needed to be more proactive. Anything to help cage O'Malley. His proposal had been approved, and a new training program had been funded.

The project had closed down after three months due to budget cuts.

"Jet?"

"It's nothing," I said, though I couldn't take my eyes off the proposal. "I remember Michael's reaction to this project being cancelled. No one could bring it up without him going off on a twenty-minute rant about short-sighted bureaucratic bullshit. I'd never seen him so angry."

The memory evoked a smile until I remembered his rage in the car over our current situation. Back when this project had ended, I'd been able to calm him down before his ability to suppress kinetic energy had left everyone close to him rooted to the floor, unable to bat an eyelash. Now he was hesitant to listen when I talked about the danger he was in.

How far we've come.

"It wasn't the first time one of our projects got canned, but this was a big one."

I made to return the document to the stack when the one beneath it caught my attention. A briefing note about the rising cost of security measures around the office building. Another one of ours. Our chief security officer had concerns about one of the elevator shafts being used by flight-abled supernaturals to make their way to the SMOAC floors. They'd requested funding to purchase high-pitched frequency alarms that would mess with any intruder's perception and render them flightless. The request had sped through approvals until the powers that be had done an about-face and rejected it.

I flipped through a few other notes until I found a third one with Michael's name on it. An updated report on a project that used local supernatural community centres to recruit and train new soldiers, either from within the department or as on-the-street resources. The project had been shut down due to lack of funds.

I rose from my chair, my surging adrenaline making it impossible for me to sit, and pored over the pile of documents more closely than I had with Madison.

Gideon's chair squeaked across the floor as he pushed it back, but I didn't look up when he came to stand beside me. The warmth of him brushed against my arm, soothing the goosebumps bubbling over my skin.

"What do you see?" he asked.

"So many of these are ours. I never noticed before how many of our requests were shut down like this. Approved, then cancelled. Approved, then cancelled. The same pattern as all the other notes Madi flagged."

I set the document aside and chose another one at random. There was nothing to get excited about yet. None of this meant anything. My desperation to find a clear path was so strong I was reading too much into nothing. SMOAC cancelled projects all the time. Being a super-secret government department meant we were always facing budget cuts in favour of the mundane, more mainstream areas of government. Or, at least, that's what we'd always been told.

A ball of uneasiness lodged in my throat as I sorted the task force-related notes into their own growing stack.

Gideon started in on another pile, laying them out in a row so I could sift through them more quickly. There were a dozen already, all from the last six months.

"Madison didn't notice this?" he asked.

"She couldn't have known. Some of these projects were peripheral, issues we had a hand in but weren't necessarily responsible for. The only reason I remember them is because Michael says most of his grey hair came from trying to push them through. Make them successful so our branch could be more efficient. Sometimes he got them off the ground for as long as a few months, sometimes only a week. Too often, though, something shut them down before they got out the door. He's been getting more and more frustrated about it. I think that's why he blames Meril for being useless and dumping the burden of protection on us when we don't have the money to do it properly. So much anger about the time and effort wasted on setup that never paid off. I just—" I raised my eyes from the papers to look at Gideon. He watched me, silently encouraging me, but I didn't know where I was headed. "I assumed it was the regular government runaround, you know? Moving as far as you can before the red tape kicks in, sometimes breaking through it, other times not. I never thought—"

My gaze fell once more to the papers strewn in front of me. Over a year of lost projects, all of them approved when the minister had been away, meaning he'd probably never seen them. All those times Michael had railed against the empty head in a seat of power, he'd been pointing his finger in the wrong direction. Someone else had been calling the shots.

Hand shaking, I picked up my phone and found the photo of the shipping authorization. I zoomed in on the date and compared it to the calendar Madison had printed off for this month. The evidence glared at me. Bastien had been out of town that day and the day after. There was no way he could have signed off on the shipment.

I dropped my phone onto the table, sank onto the chair, and buried my face in my hands as more memories washed over me. Boardroom sessions, brainstorming emails, logistics and strategy meetings. Always Michael, often me, and always Deputy Minister Gagnon directing the conversation.

Gideon crouched in front of me and took my cold hand in his warm ones.

"These projects," I said, jerking my chin to the documents on the table, "they were the brainchildren of the deputy minister. He's the one who came to Michael and asked him to prepare the research to present his ideas to the minister. He requested all of these. He wanted to strengthen the community, he said. Make sure SMOAC was seen as the protective force it was created to be, standing for the rights and well-being of supernaturals across the country. Each initiative would have been a step forward in solidifying our foundation on this side of the wall." I looked at Gideon. "With the minister dead, Gagnon's sitting pretty at the top of the chain."

Gideon's eyes widened. "You think he's one of O'Malley's connections?"

"If I'm right, it's more than that." My team showing up in time to let Dougall get away, informants being outed and either killed or vanishing without a trace, O'Malley always knowing where we would search for him next… "What if he's not supplying O'Malley with information? What if he's leading the charge?"

Did I have enough evidence to back me up? This was a big accusation. One I would never recover from professionally if I turned out to be wrong. After all, we'd been wrong about Bastien, hadn't we? The people behind this conspiracy were pros at laying the blame at someone else's door. And if I'd landed on the right track, what about the FoSA guinea pig project? Was it real, or another cover to hide the missing money?

"All arrows point to him. It might be another misdirection by our friendly neighbourhood mole, but now that I see it, I can't ignore it."

For a moment we sat in silence, Gideon lost in thought and me trying to wrap my head around the significance of what Gagnon's involvement would mean. The acting head of the department. The man who had the power to bring the wrath of SMOAC down on our heads without being second-guessed. Was this the enemy we had to go up against?

I hoped that whatever Madison was up to, she'd be prepared for this fight. If we moved forward and we were right, there was no telling how big this could blow up.

Chapter 29

Madison

I'D HOPED MEETING with Sercario would help me figure out what to do with my swiftly moving hourglass and slowly growing army, but after I'd settled the bill and separated from my uncle, watching him melt into the shadows on Elgin Street, my path was no clearer. My thoughts were too busy with the timer in my head counting down the seconds. As though I were back in SMOAC's boardroom with a ghostbomb tied to my lap.

All right, that's a little extreme, I scolded myself, remembering Serc's gentle reprimand. *Being recalled to court is not as bad as being obliterated by a bomb. By much.*

At least in the realm I would be alive, even if every heartbeat was at the queen's discretion—and a privilege she could revoke whenever she wished. No matter what Serc said about Meril's love for her people, I didn't have enough faith in her mercy or magnanimity to believe my life across the wall would be happy and safe.

Before my brain could kick off in another panicked spin, my phone buzzed in my purse. I pulled it out and frowned at the familiar number on the screen. A too-familiar number that should not have had knowledge of my new one. "Nan?"

"Hello, *chailene*. Sercario told me how to contact you," my grandmother said, getting to the point by knocking both greeting and explanation out of the way. Never one to waste time, my Nan. "He thought you might need a friendly voice."

I rolled my eyes. "At this rate, I may as well have kept my old phone." Though I couldn't deny the sound of her warm gruffness was a balm on my frazzled soul. "He told you what we talked about?"

"A quick summary. Enough that I can say goodbye to sleep for the rest of the night."

I cringed and checked my watch. Three-thirty. "Sorry, Nan. It could have waited until tomorrow."

She hmphed. "It most certainly could not. How am I supposed to get any rest when my granddaughter is putting together an army to save the world?"

Despite myself, I smiled. "That might be over-exaggerating the situation slightly. Have you been up late watching *Lord of the Rings* again?"

I turned the corner and headed south on Elgin. I had no particular destination in mind, but the night air was cool and refreshing, and I needed to clear the fog in my head. I hoped

Jet had been smart and gone to sleep instead of waiting up for me. I would be useless if I didn't get home myself, but the idea of being confined in my room with nothing but silence and the future closing in on me was suffocating.

"If this were a story, the ending would be predetermined," Nan said. "This is life, where nothing is guaranteed. What is happening, *chailene*? When we last spoke, you were getting ready to disappear, and now you're having meetings with your uncle? Preparing for battle?"

"I don't know where to begin." I turned towards the organized streets of the Glebe. The large houses with their sunrooms and balconies looked so quiet and secure, and I wondered how many supernaturals lived here, as concerned by the growing troubles as we were. "One seemingly random attack has turned into a maze of suspicion and... well, evil. People are dying, and some of the people doing the killing don't realize they're fighting for the wrong side. I'm a public servant, *adale*. I've spent most of my adult life doing paperwork and helping my father's friend manage our corner of the country. Now Jean-Luc is dead, and our corner is under fire. How did I wind up in the middle?"

A soft sigh came down the line. I pictured her in her small apartment, the living room light on as she settled into her favourite armchair. A half-finished jigsaw puzzle would be laid out on the coffee table, a sheet of glass over top to ensure her tortie, Miga, didn't knock off the stray pieces while she wasn't working on it. It should have been a normal night for her, and instead she was on the phone with me, talking me down from the ledge I'd voluntarily walked out on.

Guilt and fear choked me, not mixing well with the stale coffee and cold French fries.

"I'm sorry, *adale*."

"For what?" she asked, sounding genuinely surprised. "You've only done what you believed necessary, and not once in my life have I doubted your judgement. If you see something happening that you need to fix, then what choice do you have but to take risks and stay strong? All I want is for you to be happy and safe, and if I can't have either of those, then I want you to be smart. I trust you to be what the department—what the *country*—needs."

"As much as I'm able to accomplish in the next few days," I said, the ever-shrinking amount of time making everything seem so out of reach.

"Why put such pressure on yourself?" Then, with a note of wariness, she added, "Unless you've learned something else you haven't told me?"

I pulled up short, tripping on a curb as ice spread through my heart. "Did Serc not tell you?"

"Tell me what?" she asked.

Of course my uncle had left it to me to break the news of my recall. He'd hoped to avoid the bleeding eardrums from Nan's tongue-lashing, no doubt. The man was far from a coward unless my grandmother was involved, and who could blame him? She'd proved time and again she was Great-Grandmother Clarissa's daughter. Stubborn, single-minded, with the ability to twist the strongest minds to her will and snap the weak ones. I'd trained with her most of my life and still felt leagues behind. Especially when I had to give her bad news.

"Her Majesty has put out the call. I've been summoned to the Shadow Council."

There was a sharp inhale, followed by a stretch of silence, and then, "When?"

Meril help me, it was hard not to cry, to keep one foot moving in front of the other, doing my best to sound strong, like I had it together. What I really wanted to do was hop on a plane, fly to Winnipeg, and rest my head on Nan's knee while she combed her fingers through my hair and told me everything would be all right.

"Serc is dragging his feet for me, but that might gain me what? Another couple days? I don't see any way of avoiding her that wouldn't put him in danger." That pesky lingering hope reared its head again, pushing me to ask, "Do you?"

A long, drawn-out exhale. "No, *chailene*, I'm afraid you're right. It will be much worse for everyone if you don't go willingly. But perhaps it won't be as bad as you think. She'll need good people on this side of the wall to fight the coming battle and to help rebuild once we've won. Don't give up."

I paused and leaned over the railing to stare into the

Rideau Canal. The water was dark, but far from still. This hour was prime time for the mermaids, and they swam close to the surface, their hair creating ripples that lapped against the concrete sides. Were they nervous about the changes in their city, or did they not care? Water creatures never paid much attention to what happened on land. Ghost attacks didn't affect them, and neither did anything else the syndicate threw at the rest of us. If the threat blew their way, they could travel down the locks and follow the river out of Ottawa before anyone noticed they were gone.

Never in my life had I wished I possessed fins instead of legs, but right now, the advantages were infinite.

"When are you going to go?" she asked. The question I'd dreaded. The question I still hadn't answered myself.

"I need to talk to Jet." I pushed away from the railing and started back towards Centretown, veering left to follow the bike path along the water. "We're in this together, and I'm afraid for her." I'd spent the night setting up potential backup that would be ready when the call came, and I wasn't sure our captain would be ready to lead them. I couldn't abandon her until I knew she had a plan of her own. "She lost someone. Someone important. And the people who took him away from her are the same people she's fighting to protect."

"Poor *amuera,*" Nan said. *Poor love.* "It's a heartbreaking side effect of ambition. Everyone is so focused on reaching their goal, they don't consider everything they destroy along the way."

I couldn't have phrased it better.

"Promise me you'll be careful," she said.

"I promise." A bitter laugh rumbled in my chest. "I don't have the option to be rash. Someone needs to keep a clear head to move things forward. If I'm not prepared, or if Jet's not up to the task, there won't be anyone to stop these people from overturning our world for their own gain."

"You're not alone. Hang on to the people you trust and know we're here to help where we can. Even if it's only to listen."

"Thank you, *adale*."

"Of course. You're the heart of my heart, the light in my darkening days. Anything I can offer, I will gladly give. In the meantime, I'll send you more tea. There's nothing like an emotional reset to make the most jumbled puzzles clear."

I thought about how long it had been since my emotions were as level as I needed them to be. While I didn't think her tea would end the maelstrom, at least I could escape for a few minutes to float through the calming steam of lavender and lemon. For now, I would have to find my pleasures in the brief, stolen moments that would no doubt come fewer and farther between as the days passed.

"You're strong enough to survive this," Nan said. "Right now you might not think so, but you are my granddaughter, the great-granddaughter of the woman who helped make life possible for our kind outside the realm. No small feat. She faced Meril's disapproval, risked starting a civil war because of it, but so firmly did she believe the department was worthwhile, she fought for every inch she gained. It won't be easy, but it's *possible*. That's what you need to remember."

A breeze stirred through the trees around me, and I turned my face into it as though it were a message from Clarissa herself. Nan wasn't wrong. From where I stood, I didn't see how we could win, but I had to believe it was worth the attempt.

I gave my grandmother the address of the safe house, along with a name to use on the package, told her I loved her, and hung up.

The night seemed lonelier without her confident voice in my ear. In its absence, all I picked up were the rustlings in the bushes of waking squirrels and treekins, the lap of water as the mermaids headed to the depths of the canal to remain out of sight of the coming dawn, and the stirring of crickets. No one else was around to disturb the peace, and I allowed myself to take in the silence.

It was blissful.

Rarely was I able to drop my guard, but this time of morning, before anyone else had risen, offered a glorious reprieve.

Except I wasn't as alone as I'd thought.

As I opened myself to the world around me, I detected the unmistakable buzz of someone's aura. I spun around to find the source, and when no obvious figure revealed itself, I backed away from the shadows of the trees near the river.

Every darkened angle reached towards me, and I focused my attention on the unseen current of emotion, trying to interpret the intention that accompanied it. Was it some creep looking to prey on a woman walking alone at night? A couple looking for privacy? Someone out for a walk, hoping not to be disturbed?

The further I reached into the person's mind, the more confused I became. No anger wound through their brain chemistry, no curiosity, no joy. What I sensed was more like a blanket of white light—a pure neutral. My mouth went dry. I only knew of one group whose members were capable of achieving such a complete level of calm. Vessels more than individuals. Their personalities buried beneath the needs of someone with a will so much stronger than theirs.

No. Please. Not yet.

Branches ruffled as the figure stepped out of the trees and into the yellow glow of the street light. Her eyes were white, as though they'd rolled back in her head, but I knew she could see me well enough. As could the woman who'd sent her.

Serc had been right, though he'd misjudged the time frame.

The queen's Eyes had found me.

Chapter 30

Gideon

I WATCHED JET pace the living room. By the clock, she hadn't stopped for the past ten minutes, her features screwed up in thought, her third eye snakelike again.

There was no point in asking what she was thinking about. Better to let her run through her ideas first and be there to bounce them around when she was ready. In the meantime, I sat in the armchair beside the one I'd passed out in. That one was a lost cause, covered in more blood than it would be worthwhile to wash out. I used it as a footrest, elbows propped on the armrests and my hands clasped over my stomach.

A posture of habit. I'd learned early in my SilverGuard days that a pretense of relaxation made people drop their guard and underestimate me. Under the surface, I was coiled and ready to move whenever Jet called.

Her suspicions—and the more she'd run through them,

the more logical they sounded—would have serious repercussions on both sides of the border. Serious enough that I would get my ass handed to me if I didn't pick up the phone right now and make my report to Dark Wire, with or without confirmation that she was right. Even the possibility that Gagnon was the mole would throw me in hot water for not excusing myself and bolting. No involvement in foreign politics, they'd told me. They'd been quite clear about the consequences on that point, but I had no way of escaping it. The government mole wasn't a peripheral problem, not a minor player in the bigger game, but potentially the core of every other concern.

A revelation like that deserved an immediate report to my people, warning them to hunker down and prepare for a shitstorm that would radiate across countries. But I had no intention of making that phone call. To say the acting minister was involved in a murderous conspiracy before we were sure—*really* sure—would draw a lot of attention from multiple authorities and leave Jet dead in the crosshairs.

I would accept the fallout of staying silent and cross my fingers everything would work out in the end. If Jet's clumsiness had helped her stumble on the missing piece, then it was possible we had our way forward. We could make a plan. Solve the problem. Not easily, and probably not cleanly, but we could get it done. Then I could go home, explain that my radio silence was because the situation had been too unstable for me to reach out, and hopefully receive endless accolades and a good long vacation.

And a genie could pop out of the table lamp beside me and grant my heart's desire.

Whatever. If all I had right now were wishes, I would hang on to them.

Finally, Jet drew to a stop in front of me. "I need to call Michael."

After so much pacing, I'd expected strategy, a clever, tactical approach. I lowered my leg to the floor, cringing as the muscles in my stomach flexed and stretched the skin across my chest, and rested my elbows on my knees. "Are you sure that's a good idea? Didn't he write off your theory about the failed projects?"

She let out a frustrated scream as she threw herself into the dining chair across from me.

"I know," she said, and though the words came out sharp, for a blessed change, her anger didn't seem to be directed at me. "I know exactly what he'll say if I call him. He's already explained the paperwork. This isn't about the syndicate, it's about the drugs. I know, I know, I *know.*" She raked her fingers through her hair, then curled them into fists. "But he can't realize the cancelled task force projects are part of it. If they're linked to the FoSA project, wouldn't he have known? He wouldn't have gotten so furious." She groaned again. "I can't get my footing here, Gideon. Madison's discovery that someone was messing with Bastien's authority was hard enough to swallow, but for Gagnon to be involved—for him to have manipulated us like this—and we bought right into it, handed him control of the entire department."

She dragged her fingers across her face and met my gaze, the darkness of her fatigue, fear, and confusion screaming for help I couldn't give.

I reached out and grabbed her hand to ground her in the here and now. "You're spinning. If you want to see this clearly, you have to remember where you are. Here, in this room. With me, and only me."

Jet closed her eyes and squeezed my hand. When she looked at me again, she appeared to have regained some measure of calm, and I loosened my grip on her, leaving her free to pull away if she wanted to. For now, she let her palm rest on mine.

"There has to be someone else you can call until we find something to back us up," I said. "What about checking in with your sources?"

Now she pulled away and pressed her fingertips against her third eye, massaging the creases around the faint ridges. "Checking in feels like a waste of time."

"Why? I know you said Travis would have reached out to you, but you could tell him what you've learned. It might trigger a memory, something he heard but didn't realize mattered."

"You think a car thief masquerading as a mechanic is going to know the secret goings-on of our deputy minister?" she asked as she sagged into her chair. "If this goes as high up as Gagnon, he won't know anything. Even if he did, even if Gagnon carried out his business right in front of him, what are the odds he'd risk passing it along to me? Ratting out some low-ranking paper-pusher passing government secrets to the syndicate is one thing, but the head of the department?"

She stared out the window, and I pinched the bridge of my nose. I didn't like where her thoughts were headed. She was making excuses, refusing to look at her options. She'd latched on to the idea that her commander would be able to fix everything, and no matter who else I suggested she contact, she was as stubborn as she was loyal. I could suggest she wait for Madison to get back, and she'd probably have an argument ready for that, too.

It wasn't that I didn't understand. Almost from the day we met, she'd talked about Michael Torrence, her stand-in father figure while her real father was three provinces away. Of course she would rely on him to help.

But I'd never met the guy, and although I trusted Jet about most things, I had to take her blind spots into account. He'd directed her to the minister's office, she'd given him what she'd found, but that had been hours ago. What had he done with the information? When would he decide to loop Jet in for the next step?

Based on his decisions so far, I didn't trust him not to take what we'd learned and order Jet to sit on it until he had an opportunity to investigate himself.

If calling him now meant us having to step aside, I voted to keep him in the dark. I wasn't ready to lose sight of the field.

"Will he let you take the lead on this?" I asked, trying to get her to see reason.

She rolled her gaze to meet mine, the rest of her remaining still. "Probably not." And as though speaking the words aloud unlocked her joints, she slid forward to lean on her knees, mirroring my position. "No, definitely not, but this is more important than who calls the shots. Michael is poking around in this, too, but with no clue he's in the middle of the lion's den. What if he takes his suspicions to Gagnon?" She blanched. "What if I'm already too late, and he used the shipping authorization as evidence the minister was corrupt? With the minister dead, Gagnon's cover is blown for anything he wants to do going forward, and if he thinks someone is onto him… I need to warn Michael before he gets himself killed."

A shudder ran through her, but before I could offer any kind of reassurance, she pushed herself out of her chair to pace the room again. When she crossed back towards me, I spotted a phone in her hand. The new one Madison had left her was still on the counter, so this had to be her old one. I hadn't even noticed her picking it up off the dining table.

"When I talked to him before, I left out most of what we learned to protect Madison," she said. "What if that was a huge mistake? If I told him everything, he might have believed me. If I can convince him I'm not crazy, that this conspiracy really is as big as I think it is, we can work together. He has to have seen more than we have, even if he didn't realize what it meant. Gagnon will have needed to tell him some version of the truth to get him to go along with things so far, and if I hear his lies, maybe we can work backwards to figure out his plan."

She scrolled through her phone and hit a button.

"There's no way to talk you out of this, is there?" I asked, fighting against the urge to tackle her to the ground and kick the phone out of reach. Was I being unreasonable? Distrustful? It probably didn't help that one of her team had shot me less than twenty-four hours ago, but her panic hadn't done anything to untie the knots in my gut. She was so desperate to keep faith in her team.

She pressed her phone to her ear, and even though she was across the room, I heard Michael's muffled voice as he said, "Hello?"

"Michael? It's me."

"Jet? What's wrong?" To his credit, he already sounded more awake and full of concern.

I clasped my hands and bowed my head, the crooks of my thumbs pressing into my brow. I disagreed with Jet's move, but I couldn't help straining my ears to pick up every word.

"I know you think I'm nuts, but I found something else to back up my claim that the mole is after more than drug money," she said. "Can we talk? Somewhere safe?"

I flinched. The man already thought she was paranoid, and

she was suggesting a secret meeting? I was amazed he didn't hang up on her.

"Are you all right?" Michael asked.

"I'm fine. Or at least, I will be. Can we meet?"

"Yes, of course." In the pause that followed, I pictured Michael rubbing his forehead as he sat up in bed, wondering how the hell his day had gotten off to such a confusing start. I empathized. "How about the Labyrinth? Meet me there tonight. Around eight?"

I glanced at the clock. That was sixteen hours away. Could Jet manage to wait that long without her head exploding? I watched her impatience skitter across her face, but she nodded.

"I'll be there."

She hung up and collapsed into the dining chair, her bare legs stretched out to intersect with mine.

"He didn't shrug me off," she said, the exhausted relief in her voice palpable.

"What's the Labyrinth?" I asked.

If it bothered Jet that I'd eavesdropped on her conversation, she didn't show it. "It's an underground through-way. A network of storm sewers and tunnels that run under the city. The mundanes forgot about them ages ago, so they don't show up on the municipal blueprint."

I rested my chin on the pads of my thumbs so my index fingers pressed against my lips, preventing me from saying any of the opinions that sprang to mind. I shouldn't have wasted the effort. My silence obviously spoke volumes.

"You don't think I should go," she said.

"To an underground sewer when the syndicate and possibly the head of your department are after you? No, I can't say I do." So much for me biting my tongue. "What if someone finds out about the meet and comes after you?"

"I'll know if they do." Although she made no move towards her third eye, she may as well have. "Unless you can come up with something better?"

I couldn't, and Jet knew it.

"At least let me come with you."

She started shaking her head before I finished talking. "He thinks you're dead, and it's probably better to keep it that way." She leaned forward and took my hand, her palm cool and steady. "He's my commander, Gideon. My mentor. He won't let anything happen to me."

I caught her gaze but said nothing. Michael could try as hard as he wanted to keep her safe, but with the people we were up against, there was no guarantee he would be enough.

If anything, she should have been scared for them both.

Chapter 31

Madison

FOR ONE RIDICULOUS moment, I thought about running.

While there was any opportunity to avoid this confrontation, I wanted to hightail it back to the safe house. My body was tensed and ready to flee. A week of fear, panic, and adrenaline had left me primed to give it my best shot.

The whispering voice of reason held me in place.

One Eye activated meant all Eyes would be looking for me. Dozens of white stares searching street corners and walking paths, spying out windows. And behind them all, Meril's judging gaze.

So no, running wouldn't help, which only left fighting. Not with fists, but with words. I was the queen's descendant, not some simple subject with no power of my own.

My odds were slim, but it was worth a try. Better than standing here, stunned, holding myself back from begging and blubbering.

I raised my chin and clenched my fists at my sides, hoping the shadows were deep enough to hide my shaking legs. "Do you seek me, Your Majesty?" I asked. There was a distinct tremor in my voice, but with luck she would interpret it as anger.

"I am but the queen's messenger, sent on her behalf," the Eye said, her voice normal, not the dual strain of the queen speaking through her. I nearly collapsed with relief, but the blood rushed out of my head again when she added, "For now."

Trust Meril's people to play games.

She stepped closer, and I took in the faded jeans, bright yellow T-shirt, and grey hoodie. Never in a million years would I have pegged her as the queen's pawn if not for those eyes.

"Though Her Majesty does wish to know why you have avoided her summons for so many days. Disobedience is a step away from rebellion, and she will not allow her power to be questioned."

I swallowed hard. *Stay strong. Our reasons are sound.* "We needed time to form a full report. I'm aware Her Majesty does not appreciate half-measures."

"Consider your time at an end. You're to cross the wall and stand before Queen Meril at noon tomorrow."

She may as well have punched me in the gut. Noon. That was less than thirty-two hours away. *Not enough time!*

I drew in a shaky breath to steel my nerves. "If I'm to leave my friends without support, I need to put protections in place.

I need to ensure I have taken every possible step to prevent a war. Give me seventy-two hours. Time to ensure the safety of thousands. Millions. Please. A few extra days is all I ask."

It will always be a few more days. I realized it as I stood staring into the eerie white eyes that would soon be a constant part of my life. I would always find a reason to bargain, a reason to stay. I wasn't ready to leave this world behind.

"You should be grateful Her Majesty is offering you the time she has," she said. "Noon tomorrow, and no later. Don't make us come looking for you."

For a minute that felt like years, she held my gaze, and it took every last effort for me to meet it. I would not be the one to break. If Meril had sent her Eyes to test me, she wouldn't find me lacking in stubbornness or will. As she never failed to remind me, I was the blood of her blood, which meant she had to reckon with everything I brought with me once I joined her court. Not someone who would lie down and follow orders like a meek kitten, but someone who would stand her ground. It was best she learned that now.

The stare-down finally ended, and without a word or change in her stony expression, the Eye melted into the shadows and was gone.

Now alone, my strength gave out, and I sank into the damp grass. Official, then. No more hope of a last-minute reprieve. No chance that Serc or Nan would help me find my way free.

Less than thirty-two hours. And the Eye was right, I *should* have been grateful Meril had given me that much, though right this second I didn't feel it.

I can't waste any of that time sitting here, I told myself, and though they needed a lot of prompting, my strength and courage returned to help me to my feet.

My phone buzzed, and I wiped the tears from my eyes before checking my messages. Jet. Back at home. Ready to talk when you are.

My throat closed around everything that needed to be said. How would she take losing her last ally, both me and Gideon taken away from her without warning, so soon on the heels of losing most of her professional family? I'd hoped to talk her into coming with me, but how could I do that when we needed someone on this side of the wall to coordinate whatever reinforcements Lilith and Serc brought in? I had found them, but it would be on Jet to decide how and when to use them.

Could she do it? The last time she'd ordered troops to march, half of them had died. She'd been afraid of bringing Gideon with her to the protest because she hadn't trusted herself to keep him safe, and Eric had killed him.

Jet would have to be my priority in my remaining hours. Before I left, I would make sure she was ready to lead. I would remind her who she was—not a fugitive on the run, but a SMOAC task force captain whose job it was to protect her people, her country, and her department. In that order—no matter the consequences. If I could get her to believe it, we stood a chance.

I shoved my phone into my purse and continued the walk to the safe house, my thoughts no more settled after my run-in with the queen's Eye than they'd been before. The update to the ticking clock, the laundry list of tasks danging in front of me—none of it made things easier.

And somewhere in all of that, before I left her, I needed to make sure Jet was emotionally okay, that she would give herself time to grieve and find support where she could.

At least she and I could say goodbye, a privilege she hadn't had with Gideon.

Right when they'd started to find their footing and face some of their problems. Right when the possibilities were branching out.

Like me and Colm.

I drew to a sharp stop, my breath lodging in my chest, a solidified lump of rock.

He'd never been out of my thoughts. Not really. Especially not since I'd spoken to Serc and received the forewarning about my summons. But I'd kept setting him aside as a future issue. Not one I had to deal with yet. I'd pretended my troubles would blow over and he and I could have our dinner.

That layer of denial was gone now. Meril had pulled the rug out from under me.

Now I had to face the truth and decide if I wanted to try to come up with a believable story about why he would never see or hear from me again, or cut and run.

I pulled out my phone, opened my chatting app, and scrolled through his messages. Months of back and forth, complaining about work, exchanging public service memes, arranging lobby meets for an afternoon break. If I said nothing and disappeared, he would never know how bearable he'd made all those late nights at the office.

The desire to break down and tell him the whole truth nudged my thumb towards the digital keyboard, but my mind went blank. What could I possibly say? *My royal relatives have called me home… If you see witches fighting each other in the streets, please stay out of their way.*

The man would think I was delusional.

With a frustrated grumble, I shoved my phone into the bottom of my purse and resumed my walk. Colm was a mundane. He wasn't prepared to have his eyes opened without warning. While I didn't have Jet's cynicism, I was terrified he would turn his back on me. Either believe me and see me as a monster, go to the news and out us, or not believe me and think I'd lost my mind. Jet was right. I couldn't take the risk. Gideon was one of us and look what had happened to him. I had to keep Colm safe, and that meant forgetting about him.

For the third time, I pulled out my phone. The streetlights cast their yellow glow over the sidewalk in front of the darkened storefronts and spilled across the screen.

It would be better to remove the temptation of reaching

out to him. Delete his name, his number, our messages. Better to cut him out of my life and leave it at that. If by some miracle I made it back here and regained some kind of normalcy…

I couldn't finish the thought. Hopes and dreams would not help me do what needed to be done.

And yet I couldn't bring myself to get rid of him. He was one of the few strings tying me to the Madison Prince of a week ago. The woman who had known what she was doing in a boardroom, who had busted her butt to improve the quality of life for supernaturals across the country. A woman who had no idea that seven days later she would be standing on Bank Street at four o'clock in the morning, delaying a summons from the queen of the realm while the whole of SMOAC and the Death's Head Syndicate came after her.

So if I couldn't delete him, I had to not be a coward. No more pretending everything was fine. No more giving him hope when there was none. It would be cruel to leave him in the dark, and I faced enough cruelty that I didn't want to inflict it on anyone else. With my teeth clenched against the ache, I started typing.

HEY COLM. HOPE YOU'RE DOING WELL. SORRY FOR ALL THE MIXED MESSAGES LATELY, BUT LIFE HAS BEEN… COMPLICATED. SOME FAMILY STUFF HAS COME UP, WAY BEYOND THE USUAL DRAMA, AND I'M HEADING OUT OF TOWN TO HELP DEAL WITH IT. I DON'T KNOW WHEN OR IF I'LL BE BACK, AND I'M SORRY WE MIGHT NOT BE ABLE TO RESCHEDULE OUR DINNER AFTER ALL. I WAS LOOK-

ING FORWARD TO IT. TIME WITH YOU HAS KEPT ME SANE, AND I'M GRATEFUL FOR YOU. I WISH I COULD TELL YOU IN PERSON AND NOT OVER TEXT AT 4AM, BUT I DIDN'T WANT TO LEAVE YOU WITHOUT AT LEAST SAYING SOMETHING. THANKS AGAIN FOR EVERYTHING. Mx.

I hit send before I overthought or reread the message, and as soon as it was gone, a wave of fatigue swept over me. I wavered on my feet, blackness dancing on the edges of my vision.

"Hey, lady, you all right?"

A dark shape slunk out of the shadows towards me, and my first instinct was to recoil at his stringy dark beard and stale odour. But no white eyes stared out at me, and when I opened my mind to him, all I sensed was concern, no threat. He remained a few feet away from me, put off from coming closer by my reaction, so I smiled at him. "I'm okay, thank you. Just tired."

"Do you have far to go? Want me to walk you there?"

He sounded as exhausted as I felt, worn down by whatever had happened in his life to bring him to this point. Jet would have been able to reach out and know most of his life story at a touch. All I knew was that he somehow still managed to give a damn after years of having the world stomp on him.

"I'm just on the corner, but thank you," I said, and reached into my purse.

He raised his hands. "No, ma'am, that's not necessary. I didn't want you face planting in the middle of the street. The cops don't like it much."

The warmth in my heart grew at his kindness. My life had become so bleak, I'd almost forgotten moments like this existed. Random decency. Simple generosity. "Thanks to your wake-up call, I might get home without that happening. Please, have some breakfast on me. It's the least I can do for helping me not wind up with a broken nose."

He accepted my twenty with a hesitant nod. "Thank you, ma'am. Get home safely now."

He returned to his shadows, and I returned to mine. His sunny aura faded as he drifted around the corner, but the influence of it remained with me. Even under the harshest conditions, goodness persisted, and the reminder filled me with a hardened resilience. Let the world stomp. I was ready to stomp back.

After I got a few hours of much-needed sleep.

I needed to be at my best to make the most of my last day.

The safe house was dark by the time I reached it. All was silent, and I was too exhausted to detect anything other than soft waves of emotion cascading through the apartment, seeming to sweep over me from all sides. As though Jet's grief had permeated the walls themselves. Though the weight of it wasn't as heavy as I'd expected, less dark. I chalked it up to her being asleep and wished her some wonderful dreams to break up the horrors of her reality. With luck, I would experience some of my own.

Tomorrow loomed like a disgruntled parent tapping an impatient foot and leaving no room to relax, but I turned my back on it. I wouldn't let its grim face rob me of all the good I meant to do in the time I had left. On the contrary, my stubbornness rose, urging me to create as much change as possible. Soon enough, I would be at someone's beck and call, but for now I was my own person, and this person wanted to crawl under the blankets, pull them over her head, and make the world disappear for a short while.

I closed myself in my bedroom, changed into my favourite pyjamas, and collapsed on the bed. I barely gave a thought to turning off the bedside lamp before sleep arrived to sweep me away from my nightmares.

Chapter 32

Gideon

I DIDN'T KNOW what had woken me up. The apartment was quiet, my room was dark, but I sat up drenched in cold sweat with an instant awareness that I wouldn't be going back to sleep.

My chest groaned with delayed pain at my sudden movement, but compared to how I'd felt last night, I was ready to do backflips. At least my rest had been good for something, because exhaustion clung to me in a fog.

I'd been having the most incredible dream about me and Jet, a continuation of our reunion, and I half-expected to find her lying beside me until I remembered I'd gone to my own room after we'd sorted out the details of her meeting with Michael. I'd wanted to join her in bed, keep her close so we could face the uncertainties together, but somehow sleeping beside her, actually sleeping, had struck me as too… intimate. With a little encouragement, I might have been convinced to overcome that hurdle, but Jet had been distracted, no doubt running through all the possible ways her meeting might go wrong.

I checked the clock and frowned at the bright green *19:00* staring back at me. A whole day gone. The meeting was in an hour. Jet would want to get an early start, and would probably be a treat to deal with until then, but that wouldn't stop me from taking another stab at persuading her to let me go with her.

Even if she said no, what was she going to do? Collar me and leave me behind? I wouldn't leave her without backup, no matter what stupid arguments she threw at me.

My bladder squeezed, and I passed a hand over my face as I rolled—gently—out of bed and shuffled down the hallway to the bathroom. Sunlight shone through the living room windows, the sudden glare making me squint after the protection of my heavy bedroom curtains. No noise came from the other rooms as I took a piss and brushed my teeth, and I found it weird that Jet wasn't up and about yet.

I imagined going into her room and waking her up, a softer, gentler wake-up than mine had been. No sex, she wouldn't be in the state of mind for it, but a nice, positive note to start the day—or night, given the time—on.

I found myself smiling as I rinsed my mouth and flicked the light off, but when I reached Jet's room, my stomach dropped. Her door was open.

Had it been open when I'd gotten up? I wracked my brain trying to remember, but I'd been half-asleep. I lurched to the doorway and cursed on finding her bed made and no sign of the woman who should have been sleeping in it.

She'd said she was going to the Labyrinth alone, and I'd been too tired to push harder last night, but she must have known I wouldn't drop the issue and left early to avoid me. In a moment of weighted dread, I realized her leaving the apartment was what had woken me up.

But if so, she hadn't been gone long. I returned to my room, dug my new phone out of my pants pocket and called her.

The answering ring came from her bedroom.

"Shit!"

What are you doing, Jet? You idiot.

Seven o'clock. That gave me an hour to figure out where this Labyrinth place was and catch up with her. Fine. It was going to be fine.

I told myself not to overreact. She knew to be careful. She knew there were people looking for her. Jet might have been desperate, but she wasn't reckless.

No matter how hard I tried to talk myself down, the alarm bells in my head wouldn't shut up. She shouldn't have gone alone.

I hurried to pull on my jeans and a clean T-shirt, forming a rough list of people I could contact to learn more about the Labyrinth. Jet had said the tunnels ran under the entire city, which meant there had to be multiple access points. I crossed my fingers the one she'd used was within walking distance.

I laced up my second boot, strode into the kitchen ready to start my search, and stopped short on finding Madison standing in her pyjamas in front of the fridge.

She turned when I entered the room, and her eyes and mouth widened into round O's. It occurred to me that in the rush of our reunion, Jet and I had neglected to give Madison a heads-up that I was, in fact, not dead.

To her credit, she set the milk carton down before she dropped it and rested her hands on the island to hold herself steady.

"Are you really here?" she asked. Calm as could be. As though, if I told her no, she would nod and carry on, the information no stranger than anything else she'd experienced over the past few days.

"Yeah," I said. I wanted to get moving and save the explanations for later, but if Jet hadn't had the opportunity to tell her about me, she also hadn't told her about the meeting with Michael. Madison likely knew how to reach the Labyrinth, which would save me time, so the least I could do was give her a second to process that I was still wandering this side of the afterlife. "Sorry. We should have told you."

"But—" She came around the island and approached me. "How? What happened? How?"

"Touch and go, but lucky for me, my body knows how to hold itself together in a pinch. I can't say I'm tip-top, but I'm alive."

She stared me up and down, her eyes dull with shock. "Does Jet know?"

I nodded. "She found me last night. Sorry about your chair. I wasn't exactly in a frame of mind to land somewhere washable."

With what sounded like a sob mixed with a laugh, she threw her arms around my neck. "Thank the sweet heavens and all that's merciful you're here." Then she pulled back and gave me a solid smack on the arm. "That's for not letting me know earlier and keeping me in panic attacks all night." She peered around me. "Where's Jet?"

She might have been the empath, but I couldn't miss her apprehension—almost outright anxiety. Her gaze wouldn't settle, and she didn't stop moving, faint little taps and tics. What had she texted Jet last night? That they needed to talk? If I had to guess, based on the state she was in, the conversation wouldn't be a happy one. Under the circumstances, I hated to be the bearer of bad news myself, but what choice did I have but to tell her Jet was out in the city somewhere taking stupid risks?

"She's not here," I said. "She left to meet Michael."

I realized too late I'd left myself open for an ass-kicking about why I hadn't done more to stop her from going alone, but though I caught the glimpse of disapproval in Madison's eyes, it quickly gave way to something more knowing. I wondered what she sensed in me that I wasn't aware of myself.

"What pushed her to do that?" she asked, making an impressive effort to sound neutral. "Or did he call the meet?

Does he have another lead for her to follow?"

"No, this was her idea. She went through your papers again last night and stumbled on another possible pattern. One that might mean Michael's in danger. Something that proves her blue-eyed soldier boy was wrong and there's more to the cancelled projects than some federation."

Madison stilled. "What federation?"

I shrugged, nonchalant, though I watched her closely. "Supernatural Affairs or something?"

She tugged on her hair and moved to the table. "What the hell, Jet? I haven't spoken to her since she got back to her apartment after *someone killed you*." She shot me a dirty look I hardly thought I deserved. "Obviously she left out a few massive details. Do you know what Eric said about FoSA?"

"Not really. She said you'd understand more. Something about a deal Gagnon was looking into? A test project to see if reaching out to them made sense?"

She riffled through the documents until she came to a red folder. "This is where I found mention of them. Lucien recommended Jean-Luc consider working with them to take the pressure off some of our social programs, but the minister declined."

"I guess your DM decided to go ahead without him."

Madison frowned at the paper in her hand.

"What is this group?" I asked.

"I don't know. Their website is pretty nondescript. I'd love to have more information to see how it ties in to everything else."

"Could be another front to hide whatever the mole and syndicate are up to."

She huffed and pinched the bridge of her nose. "As if we need another layer to peel away." She dropped her hand to her hip and glared at me. "What is this pattern Jet found?"

I stepped forward to show her the new pile we'd made among the stacks. "All these projects are related to her branch, and all of them, but maybe more, were started by the deputy minister."

Madison's hands froze on the edge of the table. "Lucien? But—"

She dropped her attention to the papers and riffled through them again, starting with the files Jet had set aside, then moving to the rest. I tried to read her expression, but her face remained blank, her gaze darting here and there, scanning random pages. Finally, a faint pink blush filled her cheeks. She dropped into the nearest chair and buried her face in her hands.

"I never noticed."

I pulled a second chair closer to her. "Jet said there's no way you could have. She kicked herself for not looking more closely earlier."

Madison lifted her gaze to mine. "So she called Michael?" There was something in her question. Something that sent those alarm bells in my head clanging.

"She was worried he might be in danger because of how

closely he works with Gagnon. She thinks his devotion to the department blinded him to what's really going on."

"Where are they meeting?"

"Somewhere called the Labyrinth?" I passed my hand over my eyes. "I told her I should go with her, but she said it's better if no one knows I'm back from the dead. She snuck out of here about fifteen minutes ago."

Madison hesitated, her gaze darting around the room again.

"What is it?" I asked, hoping she'd tell me my fears were all in my head.

"It's probably nothing. He loves her like a daughter. I've sensed it."

I didn't need her empathy to know she was holding back. I didn't want to ask. I didn't want anything else to add to the gnawing dread building in my gut.

"Well," she said at last, "Jet knows him best."

My gut clenched, the suspense of whatever she wasn't saying pushing me to the limit of my patience. "But…"

She tapped her fingers across the funding requests, sorting them as she sorted her thoughts, and caught my eye once more. "But Michael's signature is on all these documents, too."

My mouth went dry, my mind numb. Madison was right. It couldn't mean anything.

"You know where they're going?" I asked.

Madison nodded and rose to her feet. "I can be ready in three minutes."

Chapter 33

Jet

THE LABYRINTH WAS a shithole.

Not literally, thankfully, but by such a small margin I'd often wondered how SMOAC's infrastructure branch had gotten so lazy. It was quiet, secret, and laid out in a way that made it an ideal route across the city when required, but it was also dingy, damp, and reeked of mould and whatever creatures had crawled here to die.

I hated coming down here at the best of times, but tonight, when I had so much waiting for me at the apartment, the darkness and grime were especially obnoxious.

I'd left the safe house around seven o'clock, having slept the entire day away. Madison's door had been closed when I'd woken up and I'd sensed someone inside, so I assumed she'd made it home safely, and only my opinion that she needed rest as much as I did had stopped me from knocking on her door to fill her in. There was still the matter of whatever she needed to talk to me about, but I couldn't have anything else on my mind during this meeting. My goal was to convince Michael I hadn't lost my mind and that he should look—carefully—closer to home for the mole. That would be enough of a challenge without whatever added stress Madison wanted to heap on me.

Gideon's door had also been closed. I wouldn't have minded if he'd come to bed with me this morning—something to help pass the time—but he'd kissed my forehead and wished me a good sleep before shutting himself in his room. The huskiness of his regret had prevented any sense of rejection, and although I'd crawled into bed disappointed, I accepted he'd made the right call. Although he'd proved he had the vitality of twenty men, he looked like something my parents' cat might have dragged in from the streets, and by the cautious way he moved, I suspected he'd pushed himself too hard. He needed a chance to heal, and I'd needed the sleep.

The privacy had also given me the opportunity to slip away without waking him up. He would have fought to come with me, and I hadn't wanted to waste time assuring him I would be fine. As much as a pep talk before I headed out would have been nice, I was better off facing this alone. I probably wouldn't have gotten one anyway. Gideon thought I was making the wrong move, and Madison would no doubt agree with him. It was why I'd left my phone at home. I didn't want to be bogged down with lectures when I'd already made up my mind.

I saw his point, but as long as I paid attention and watched my back, I held firm that gaining Michael's support was our best chance of finding out the truth about Gagnon and, if our suspicions were right, taking him down.

Traffic sped overhead, the lighter cars doing little more than echoing against the concrete, the heavier vehicles causing the walls to shake and the magic-infused bulbs to tremble in their metal cages. Bugs and dirt clogged the cages themselves, obscuring the yellow glow that attempted to light my way through the twists and turns.

To avoid touching the sludge creeping along the walls, I stuck to the middle of the dried-out path. These storm sewers and access tunnels used to be fully functional, but as the municipal government had updated the city's infrastructure, SMOAC had commandeered them. Now the only water pooling on the ground was what seeped through the walls and between the cracks. Not much more than a lingering moistness beneath my boots, which softened my footsteps and prevented the echoes created by every other minor noise. Even my breath bounced off the walls a few decibels too loudly.

At one time all these tunnels must have been well maintained—they were used as official routes for supernaturals who had a harder time getting around in public—but over the years, many passages had fallen into disrepair, used for shadier dealings by shadier supernaturals, and no one dared to go down them unless they had money or wanted to be impaled by a horn or claw or talon.

So far I'd seen and heard no trace of Michael, but I expected to find him at the hub, the point where the tunnels joined. Once there, we would have half a dozen exits available if anyone came after us. Not only would our position have a tactical advantage, but the fact he'd chosen it told me he was willing to take me seriously. At least until he heard me out. I would have to make my report good and quick, because he wasn't likely to give me much time, and as I walked through the tunnels, navigating my way towards the centre, I tried to figure out how best to present my case.

I turned another corner, and the tunnel widened into a cavernous arena. The ceiling rose from seven feet to fifteen, light from a dozen fixtures filling the room with shadows around six concrete pillars. Including the one I'd come through, six archways sat on my level, extending to various points across town, and on the west side, a staircase led up to a seventh, an access point that eventually connected to the tunnels under Carleton University.

I'd reached the hub.

I checked behind each pillar for any unexpected guests before settling my back against one to wait. I was a few minutes early, having wanted to clear the place before we met, and Michael was nothing if not punctual.

My guts twisted with nerves, and every small sound had me reaching for air, raising half-hearted shields I could strengthen if needed. My left hand rested against the small of my back, close to the hunting knife I wore sheathed under my jacket. While I trusted my commander with my life, I didn't trust anyone else who might find me here. Not even the rats.

"Dawson?" Michael's voice reached me in an echoing greeting from my left.

I pushed away from the pillar and stepped into a pool of light. "I'm here."

He came forward, relief etched into the lines around his eyes. The yellow glow caught the angles of his jaw and cast shadows across his cheeks, making him look older and more haggard than he had in the car yesterday. Whatever was happening here had aged my mentor a hundred years in seven days, and I was as furious about that as anything else.

He wasted no time closing the distance between us, his gaze scanning the exits behind me as I did the same behind him. "You're alone?"

I nodded. "Who else would be with me? Eric shot the only man who'd agreed to work with me."

I hated guarding my words with Michael. I'd come here to tell him everything, but only to a point. Although I was prepared to fill him in on more of what Madison had found, if I could do that without sharing her name, I would. As for Gideon, he was still wanted for questioning by the department, so regardless of Michael's feelings about the mole, he would feel obligated to hunt him down and bring him in if he learned he'd survived. I hoped my silence about their involvement would keep them out of the mole's sights, even if it meant sacrificing the same advantage for myself.

"What about you?" I asked.

I wouldn't put it past Michael to bring Eric with him. He'd confided in my lieutenant, trusted him with his private investigation. It only made sense he'd want to keep him in the loop with whatever wild theory I spouted. But I wasn't ready to share my theories with anyone other than my commander. Not when I suspected his reaction would be as full of skepticism as my first response had been.

Thankfully, Michael nodded. "You asked me here in confidence, Dawson. I wouldn't betray that."

"Thank you. I'm sorry. It's not that I don't trust you. I'm just—" I shoved my hands in my jacket pockets, and all at once, the strain of the past week landed on me. This was the first time I had seen Michael when neither of us were on duty. All week we'd had people watching us, needing something. We'd been trapped by our roles of colonel and captain. All this time, I'd wanted my friend. "I don't know which way is up anymore."

"Hey, talk to me." He rested his hands on my shoulders until I met his gaze. The deep understanding, the willingness to listen, bolstered my courage. How ridiculous I'd been, worrying about meeting him. Gideon's fear had crawled into the back of my head and nested there, but this was Michael. "I get that you're overwhelmed by what's happened. How can you not be? You've got the syndicate riding your back, you found the minister dead, you've survived three ghostbombs, you lost your team, and your family hasn't even gotten on a damned plane to come check on you. But you've got me, kid. I'm right here."

I gripped his arms as though his solidness would steady the world.

He squeezed my shoulders and let me go. "You said you learned something new? Let's talk it out. I'm stumped on my end. That shipping authorization tells us O'Malley's getting big for his britches, but I haven't been able to track down the actual shipment to see if it's moved yet. While I'm not happy you poked around on your own—*again*—" he gave me a hard stare, but the corner of his mouth curled upwards "—maybe your disobedience can get us out of the rut."

He made himself comfortable leaning against the pillar across from me, arms crossed, one foot over the other. I wished I could mirror his casual assurance.

"I don't think O'Malley's moved at all." I tucked my hands behind me so he wouldn't see my fingers trembling. "I think Kingston's been a smokescreen this whole time to distract us from what's going on at home. Real close to home."

"Oh?"

I took a deep breath, braced myself for his reaction, and said, "I have good reason to think Gagnon is one of the moles. In fact, I think his role is bigger than feeding intel to the syndicate. I think he ordered the de Lauer attack." I'd played this conversation through my head so many times on the way here, and while I knew how incredible it sounded, hitting the punch-line first stood a greater chance of grabbing Michael's attention and hopefully busting through his denial.

"You what?" His eyebrows crawled towards his hairline as he straightened away from the pillar. "You can't be serious."

Was he considering walking out? Tackling me and dragging me to a nice, quiet padded cell? The clock was ticking now to share as much information as possible before his shock wore off and he stopped listening. This was my best chance to get him to see the whole picture. Probably my last chance.

"I've never been more so," I said. "Everything I've dug up points to it. I told you about the failed projects, Colonel, and you told me they're unrelated, but I took another look, and the pattern points to something more than extending our resources. Think of all the task force projects that never got off the ground. Each one shut down *after* the money was granted. The same pattern across every branch. All of them headed by the deputy. Eric says this has something to do with FoSA, but where did that money go? More than that, every one of those projects and their cancellations were signed when the minister was out of town and had no way to read or approve them."

I'd lost him already. The doubt in his eyes screamed as loudly as if I'd said the Man in the Moon was behind it all. Hell, for all I knew, the Moonman *did* have a role in this that I hadn't discovered yet. At this point, nothing would surprise me.

"Dawson…"

"I know how it sounds," I said, "but would I have asked you to meet me if I didn't have proof? I might sound paranoid and insane, but I'm not. My troops are dead, these ghostbombs are real, and I would not waste my time or yours hunting shadows to find out who's responsible. Not when the department is doing so little to seek justice for my team." My lungs burned, and I pressed my fingers into my sternum to ease the spasm. I couldn't lose myself to emotion. Not over something so important.

He watched me, head tilted, a furrow deepening his brow. "You say you have proof? What kind of proof?"

I licked my lips. I'd known these questions were coming. I'd prepared for them, a mix of truth and fiction. "Files. I took a flash drive from the minister's desk when we found his body. It was tucked underneath him, so I thought it might be important. I was so desperate to find answers."

A lie, and one that didn't put me in the best light, but it was better than admitting Madison had accessed the system before IT cut her off.

"That's not—" he started, then pressed his lips together and didn't finish. His gaze jumped from tunnel to tunnel, and I wondered what was going through his head. It finally rested on me again, sparking with intensity. "Where have you been staying, Jet?"

I started, not having expected *that* question. "What do you mean?"

"You've changed your phone number, your new one comes up blocked, and you haven't been home. Even before Eric dropped you off yesterday."

I drew my shoulders back and narrowed my eyes. I hadn't forgotten my chase through Centretown to escape O'Malley's goon, but how did Michael know my whereabouts so well? Yesterday I'd told him I had a place to stay, but before that?

Michael snorted a laugh and passed a hand over his face. "Don't give me that look, Dawson." He stretched his hand towards the tunnels. "There's a madman out there making ghostbombs, and you've evaded three of them. Of course I'm going to keep tabs on you." He rested his hands on my shoulders again and ducked to catch my eye. "You're the best I have, more a kid to me than my niece and nephew. I want to make sure you're okay. Especially when it looks like O'Malley's got his eye on you, too."

I riled under his gentle reprimand, but he was right. Only luck and a herculean effort had helped me escape Sammy G. I didn't know what he would have done if he'd caught me. The look on his face haunted me. As though my escaping him had been exactly what he'd wanted…

A niggling thought worked to get my attention, but when I reached for it, it slipped away, and before I could search harder, another one slammed into me.

"You still don't believe me about the projects, do you?

You're focused on Dougall and his bombs, but I'm telling you, this is bigger than him. The drugs, O'Malley, even these protests are playing into something huge, and everything points to Gagnon. With Bastien dead, he has all of SMOAC at his disposal and no one looking at him too closely."

I knew I shouldn't be surprised he didn't want to hear the possibility that he'd missed the obvious. I should have brought the paperwork with me but hadn't wanted to take the chance the documents would lead back to Madison. I'd hoped my word would be enough.

"I don't know what you think a failed surveillance project proves," Michael said, his tone gentle, tired. He sighed and ran his hand over my hair before stepping back. "Maybe there is a pattern, but do you honestly think a man like Lucien Gagnon would move against his own people? He swore an oath to protect them. He is devoted to his country and the supernatural community within it. Why do you think he wants this federation to step in and help? He knows SMOAC lacks the budget and personnel to do right by us. He sees what Bastien refused to accept. He's exactly what the department needs. So we can finally get free of the wall's shadow."

Passion flickered through his words as his anger grew. I'd known my news would surprise him. I hadn't expected it to offend him.

My earlier unformed thought wriggled again at the back of my mind. A teasing, taunting tickle that grew louder as Michael talked.

He walked around the hub, and I took the time while he regained his composure to run through our conversation and figure out what bothered me.

I'd told him everything, and he didn't believe me. Nothing there was unusual or, though disappointing, unexpected. I'd come here accepting this would be a challenge.

I played through his arguments again, and only after the third time did I land on a giant red flag. My breath caught in my throat.

The surveillance project.

Without hesitation, he'd remembered exactly what projects I was referring to, but why the confused look on his face when I'd lied about finding proof in the minister's office? *That's not—* What had he been about to say? Not what? Not possible I'd found a USB stick under Bastien's body? How would he know?

Unless…

I couldn't let myself consider it.

Eric was right. Michael was right. I was paranoid. Seeing monsters at every turn, and now even the most familiar, friendly faces were turning ugly.

"So maybe I'm wrong," I said, "but have you found any evidence pointing to someone else?"

He drew to a stop a few feet to my left and frowned. "Not yet. I told you, Dawson, I'm stuck on where to look next."

"What about Carstairs? Have you looked into him yet, figured out what his end game might be? Who lined him up to join my team?" It pained me to hold the smallest suspicion over the man who meant so much to me, but I had to know. If I was wrong, I was wrong.

I prayed I was wrong.

"Carstairs?" he asked. "What about him?"

I blanched. I'd told him the man was a syndicate thug. I'd told him what he'd done to Gideon. How could he have forgotten? How could my accusation have meant nothing?

Unless…

Again with that word, but I couldn't hold back my growing horror.

Unless he'd already known before I told him. Unless my news—a revelation to me—wasn't nearly as surprising, and therefore worth taking in, to him.

The air in the Labyrinth grew thin, the space dark and confined. I wished now I'd suggested somewhere more public.

Fear struggled against denial.

I was reading too much into his forgetfulness. The man had a lot on his mind. What were the ravings of someone he suspected was off her rocker? To even consider it might be anything more was a betrayal of everything he'd done for me. He'd trained me, moulded me, morphed me into the wolf I was today. The leader of my pack.

A pack that had been horribly, brutally cut down by a bunch of cowards who hadn't bothered to show up in person to look them in the eye when they killed them.

And I was considering the possibility Michael was involved? In the murder of his own troops?

An incredulous laugh nearly burst out of me, but my growing confusion held it at bay as my years of trust warred against what he was saying.

This man was family.

This man had protected me from losing my stripes.

This man knew that my finding a flash drive under the minister's shoulder was impossible and refused to believe at every turn that the mole had burrowed deeply enough into the department to embezzle money and influence who knew how many aspects of our lives.

My head throbbed with the effort to parse through it all, suspicion and disbelief bouncing back and forth, refusing to let me settle on one side or another.

"Dawson, what is going on?" he asked, and the paternal concern in his eyes contrasted so sharply with my rising doubts that pain shot through my head. My chest tightened. I couldn't breathe. What was real? What was the lie?

"Come on, kid, talk to me. I can't explain if you don't tell me what has you so wound up. Whatever you think you know, there's a reason for it. Walk me through it."

Beyond the pounding in my skull, beyond his words of reassurance, I sensed a shift in the air and my third eye detected two shadows approaching us from above. I raised my head to get a better sense of their direction and followed the stairs that led to the second-storey tunnel.

"Michael, you should move," I said. Whatever else he and I needed to talk about, I had to make sure we survived long enough to do it. If danger had found us, we would fight it together.

"Wha—"

He stepped towards me and followed my gaze to the upper level as two large men stepped into view.

Familiar, though it took me a moment to recognize them.

When I did, my blood ran cold.

Sammy G had found me, and beside him stood Storms Anderson, O'Malley's second top guy.

I pulled my blade and looked to Michael, expecting to find him shocked with the realization we'd been followed.

What I found instead was a flash of irritation. No surprise, no fear, just the same frustration I'd seen in his eyes every time a mission failed to go according to plan.

He shifted his gaze to meet mine, and in the depth of his stare, in his relaxed posture at the sight of the newly arrived enemy, I saw the truth I'd been too busy to notice before.

He hadn't been blind to the real corruption in the department.

I had.

Chapter 34

Jet

I WAS SIX years old when I discovered I'd inherited my father's supernatural genes. Until then, my life had been normal. Father, mother, brother, all of us close, my father's mother a regular host and visitor in our weekly routine.

I'd wanted to be an astronaut.

That wish was what pushed me one day, while playing in the backyard with my brother, to throw myself off the swing at the top of the curve in an attempt to launch myself into space.

Gravity soon kicked in.

My fall was short. About halfway down, I caught the air, wrapped it around me, and stayed hovering for a good thirty seconds before I overthought what I was doing and lost my grip, tumbling the rest of the way to the ground.

I broke my arm, but that didn't matter. Curtis, two years older than me, had seen what had happened. He told my parents, and they immediately knew what it meant. After that, my father and grandmother brought me even closer, teaching me, explaining the ways of the world, helping me develop my abilities. As my strength grew, the odd ridges on my forehead opened and turned out to be a working third eye. My mother grew cold, detached, and my brother, my best friend in the world, turned his back on me.

That betrayal had rocked me, tainted everything, and touched my life with a bitterness twenty-eight years hadn't shaken.

It was nothing to the betrayal that rocked me today as I stood in the bowels of the city, staring into the familiar grey eyes of a man I'd just learned I didn't know at all.

With seeming reluctance, he broke eye contact with me and snarled at the men up the stairs. "What the hell are you doing here? I told Lucien I had this. I needed a bit more time."

"The boss says you're out of time."

Sammy's deep voice echoed through the hub, and I grounded my feet against the cement to give myself a solid launching point. His ability was notorious, how he could create a sonic boom that knocked people off their feet. He wouldn't find me unprepared.

"Kill the soldier, stick to the plan," Storms said. His eyes darkened into black pools, and my skin prickled with the shift of electrical energy in the air.

He reached for the gun at his hip, and I didn't hesitate. Drawing the air in the room closer, I stretched it taut and launched it forward, knocking all three men backwards. In the few seconds it took them to regain their balance, I was already halfway up the stairs, more air wrapped around my fist to throw a punch into Sammy's throat.

Take out the greater threat. Don't give them a chance to use their advantages.

Michael's voice sounded through my head, all his years of teaching me, training me to become the best soldier on his team.

And yet, even as I remembered his words, I accepted that I was ignoring them. The greatest threat in this space was Michael, but I couldn't bring myself to turn on him. Instead, I kept my distance, removing his opportunity to manipulate my kinetic energy, and focused my attention on O'Malley's lackeys.

My frenzied onslaught had taken them both by surprise, but the initial shock wore off sooner than I'd hoped, and the reason for their status in O'Malley's top tier became obvious. They were quick, and they worked off each other, Sammy's booming voice and Storms's electrical surges leaving me disoriented, caught between thunder and lightning.

I drew the air close to me again, but Storms released an electric charge, and I had to drop my hold, ducking to the ground to prevent the static from shocking me from head to toe. My sudden drop caused Sammy's punch to swing over my head. I swept out my foot, connecting with his ankle and taking him to the ground, but by the time I stood back up, Storms was there to land a blow in my gut. An electric charge passed through me, made my heart stutter and my vision flash black, and only by trusting my instincts to duck into a crouch was I able to avoid Sammy's tackle.

He stumbled over my stooped frame, and I threw my elbow. It slammed into the side of his face, bones crunched, and his muffled grunt sent a rush through my veins, urging me on.

Through the bars of the railing, I spotted Michael. He hadn't moved from his place on the ground floor, and though I only caught a glimpse before Storms drew my attention, I swore he was smiling. Glee? Relief that I would finally be out of his hair? Pride that even in a two-to-one fight, I was holding my own?

I didn't care. What I wished was that he'd throw himself in with the rest of them so I could kick his ass, too.

Sweat dripped into my eyes. I blinked it away, ignored the crack and pop in my shoulder as my already strained muscles warned me to stop, and the moment's hesitation prevented me from spotting Sammy coming at me again. His weight pushed me towards the stairs, but I refused to let him control the manoeuvre. With a twist of my hips, I turned us around mid-fall and hauled him with me over the railing.

My stomach lurched as we hit air, but I wrangled myself so I was on top when we landed, my elbow buried in Sammy's sternum. His face turned purple at the lack of oxygen, his swollen, bloody cheek darkening another three shades.

I rolled to my feet and didn't give him an opportunity to join me. With all my strength, I brought my heel down on his windpipe, and he sagged against the ground.

Storms let out a bellow of rage as he tore down the stairs. Static raised the hairs on my arms, but this time I didn't let the shock of pain stop me from grabbing hold of the air. I sent it upwards to the water pipes running beneath the city streets and twisted the metal until it cracked in half. Rain poured over Storms's head just as he prepared to stun me with another charge. What he got instead was an electric shower. He twitched as the power doubled back into his chest, and I drew my knife from its sheath and hurled it into his heart. He collapsed to his knees and face planted onto the muddy stone.

Silence fell, broken only by the spilling water and the blood rushing in my ears. My lungs spasmed, my chest rising and falling with ragged gasps.

Not ready yet to move past what had happened to what had to come next, I staggered over to Storms to retrieve my knife, wiped the blood on his T-shirt, and returned it to the sheath at the small of my back.

I straightened my ponytail, smoothed the creases from my jacket. Gradually, my heartbeat slowed and my vision cleared. The sweat running under my shirt mixed with the water spraying from the open pipes and left me shivering against the pain of my discovery. I squeezed my eyes shut to fortify myself against what waited behind me, then straightened my spine and turned around.

Michael hadn't moved. He stood by the wall staring at the corpses on the ground, his mouth twisted with disdain.

"Lucien's short-sighted, and O'Malley's a fool. I hate working with these amateurs, but needs must."

Words failed me. This was a nightmare. It couldn't be real. He couldn't be involved. Not Michael.

But in the face of the battle I'd just fought and won, to cling to denial would make me the fool.

"Why?" I asked.

Pity filled his eyes. As though I were the stupid one for not seeing his purpose in committing treason. But how was I supposed to see his reason for killing so many of his own people?

"I guess I should have suggested we meet somewhere with chairs," he said, offering a smile that didn't fit with anything that had happened in the past… however long it was. Hours? Days? "If these assholes had given me a chance to explain first, maybe you'd have been more willing to listen, but Lucien's gotten impatient."

He shook his head and rubbed the back of his neck.

"You have my full attention now," I said, my voice stony. He wanted to explain? Perfect. I was all ears. In spite of everything, I still hoped, deep down, that he'd gone undercover. That his involvement had been a ruse. Any second now, he would tell me the truth behind his familiarity with these people.

"You've already uncovered a good chunk by the sounds of it." He chuckled. "After all your days running around chasing shadows, the last thing I expected was for you to go digging into things that actually mattered. Always a woman of action.

It's why you're my favourite."

Laughing? Amused by what I'd brought forward?

None of this conversation was going the way I'd imagined.

Then again, I'd never in a million years imagined having this conversation.

When I did nothing but stare, he raked his fingers through his hair and shrugged. "I told Lucien to stop putting things on paper. It was only a matter of time before someone caught on. But he thought someone would notice sooner if there wasn't a paper trail. Bastien was a thorough son of a bitch. Always paying attention to where money was being channelled and where his people spent their energy. I tell you, he was the biggest bottleneck to doing anything that would create actual, necessary change. Doing something right for our kind."

The ground beneath my feet wobbled.

"Excuse me? Something *right*?" He had the nerve to say that? To me?

He frowned. "Of course. What do you think we're doing, Dawson? All of this, everything we've done, is for the benefit of our people. I never lied to you about that. Whatever you think you've figured out, if you don't see that, you've got it wrong."

He started walking again, pacing between pillars, avoiding the corpses on the ground and the water splashing against the dirty stone. I set my back against one of the pillars out of range of the cold spray, not wanting to give him—or anyone else— an opening to sneak up on me. Gagnon had already sent two people after us—how many more waited in the wings?

I opened my third eye, stretched my sight down all seven tunnels as far as I could, but detected only Michael. As if that weren't enough. How could I trust my abilities when I'd missed the biggest liar of them all?

"You're thinking short term, Dawson. Just like Bastien. You can see what's right in front of you and catch glimpses of what was, but you can't imagine life outside the status quo." He bowed his head. "I know I should have brought you into this sooner. You might have helped us find another way forward without bringing in that snake Dougall, but I know how stubborn you can be. You're so set on black and white, you don't leave room to get your hands dirty. It makes you a great captain, but a lousy visionary. And that's what we need here. That's what we're aiming for. A revolution."

He spoke with such passion, my heart stirred. He'd always been good at the motivational speeches, but I doubted he ever would have talked me around on this one.

"We're working to protect our people," he continued. "To elevate them to the level they deserve. Not by some big *war* or whatever you seem to think. We're talking policy. Contracts. Trade agreements."

"FoSA," I murmured through numb lips.

Michael nodded. "Exactly. You see? I've been honest with you, kid. I told you what their involvement means. Major change. Money, resources, everything we need to do our jobs that this mundane government can't give us. We're making progress on a greater scale and with more speed than the country's ever seen. Under Lucien's guidance, the department is running the way it should have since its inception. No more slowing down to avoid the muns figuring out the truth. We've got one goal, and we won't stop until we've reached it."

His voice wavered in my ear, drowned under the memory of the blast vibrating through the soles of my boots. The screams of nine people tearing each other and themselves apart. A heart monitor flatlining in a cold, sterile hospital room. Bile rose up the back of my throat, chased by a cottony weightlessness that made my limbs feel heavy and disjointed.

"You killed my pack for this?"

My question checked his enthusiasm, and his face fell, his hands dropping by his sides as he slowed to a stop. "That was a damned hard call to make. You weren't supposed to be caught in it. You were supposed to be upstairs with Sampson. But I had to do it. Sacrifice is always needed for change." When he raised his gaze to mine, it shone with fresh vigour. "If your fallen troops could see what their deaths are helping us achieve, they'd be proud to have given their lives for it. Our people had to be woken up. They had to demand change. Now Lucien can offer it to them."

My numbness ebbed as the nausea returned. I wouldn't cry—I was too stunned for tears—but I did want to lodge my fist in his face.

"What do you say, Dawson?" he asked, as calmly as if he were oblivious to my growing rage. Just as I'd been oblivious to his treachery. "Will you join us? Will you sit down, hear us out, and play a role in saving our country? Your rightful role, Captain. The one you should have held from the start."

He spoke as though he were offering an olive branch. A reasonable job opportunity in the middle of his indifference. His delusional self-righteousness.

Fiery rage sparked deep in my middle and rose to fill my limbs. "Are you joking? You have got to be out of your fucking mind. *Join* you? I don't care what warped vision of the future you have. If it comes at the cost of people *now*, then it isn't something I will ever be a part of."

"You wouldn't be alone at my side. Sampson sees what we're striving for."

My heart stopped, and I forgot how to breathe. Eric? "Impossible. He can't know everything."

"He's the one who told you about the federation, isn't he? He knows where his loyalties lie. SMOAC doesn't only exist when you agree with it, Jet. It isn't a charity organization you can turn your back on. The department is still here, and it needs people in power to keep it functioning. Sampson understands that. He's the soldier you trained, as dependable as you made him. Do you have any idea how disappointed he is that you, his trusted leader, turned out to be so unfaithful?"

His verbal blow hit so hard I saw stars.

"Me? You're calling *me* unfaithful? When I earned my stripes, I swore to uphold the safety of my community, *Colonel*. That means protecting our kind from madmen who set out to destroy everything that matters to them."

"To what end?" he barked. "You think things are going to stay the way they are now? With the rise of social media, of smartphones, of TikToks and Twitters, you think our lives will maintain their current level of secrecy and security? You're naive. We need to be ahead of the curve, ready to form a new cover when the old one is so frayed the light shines through the seams."

"By allying yourself with criminals?"

"Needs must, Dawson. It's the way it's always been and the way it always will be. The problem will keep getting bigger, and the government is too slow to outrun it. It doesn't matter what nasty taste it leaves in my mouth. If the result keeps our people safe, I'll suffer whatever bedfellows I have to. As a loyal soldier. Loyal to my department and my kind. You may not choose to see it, but I'm doing this to keep you safe, too. And people like you. People whose family and friends turned their backs on them when the truth came out. But I have always been there for you, even when your family wasn't. I shielded you from the minister's blame, from the media, from Lucien's suggestion we throw you to the lions. I'd do it again. You mean too damn much to me to watch you burn. So come with me. Work with me on this. You, me, and Eric, as it's always been."

As it's always been.

Years of memories swirled through my mind. Always the three of us. His star players. Seeing our potential and preparing us for bigger and better.

For this?

For how long? And when had he decided to leave me in the dark and focus on Eric instead? The obedient pup always so eager to follow.

Michael was right about one thing, though. Since the blast in the de Lauer subbasement, he had gone out of his way to protect me and my reputation. Offering to look the other way, brushing my insubordination under the carpet, downgrading the consequences. I'd thought it was compassion, or unofficial encouragement to keep pushing, but he'd been tying strings around my gratitude. Isolating me from anyone who might listen to me or show support.

Right from the start, he'd been manipulated me.

Every fluid in my body—spit, blood, bile—turned to acid, corroding my insides with shame and humiliation.

All that time he'd been playing me, and now we were here and he expected what? More gratitude? Continued devotion?

He would be disappointed. While he was right about most of my situation, he was wrong about one crucial detail: I wasn't alone, and now Madison, Gideon, and I would know the truth.

I steeled myself, clenched my fists at my sides. "I will never join the people who killed my squad, and whatever you're trying to do, I will stop you."

He bowed his head. "That's a shame, Dawson. A real shame."

I readied myself for another lecture, a warning of what I faced if I stayed on their heels. But in a smooth move—so quick I didn't see him raise his hands—he drew a pistol and aimed it at my head.

Shock held me frozen for a second that stretched into eternity. Michael Torrence, my commander, my mentor.

Not anymore.

I had no time to process the significance of the change. Self-preservation kicked in, and I grabbed his wrist to shift the barrel away from me. He kicked out with his leg and caught me on the ankle. I stumbled, but didn't fall.

My moves were stiff, jerky, as Michael's ability wove around me to stifle my kinetic energy. I may as well have been punching through water, each blow losing momentum as it swung towards him. I couldn't deal any damage, but he couldn't hold his shield up forever. I had to keep at him, take any opportunity to bring him down.

Bring down Michael.

The words made no sense. The truth was right in front of me, but I couldn't accept it. Every move I made was automatic, without heart, almost against my will. My heart burrowed in my throat, my vision growing dark around the edges as I struggled to draw in air. My entire world was on its head. Only training and instinct kept me moving, wading away from his blows, directing the barrel of the gun anywhere but at me.

My primary advantage was the twisted fact that this man had trained me. Almost everything I knew, I knew because of him, because of all the time he had taken to turn me in the soldier he'd needed me to be.

The advantage let me regain control of his wrist when his ability slipped, and I twisted until he lost his hold on the gun. It clattered across the concrete floor, well out of reach, but I had no time to catch my breath before the heel of his palm swung towards my nose. I jerked my face away, and the thrust struck my cheekbone. Stars burst in my vision, and I spat out blood.

"It doesn't have to go this way," he said. I felt as though I'd been running for days, having fought so hard against him, but he was barely winded. "You can still change your mind."

He was talking to mess with me. I knew the trick. I'd used it myself so many times I'd become almost incapable of keeping my mouth shut during a fight. The tactic worked for a reason. No matter how hard I tried to tune him out, his calm voice, the cadence I'd come to associate with confidence, cleverness, and guidance, wormed its way into my ears, throwing me off balance more effectively than any blow.

"You're only hurting yourself," he pressed, blocking another of my slow-moving punches. "Cutting yourself off from the people you care about. From the people who care about you."

He shifted towards the gun, but I spun to block him, drawing my blade in the same motion.

I had to ignore him. He was a snake, and his words were venom. If I paid them any attention, they would crack my resolve, corrupt my thoughts until I was too distracted to put up a solid defence. Worse, until I doubted myself.

My stomach churned, and I made myself fight through the nausea.

He darted in, and I caught the falter in his shield. I grabbed the opening and slashed, pushing him back.

How could he believe he was doing the right thing? When had my mentor lost his mind—and why hadn't I noticed?

"What are you hoping to achieve, Dawson?" he asked as I raised the knife between us again. "Are you going to kill me? *Could* you kill me?"

Ignore him. My head throbbed with the effort, and the sweat dripping down my back sent chills running after it. I was losing control. I had to stay focused.

"If you succeeded, do you think this would be over? You were right, what you said in the car. This is so much bigger than me. So much bigger than either of us."

He moved in closer, tried to slide around me. We were dancing, circling each other. Neither of us had taken the shots we could have. While I judged myself for hesitating, I understood why I did. The only reason I could come up with for his lack of effort was that he meant what he said. He wanted me to join them, to see things his way. Despite everything, he still wanted to take care of me.

Son of a bitch.

"Standing against me, you're choosing the same shit you've always had. The same problems. The same failure to protect your country. Always fighting against a brick wall, never gaining ground." His voice rose, touched with passion and anger, and I flinched away from him, once more caught in the molasses-like tide. He grabbed my wrist and twisted the knife away, but he didn't let me go, wrenching my arm behind me until my hand pressed between my shoulder blades.

My muscles and joints ached too much from my previous days of exertion to summon the full strength of the air, but I pulled it closer, slid it between us, and threw him off me. He grunted as he slammed into the concrete wall.

I drew my arm close to my chest and glowered at him as he struggled to catch his breath, then stirred up the air around my knife. The steel clattered against the ground as it rose to hover between us, the point directed at his chest. My body trembled with the effort it took to control the air, but I couldn't let myself get close to him. I was too exhausted, too confused to pit myself against his strength and ability. It would be too easy for him to get the better of me. I couldn't give him the chance.

I had to kill him.

I knew it.

I also knew I'd never be able to do it with my bare hands. For all that I strove to be a hero, he was right. I was a coward who hated getting her hands dirty.

Come on, Dawson. Make it quick.

All I had to do was hurl the blade into his throat. Over and done.

His red face darkened as he spat on the ground. "Tell me what else I was supposed to do, Dawson. Show me any major progress that came without sacrifice. If you can do that, you may as well spit in the eye of each of your troops and tell them their deaths were worth nothing."

"Stop it."

"That *they* were worth nothing."

"*Stop it,*" I shouted, and with a sweep of my hand, I launched the knife at him.

He'd anticipated it. Of course he had. The blade made nothing more than a gentle *ting* as it glanced off the concrete wall. Michael had already moved, dropping and rolling towards the gun on the ground.

I shifted the air surrounding me, summoning it closer so I could throw it at him.

He was on his feet before I raised my hands, his weapon once more aimed at my head.

"I'm so sorry, Jet," he said.

He pulled the trigger, and a burst of white powder blew into my face.

Chapter 35

Gideon

"THIS PLACE IS a shithole," I grumbled as Madison and I made our way through the dingy series of tunnels.

"What did you expect? Marble halls and a red carpet?" she asked.

"At least an occasional pass with a broom. This is where you people conduct your hush-hush meets?"

"Trust me, it wouldn't have been my first choice. They're here, though. Somewhere up ahead."

I clenched my fists at my sides, ready to mist, but before I could ask, she shook her head. "It seems fine. Neutral. On edge, but steady."

She closed her eyes and held up a hand for me to be quiet, the third time she'd shut me up since we'd entered the tunnel. When she opened her eyes again, she pointed to the left, and we took a turn.

So far, we'd kept a slow pace, reducing the echo of our footsteps. Now, though, I couldn't miss the way she quickened her pace.

"What is it?" I lengthened my stride to keep up with her.

"I spoke too soon. Something happened. There's fear. Anger."

She paused again and turned to the right. I followed, wishing I didn't have to. I wanted to mist ahead, but I couldn't take the risk of getting lost and wasting time. If anyone knew how to read a room, it was the woman beside me who could literally read a room, and if she sensed trouble, I needed to reach Jet.

I'd gone back and forth on our way to the Labyrinth access point about whether we were making the right decision in coming after her. While I disagreed with her about going without backup, her arguments for not tipping our hand made sense. I was dead, and Madison was in the wind. That was what her people believed, and it worked to our advantage to keep it that way.

But how could I sit around at the safe house and watch TV while Jet took the danger on herself? Especially when she'd left her phone at the apartment. To not be able to call her, to not have her able to contact us if she needed help, was more than I was willing to accept. If she was fine, I wouldn't get in the way, but if Michael tried anything, he would have more than her wrath to deal with.

Madison sped into a run, and her urgency drove mine.

I almost asked how many people she sensed, but reminded myself she wasn't Jet. She picked up emotions, not shadows. There could be a hundred people waiting for us in the middle of this maze, and all we knew was they were angry.

She took another left, and another, and the deeper we progressed into the tunnel, the harder she pushed herself, the tenser her expression became. And all I could do was keep pace with her. I hoped she knew where we were going and that we would find Jet before she needed us. Fifteen minutes of wandering, and I only had Madison's confidence we weren't going in circles. The bug-infested lights and grungy walls gave away nothing about where we were. No signposts or convenient arrows directed us to the hub. All we had were Madison's knowledge of the tunnels and the emotional trail she followed.

When we rounded the last corner, every thought faded as a gunshot rang out.

I stared across an open space, partially hidden by a wide, rounded pillar. Two dead bodies on the ground. A pool of blood mixed with water dripping from a broken pipe. A man standing in front of a woman. A burst of powder. The woman falling.

White particles drifted through the stale air, and I only just had the presence of mind to cover my nose and mouth with the crook of my elbow as I ran in and, sliding on my knees, caught Jet before her head hit the stone floor.

Michael was gone, having torn down a different passageway by the time I reached her.

Madison raced in after me and stood frozen at my side, staring in the direction he had gone. As soon as the echo of his footsteps faded, she flew to Jet's other side and took her hand. Like me, she'd covered the lower half of her face with her arm.

Propped up against me, Jet twitched. Her face was white, covered in fine powder, and underneath it, a sheen of sweat coated her pale forehead. Her eyes were closed, and although she drew breath, the rise and fall of her chest was quick and ragged.

I knew we had to hurry, get out of here before we breathed in the white dust, but I couldn't bring myself to let her go even long enough to pick her up.

Ghost.

Breathing ghost.

Fucking bastard, I'll fucking kill him.

Jet, wake up.

For fuck's sake, wake up.

I had no idea how much I spoke aloud or how much was a blur in my head. I couldn't think straight, I couldn't see anything but her. How had I lost her when we were just finding our way back? If she slipped away from me, Torrence, Dougall, O'Malley, they would all suffer the agony of their insides being pulled out through their throats. If she died, my mercy died with her.

The moment her eyes opened, her dark gaze clear and lucid, the air was sucked out of my body. Without thinking, I dropped my arm and brushed her hair out of her eyes, incapable of not touching her. Whiteness covered the ridges of her face and her eyes were red with irritation, but there was no wildness, no sign of an altered mind.

I looked at Madison, who sat back on her heels and lowered her arm, dazed.

"Is she all right?" I asked, desperate for some confirmation that my heart was allowed to beat again.

"Her brain chemistry is fine. Stressed, but not overloaded. It's not ghost."

I returned my attention to Jet. Not ghost. *Thank god.* Not ghost? What had the crazy son of a bitch shot her with, then? Baking powder? Why? What was the point? To give himself time to get away?

Jet gave her head a shake and eased herself into a sit, but I kept my arm around her waist, ready to catch her if her strength failed.

"How do you feel?" I asked. My tongue felt swollen with adrenaline and terror, but my pulse had started to slow on seeing her so… normal.

In a heartbeat, I'd gone from fearing she was dead to knowing I hadn't lost her, and I felt as though I'd grown fucking wings, ready to soar out of here on a current of relief. Was this how Jet had felt after seeing me get shot and finding me in the safe house? Had her happiness been anywhere close to mine? Part of me hoped so. The other part of me was terrified about what it meant for the personal and emotional guards I'd kept raised around me for so long.

"I'm okay," she said, and her voice sounded solid. "Confused and heartbroken, but okay." Her eyes filled with tears, and she brushed them away. "Betrayed, but alive." The tears returned, and this time she didn't bother to get rid of them. "Michael is one of them. He killed my pack."

Her whole body convulsed, and she wrenched to the side, away from Madison, to bring up the contents of her empty stomach. When she finished retching, I wrapped my arms around her, pulling her close as Madison reclaimed her hand.

"He admitted it," Jet said through chattering teeth. "He—"

It was all she got out before she broke down. I bundled her against my chest and held her, catching Madison's gaze over her head. Her calm hazel eyes stared back at me, filled with opinions and suggestions I didn't want to guess at. I didn't care what she sensed from me. It didn't matter. I was who I was, and whatever ideas she had about me and my future, they were impossible. No matter what I wanted, so much of my life was out of my hands. I broke eye contact, and Madison turned her fussing to Jet, rubbing her warm hands over Jet's cold ones, using her sleeve to wipe some of the powder off her face.

Gradually, Jet's shaking subsided, and she sagged against me, her head resting in the crook of my shoulder.

"How am I supposed to stop him?" she asked in an empty voice. "How can I fight against the man who knows me better than I know myself most of the time? In the eyes of anyone who can help, I'm a disgraced agent and he's a national hero. He holds all the cards."

Madison gently pulled her away from me. I took my time releasing her, not ready to let her go when she looked so shattered, her narrow frame appearing so frail, her expression tight with the effort of her self-control. Only once I was sure she was able to sit up on her own did I loosen my grip, though I stayed close enough to be there if she needed me.

"First, we're going to clean you up," Madison said. She pulled some tissue out of her pocket and set to work cleaning whatever her sleeve had missed. I watched the way her eyes traced the lines of Jet's brow, her nose, her lips, her chin in the dim light, searching for any trace of what Michael might have done to her. I performed my own assessment as Madison worked but noticed nothing beyond a faint redness around Jet's three eyes and her nose. Whatever the powder was, it didn't appear to have caused any damage.

Once the worst of the whiteness was gone, Madison held out her other hand, and Jet took it.

"Then we're going to get out of this pit," she said as she eased them both to their feet.

I rose with them, light-headed after the rush of horror and the high of relief. Jet wobbled, and I held out my hands, but she steadied herself.

"The three of us are still standing," Madison said. "Still

fighting. Whatever Michael hoped to accomplish by bringing you here, he failed. He might think he knows you, but if that were true, he never would have tried to deceive you the way he did. He doesn't know me, he doesn't know Gideon, and he doesn't know how ready we are to tear them apart piece by piece. Don't lose hope yet, Captain Dawson, do you hear me?"

Jet forced a smile, but by the way her shoulders straightened and her chin lifted, I suspected her friend's words had gotten through to her.

They had a similar effect on me. If I hadn't had enough motivation to bring these assholes to heel for what they'd done to me, Michael's betrayal of Jet set my blood on fire.

I imagined driving a knife into the man's heart and twisting slowly, not letting him slip away too easily.

The only thing that would hold me back—the only reason I would leave him alive—would be to let Jet finish the bastard herself.

Chapter 36

Madison

WE ARRIVED BACK at the safe house around midnight. A package waited for us at the door, and I picked it up without looking at the return address.

No one spoke.

I doubted any of us had the strength to voice a syllable.

Gideon walked like a man who, well, had died and come back to life. Not only in the way he carried himself, cautious of how he moved the left side of his body, holding his arm close to his middle as though to shield his healing injury from any further trauma, but also in the way he couldn't take his eyes off Jet.

He knew I'd noticed. It was obvious by the way he avoided looking me in the eye, but I couldn't stop watching him. So much was loaded in his stare I had trouble breaking it down. It probably would have been polite of me not to try, but I needed something to keep my thoughts off Jet's horrible discovery. Lucien and Michael, traitors. Two of the most powerful men in the department working with the syndicate for their own ends. I wasn't ready to process it yet. So instead, I focused on Gideon's concern, his wariness, his faint trace of desire tempered by an emotion I would never dream of naming love before either of them spoke the word first.

When he'd walked in on me in the kitchen and nearly scared me into an early grave, I'd thought I couldn't be happier he'd survived. I'd been wrong. Now, given Jet's current state, I hoped his presence, his strength and simmering anger, would be enough to keep her moving.

Because as it stood, I wasn't so certain she could do it on her own.

She moved with zombie-like stiffness, her feet shuffling forward because we were guiding her, her lungs taking in and expelling air because they didn't know what else to do. I didn't think she'd even blinked since we'd left the tunnels.

Her shock was so potent, I detected almost nothing else from her. A blanketed emotion that blocked everything out and brought her so close to pure neutral an Eye might have been confused.

She had gone into the Labyrinth expecting to warn Michael of the dangers ahead. Fourteen years of following his lead, meeting his exacting standards, respecting him more than anyone else in her life… only to have reality come crashing down on her head.

Or blowing up in her face, as it happened.

How could she feel anything *but* shock? How would she trust or have faith in anyone again?

And in the middle of this, I somehow had to tell her I was leaving.

So I thanked Meril that Gideon was alive and that he'd chosen to come back to her. She would need him. The layers of this conspiracy squeezed tighter and tighter, creating a claustrophobic ring they would never penetrate if they didn't work as a team.

My speech to her in the hub had done the trick to get her home, but I wondered if it would jumpstart her into action.

I considered reaching out to calm her mind so reason and practicality could overpower her pain, but I was too nervous to try, my own emotions too shaken by everything I'd sensed in the Labyrinth. I'd warned Gideon of the fear and anger, but hadn't had time to tell him about the grief. I'd nearly drowned in the deluge of hatred and loss, of desperation. It had taken every ounce of strength to raise the guards around my ability so they didn't overwhelm me and render me useless.

The worst part was, the emotions had come from Jet *and* Michael. None of them one-sided. His grief had been as strong as hers, his desperation as great.

What I'd felt changed nothing, of course. He was a traitor, his crimes worse for acting against his conscience and turning on a person he cared for as deeply as he did.

If anything, the depth of his pain turned him into even more of a monster in my eyes, and I would feel no remorse when Jet struck him down.

On the walk back to the safe house, along streets as dark and quiet as one would expect in the middle of the night. I'd looked over my shoulder every few steps. I didn't sense anyone nearby, but I was terrified someone might follow us and discover we'd hidden in plain sight. Only once I locked the apartment door did I relax and appreciate the peace of our haven.

Which seemed smaller, somehow. As though we were standing in the last safe place in the city.

I couldn't remember ever feeling so lonely.

Jet went into the living room, dropped onto the couch, and turned on the television.

The inane babble that cut through the silence was a blessed respite. It prevented any of us from sitting with our thoughts, which could only be a good thing for now. Everything was too new and raw. In the morning, once the sun rose and the shadows receded, everything would be clearer. Less hopeless. Or so I wished.

Though Jet might have chosen a cheerier channel. A replay of the earlier news flickered on the screen, reports of protests across the country devolving into riots in Vancouver and Montreal. The subjects of the protests conflicted across stations as Jet flicked through, but the truth was easy enough to see for anyone in the know.

The supernatural community was rising up as the recent Ottawa attacks caught national attention, the reaction snowballing as the anger grew. The louder our people became, the better the situation for Lucien and the sooner the queen would get involved. Lucien had to know he was fighting within a narrow window. How close were we to the tipping point?

How soon after I crossed the wall, after I abandoned my friends, would this come to a head?

I can't leave them.

From the moment Serc had told me of my summons, I'd accepted my fate, but now more than ever, as we closed in on the eleventh hour, I wished we had another option.

Jet finally landed on a fluffy sitcom and dropped the volume until all I heard from across the room was the staccato laugh track and the cadence of witty banter.

Leaving her to the television, with Gideon at her side as her vigilant guardian, I turned my attention to the parcel sitting on the kitchen island.

At the sight of the familiar handwriting printed in neat script across the envelope, some of my tension melted away. My grandmother had come through, and her timing couldn't have been better. Thank Meril for supernatural couriers.

I switched on the kettle and opened the envelope. The cannister of tea rolled into my palm, and I twisted off the cap to inhale the faint hints of lavender. The bitter sweetness swept into my lungs, revitalizing me, and I didn't bother to ask before taking three mugs out of the cupboard.

Tonight wasn't a matter of *wanting* a cup of tea, it was a matter of *needing* one. Or so Nan would have said.

When the kettle clicked, I poured the water over the home-made teabags and let them steep. I debated joining the others while I waited, but the opportunity for a few minutes of quiet reflection took priority, and I stayed where I was, my back to the living room, breathing in the dancing steam. The herbs braced me against what I had to do next.

Jet wouldn't take my news well. Gideon would do his best to stay strong for her, but how much could he ask of himself when he was still healing? Handling this on their own was too much to expect from either of them.

I'd readied some allies, but how would we know how many of them were on our side? If *Michael* stood with Lucien, how many of the people I'd called today also believed in Lucien's grand ambitions?

Only one group came to mind that I knew with certainty never would. One person who would bow to no one, and who would stand as firm as stone against the threat to those she saw as her people.

I didn't want to leave Jet and Gideon alone, didn't want to give up any of the few precious hours I had left in this world… but what if I could obey the summons and get what I wanted? We knew who was involved now. We knew more of their plan.

Although our odds were still poor, three people against a government department *and* a crime organization, we were in a better place to stop them now than we'd been this morning. It would all depend on whether Serc was right: would Meril weigh the importance of the department against her own bid for power?

It was a big if, the chances of failure astronomically high, but while the hope remained, I couldn't let the opportunity slip past me. What did I have to lose but a little time?

The end credit music of the sitcom lurched my thoughts into the present, and the room fell silent as Jet turned off the TV.

With a deep breath to summon my courage, I set the mugs on a tray and carried it into the living room. Gideon took his tea and sniffed at it with a marked look of skepticism but tried a sip without complaint. The effects were immediate as he relaxed into the cushions and the hard lines around his mouth eased. I don't think he noticed, but that was the wonderful nature of my grandmother's tea. Nothing forced, nothing fake. It reminded me of a warm hug—the kind that made everything a little bit better.

Jet wrapped her hands around her mug but didn't drink. Her brow was pinched with pain, and her pale face stood out against her dark hair.

"Jet?" I asked as I set the tray on the table and dropped into the armchair beside the couch.

She closed her eyes and leaned against the cushions. "I'm all right," she said. "I have a headache, but it's nothing."

"What's 'nothing'?" Gideon asked. He pulled one of her hands away from her mug, and I noticed the way his thumb stroked her palm, the way Jet's fingers curled around his.

Whatever had happened between the time Jet discovered he was alive and the time I did, the connection between them had changed. I detected nothing but warm affection from him, and none of the ever-familiar hostility in Jet.

In fact...

I frowned.

There was something odd about Jet's chemistry. Something different, twisted. I opened myself up to it but couldn't get a read. If I'd been pushed to describe it, I would have said it was an urgent... *need*, like a hunger, but so faint I barely picked it up.

I didn't understand what it meant, but as long as I stood by her, I would pay attention to it. Michael had used that weapon of his for a purpose, and I doubted it had been to give Jet a makeover. He could have killed her. He hadn't. That didn't mean she had walked away as unscathed as she appeared.

"I'm used to aches and pains," she said. "I'll get over this."

She took a sip of her tea, and I was relieved to see that even for her the herbs worked their magic. The furrow on her brow smoothed, and her breathing fell into a gentle rhythm.

I wished she had time to sleep. Meril knew we all needed it.

But we couldn't afford the break just yet.

Reluctant as I was, I set my mug on the table and clasped my hands between my knees. "I know this is hardly a good time—but I don't think a good time exists for what I'm about to say."

Both Gideon and Jet turned to face me. Exhaustion deepened every line of their faces, weighed down their eyelids, and their expressions were almost resentful that I had more to throw at them. I regretted the necessity but had put my announcement off long enough.

"I've been recalled to the realm."

I may as well have electrified Jet's seat and thrown the switch for the speed with which she sat up, her eyes wide. Tea sloshed over the side of her mug, but she didn't react to the hot water spilling over her fingers, as though she hadn't registered the pain. Gideon looked on, accepting the seriousness if not appreciating the significance.

"Madi, no," Jet said. "When? How?" Awareness sank into her expression. "Your text message from last night."

I nodded. "Serc told me first, and then an Eye tracked me down with the official order. I have until noon to cross the wall."

Jet sank into her seat, and I swallowed hard against the fear that my next words were pointless. I had no guarantee of how Meril would choose to act, and I didn't want to get my hopes up only to have them crushed.

But short-lived hope had to be better than no hope at all.

"I have an idea," I said. "A way we could twist my summons

in our favour."

Jet met my eye, too stunned to respond, but Gideon's interested stare, the spark in his eyes when I'd used those magic words, motivated me to continue.

"If we want to stop Lucien, we need to move through different channels than the ones we've reached out to already. In this city, there isn't a single group not watched or controlled by the department. Every group, every potential ally we find here will have someone with connections to SMOAC, a connection we can't risk drawing attention from."

Jet frowned. "We can't expose their plans and take them down on our own. The three of us have made it this far, sure, but if Michael is involved, and Eric—" she stumbled, cleared her throat, and pressed on— "Eric is now leading my squad, then the entire task force will come after us, on top of whatever protection Lucien has at hand. The deputy minister is running the syndicate."

She stopped and froze, as though the weight of the truth had fallen on her again.

I swallowed through my own pain and persevered.

"That's why I said different channels." I shifted in my seat. hating that the situation had narrowed us down to this final option. "The fact is, even if we reached out further than we have, we're going to lose our standing. One way or another, word about what's happening will spread, and against Lucien's version of events, no one will believe two shamed public servants and a foreign spy. Our allies are more likely to turn us in than help us."

Jet took another sip of tea as her curiosity overcame her horror. Gideon drained his mug and set it on the table beside mine.

"You think the queen will help?" he asked. "I thought you were afraid of her tearing the world apart if she came anywhere close to taking action."

"I was." I fought my creeping dread over how vulnerable we would be if we put my idea into practice. "I am. But my uncle tells me I'm wrong. He says it benefits Meril as much as us to have SMOAC running strong."

Jet snorted, and I understood her disbelief.

"Regardless, it's worth a shot," I said. "What else do we have to try?"

It wasn't the most inspirational speech, but I had nothing else to offer.

Gideon looked from me to Jet, who sat staring at me. I sensed her fear, though I couldn't place its source. Fear that I might have to leave her? Fear that if my idea failed, she would be left with only a toothpick to battle a mountain ogre? Or two ogres, if Meril opted to roll her way through town.

Yet beyond the fear, deeper, more powerful, came a wave of sympathy, and my chest tightened against it.

Jet knew how far I'd come from my origins, how hard I had fought to maintain my independence from that side of my family. She also knew the dangers that would come with taking this step, and, if we succeeded—*especially* if we succeeded—the debts we might need to pay when this was over.

Even if I persuaded Meril to let me stay and fight, even if she promised us the resources to defeat Lucien and his allies, there was a strong possibility I would only be buying more time—and that Jet might not go untouched, either.

It was why I had to leave this part of the decision up to her. My choice had been removed—I had to be in Meril's court by noon or suffer the consequences—but the only way I stood a chance of coming back was if Jet agreed to stand with me.

"All right," she said, and the determined fire returned to her eyes. "If we want to win, it's time we step up our game. Let's cross the wall and request an audience with the queen."

AUTHOR'S NOTE

When I decided to set this series in Ottawa, I made up my mind to go all in.

Everything Ottawa.

From the cover designer to the editor to the funding, everything.

This city has so much to offer. Yes, it dominates as a government town, but beneath the suits and ties and pubs (so many pubs), is an artistic streak so beautiful and diverse, it lights up the streets.

You walk up Bank Street and there are breathtaking murals on empty walls.

You look at the social calendar and there are festivals or indie performances almost every night of the week.

Unfortunately, though, you often have to dig for it.

Which is why I wanted this series to serve as an opportunity to uncover some of the beauty that brightens the bureaucratic edges, the colourful underbelly.

Having followed photographer John Wenzel's work for many years, I jumped at the opportunity to work with him on Ghostmaker. His eerie, macabre, twisted views in his art were a perfect match to the vibe I was going with, and the results speak for themselves.

Even better? He was a dream to work with. Professional, enthusiastic, willing to try something new and play.

Through him, I found my Jet (Melysa Parent), Madison

(Karolina Roussakis), and Gideon (Thomas James), all Ottawa-based models I was honoured to work with to make my characters step off the page.

My editor, Sadie Hall, called Ottawa home for most of her life, giving her the insight necessary to help me navigate our streets. Her excitement when she recognized certain places I described assured me I'd gone in the right direction.

Alas, the Ottawa-based funding didn't pan out, but I wasn't about to let that stop me. Not when this project had embedded itself so deeply in my soul that not even four years, a pandemic, a tornado, a nine-day power-outage, or a pregnancy—and now toddler—were enough to hold me back.

If Ghostmaker introduces one reader to any of the amazing Ottawans I worked with to create it, then I've done my job properly.

Thank You for Reading

Thank you so much for taking a chance on an independent author. We're living in a wonderful age where it's easy to upload a book to the internet, but that doesn't reflect the blood, sweat, and tears that go into making a book the best version it can be. It takes time, patience, perseverance, and to have the final result end up in a new reader's hands is the best reward. You are the reason we keep writing, so thank you.

If you enjoyed the read, please help support the author by leaving a review at the retailer where you purchased the book. Reviews make a world of difference for an author, helping us reach new audiences and bringing more people into the worlds you've spent time in.

For exclusive character content, announcements, promotions, and special offers, sign up for Krista's mailing list at https://www.kristawalshauthor.com/newsletter

ACKNOWLEDGEMENTS

In some ways sequels are easier to write than first books. So much has already been sorted out with regard to character and plot, and author and reader are already invested in what happens to bring them to the end.

In other ways, it's a million times harder. Expectations are higher, and the stakes need to be so much stakier.

Thankfully, I'm surrounded by so many wonderful people who helped me get there.

John Wenzel and Thomas James, one for his mad skills behind the camera, and the other for stepping so perfectly into character he walked off the green screen and onto my cover.

Kate Sparkes, always and forever, for helping me lift up my muddling middle and convincing me the spicy bits should stay on the page.

My Writerly gang (Jean Malone, Angi Black, Mark Benson, Megan Paasch, Jennifer Iacopelli, Jennie Davenport, Christian Berkey, Sarah Henning) for the reads and help with my cover copy.

Sadie Hall, for helping me clear away the final cobwebs on the plot to make sure every single corner shines as brightly as it can.

Traci Otte and Wendy Smith, my amazing beta readers, for boosting my confidence on the high-stakes second book.

Tim Scapillato, for catching my last-minute errors.

My family, for not reading the steamy parts of this book.

Seriously. Don't read them. Or at least don't tell me you did.

Chris Reddie, husband, father, production manager, chef, launderer, therapist, motivational speaker, bartender… you are my everything.

My daughter, my LilBit, for your smiles and babble and snuggles that remove every stress, even when you make sure they happen at 1 a.m.

My readers, for your reviews, your kind words, your emails, your encouragement. I say it often, but because I believe it deserves to be said: this is a hard job, and it's one I would never find the courage or the energy to keep doing if it weren't for you.

Thank you all for being with me on this adventure.

Because of you, we successfully made it… to book 3. See you there!

About the Author

Known for witty, vivid characters, Krista Walsh never has more fun than getting them into trouble and taking her time getting them out.

When not writing, she can be found reading, gaming, or watching a film – anything to get lost in a good story.

She currently lives in Ottawa, Ontario with her husband, toddler, and epileptic blue heeler.

You can find her at www.kristawalshauthor.com or at the local Second Cup coffee shop... but only if you come bearing a Vanilla Bean Latte, half-sweet.

Other Works by Krista Walsh

The Meratis Trilogy

Evensong

Eventide

Evenlight

The Cadis Trilogy

Bloodlore

Blightlore

Bladelore

The Nayis Trilogy

Veilfire

Dreamfire

Cairnfire (coming soon)

The Dark Descendants

The Invisible Entente prequel novella

Death at Peony House

Song of Wishrock Harbor

Shadows in the Garden Hotel

Howl of the Fettered Wolf

Light of the Stygian Orb

Gods of the Stone Oracle